Just a Normal Day

Copyright © 2022 Craig Baumken

ISBN: 978-1-7387150-1-5 eBook

ISBN: 978-1-7387150-0-8 Paperback

This book is a work of fiction. The names, characters, places, things, incidents, businesses, and organizations, are a product of the author's imagination or are used fictitiously. Any resemblance to actual persons, living or dead, business establishments, events, or locations is entirely coincidental.

Just a Normal Day

A novel by **Craig Baumken**

For Bill Land, aka; Coach Billy.
A puck brother extraordinaire. I miss you.
Don't worry, I captured the spirit of the thing.
Rest in peace my friend and save me a spot in net.

Prologue

"HEY! WE'VE GOT to get out of here *now!*"

"Huh? What did you say?" I yelled, ducking as a bottle whizzed past.

"Look out!" she barked.

I ducked as she tomahawked a punk in a lumberjack shirt sneaking up behind me. "Watch it!" I pushed her roughly out of the way and batted away a bottle, slumping down, groaning, holding my arm.

"Hey, you okay?" She pulled me up by the scruff of my jacket.

"Yeah," I said, rubbing my arm. "Sorry about that."

She grinned. "It's okay, I won't break, but we gotta go. The cops! We gotta go now!" Dropping the pool cue, she ripped mine out of my hand, tossed it aside, and yanked me forward. Racing up the stairs, she stopped abruptly at the landing. "My helmet."

"Your what?"

"My helmet, I threw it protecting your ass."

"My ass doesn't need protecting," I snapped.

Tilting her head, she smiled. "Funny, it looked like you needed it."

"I had them you know."

"Sure, sure."

"So, are we going to stand here arguing, or are we leaving?"

"As soon as I get my helmet."

"Where is it?"

"I think it's somewhere in there," she said, pointing to the dance floor. "Can you get it? I will stand guard here."

"Down there?" I gulped, "people are fighting."

"Yes, please."

"But you threw away my stick," I pleaded.

"You don't need it to get my helmet, and besides, I will be right here if you need me. You'll be fine, but you better hurry," she patted me on the chest, winking.

"Brat," I grumbled, looking down at the floor.

"What did you say?"

"Nothing."

I stood glumly watching the pier-six brawl, I no longer wanted any part of, even if I was the one who started it.

I felt a hard shove and stumbled down the steps. Keeping to the fringe, I gingerly stepped over the bodies, sidestepping an overturned table. Body checked from behind, I lunged forward, instinctively tucked my head down, and scampered on all fours in the other direction. I heard a voice and cautiously looked up to see her standing at the top of the railing, pointing at me.

"Hey! Hey! You're going the wrong way! It's over *there*," she pointed in the opposite direction.

Following her hand, I spotted the table in the corner, the same table she was sitting at when I came in earlier, and lying underneath, was a lime-green motorcycle helmet.

"That it?" I pointed. She nodded, and checking to see if the coast was clear, I ran hunched over to the table and reached down for the helmet, but as I stood up, I was face to face with the punk I had started the brawl with. *Fuck! Where did he come from?*

"There you are, motherfucker," he snarled, grabbing my jacket, his face inches from mine. I could smell the beer on his breath and drool was hanging at the corners of his mouth, mixed in with the blood streaming down the side of his face.

The punk's fist was cocked, and strange in that moment, all I could think of was — careful for what you wish for. Wasn't it only a few weeks ago I was perched on a bar stool in my neighbourhood watering hole back in Ottawa, lamenting how disconnected from life I had become, and how I needed a change? And now here I was up in Timmins of all places, about to be on the receiving end of something I hadn't bargained for. Wincing, I shut my eyes and braced myself; there was a loud crack, then everything went quiet …

1

"ANOTHER BEER?"

"Yes, please."

Patty, the bartender, placed the Barking Squirrel in front of me, and noticed the journal lying open, the white pages bare. "What are you writing?"

"Nothing."

"Yes, I can see that."

I looked at her, pen in my hand but didn't reply.

"Then what's it for? A new way to pick someone up?" she teased.

"No, I just can't think of anything to write."

"A place like this," she said, sweeping her arm out, "and you can't think of anything to write? Then I'm afraid you're a lost cause there, Pete, and even I can't help you." She turned and moved to the other side of the bar to serve a customer.

She was right. I was a lost cause, but that wasn't always the case. At one time, I had my *cause*, my purpose, or so I thought because everyone told me so. Then, one day, when I wasn't paying attention, everything unraveled, and I lost my purpose along with the white picket fence that came with it. Things would never be the same again.

I took a long pull on my beer, holding the pen over the blank page, poised, ready to strike, but my hand remained motionless. Flicking the pen down in disgust, I slid off the stool and headed toward the john. As I passed the open fireplace, someone called out asking me to drop another log on the fire. Waving my hand in response, I reached down, picked out a log from the pile, and dropped it on the small fire. I jumped back as orange embers spit out, followed by loud cracking and popping, then more embers spit out, sparking into the air before disintegrating.

Returning to my stool a few minutes later, I looked at the blank pages staring up at me, sighed, flipped the book closed, and reached for my beer.

Have you ever felt disconnected—from life, from yourself—and not connected to anything substantial? Feeling lost, adrift, rudderless on the ocean of life, emptiness as far as one can see and going through life without a purpose, or as all those self-help books like to call it, "Living a purpose-driven life."

Yet, strangely enough, at the same time, you do find yourself connected to something. Everyone needs connection and purpose of some sort. The problem was my connection was not a meaningful one, still, it was a connection, with its own unique purpose attached to it. That had to count for something, right? And that described me to a 'T'. I was disconnected from the right thing, and I was connected to the wrong thing.

Hmm ... I couldn't be the only one, could I?

So, my connection was Sharkees. A nondescript bar nestled in the far corner of a strip mall in Ottawa's south end. My go-to place.

Sharkees was a cool-sounding name. Even the spelling of it dripped in cool, written out in fancy script with splashes of blue and green finished off in shiny neon. Attached to the roof above the bar, the flashing neon lights made it seem bigger and brighter than it actually was. It was a safe harbour when battling the raging seas of life—sinking, swimming, bobbing, trying to keep your head above water—Sharkees was the shining beacon in the storm, bringing you home, guiding you safely ashore.

From the outside, Sharkees didn't look like much. Plunked down at the end of the L-shaped strip mall, it had a simple storefront entrance. There were no heavy oak doors with large fancy handles nor a cobblestone walkway with potted ferns guarding the entrance. Though at least lights were burning in the windows meaning someone was home. And of course, one couldn't miss the main attraction: a patio tacked on the end extending out over the parking lot.

The patio, large enough to accommodate two baseball teams—as long as the outfielders stood—was held together with puke-green pressure-treated two-by-fours and filled with cheap white plastic chairs and two heavy wooden picnic tables. Strung along the top of slatted fence from end to end were white Christmas lights, with patio lanterns crisscrossing above. Pennants were hung haphazardly from post to post and flapped continuously, promoting cheap beer and summer coolers. Paved paradise it wasn't, but for me, it held an instant undeniable attraction.

And this is where the purpose part came in. You see, Sharkees was walking distance from my townhouse, and on the so-called Sharkees Specials days—which was every day the week and twice on Saturday and Sunday—staggering distance. The journey home after was an easy trek across the paved parking lot, through the woods, over the train tracks, and voilà! Home. But when drinking was involved, it was a journey akin to Little Red Riding Hood's adventure through the forest, and we all know how that turned out, don't we? So, you can see why I felt connected and not wanting to miss out on the daily specials and the journey home after.

What made Sharkees unique, despite its less than glamorous setting, was there was no escaping an entrance at Sharkees. Upon entering through the double set of doors, pulling on the handle of the outer door, there was a loud bang followed by a whoosh of air, the door banging hard behind you, then pulling the handle on the inner door, made everyone stop and look. Then someone would immediately belt out a greeting, giving you a name if they didn't know yours or didn't care, making one laugh and feel welcome. That was the beauty of Sharkees; it felt like home, where you could be yourself.

After passing through the double set of doors, announcing your entrance, straight ahead was the U-shaped bar, open at the far end, with a floor to ceiling stone face fireplace on the back wall. A fire burned perpetually no matter the temperature outside. To the right was a small stage with an even smaller dance floor in front, bookended by a picture window facing the parking lot. Stretching along the wall to the kitchen were a row of booths. On the other side of the bar, along the outer wall, was a standing area for patrons with a ledge to place their drinks. Large windows faced out to the patio, and on the other side of the patio entrance stood an old western saloon piano. The décor was stylish, dark, with wooded paneling throughout, the hardwood floor creaking under your feet. Soft yellowish lighting added to the feeling of warmth while classic rock played overhead.

Sharkees was noticeably quiet today, a sweltering summer Saturday afternoon giving new meaning to the dog days of August. It was one of those days when no one wanted to be anywhere, but here I was, connected to the bar stool. Today, everyone was inside, the patio deserted, the pavement shimmering in the heat, steam rising from a brief sun shower. The pennants hung limply, too hot even for them. To my left sat a middle-aged couple on a blind date, excitedly sharing photos of their respective, now adult children; both were ooh-ing and ahh-ing over how great they turned out, despite what a deadbeat the other parent had been, or still was. To my right, a pair of retirees were burrowed in today's newspaper, silently sipping on their draft beer. Above me, over the bar, were three muted large-screen TVs, a different program on each one. A tennis match at one end, and typical of Saturday, at the other end, a man's-man wearing a tan vest, with shiny things hanging off his hat, was instructing the viewers how to put the worm on the hook.

On the TV above me was, ugh! CFL football. Even after all these years, I still couldn't connect with it, the field wider than the TV, the score 3–1 in the second quarter. So many questions. Just why was a single point called a rouge? Never mind that missing down. Why were there only three downs? Where did the other one go? Did someone lose it, and that's why they only played with three? Shuddering at the thought, I downed my beer.

I looked for Patty, Sharkees' resident bartender and manager, and like the name, she too was cool. Perky, with short dark hair and colourful tattoos on her forearms, she barely topped out at five feet, but crammed inside was ten feet of spunk, spit, and nails—one person I would not want to meet late at night in the woods. Today, she was in black low-cut Converse runners, jean shorts, and a bright green Sharkees tank top that matched her bright round green eyes. At the moment she was doing shots on the other side of the bar with one of the regulars. I waved my bottle, catching her eye, and she motioned she would be right over. While I waited, I gave the stool a kick, twirled around, and looked out the window.

I had only started coming here a few weeks ago. I had been meaning to check out the place for ages, noticing the flashing neon at night from my bathroom window. A lazy Saturday afternoon, bored, I went for a walk when the midday sun became unbearably hot, so I sought refuge. I wasn't in the best place, in fact I was feeling lost, disconnected from everything. Walking into Sharkees that day, despite the intense heat, it was warm and inviting. A small fire was crackling, burning brightly, as I walked through the double set of doors—the loud bang and whoosh of air startling me—and after being greeted heartily, feeling like I was about to receive an award, I found an empty stool at the bar and plopped myself down. And just like that, I had my instant connection with its instant purpose.

Patty returned with another Barking Squirrel. Flipping open the journal, I took a drink for courage, put pen to hand, and stared at the blank page. And stared and stared. I waved to Patty for another beer.

I had been running for quite some time, the footsteps getting louder, and I knew it was only a matter of when. Dr. Jayne, my therapist, said journaling was good for one's soul and that I should give it a try, something about writing out what was on your mind being therapeutic. She said people journal all the time and that putting down one's thoughts helps heal whatever is bothering them inside. If that was the case, I would need a *War and Peace*-like tome and not this thin notebook.

Today was more than that. I needed a spark, a change, anything to snap me out of this funk. And strange? Something about today did feel different. I could even feel it in the hot, humid air. I couldn't put my finger on it, but there was something about *today*. So, all I had to do then, was be patient and wait. *Have you met me?*

Licking my thumb, I flipped through the pages of my journal, glancing over what I had written previously—hangman, x's and o's, stick figures, phone numbers. All in all, some nice artistic doodling. Wait! I did write something three weeks ago. Thumbing through the pages, I found it:

It's been a long, strange trip, July 27, 2005
- Pete Humphries

"Well, Pete ..." said Dr. Jayne at our next session, "that's a start."

But then she chided me that until I was ready to commit to myself, we were wasting each other's time. Deep down, I knew she was right. I also knew if I could just get started, it would flow. That was a double-edged sword. I was afraid of what was stuck inside. What happened if I let it out and couldn't deal with it? What then?

I was an expert at deflecting and pushing things away. I had lots of practice: my dad, the incident that day on the dock, Tina, Joanna, and later abruptly leaving the police force. I could deflect, push, roll-off with the best of them. The 'dealing with it' part wasn't any fun, so I avoided it. I mean, you would too, if something constantly hurt. Denial is such a neat place. One can live rent-free, and as the song says, you can check out anytime you like; you just can't ever leave. And isn't that where the term *let sleeping dogs lie* came from? Living every day in denial, avoidance, tiptoeing through life, afraid to disturb Fido.

Catching myself before plunging headfirst down that rabbit hole, I returned to my journal. Giving it the old college try, I started to write and without thinking—forty-five minutes later—I had written five pages. *Wow! I guess this isn't so bad after all.* Maybe Dr. Jayne was right. Scribbling furiously, I looked up for Patty, but there was no one behind the bar.

Whoa! Wait! what's this? A new face? Where did he come from?

Parked on the stool beside me was a giant hulking dude in an orange ball cap. He was wearing a matching orange tank top, bearing a large white cow horn covering the front. *A cow horn?* How could I miss that? I peered over at the huge mass and thought tank tops looked great on women. At least he filled it out properly.

This was one big dude. Pie-faced, with baby fat puffy cheeks, round puppy-dog eyes, and a mouth formed in a permanent tight-lipped grin. I guessed him to be in his mid-thirties. Even sitting, he looked to be 6' 6" and 240 easy. He was wearing long thick arms attached to coat hangar shoulders, and his hands could easily wrap around a football, while his biceps were the size of my thighs. Tufts of blond hair poked through the sides and opening of his cap, which he wore backward. Sitting forward, his head still, lips moving, he was glued to the TVs above. What was he watching? Fishing? No, I don't think he had the patience. CFL? No, he didn't look the type. Check that, no one watched the CFL—no one cared—but maybe he knew where that missing down was. Following his eyes, bingo! College football. I looked up at the TV, then back at him, and that was when I made my mistake.

I made eye contact with a complete stranger.

First down: Run

"Hey! Buddy! LOOK! LOOK! See that?"

Jet plane take-offs have been quieter. I dropped my head and started scribbling furiously.

Grabbing my shoulder, he turned me toward him. "Hey! Buddy, check this out. Look, look," he said, tugging at my arm.

I had no choice but to look up. He was gesturing at the TV, pointing, telling me how the Texas Longhorns were his favourite team. He had just scored tickets to see them play, cheap flight too.

"Cool," I answered.

Things were quiet again. I continued writing, but his presence had broken the mood. I started another game of hangman: five letters, two vowels ... gee, that's funny, why has everything gone dark? I looked up to see an orange cap leaning over, trying to peek at my journal. *Lucky me, I have a new best friend.*

"Have you ever been?" he asked.

"Where?"

"To see the Longhorns play," he responded matter-of-factly, like I should already know.

I shrugged. "Who?" I kept my head down, trying to avoid making eye contact.

"The Longhorns! My team, the Texas Longhorns," he said eagerly.

"No," I answered, wisely leaving out that I didn't care.

"It's awesome! This will be my third time!" he said, sounding like an eight-year-old after too much birthday cake.

"Cool," I replied again, lowering my head, wishing I was anywhere but here. I poked at the page with my pen, but the light kept changing, the orange cap twisting and turning, trying to see what I was doing.

"What are you writing?" he asked, peering over my head.

"Oh, just stuff."

His head moved in closer, and I could feel him breathing on me. Leaning forward, I covered the pages, trying to block his view, not up to having my feeble hangman attempts viewed by anyone.

"Wait!" he exclaimed, "You're a writer, aren't you? I can see it! You're a writer!"

I didn't know whether to take that as a compliment or an insult.

"No, no, I'm not a writer." Flustered, "I'm just writing in my journal, that's all." I waved my hand and tried to shoo him away like a fly.

"Well, that still makes you a writer, right?" he said, undeterred, ignoring my fly swatter.

I thought for a second, *He has a point.* It was true in a way; I *did* write stuff. I could fill the pages equally with hangman and x's and o's, and my grocery lists were written out neatly with straight lines drawn through each item. And, I always drew the head in a full circle on the stick figures. All that had to count for something, right?

"Hey!" My new name apparently. "Wanna do some shots?"

"No."

"Come on, let's do some shots," he playfully tapped me on the shoulder.

"No," I said, head down.

"Hey, Amy!" he bellowed.

Why is he always yelling? Does he not have an indoor voice?

"Amy! Amy! Shots for my new pal and me."

Pal? I'm not your pal. I don't think I've ever been anyone's pal. Well, maybe when I was six. My head remained down, looking for the trap door handle.

"Hey!"

"Yeah?" I didn't bother to look up.

"What's your name?" he said. "Mine's Teddy, Teddy Polson. What's yours?"

I felt like I was in the playground sharing the sandbox. I hadn't missed those days. I know some did, but I wasn't one of them. Forced to re-engage, I looked up again.

"Pete," I sighed heavily, hoping he would get the message.

"Pete, what?"

I surrendered, fighting off the urge to say something stupid, especially since it would take three of me to fit in his tank top. "Pete Humphries."

"Cool! Pete 'n Teddy doing shots!"

Lovely. I've never been part of a nursery rhyme before.

"Hey Amy!" Another jet taking off. "Shots for you too."

It went quiet, and peeking up, Teddy was staring at the football game. He followed the play with his head perfectly still, lips moving, his beady eyes moving side to side. I wondered if he struggled in school with his attention span. I looked down at my journal, then back up at Teddy; Amy's back was to us as she poured the shots. *What if I just got up and left? Would anyone notice? Would anyone care?*

Looking at my half-empty beer on the counter, I didn't want it to go to waste—no matter how dire the circumstances, never leave a man behind, as they say. I resolved myself to my fate. I did say I was feeling disconnected and looking for a change. I needed to start wishing better.

Amy brought over a tray holding three shots—vodka surprise. Teddy didn't notice, and snapping my fingers, using my indoor voice, I tried to get his attention.

"Teddy, Teddy." No dice. I looked up at the TV. It was on a commercial. Good lord! I had no choice. Jet takeoff time.

Leaning over, "TEDDY!" I yelled into his ear.

"What?" turning his head just enough to keep one eye glued to the TV.

"Er, um, the shots are here. Remember? You ordered shots."

"Oh yeah, shots."

He looked down from the TV, taking a glass from the tray. "Drink up!" he said, motioning to Amy and me. "What do you wanna drink to?"

Glancing at Teddy's massive biceps, once again the urge to say something stupid fortunately retreated quickly.

"Oh, I dunno. How about we drink to Texas?"

"Texas. YEAH! Texas!" he whooped.

My new best friend slapped me hard on the back and downed his shot. Gasping for air, I dropped the shot glass on the bar, reaching for my throat, coughing and sputtering.

"Are you okay?" Amy asked in alarm.

"I just need a sec," I gasped.

Teddy, alternating between the TV and me, expressed concern also. "Hey! You didn't drink your shot. Come on, hurry up! I'm ready for another."

Second down: Pass

Spread out in front of me were six empty shot glasses. Spread out in front of my new best friend were six empty shot glasses. Spread out in front of Amy was a single shot glass. One of us got it.

The afternoon sun had shifted, long shadows slashing across the deserted patio, the umbrellas hanging limply. Teddy was on his stool, turned sideways, his head cocked to the right, playing shadow puppets with the long shadows, while I tried to keep the bar from falling into the sea, both hands firmly secured to the outer edge. The winds had picked up, the sea full of white caps. When did *that* happen?

"Boy! Is it wavy in here. When did it get stormy?" I asked no one in particular. Turning, I gestured with my head towards the patio. "Look! It must be one of those freak storm thingies where it rains and shines at the same time. Wait! Wait! That's a song, right? There's a song about that, I just can't remember from where. Amy! Amy! AAAMMMYYY! Where's the jukebox? Have you seen the jukebox? I gotta find that song!"

I was swaying to the rhythm of the rolling waves. "Oh, wow! Look at me! I'm just like my new sandbox buddy Teddy. HEY TEDDY! I can talk in one long sentence just like you."

Amy appeared, hands on her hips. "All right guys, keep it down, or I'm going to have to kick you out."

Steadying myself, I snapped to attention and saluted. "Aye Aye, Captain."

Hearing me, Teddy, carefully holding his shadow puppet, gave a sloppy, half-hearted salute, slurring, "Aye oh eye, sister."

Halftime

"Guys? Guys!"

"Huh? What?"

I looked up. It was Amy, and her lips were moving.

"Can you give us a sec? We're in the last round of our shadow puppet fight." I turned to Teddy, furiously battling a little longer, then announced, "DING! DING! Round over, I win."

Teddy mumbled something about me always winning, and I playfully socked him in the jaw. Putting our hands down, we turned on our bar stools and faced Amy, wearing angelic grins. "Yeeesss, Amy?"

She shook her head at us. "Listen, why don't you guys go get some air for a bit?" she said, trying to keep a straight face.

"Good idea! C'mon sandbox buddy, let's go outside." I grabbed my new best friend by the arm. We slid off the stools, standing like newborn foals, locked arms, and holding onto each other like two little old ladies on a windy day, staggered outside.

Squinting, shielding my eyes, I turned in a circle, trying to find my bearings.

"Where did the day go?" Teddy asked.

"Good question," I replied, "I thought it was right where I left it."

Teddy spotted a guy having a smoke and called out to him. "Hey buddy! Have you seen the day? I think we lost it."

The guy looked at him, said nothing, puffing on his cigarette.

"Well, he doesn't have it," Teddy sighed, disappointed.

Third down: Punt

Back inside, we informed Amy that just now, each of us had an epiphany at exactly the same time—I mean, how crazy was that? And in a moment of sheer brilliance, we had given each other nicknames.

Reaching up and putting my arm around Teddy, "I'm Pistol, as in Pistol-Pete, natch, and Teddy here is Texas, cuz he's just so darn big like the state. And from now on, could you please refer to us by our new nicknames."

"A pair of dickheads is more like it." Amy rolled her eyes, disgusted with our behaviour.

Teddy and I … oops, I mean Texas and Pistol were back on our stools, watching the CFL game. Courtesy of Amy, we were each nursing a scotch.

"I don't think Amy likes it when we do shots," I said to Teddy. He didn't respond, his eyes glued to the TV.

"Do you know what we should do?" he said out of the corner of his mouth, staring up at the game.

"No, what?"

"Pistol, we should go looking for that missing down. Fucking CFL shit! I mean, really. Can you imagine my Longhorns playing with only three downs? How the fuck do you play with just three downs anyways?"

Suddenly upset, Teddy banged his fist on the bar, and leaned forward, his head in his hands. His head shaking slowly, his forehead now bumping on the bar, I could hear sniffling. *Wait? Is he crying?*

I reached over to console him, rubbed his shoulders, leaned in, and whispered in his ear. "It's okay, big fella. The missing down is here somewhere. I know it. I'm sure it's just been misplaced, and someone will find it and put it back. Maybe it fell out of one of the equipment bags? It's only a matter of time, is all, I'm sure of it."

Fourth down: I knew it was here all this time
Despite my best efforts to console him, Teddy was in an ever-increasing state of misery.

Okay, that can't be all because of that missing down, could it? And I did promise him that we would find it.

I rubbed Texas's shoulders as he picked at a drink coaster. Turning his head, his eyes were moist, and he wore an expression of sadness. "Speaking of missing, my sister is missing. She's been gone for almost three months."

"Huh? What? Aw, I'm sorry big guy. Have you contacted the police?"

"Yeah, a few days after she went missing, but the cops never found anything. I don't think they tried very hard."

Teddy's tone was matter-of-fact, and almost had me convinced. We sat in silence, staring up at the game, and I wasn't sure whether to believe him when Teddy face planted on the bar, hands over his head, and moaned. At that moment, my gut instinct sounded the alarm, and everyone went shimmying down the pole and raced to the trucks. And me being me, of course, I chose to ignore it, thinking, *ahh, it's nothing more than a fire drill.*

I should have known that it was the signal to cut my losses, chalk it up to one of those Sharkees moments, and call it a day—buy the T-shirt on the way out, and catch up with Little Red Riding Hood on the way home. But I didn't do that, of course.

2

WIDE-EYED, MOUTH DRY, hands clammy, I gawked at the black canvas bag on the bar in front of me; the zipper pulled back, the bag was filled with nothing but stacks of brown. Instantly, I was sober. Funny how that works, huh? Have you ever noticed, how quickly it gets your attention, when the topic turns to money? Teddy reached in front of me and picked up the bag, my eyes glued to it like a child when Mom takes away their favourite toy. Pointing to an empty booth on the other side of the bar, he beckoned me to follow him.

Pete! Pete! Get a hold of yourself! Get a grip! My inner voice screamed as I nipped at Teddy's heels, not wanting to let him, or the bag, out of my sight. We slipped into the booth in the corner, Teddy with his back to the wall, while I faced him with nowhere else to look. He caught the eye of a server. "Two coffees black."

While we waited for our coffee, my eyes glued to the bag, I made a quick recap of the day's events: hanging out at my favourite bar, minding my own business; a stranger appears—my new best friend; heavy drinking ensues; a story about a missing person, culminating in a bag full of money. *Just your normal day, right?*

Already, things had gone too fast, too far, but I couldn't turn back now, could I? Usually, this stuff I picked up on quickly, never allowing it to get ahead of me. This time, though, it had. Why? Not like me at all. But then again, I had not been myself for quite some time, so who was I kidding? I was ripe for the taking.

You see, I was desperate. And that was never a good thing because, from desperation, wrong choices are made and with wrong choices come repercussions. Nothing good ever came from desperation, nothing. Have you ever felt desperate? Have you ever been in a desperate situation? Have you ever been down to your last dollar? And not knowing—and I mean *really* not knowing—where the next dollar was coming from? Have you ever wondered how in the hell you got there? What happened? One minute everything was fine, then the next minute it wasn't. When that happens, things change. People change. *You* change. One does things one would normally never do. Desperation does that.

Then when money enters the equation, the scales are tipped even further. Do the math: the more the money = the more the desperation it stirs up = the greater the changes. And true to form, things do not end up as you would expect or hope. In situations like this, you better be thinking clearly so you choose wisely because there are no do-overs. But most people don't—think clearly that is—instead trying to fool themselves into thinking they are, and it's not until later, much later, when reality does its thing and bites hard.

Remember how I said today felt different? That something was up? And here it was, right in front of me, just not what I was expecting. But that's how these things work. I had an opportunity here to make a choice. Choose wisely, which would have been the smart thing to do, and walk away unscathed. Or I could choose out of desperation and live with the ensuing consequences. Three guesses as to which choice I made.

A different server delivered our coffee, and we were now in the care of Tony, a bald, muscular, heavily tattooed creature with a quick, friendly smile. However, I immediately sensed something dark and sinister about him and made a mental note to make sure my back was never turned when he was around.

As we sipped on our coffee, Teddy filled me in on the disappearance of his sister Sara Polson—"Sara, no h," he said. He said Sara vanished one night three months ago after having a beer together at Sharkees. She had left on her bike, and he had not seen or heard from her since. Teddy said he waited forty-eight hours before contacting the police, and playing detective himself, he traced her last remaining days and steps, canvassing door to door and placing posters all over suburbia. He even offered a fifty-thousand-dollar reward for information leading to her whereabouts, but the trail was cold, and he was crushed.

People go missing all the time, the police told him, sometimes they want to go missing, and they return when they're ready. But Teddy didn't believe that theory for one moment. He and Sara were close; she was all he had. He said their parents had died when they were teenagers, leaving them a trust fund. The trust fund afforded them the luxury of not having to work for a living, and all they had was each other. He wanted her back, and he didn't care what it took or cost. He just wanted her back. Money was no object, Teddy said. He was desperate, and so was I. A bad combination. (You think?)

Teddy opened the black canvas bag, reached in, and pulled out a stack of hundred-dollar bills. He thumbed through the thick wad, counted them out, losing track at around ten-thousand, and placed the money on the table in front of me. He offered the stack to me—and if not me, if I knew of anyone willing to look for his sister, that huge stack of cold hard cash would be theirs if they just made an effort to look for her. Just simply L-O-O-K. Anyone can look, right?

And I wasn't just anyone. I was Pete Humphries, ex-cop, who had loads of experience with dealing with people who were lost—so I jumped at the bait. Took it hook, line, and alcohol poisoning. Wouldn't you? I puffed out my chest and said to Teddy that I was his guy, and I would look—no wait, better than that—I would *find* his sister, Sara.

See? Desperation leads you to do things, say things, make questionable choices, even when the little voices in your head are screaming at the top of their lungs to run as fast as you can in the opposite direction. Reaching across the table, shaking Teddy's hand, I was back in the game. Funny, deep down, my instinct was Sara wasn't missing, and that all this nothing more than a ruse of some kind. But hey, who listens to gut instincts? I had a spanking new normal day, starting right now, wearing my favourite shade of brown.

Next morning, soaked in sweat, sleeping fitfully, dreaming of being chased by trees wrapped in hundred-dollar bills, I woke to the sight of a stack of hundred-dollar bills on the nightstand. I shook my head and sat straight up. I reached out to touch the stack but pulled my hand back quickly and stared at it. Still not sure, I closed my eyes and counted out loud to ten and opened them, I broke into a huge grin and let out a whoop. Smiling, I dragged my ass out of bed, threw on a T-shirt, and stumbled out to the kitchen, all the while looking back at the nightstand.

This was a breakfast of champions moment if there ever was one. Opening the fridge, I pulled out a can of courage and worked my way out to the front steps of my townhouse, but not before another look down the hall into my bedroom. Stepping outside, I was greeted by the blinding sun and thick as soup humidity.

The neighbourhood was empty, as everyone was hunkered indoors, typical by late-summer when everyone forgot the winter blues, tired of the constant heat and humidity. Looking to the left, my next-door neighbour Mary was sitting on her front steps, a cigarette in one hand and a bottle of beer in the other. Lying next to her was a set of crutches, her foot wrapped in a bright white cast. She looked up and gave a half-hearted wave.

"Hey."

"Hey."

"So, what did you do now?" I called over, smiling.

"Oh, nothing really, I broke my ankle having sex."

With Mary, you just never knew, and I answered back laughing, "Cool! Might as well have been while you were having fun."

She nodded, then abruptly grabbed for her crutches. "Shit! I left the water boiling on the stove. Shit! Shit! Shit!" Firing her cigarette in the garden, she propped herself up on her crutches, knocking over the beer, the bottle clinking on the pavement. "Bye, Pete," she hollered while fighting with the door handle. "Take care, drop over for a beer sometime."

She got the door open, and I nodded, lifted my can of courage, and waved as she hobbled in.

Rolling my beer across my forehead, I opened it, slurping at the foam, then with a couple of loud gulps, polished it off. Leaning back against the step, the courage starting to work its magic, I mustered a rather impressive, loud and long, belch. Pleased with myself, I closed my eyes and let my mind drift.

Was this just another normal day in the life of me, Pete Humphries? Or was it something brand new, entirely different? Perhaps even an adventure?

Questions, questions, questions. I needed more courage. An hour later, after two more trips inside, empty beer cans littered the steps, and my courage was replenished. The steaming humidity worked its way through my pores, extracting the day-old alcohol and forming into beads of sweat, which dribbled down my arms. The sun, becoming unbearably hot, forced me back inside, which was just as well, as I needed to get started on what came next.

Teddy said Sara was a biker-chick and a pool hall junkie who loved playing eight-ball. A match made in heaven—pool *yes*, bikes *no*. He said Sara would get on her bike and ride until she found a pool hall, and for the rest of the night, she would own the table. He said she had been frequenting a place called the Lucky 7evens in Peterborough. At the word Peterborough, my blood froze, tingles shooting up and down my spine. Recoiling inwardly, I went straight back in time to that day on the waterfront. I hadn't thought about that day in years, it remained parked in the cold, damp, dark basement of my mind among the stuff Dr. Jayne had been wanting me to write about.

I reached for a bowl from the cupboard and poured myself some Cheerios and eating over the sink, thought back to my conversation with Teddy. Despite my misgivings about Peterborough, I was certain Sara had disappeared on her own terms. I placed the half-eaten bowl of cereal on the floor, and let Cat, who had adopted me one night as I staggered home from just another normal day at Sharkees, finish it off. Watching him eat, I thought, *This could buy me some time. Perhaps, I can make this work for me, maybe even a chance at redemption?*

Redemption for what exactly? My dad? Tina? That day on the dock? Joanna? The force? Dale?

Mentally exhausted, I stopped. There were way too many redemptions, two or three lifetimes worth. I pulled the bowl away from Cat, refilled it, scarfing the Cheerios down, as Cat looked up at me longingly. Smiling, I put the bowl down and let him finish it off. I kept coming back to how Teddy appeared to be exaggerating his sister's disappearance, making it seem worse than it was.

Then, why all the money? I had no answer to that.

Teddy had said to meet him the following Saturday at Sharkees, so I had time to get a start on things. And if I were as smart as I thought I used to be, I would take advantage and stretch things out, my instinct being that Sara was alive and well, probably hiding out somewhere, and needing a break from Teddy. Teddy appeared intense towards his sister, and I had seen that dynamic before, the smothered sister needed space from their overbearing brother.

I meandered down the hall and stood in the bedroom doorway, staring at the stack of money on the nightstand. Dammit, I needed my wheels! Time to get them out of hock. I made a call to my car guy, Otte, and said, "Unwrap her buddy, Poppa's coming home!" Otte laughed and said to give him a couple of days, then it would be ready for pickup.

Ahh, my wheels, my 1973 Chevy Nova SS—factory restored, candy apple metallic red with a 350 cubic inch, 5.7L V8, Mickey Thompson 33x15-15 racing slicks, Hurst shifter four-speed, hood scoop, and black leather bucket seats. She was a beauty, all right. My pride and joy, my baby, the love of my life.

After everything fell apart, Otte had sold it to me, as a form of retail therapy. I had moved to Ottawa on a whim and landed in Otte's dealership one day looking for some new wheels. We got to talking because we were guys, after all. Otte was a big man, standing 6' 2", with a black goatee, buzzcut, friendly eyes, and with a firm handshake. As we talked, he realized he had the perfect car for me and took me over to a side lot, and as soon as I saw her, I knew. He had come across it at one of the auto auctions, bought it for himself, and restored it with the intention of flipping it eventually. That was his hobby, he told me. Taking it for a test drive, I said we had a deal if he could install an eight-track system. An eight-track *what*?

I told him it was my way of staying connected to my dad. I had inherited all his eight-tracks when he passed, and I had grown up listening to them. My dad and I took car rides together everywhere.

Saturday mornings around the breakfast table, Dad would ask, "Well son, where do we want to go today?" We would pull out the road atlas, find a place, and off we went, just like that. Me, my dad, and his eight-tracks. I guess that's where I got my love of music and driving from.

Otte went searching and found a mint condition Panasonic in-dash radio/eight-track player, installing it, along with a set of Jensen co-axial speakers in the front doors, and tri-axial speakers in the rear window. My dad's old eight-tracks now had a place to play again.

Heaven.

Anyhow, Otte had been holding my Chevy in storage for me, ever since my normal days became even too abnormal for me, because it was too costly to keep it on the road. A piece of me died inside the day I dropped her off, and I couldn't look back when I got into the taxi. I was depressed for a long time after and missed my baby. I honestly thought I would never see her, or this day, again. The one thing with Otte, though, was that I knew the Chevy was in good hands, and I would never have to worry.

I had a few days to kill until we were reunited, so next up, I needed to change the colour of my bank account from red to black. That was easy as I would walk over to the bank in the strip mall and deposit the giant stack of hundred-dollar bills. Nothing unusual about that, right? And I would make my landlord think it was Christmas, paying the three months' back rent. Again, nothing unusual about that.

I showered and put on my best pair of jean shorts and for fun, stuffed down the front of my shorts as many of the bills that would fit to form a rock-star bulge. The rest I carried in a plastic shopping bag, as I didn't want to look too conspicuous. It felt good, looking down at the bulge, and I looked good, too. As I walked, I pictured women looking at me, then down at the bulge in my shorts and smiling. You know the rock-star bulge? Remember all the seventies rock stars in their tight jeans, commando-style, the large hook drooping down the left or right side? If you don't, just google David Cassidy, trust me.

I deposited my money—but not before enduring questionable looks from the bank teller—and walking home, I felt better about things. Though my rock star bulge was short-lived, my bank account was back in the black, and doing some quick math; my $50K was down by only $10K. If I played my cards right, there was more where that came from.

Whistling loudly, I strolled along the sidewalk, the intense heat and humidity no longer a bother. I felt giddy as I cut through the empty baseball field and stopped at home plate. Looking out onto the playing field, it was like old times, as I gathered myself in my batting stance, squaring my feet in the dirt, windmilling my imaginary bat, I settled in. Waiting on the pitch, I took a mighty swing, the loud crack of the bat, the ball soaring into deepest center field. Flipping the bat, I took off around the bases, squealing like a little kid, rounding third, headed for home, I dove headfirst and in a cloud of dust and dirt, slid face first across home plate. Jumping up, dusting myself off, spreading my arms wide, I yelled out, "SAFE!" turning and waving to the imaginary crowd.

Two days later—Christmas morning August-style—found me waiting at the curb in front of my place, barely able to contain my excitement, pacing back and forth on the sidewalk. Otte sent a car to pick me up, and I talked non-stop to the poor driver the entire way out to Stittsville. My Chevy was out front, gently idling, rims sparkling in the sun and the Mickey Thompson's glistening. The windows were down, the faint sounds of rock music coming from inside.

Handing over the cash in hundreds, I eagerly went for an inspection of my baby, and for the next ten minutes, I checked out every inch of rubber and metal. I popped the hood, marveling at Otte, who had kept the engine in pristine running condition. Hopping in the front seat, I lovingly gripped the steering wheel, twisting and turning it, taking in every nook and cranny of the interior. Instinctively, I reached behind the seat, feeling for the eight-track case, finding it exactly where I had left it. Thinking ahead, Otte had popped a Doobie Brothers tape in the deck for me. If I had a will, Otte would be in it, at the very top. I revved the engine, feeling its soothing rumble underneath, gripping the wheel, I paused to reflect.

Overnight, my life had taken an unexpected turn for the better. This was my kind of *normal day*, the one I had been longing for. And it had been that easy. I had money in the bank, my beloved Chevy back on the road, the back rent paid, and—most importantly—I was reconnected with a purpose. I felt alive again like I belonged. Like a phoenix, I had risen from the ashes once more. The rising had always been the easy part, I had lots of practice. It was the staying that was the hard part.

Buckling up, revving the engine, I shifted into gear, waved goodbye to Otte, and wound my way through Stittsville and the midday Kanata traffic. In no time, I was on the 417 heading back into the city, my arm out the window, the wind in my hair, the volume on the eight-track player set to eleven.

Life was good again.

3

TEDDY WAS PERCHED on the bar stool in Sharkees while his sister was on the other side, moving between the coolers, taking inventory. He took a long pull on his beer, wiped his mouth with the back of his hand and belched. They were the only two people on the bar side and could talk freely. Ignoring the belch, Sara stopped what she was doing and turned to face her brother.

"Do you think he knows?" she asked.

"Knows what?" said Teddy, adjusting his orange Longhorns hat.

"That he's being played."

"Who?"

"That guy."

"What guy?"

"The guy you met in here the other day. The guy you were drinking with."

"Oh, that guy."

"Yeah, oh, that guy. Shit, Teddy! Aren't you tired of this by now?" Sara sighed, exasperated.

"No, never. Besides, this one's different," he answered.

"Different how?"

"Because."

"That's it? Just because?" She shook her head. "Seriously? Just because? You want to fuck someone over just because."

"Yes and no."

"Yes and no? Fuck Teddy! What is wrong with you?"

"Nothing."

"I beg to differ, little brother," she glared at him.

Slowly shaking his head—knowing she didn't understand—he looked down at his beer. "Sis, I want payback. I want revenge," he said, staring off into space. He took a drink, then placed the bottle on the bar, still looking straight ahead.

"Payback? Revenge? For what? What the fuck? You don't even know the guy!"

"No, that's where you're wrong, sis. I do know him."

"How? From where?" She slumped down to the floor, her back against a cooler, looking up at him.

"I know him all right." Teddy sighed, taking another pull on his beer. Swallowing hard, he emitted a loud and prolonged belch.

Sara, disgusted, muttered, "Brothers ..."

"Pete Humphries," he said.

"Pete, who?"

"Pete Humphries. I know him all right...what a dick ..."

"*How* do you know him?" Curious now, she cocked an eyebrow.

"Our paths crossed years ago."

"Really? Where?"

"I was seventeen, summer in Peterborough, the marina on the waterfront."

"Huh? What? Wow. You still remember that? What happened?"

"Remember Mom and Dad's place near Lakefield?"

She nodded. How could she not?

"Remember how on weekends I would hitch a ride into Peterborough and work at the marina pumping gas?"

She watched his eyes as he spoke; aglow, his face lit up. She remembered those times, of course, just not as fondly as her brother.

"It was quite a time, all right," he said. "The waterfront was always buzzing, I loved it those days ..." He drifted off, lost in the thoughts of those teenage-angst good times, wishing it was still then.

Sara let him be, got up and reached for the coffee pot, pouring herself a cup.

Reaching down into the cooler, she brought out the milk carton, poured some in, stirred it, then tilted the spoon against the side of the carton. Leaning against the bar, she took a sip, ignoring the giant knot in her stomach.

"There was always stuff going on. Boats, beer, girls, boats, beer …"

Sara rolled her eyes at the thought, shaking her head the way only big sisters can do.

"Anyhow, one day I was pumping gas on the dock. And it was hot that day, busy too! Man, I don't think I had seen it that busy."

Sara smiled. Her brother lived for days like that.

"It was great! Free beer after, and the—"

"Yeah, the boats … I get it."

Teddy laughed, a big hearty belly laugh, his cheeks and shoulders jiggling in unison. The kind of laugh she had not heard in years.

Teddy knew boats and the connecting lakes and locks like the back of his hand. He was totally in his element. At the marina, no one—specifically their parents—could take that from him or question what he was doing. It was his choice, his life, what he wanted, and not what their parents wanted or expected of him. There, on the waterfront, he was *someone,* someone *important.* He pumped gas, worked the dock, and offered assistance to the weekend warriors. He loved what he was doing. He was only seventeen, just a kid, but he fit. He mattered, he was respected, and accepted for who he was, not who his parents wanted him to be.

"Anyway, I'm working the pumps, and the boats were lined up two deep when one of the pumps ran out of gas. Now we're down to one pump. I had no idea how much was left in it. The lineup of boats kept getting bigger. They were getting frustrated, and who could blame them? I had just turned off the pump when I heard a voice from across the water. 'Hey, asshole! Turn the pump back on!'

"I looked up to see where the voice was coming from, and it was a guy about my age. I didn't recognize him at first but when he yelled again, I remembered who he was. He came by all the time in Daddy's boat, always showing off. I guessed he was pissed there was only one pump now. But there was nothing I could do. I called out, trying to explain, but he wouldn't listen. He just kept being an asshole, going on that I was purposely fucking him over. What was I supposed to do, wave my magic gas wand? That guy made me feel like shit. The other boats were watching us bark at each other, when my manager came out, wanting to know what all the yelling was about. I told him, pointing at the boat on the water. The guy was yelling again, and my manager started yelling back at him, telling him to piss off and get back in line. It was great! He patted me on the back and told me to help out with the other pump, then he went back inside.

"I looked for the boat, and when I didn't see it, I thought, okay, he's gone—when that asshole came out of nowhere, backing his boat to the edge of the dock then blasting everyone onshore with water. It was crazy, water was pouring over the dock, the other boats tied up were slamming up against the side. Then the gas hose got loose and sprayed Angie with gas. You know, she never came back after that. It was crazy. What an asshole!"

"So, then what happened?" she asked. "What did you do?"

"Nothing. I didn't do anything. Well, other than clean the mess up."

"Huh? Did they find the guy? Did you call the police?"

"No, he took off. I mean, I wanted to. I wanted to punch his head in. I thought of jumping in the dinghy and going after him. Everyone else was pissed. I wished I had now, but I didn't, I was soaked. I looked for him the rest of the summer, but I never saw him or the boat again. I knew if I ever ran into him, I would have torn his head off ... that fucker ... he had no right to do that."

"Brother, you're losing me here. What's the big deal, then? Dad would yell at us worse than that because the sun didn't come out when it was supposed to."

"I know, sis. I don't know. Maybe it was the way that guy yelled at me and expected me to magically fix everything? Dad used to yell at me the same way, you know?"

Sara nodded at the memory, the knot in her stomach twisting tighter.

"Brother, this seems different than what Dad did, and you and I *both* know you are the king of not letting things go. Why can't you just let it be?"

Abruptly, like a switch, Teddy turned his attention to the TV overhead, his mood dark. *Like father, like son,* she thought. She knew to let him be when he got like this, knowing too well Teddy's dark side and how fast it could change.

Ah that blessed Polson trait. Thanks, Mom. Thanks, Dad.

Sara picked up the clipboard, turned to the wall of bottles, and resumed counting. A few minutes later, like a switch, Teddy continued, even though her back was to him.

"Pete Humphries … I heard his parents had money. Fucker would take girls through the locks on Daddy's boat and hang out in front of the marina. His boat was always getting in the way, and he would dock it where he wanted instead of following our direction."

Sara wondered if there was more to this than just some guy being a jerk. Perhaps it was the jealousy of not having a boat like that guy Pete had. She guessed his father let him have the boat anytime he wanted, and her brother, thanks to *their* father, never had that opportunity. Maybe it was that.

Teddy was never allowed to take the boat out on his own. Yet, Teddy had a knack for boats; it was like they were joined together at the hip. He treated boats better than he treated girls, and it was no wonder Teddy struggled with relationships. Sara always said, "If a boat were a girl …"

Teddy would rage late at night over the injustice of it. He could never accept that his father simply didn't trust him, and stubborn, just like his father, he refused to take no for an answer. That fateful summer Teddy had been on his father for weeks about wanting to take a girl out in the boat, but the answer was always no. Then one day, very unexpectedly, he said yes, Teddy could take the boat out the following Saturday. Teddy could hardly sleep the night before he was so excited. Sara suspected the girl was nothing more than an excuse to take out the boat.

That one time …

That one time turned into the last time, and nothing was ever the same again—not for Teddy, not for their father, and not for her. Unbeknownst to Teddy, Sara carried the burden of that *one time* also, carrying it much more heavily than her brother. He just never knew. For that, she had paid a steeper price than anyone could have imagined. Over the years, through the sleepless nights, she had struggled with telling Teddy what happened that night. What happened, after he had stormed off, and what she had done.

Just then, Patty walked behind the bar.

"Amy, can you unlock the front door, please? It's time to open."

4

FOR THE PAST hour, in the sweltering heat, I had been sitting in my Chevy, in the far corner of the strip mall parking lot, watching Sharkees from a distance, trying to quell the nagging alarm bells that were exploding in my head. My T-shirt was soaked through, that sweaty, clammy feeling adding to my growing discomfort. As much as I didn't want to admit it, deep down, I knew I had jumped at the opportunity too quickly. But something bigger was at play here, I just couldn't put my finger on it, yet.

Squinting through the windshield, I saw Teddy exit through the wooden gate of Sharkees' patio followed by that server, Amy.

Strange, I hadn't thought they knew each other. Huddled on the grassy median, they were too far away to hear properly, the best I could tell, however, they were in a deep discussion of some sort.

Amy, at least a foot shorter than Teddy, was standing close to him, looking up, hands out to her sides, gesturing. She appeared angry with him. Teddy occasionally raised his hands in defence, gesturing in return. Just then, maybe in the nick of time for Teddy, Tony, the beefy server, exited from the same patio gate and walked over. Standing back, he waited until Amy stopped speaking, then stepped forward, handing Teddy an envelope. They talked briefly, shook hands, and Teddy pocketed the envelope. Tony kissed Amy on the forehead, then went back inside, but this time through the front entrance. Teddy and

Amy were still talking, but I had seen enough. I started my Chevy and exited the far end of the parking lot.

Three days later, I was parked in the same spot, early for my meeting with Teddy. I had spent the past couple of days getting ready. I packed light, thinking I would only be gone a day or two. I threw in a couple of T-shirts, then, as an afterthought, tossed in a pair of jeans. I left enough food out for Cat, and asked my neighbour, Mary, to keep an eye on my place, her broken foot making her a good watchdog. As it was, there wasn't much to watch in the way of possessions or furniture. An old, four-poster bed and dresser combo filled one of the bedrooms, and no need for a kitchen set, as I ate standing up. In the living room was a large flat-screen TV I had liberated one night from the end of someone's driveway, stumbling home from Sharkees. After plugging it in, and turning it on, it didn't work, but I had a knack for finding fortune at the most opportune time. I traded a favour with Mary, who worked at an electronics store nearby, and she had the TV fixed. Oh, and the favour? Nothing much, really.

A few nights after finding the TV, while sitting outside since there was no TV to watch, Mary had ended up in an altercation on her front lawn with an old boyfriend. He wouldn't take the hint and leave, and not taking kindly to women being beaten up on their front lawns, I intervened. In most cases, that will get your TV fixed, and more. Fortune, meet opportunity.

My most prized possession was my stereo and record collection, coloured milk crates filled with albums, covering the living room floor. The only piece of furniture was a red and white patterned aluminum lawn chair, sitting in the middle of the room, pointed toward a pair of giant speakers. Late at night, I would sit in the chair, facing the speakers, playing album after album.

Then there was Cat. He wasn't mine, and I had no idea whose he was. Stumbling through the baseball field one night, I came face to face with a black and white cat sitting on the bench. Meowing loudly, trying to get my attention, it stood up and wanted to be petted. Reaching down, I patted it on the head, and he up and rubbed his nose on mine, and that was it. He followed me home, taking up residence like he owned the place. At night, he would keep me company, purring softly in my lap, on the chair in the living room, as the music blared—both of us giving each other what we needed, which wasn't much.

~

A taxi pulled up in front of Sharkees; after a moment, Amy got out and walked inside. Maybe, this was my chance. There was something femme fatale about her, and I had lots of experience in that department. I pulled forward into a parking spot closer to Sharkees and went inside. It was still early, the oppressive humidity after the morning's storm had returned, and walking through the double set of doors, I stood in the entranceway, arms outstretched, absorbing the cool air of the a/c. Straight ahead, a small fire was burning, which seemed surreal, but it was the perfect counterbalance against the a/c. I looked over to the right, the restaurant side was empty except for a lone server who was moving about the booths and didn't notice me.

I moved to my left and casually trailed my hand along the front edge of the bar's surface and slipped silently onto a stool. Amy was behind the bar, head down, buried in her phone, pecking away. She didn't notice me, so I sat patiently and waited. When she still hadn't looked up, a smile came to my face, and I couldn't resist. Clearing my throat, she jumped, dropping her phone. Fumbling, she juggled it, catching it between her knees. Flustered, looking up, she smiled at my devilish grin.

"Oh my God! I'm so sorry. I didn't see you."

"I've only been sitting here for like five minutes. I was in no hurry anyway. It's not like I'm dying for a nice cold frosty beer, after walking five miles in bare feet, on the burning pavement, this being my last day on earth and all."

Slipping her phone in her back pocket, she stepped toward me; eyes sparkling, a huge grin forming, the lines on her face creasing around her eyes.

"Well, we can't have that happening now, can we? Since this is your last day on earth and all, what will you have? On me."

"Barking Squirrel please and don't stop."

Smiling, Amy moved to the cooler behind her, brought out a chilled mug, and looking at me, started pouring from the tap. Tilting the mug as she poured, she carefully filled it to the brim, then gently placed the frosty mug in front of me. A bit of foam oozed over the top, slowly wiggling down the side of the glass, making squiggly lines, competing with the condensation forming on the already melting glass.

"Ahh, there you go. The perfect last supper fit for a king."

We continued to smile at each other, our eyes locked. Amy reached for a jar of water and took a sip from her straw.

"So, Pete … It's Pete, right? Are you from around here?"

"Yes, I live over in that new townhouse complex," I replied, and turned and pointed through the window.

Amy looked over my shoulder. "Oh, I know the one. What's it like? I've been looking for a new place."

"It's nice, quiet, and not many kids. People keep to themselves. I moved in after Christmas. I haven't seen any vacancy signs, but that doesn't mean anything. You know, I can check if you like."

"Sure, sure, that would be great." She leaned back against the bar, her legs crossed, sipping on her jar of water.

Amy, unlike the other servers, was not dressed in Sharkees attire, instead, in skinny black jeans, black low-cut sneakers, a faded pink golf shirt ending just above the waistline of her jeans. Her long brown curly hair was tied up in a bun on the top of her head, loose bangs hanging down. She had friendly, soft blue eyes that drew you instantly to them. Amy was certainly not like the other Sharkees servers. There was a brief, almost awkward, silence as we stared at each other.

"So, Pete, you come here often?" she asked, and as soon as the words came out, she started blushing. "Oh my God, I'm such an idiot. I sound like a pickup line."

"What I mean is … er uh … what I meant was … well, do you come to Sharkees often? I don't think I have ever seen you here before. Well, except for the other day. And that was some a performance," she smirked.

"Oh, that …" I looked down, feeling embarrassed. My head remained down, and when I didn't hear a response, I lifted my eyes. Amy was smiling at me—that soft, innocent smile—and our eyes locked again.

I gave her a flirty smile. "I have the permanent reminder of that temporary feeling. My head didn't stop banging for two days. I've made a pact with shots—you don't bother me, and I won't bother you."

"Well, it looks like you made a new best friend out of it, at least."

"Huh?"

"That guy. Um, Teddy, I think ... That big guy that was with you ... you're friends, right? Are you here to meet him again?"

Just then, and not a moment too soon, in walked Teddy. He was still wearing the same tank top and hat. Grinning from ear to ear, he plopped down on the stool beside me, and slapped me hard on the back. "How are you, big guy? No, wait, it's Pistol. Pistol Pete, right? So, how are you, Pistol?"

He slapped me even harder, almost knocking the wind out of me. Amy smiled and shook her head. Catching my breath, I straightened up, lightly punched myself in the chest, and reached for my beer—fighting off the urge to slap Teddy back, hard. Bravely, I turned to Teddy, taking a deep breath. "Texas! How are ya? You haven't changed a bit."

Teddy laughed, this time slapping me on the back so hard I was flung face-first onto the bar.

"Teddy!" Amy snapped, then caught herself. "I mean, that's your name, right? You better stop, or you will hurt him."

Coughing and gasping, my face turned sideways on the bar, between gasps, I could see Teddy looking at Amy. Suddenly, Teddy reached over, grabbed me by the scruff of my neck, lifted me off the stool, and positioned me upright again. Wide-eyed, open-mouthed, I was powerless to stop him. Teddy winked at Amy, and I snapped out of it when I felt Amy's hand on my arm, gently rubbing it.

"Hey, you okay?" she asked, her touch setting off tiny electric shocks.

"Yeah ..." drawled Teddy, "she's right. I better stop. Listen, I'm sorry there, Pistol. Sometimes I don't know my own strength. Here, let me buy you another beer. Or how about a shot?"

My eyes bugged open. "No shots!" I shifted on the stool. "But another beer would be great."

"That we can do, pardner." Teddy motioned to Amy, who poured me another beer and prepared a shot for him. Drinks in hand, with Amy holding her water jar, Teddy offered a toast.

"To my new pal, Pistol. Salut!"

Hands raised, none of us clinked glasses, and I cringed in anticipation, but there was no back slap this time. Amy leaned back against the counter, sipping on her water, watching us. Downing his shot, Teddy tapped me on the shoulder and suggested we move to a booth. I nodded, reached for my beer, slid gingerly off the stool, and dutifully followed him. Looking back over my shoulder, Amy was watching me, wearing her infectious, innocent smile. I smiled and mouthed "bye," lifting her hand and waving, she mouthed, "bye."

Teddy and I took the same booth as before, and again I sat facing him, his back to the wall. Sipping on my beer, I decided to play along and see where Teddy took this. As he spoke, I turned my head slightly, trying to find Amy, but out of nowhere, Tony appeared, startling me. Tony placed a tumbler in front of Teddy and handed him a thick manila envelope similar to the one he had given him the other day in the parking lot.

Teddy thanked him, but Tony's eyes were on me, and a cold shiver ran down my spine. I flinched involuntarily. Teddy looking at me, winked, thanked Tony again, and shooed him away. Visibly shaken, I clasped my hands around my beer mug, steadying myself. I turned my attention back to Teddy and the envelope.

Teddy opened the envelope, peered inside and licking his fingers, started counting the bills using thumb and forefinger, "One hundred, two hundred, three hundred, four hundred, five hundred …" I tried to pretend I didn't care, changing the subject.

"So, do you have that picture of Sara you told me about the other day?"

"Oh yeah … the picture. I almost forgot. Hold on a sec."

His head bobbed as he counted. When he finished, and solely for my benefit, he took the bills out of the envelope, straightening the thick wad on the table, shuffling and flattening it in his two large hands like a Vegas card shark. My eyes glued to the table, I silently sniffed the intoxicating smell of the brown money. *Yes, Virginia, the smell is different.*

Teddy slipped the bills back in and put the thick envelope into his back pocket and reached around, pulling out a picture from his other pocket and handed it to me. Sara was your typical biker chick. Smiling and leaning against the side of her bike, legs crossed, she was tall, lean, with long California blonde hair cascading down the back of the dark purple leather jacket. Her matching helmet was perfectly balanced on her hip, and she had a dazzling white smile and her eyes sparkled. A born heartbreaker. As I studied it, he told me what he knew.

Three years ago, he bought her a Harley 883 street bike for her birthday, and he had regretted it since. She had taken to the bike like a duck to water, and what bothered him was that she would disappear for days on it. He never knew where she was or who she was with, and being her little brother, he was only concerned for her well-being. He could never keep tabs on her, and that drove him crazy, he said. Her go-to place when she had disappeared was the Lucky 7evens in Peterborough, three hours away. That much he knew.

I was rattled again by the mention of Peterborough and pushed the unpleasant thought aside.

Teddy said he bought the bike using their parents' trust fund, thinking, it would be a nice toy for his sister. She could ride around town, showing off what her little brother had bought her, and that was that.

As Teddy spoke, I felt like something wasn't right. *Peterborough?* No, that was a living, breathing entity unto itself. Then what? Tony had unnerved me a few minutes ago. Was that it? It took a lot more than some knucklehead like Tony to unnerve me, but something wasn't right. Then it hit me. I was being watched.

As Teddy talked, I looked around the bar, hoping it was Amy. I was more than okay with that. Then, I noticed a dark figure between the kitchen and the entrance to the bar. Squinting, I could just make out someone staring at me. Tony? I shivered and flinched, electric shocks running through me. How long had he been there?

Tony moved into the light, our eyes locking. Tony nodded once, winked, and pointed his finger at me—cocking his thumb, he pulled the trigger. Smiling, he turned and walked into the kitchen. More electric shocks tore through me, I shivered hard and reached for my arm.

Snap. I could feel a breeze in my face, and it was not the a/c.

"Huh? What?"

Teddy was trying to get my attention, snapping his fingers at me. "Are you listening, or is your mind on Amy? I saw. Didn't think I noticed, did you?"

"Huh?" I tried to play it coy. "Noticed what?"

"Aw, come on, Pistol. I saw you making googly eyes earlier with that bartender, Amy. You can't fool me."

Hoping Teddy hadn't noticed my encounter with Tony, I was willing to go along with this charade. "Yes, you got me, Texas. Busted! Guilty as charged. I have been having impure thoughts about Amy."

An awkward silence ensued as Teddy eyed me suspiciously.

BANG! I jumped, knocking over the mug, spilling what was left of my beer.

"Shit!" My whole body shaking, eyes ablaze, I looked at Teddy, his fist resting on the table. I tried to speak, but nothing came out, my nerves stretched tight. Teddy watched me unravel, wearing a shit-eating grin.

"Ahh, it's okay, pardner. I was just playing with you. Sorry."

At the sound of *pardner*, I flinched, raising my arms in self-defence, and pulled back. Smiling wanly at Teddy, I dropped my arms and reached for the mug, my hands trembling.

"Okay, where were we? No, wait! First, you need another beer, and I need a shot." Teddy twisted his head, looking for Tony or Amy, but neither were in sight.

"Aw shit!" Irritated, he got up, grumbling. "Fuck it! I'll do it myself." Walking over to the bar, he glanced back at me. "What is it you drink? Barking dog something?"

"Barking Squirrel."

"Oh yeah, that barking chipmunk crap."

Teddy returned, handed me my beer, sat down, placing his two shots in front of him. We took a drink, eyeing each other warily, without the toast this time. Returning our glasses to the table, replenished with courage, I looked over at Teddy.

"You were telling me about Sara and that she loved her bike, her freedom, she went everywhere on it, she was happy, and you didn't like it ... or something like that."

Teddy's beady eyes narrowed, his ready smile replaced by a frown. Remember when you were little, and you tried to hold your breath for as long as you could? I'll huff, and I'll puff ... and your cheeks would expand out, your face would turn purple, and it looked like the top of your head would blow off? Well, that was Teddy.

"Whoa! Easy big fella," I said. "That didn't come out the way I meant it. Easy now ..."

Teddy, looking like he was going to explode at any second, I tried to pour water over the burning coals.

"What I meant was, I can see why you are concerned, big guy. I mean, not knowing where your sister is at all hours of the day or who she is with? I would be freaking out over it. The world is a crazy place nowadays, right? I would love to have a brother like you, always looking out for me, always checking up on me. I mean, that's what brothers do, right?"

I raised my glass in a toast toward Teddy. "To loving brothers!"

Teddy's frown softened, and his fists slowly unclenched. He eyed me warily, and still holding my beer in a toasting position, I gestured and nodded back in hopeful approval. "To loving brothers, right?" I gestured once more, flicked my eyebrows, and nodded my head. "Hmm, hmm."

Another awkward pause, and then like the Berlin Wall, Teddy crumbled. "Aww, pardner, I can't be mad at you. You're my Pistol after all." Raising his shot glass, he met my toast. "To loving brothers!"

We clinked glasses this time and downed our drinks in one gulp, turning our heads just enough so our eyes remained firmly locked. Finished, we simultaneously banged our glasses down on the table.

"Another round! Tony! Amy!" Teddy bellowed, without even looking up. Amy appeared out of nowhere, standing beside me, her hand on my shoulder.

"Yes, Teddy. What do you need?"

"Another beer for my partner, and a couple of more shots for me, okay? We have to finish up our business here."

"Right away, Teddy," Amy replied, squeezing my shoulder, her hand warm and gentle. Teddy pulled out the thick envelope again, and was thumbing through it, counting and pulling out hundred-dollar bills.

Amy returned with our drinks, then mouthing "bye," went into the kitchen. Wearing a goofy grin, I watched her walk away.

BANG! Teddy slammed the stack of bills on the table, trying to get my attention. I jumped again.

"Uh, what?"

"Pete? What's your plan?"

I thought for a second. *Plan? What plan? There is no plan.* Reaching into my hat, fumbling around, I found a rabbit and pulled it out.

"Well, Teddy, since you said Sara likes riding, especially to Peterborough, it's not that far, so I thought, I would head there first. That's an easy drive, plus, there are lots of small towns along the way, and I could check them out. Those roadside motels too. Maybe, she's shacked up in one with some biker-guy? That mutual attraction thing." I offered an innocent smile then quickly continued, not giving Teddy a chance to react. "And of course, I will check out that Lucky 7evens. I've heard of the place, and I wouldn't mind playing some pool again. My old stomping grounds."

I sighed, not so wistfully, at the memory. Teddy's head jerked up, and he stared hard at me.

"What?" I asked nervously.

"Oh, nothing. Just thinking. Listen on the way, do you think you could make a stop for me?"

"Sure, where?"

"Havelock. It's on the way, just off Highway 7. It's this side of Peterborough. Do you know the place? It's where the old train station used to be on the main drag as you go through town. There's a bar now called the Last Caboose. I know the owner, Jimmy."

"Yeah, yeah. I've heard of the place."

"Okay great," Teddy said. He picked up the stack of bills on the table, put them back in the envelope, and handed it to me. "I need you to give this to Jimmy. I'll tell him to expect you."

Holding the thick envelope in my hand alarm bells started going off. *So … now I can add delivery boy to my resume.*

Ever feel like you've been had? It's not a nice feeling. And, did you ever notice that once you come to the realization, the person you are most mad at, is yourself? Hook line, and sinker, I had been reeled in tight. There was no turning back now.

Teddy, reading my mind, tried to reassure me. "Ahh, don't worry, Pistol. Easy-peasy. All you have to do is drop off the envelope, and that's it. Simple. A quick stop, ask for Jimmy, hand him the envelope, and I bet he will give you a free beer or two. Then you leave, just like that."

Looking down at the envelope, then up again, he dangled the carrot. "And for doing this, you can take out five thousand, okay?"

"Huh?" I looked up in shock.

"Don't worry, Pistol. I counted it. It's all there. Twenty-five K. Twenty for Jimmy, and five for you." He smiled at me reassuringly. Quickly, I snatched the carrot off the stick before he could pull it back. Let the games begin.

"Okay, so we're good?" he asked.

I nodded again, keeping my head low, trying to hide my deer-in-the-headlights expression.

"Check in every few days to keep me posted on things, other than that, I will leave you be. You promised to find my sister, and I'm holding you to it. A promise is a promise."

Nodding, I swallowed hard, pocketed the envelope, and got up to leave. I reached for my beer, finished it, and placed the mug on the table.

"I'll be in touch."

I started to walk out. As I passed the bar, I looked for Amy, but something caught my attention, tucked down on a shelf under the bar …

"Here!" Teddy called out from behind me. "You'll need this."

I turned, as he tossed me a burner phone.

5

THE SUN POKED its head through my rear-view mirror as I made my way along Highway 7, aka the Lost Highway. I had the road to myself. Glancing at my watch, it was just past 6:00 a.m., and besides the odd trucker, who else would be on the road at this time of the morning? Today was going to be a scorcher, and the windows were already cranked down, the wind swirling around the interior. The sounds of the road beneath my Chevy, with its familiar rumbling, combined with the early morning stillness, made a nice soundtrack to help clear my head. My eight-track was playing, and America reminded me that today was the day.

One can hope.

Even so, I still had an awful sense of foreboding, meaning one thing—trouble lay ahead.

The meeting yesterday with Teddy had not gone the way I expected. Surprise! And now my easy-peasy missing-persons case included a money drop, and I was in even deeper. And what about the bike helmet I saw under the shelf in the bar as I was leaving? Hadn't Sara disappeared on her bike? Could the helmet have been hers? Was this nothing more than a wild goose chase, albeit a profitable one? I also had to contend with the active playground in my mind that was Peterborough, uncertain any amount of money would be worth revisiting those good ol' days, and I wasn't sure I wanted to know if time did heal.

After getting home from Sharkees, I had spent the rest of the day tidying up some loose ends, wanting to get an early start in the morning. Peterborough was only three hours away, but I wanted to be the first one to catch that worm. I made a grocery run, extra food for Cat just in case, then went next door to give Mary a spare key. Everyone needs neighbours like Mary. Even though our paths crossed briefly, coming and going on our front steps, I could tell she was responsible, reliable, and trustworthy. I needed that; even though I didn't have much in the way of possessions, I still needed the comfort of knowing my place was in good hands. I made a mental note to make room for Mary, along with Otte, in my imaginary will. After I visited Mary, I spent the rest of my night in my lawn chair, Cat on my lap, facing the speakers, being serenaded by Pink Floyd.

I was blinded by a bright yellow-orange ball in the driver's mirror interrupting my thoughts. I blinked away the glare until I could see the road ahead of me. Where was I again? Don't you hate that? You've been driving, the miles rolling by, and you don't remember a thing? Coming around a bend there was a sign: Peterborough 152 km.

Still a ways to go yet, time to switch back to autopilot.

Summers in Peterborough. I had grown up there with my dad, and as a bonus, I grew up on boats and was a seasoned boater by the time I was fifteen. Those summers were the best times in my life, once they included girls.

Tina mostly.

Oh, to be young again. We lived right on the Otonabee River, a couple of locks up from the Peterborough waterfront. My dad's boat, a 1985 Regal Commodore 360, was the envy of the river. It was such a fun place to be, my dad let me have the boat any time I wanted. What a life. I would take the 360 out, and cruise up and down the river all day. Dad showed me everything about boating. How to operate and dock the boat, read the weather and the river's current—then left me to it. Best way to learn, he said. Then he left me to it, to teach myself. That was the best part. I could teach myself because my dad had brought me up not to be afraid of making a mistake. If the boat broke down and I was towed back, my dad didn't make a big deal out of it, simply holding me accountable. There was no anger or drama.

"Okay, what did you learn?" he'd say. "And what you will you do differently next time?"

Just practicality and common sense. I boated in every condition; the stormier, the better. It was the best way to learn.

The place to be in the summer was the Peterborough waterfront, a local hotspot for boaters, tourists, and girls. There was a Holiday Inn conveniently located beside the marina, where boats circled, waiting to gas up. And if you missed the lock closing, you could dock for the night, get a room next door, and head up George Street to catch the action.

Getting to the waterfront by boat was easy. It was a quick two-lock cruise from my dad's place, through the Peterborough Lift Locks, a tourist attraction in its own right, then a smaller lock, which emptied into the bay, with a campground and beach nestled off in the corner. I loved going through the locks, even though it could be slow and tedious at times especially in the middle of summer. Taking a boat through the locks was an art, which was another boating skill I had acquired. It was a chance for me to show off, and when you're young, that's what you do. It was an endless summer of boats, girls, water, more girls, and sun. (Did I mention the girls?)

An added bonus was the free entertainment provided by the weekend warriors in their expensive boy-toys, which came standard with the bikini-clad accessory: hot girlfriend, or bored wife, standing on the bow, holding the line. Nothing like seeing a houseboat stuck sideways in the locks. Fun times.

It was a great time in my life with only good memories, except for that *one time*.

That hot Sunday—a long weekend in August, the first summer after my dad had passed. I had tried my best to bury the memory, but much too easily, it had resurfaced. Forced to look back, it was weird. Just another overblown encounter. Hard to imagine it could have such far-reaching effects, taking on a life of its own, altering life's path, turning me into the person I became.

And isn't that what normal people do? Put bad things behind them? Move on? Proving, I guess, I wasn't normal. So, why hadn't it been triggered before now? Things happen for a reason, Dr. Jayne constantly reminded me. Was this one of them?

The blast of an oncoming horn jerked me back to reality, and I quickly moved back into my lane. Staring straight ahead, both hands gripping the wheel tightly, the truck roared past, with another loud blast from its horn. I drove in silence, rattled by the near miss. Up ahead I saw the sign for Sharbot Lake. I slowed for a gas station on my right, and I saw some motorcycles parked off to the side. As good a reason as any to stop. Motorcycles. Sara.

I turned in and parked off to the side. Two couples in their late thirties or early forties—weekend warrior types, dressed head-to-toe in matching leathers—were standing beside their chrome plated machines chatting, large takeout coffee cups in hand. The bikes sparkled in the morning sunlight, both female bikers' helmets were off and placed on their respective rear seats. A burly guy, with long stringy greyish hair was holding his helmet under one arm, a coffee in the other, leaning against the seat. The other guy, much taller and slimmer, a black bandana wrapped around his head, was doing the same on his bike. They seemed friendly enough.

I got out of my Chevy, acting nonchalant, stretching like I had been driving for hours, and walked around my car slowly, inspecting it like those long-distance truckers do, kicking each tire for effect. Looking over at the couples, I stretched again, hoping to catch their attention, and just like casting your line in the water, I caught one. The woman standing beside the taller biker, had been watching me. She was tall and slim, like her companion, dressed in black leather with a white polka-dotted bandana tied around her head, long flaming red hair hanging out, halfway down her back. This was my chance.

Smiling, I strolled over towards her. "Nice morning for a ride, huh?" I said as I came even with the group.

The other three turned—Red's eyes remained glued to me—and almost as one, seemed annoyed that someone would have the audacity to enter their space.

"Yup," the burly biker grunted.

I looked at the others, but they didn't say a word. Red was silent (but smiling).

"Okay. Um, yeah, beautiful day. You guys from around here or just passing through?"

"Why? You a cop?" scowled the heavier female biker.

"No … no … I'm not a cop," I said, caught off guard by their simmering antagonism.

"Well then, buddy," she said, "if you're not a cop, what do you want?"

I stood, silent, making me look even more like an idiot to them. Breaking the awkward silence, I made another attempt.

"I'm looking for someone. Her name is Sara Polson. She rides a Harley 883. I think she wears a black and purple helmet, maybe you've seen her? I have a picture …"

The female biker rolled her eyes at me, as I reached in my pocket, pulled it out, and handed it to her. Roughly snatching it from my hand she barely glanced at it, passing it over to her partner.

"Nope, never seen her before. Is she in trouble? And why are you so interested in her? You said you weren't a cop."

"My business," I snapped, suddenly irritated. The heavy biker-chick returned my snap with her own volley.

"Well, buddy-who-says-he's-not-a-cop, we haven't seen her."

So much for seeming friendly enough. It proved you just never know. Holding my rising temper—and remembering my past in similar situations, *and how those turned out*—I cut my losses and backed off.

"Thanks, guys. Nice chatting with you. I'm going to be on my way. Can I have my picture back?"

The picture had made its way around to Red, who walked it over to me. Smiling, her perfectly straight, white teeth gleaming in the sun, she handed it to me and let her hand linger long enough in mine. ZING!

"Thanks, have a nice day," I said, looking only at Red while pocketing the picture. I turned towards the gas bar to try what was left of my luck.

Smarting from the unfriendly exchange, I was expecting something similar inside. You know, bored cashier, buried in their phone, with an *I-don't-give-a-shit attitude* transferred back to the customers. Stepping through the door, the bell jingling overhead, I walked inside, and after a few steps, I felt this strange, positive vibe.

Looking up, stretching out in front of me was a veritable oasis of sporting gear—fishing tackle, boating supplies, tools, food, you name it. Rows upon rows, walls upon walls, of all the riches a weekend warrior could ever need. Mouth agape, I stood, mesmerized, trying to take it all in. My panoramic tour of heaven was rudely interrupted by a soft, friendly voice.

"Yessir! Your first time here, right? I can tell. Happens every time."

I turned in the direction of the voice, standing behind the counter was a man in his fifties with a high forehead and long thinning silver hair, neatly parted on the left. His hair spilled over his ears, and he had a large mouth filled with bright white perfect teeth that were smiling at me.

"What?" The best I could offer, still mesmerized by my surroundings.

"It happens all the time," he winked at me, his Spanish accent very out of place. "First time? Not what you were expecting?"

I stepped towards the counter, speechless, my mouth still open. Gathering myself, I returned his smile, as I noticed the name Carlos stitched on the left pocket of his powder blue golf shirt.

"Carlos? Wow! What a place you have! I mean, it sure doesn't look like much from the outside—" catching myself, "no uh, what I mean is—"

Carlos laughed. "It's okay, *señor*. I know what you mean. Like I said," he waved his hand out towards the store, "no one expects this."

Since it was still early, the store was empty so we could chat. I took an immediate liking to Carlos.

"Hi, I'm Pete," I said, extending my hand across the counter.

His grip was firm despite his slight physical build, and he looked me directly in the eyes. The difference between inside and outside was not lost on me. Looking around, trying to take it all in, I asked Carlos how the store came to be, as from the outside, it looked like the usual gas bar.

He chuckled. "Oh, I know, *señor*. I built all this myself. People were passing through here all the time, hunters, campers, fishermen, boaters, so it made sense. Well, with my daughter Maria's help too. She runs the store now. But I still enjoy it, and early mornings are my favourite time of the day, so I let her sleep in on weekends."

The front door jingled, and a customer entered. I stepped back, not wanting to be in the way. "Mind if I look around?"

"Sure, *señor* Pete. Take your time. I'm here all day. There's a fresh pot of coffee around the corner to the left, donuts also. Help yourself. It is free for customers. Happy exploring!"

Turning, he greeted the customer. "Hi! How are you today?"

I went off in search of a coffee and a donut, and forty-five minutes later, I returned to the front counter. Carlos, standing at the front cash, smiled at me.

"Welcome back, did you enjoy your tour? I see you are empty-handed. With that, you are a rarity. No one leaves here empty-handed."

I smiled. "There were just too many choices."

Looking around the store, we were the only ones again. Now was my chance. "Listen, Carlos. I could use your help."

"Sure, *señor* Pete. My pleasure, how can I be of help?"

Pulling the picture of Sara out of my back pocket, I handed it across the counter to Carlos. "I'm looking for someone. Have you seen her? Her name is Sara, Sara Polson. She rides a Harley 883."

Quickly, and very unexpectedly, Carlos's demeanour changed, his smile replaced by a dark frown and a look of concern. There was a long pause as Carlos looked over the picture.

"Take your time, make sure," I said, while waiting for the inevitable question of why was I looking for her. Carlos's eyes darted up and down the photograph, trying to come up with a convincing answer. Looking up, Carlos smiled sadly.

"No, I have not seen her."

"Are you sure?" Reaching out, I pushed at the picture in Carlos's hand. "Look again."

Carlos shook his head, "I am sorry, but I have not seen the girl in the picture." Carlos handed me the picture and I pocketed it.

"You had this look of concern on your face when you were looking at the picture."

"Yes, that is correct."

"I don't understand. You say you have never seen her, yet something troubled you about the picture."

"Yes, that is correct, *señor* Pete."

"Then what is it? You say you don't know the girl in the picture, but something is bothering you about it."

Carlos nodded and sighed. "Yes, I know of a Sara, who rides a bike like in the picture, but this is not her. So no, I have not seen her, but I do know of a Sara, yes. I have seen her. Many times. She always stopped here for coffee, chatting with us, the other customers. Such a lovely girl, so friendly, outgoing, but she was troubled. I never knew what, though. She would not say. I could just tell. There was an air of sadness about her. She was always friendly to

Maria and me. We never asked. We just let her be. She seemed to find comfort here. I started stocking motorcycle parts and oil for her, and she would change her own oil out back. She loved that bike."

I was surprised by Carlos's response—it had been a day of surprises, and the sun was barely up.

"Passing through to where?" I asked. "Did she ever say? When was the last time you saw her?"

The front door jingled, and a customer came in. Carlos looked at me and lowered his voice. "Hold on, give me a minute."

I nodded, stepped away, in search of another coffee. I could hear him talking with the customer, and despite it being early morning, I think I needed something stronger. When the door jingled again, I returned to the front counter.

"Such a lovely girl," he sighed.

"You speak in the past tense, like she's gone. Has something happened to her?" My mind was starting to race, I wasn't expecting any of this. Wasn't this supposed to be the easy part?

Carlos waved his hand. "I hope not. I mean, I do not know."

"When did you see her last?"

"I am sorry," he said. "It is just that we miss her. We are worried about her. I fear something has happened to her. I have not seen her since late May. She stopped in one night very late, and I was working that night. Normally, I do not work nights anymore, but I was covering for a sick employee. She seemed more upset than usual. She was not herself. She barely spoke. She made herself a coffee as she always does. I make a fresh pot every hour, you know. But that night she, she, she …"

Hmm, late May. Maybe she is missing? "She what, Carlos? She what? Do you know where she was going? Which direction was she travelling?"

Carlos looked at me, his eyes pleading. "Señor Pete, I do not know. She never told me where she was going. Never. I never asked, and she never told. It was her business. She barely spoke to me that night. She would not look at me like she normally would. She was always asking after me, Maria too. We would talk, catch up, but that night, she was in her own world. A far-off world. I started to ask her if she was all right, but she abruptly cut me off and said she had to go. She just up and left. And Maria and I have not seen her since."

"Well, could she have stopped in here since, on a day or night, when you or your daughter weren't working?"

"Yes, that is *possible*, but I doubt it."

"Why?"

"Well," as Carlos rubbed his hand through his thin hair, "for one, none of the motorcycle supplies we stock for her have been touched since that last time. No oil, rags, nothing has been bought since."

"But she can't be the only biker passing through here?"

"Yes, that is true, but we keep her supplies off to the side in a special place for her only. That is how much we liked her. So, if she did pass through, and we were not here, one of the other employees would have sold her something, but no stock has been sold since."

I nodded.

"She had this habit," Carlos said, "when she made herself a coffee, of leaving the stir stick tilted against the sugar cup, in the same place on the table every time. That is how I knew she had been here. I would see the stick tilted the next morning, and I think it was her way of telling us, I am here, I am okay. So, you see—"

Frustrated, I was perplexed by this. This was not what I was expecting at all. I figured someone would tell me they had seen her or see her all the time. Wasn't this a simple case of finding someone who didn't want to be found?

"*Señor* Pete? Excuse me, if you do not mind, but may I ask why are you looking for her?"

Did I trust Carlos enough to tell him why? I opted for yes, ignoring the little voice inside. "Her brother is looking for her. He reported her missing right around the time you last saw her, and he hired me to find her."

"Are you a police officer?"

Such a simple question, asked of me a thousand times, and barely five minutes ago outside by those bikers. Yet this time I started to fidget, fumbling to get the words out, and I answered much too weakly.

"No, I'm not a cop," I said, tumbling into a deep well of shame. I stammered, grasping for the words, trying to rescue myself, but only made it worse. My voice was shaky. "I used to be a cop at one time. Then I, well, I left."

The shame crashed over me now like a rogue wave. My head dropped, looking down and away from Carlos. Thoroughly shocked at my response to this seemingly innocent question. I had never responded in this manner before. What was happening here?

I looked up into the man's eyes, and he was smiling, nodding gently in approval. Who was this, man? He saw through me much too easily.

Recognizing my shame, he spoke gently. "It is okay, *señor* Pete. We are all coming and going from somewhere."

I felt light-headed and reached out and grabbed the counter to steady myself. The way he said that sounded so reassuring. Like he knew. How could he possibly know? We are all coming and going from somewhere.

No one had ever said something like that to me before—or maybe I had just never heard it like that before. It made no sense, yet at the same time, it made perfect sense. I felt this warmth drape over me, my arms and neck started to tingle, and my eyes welled up. Pulling myself together, I took my hand off the counter, steadying myself, I tried to lighten the mood.

"It seems I'm good at finding people who don't want to be found. And the money isn't bad either," I said, forcing a grin.

Carlos gave me a broad smile. "I hope you find her. And if ... no, *when* you find her, please tell her Maria and I miss her very much, and to come back and see us."

"I will. I promise."

I will find her, and I will bring her back here myself. Everyone needs a Carlos in their world.

I reached across the counter and shook his hand, his hand crossing over mine, clasping down on it, his touch warm, and could feel the peace emanating from within.

"Be safe, *señor* Pete. May God be with you and protect you."

I shuddered as a chill ran through my bones. I couldn't help but feel Carlos was sending me a message, a warning of some kind. I sensed real danger lay ahead, and my easy-peasy missing person's case was not going to be so easy after all. Visibly shaken, I disengaged his hand and pulled back, said goodbye, turned to head out, then stopped. Turning around, Carlos was smiling at me.

"Carlos?"

"Yes, *señor* Pete?"

"Do you remember when I came in here? There were two couples and their bikes parked outside. Late thirties or early forties all in black leather. Were they in here? They all had coffee. Did you see them? Speak to them?"

"Yes, I did." But then he stopped talking, almost like he wanted to avoid answering, but it was too late. This is what I was expecting when I showed him the picture of Sara. Were the tables turning here?

"And—"

"Yes, I saw them."

"Yes Carlos, you said that. Anything else? Did you speak with them? Are they from around here?"

"Why do you ask?" Carlos looked down, clearly uncomfortable.

"Oh, I dunno, just curious, I guess. It was strange, as I ran into them outside in the parking lot before coming in here. They appeared friendly enough until I showed them the picture of Sara, then abruptly, they turned cold, I couldn't figure it out. So, I wondered how they were with you? Did they give you any trouble?"

Carlos put his hands up in defence, waving them nervously. "Oh no, no, no … no trouble. I have never seen them before."

We both knew that was a lie, but I decided to leave it there. There was no point in pressing further, as he appeared shaken enough. Something was up all right.

"Okay, thanks, you take care now, Carlos." I smiled and turned to leave once more.

"You too, please come back anytime!" Carlos replied.

"I certainly will! I still need to buy something."

But I wasn't exactly leaving empty-handed, was I?

As I put my hand on the door to push it open, I heard Carlos's voice whisper behind me.

"Please dear, my, O Gracious Lord, please protect *señor* Pete."

Another chill ran down through me, and my hand on the door handle started to shake. I paused and considered looking back, then pushed hard on the door, the loud jingling in tune with my nerves as I stumbled out into the blinding sunlight.

6

SARA LAY IN bed staring up at the ceiling. The slowly spinning blades of the ceiling fan cast long flickering shadows across the ceiling and down the walls. The long night had been humid and still, the air too thick for even the slightest breeze. Through limp curtains she could see the faint blue of the horizon as night slowly turned into day. The birds had started their early morning rounds, chirping loudly, coinciding with the loud chirping in her head. The clock on the nightstand read 6:13 a.m.

She reached under the sheet and touched herself. Usually, when she couldn't sleep and felt tense, she would touch herself, and it wouldn't take long to relieve the tension and fall asleep. But she could tell right away that wasn't going to work.

For far too long, she had been fighting it off, and she knew she couldn't fight it off any longer. She was going to have to tell him. Deep down, she knew it was for the best, and her brother needed to know. It was the best for both of them, and she couldn't carry around the burden any longer.

A win-win, right?

What nagged at her was her fear at how he would take it. That was what had held her back all this time. She couldn't trust that he would take it well.

No one takes bad news well when it involves one's parents. She knew it would be difficult and unsettling at first and that he would not take it well, but maybe with time? That was what she hoped. Time heals, isn't that what they say? But so much time had passed already. What if he didn't come around and she lost him for good this time?

Sara desperately needed to be released from the burden. It had been eating away at her like cancer all these years. Her only release had been her Harley. That had been a godsend. *Thank you, brother.* When her shift ended, she'd hop on and ride, tearing down the highway late at night, the white lines a blur, the wind blasting in her face—that was her release. That was when she truly felt free; free from what happened that night; free from *them*, from *him*, free from her double life as Sara and Amy. Free from the crushing weight of unpleasant memories and the burden of things unsaid.

Sitting up in bed, she tried to convince herself that it was finally time. She would tell Teddy today. *I will make it quick and to the point, like tearing off a band-aid. He will understand. He'll have to.*

Just like that she felt the pressure lift. She lay back and reaching down, started touching herself, and a few minutes later was fast asleep.

~

It was still early, when Sara pulled into the empty parking lot, and parked her bike behind the grocery store at the opposite end of the mall. She had made a deal with the store's manager, when she started working at Sharkees, lying that she didn't want people gawking at the bike. But what she didn't want was anyone knowing who she really was. She let herself in through the patio entrance and went straight behind the bar to make herself a coffee. Absentmindedly, she had carried her helmet instead of leaving it on the bike, and too lazy to go back, she dropped it on the shelf below the bar. This wasn't the first time this had happened, and she knew she was playing with fire as it would lead to endless questions from Patty. She reminded herself to hide the helmet in the storage closet once she finished her coffee. Leaning against the counter, she held the mug with two hands, unable to stop them from trembling. Her seemingly concrete decision from a few hours ago was already faltering. She'd seemed so sure of it. But now …

Teddy was due to arrive at any minute. Sunday breakfast at Sharkees was a brother–sister ritual, one of their many ways of coping with what happened to their parents.

Just then, Patty saved Sara from her self-induced mind fuck, waving good morning as she breezed through the entrance, headed for the kitchen.

"Amy? Amy honey? When you get a chance, can you refill the condiment caddies up in the booths? They were supposed to be refilled at closing last night."

Sara didn't answer.

"Honey, you okay?" Patty asked, moving closer, concerned. She reached out and touched her arm. Sara jerked, pulling her arm back.

"Yes, yes, sorry ... I didn't sleep well last night with all this heat. That's all. I'm good," she lied. Forcing a smile, she squeezed Patty's hand then set off towards the booths.

Patty turned toward the kitchen, looked down, and spotted the black and purple motorcycle helmet on the shelf under the bar. *That's strange,* she thought, *where did that come from?*

7

ON WOBBLY LEGS, I groped my way across the parking lot, shielding my eyes against the bright sun. Thankfully the bikers were long gone; I didn't need any more of that. I was no closer to finding Sara, and in fact, I was even further away now. And what about Carlos's concern for my safety? That unnerved me. Wouldn't you be?

It was coming up to eight thirty when I opened the driver's door and got in, the seat leather hot against the back of my legs. I rolled down the windows letting the sun-baked air out and took a minute to collect myself. *Fuck it, Pete! Keep moving. Don't think. Just keep moving.*

I turned the key in the ignition, revved the engine a couple of times, feeling the rumble through the sticky seats, breathing life into my now battered psyche. I reached back for my eight-track case, located a new tape—Boston—pushed it in the slot, and cranked the volume. The swelling guitars slowly filled my subconscious with what I needed right now—to slip away, and fast. One last rev, I slammed the Chevy into gear; tires spinning, gravel flying, I roared out of the parking lot and continued on my journey.

Speeding along the highway, I was feeling better, the howl of the wind and the pounding music colliding, strangely in tune. My left arm bent out the window, right hand gripping the wheel, and both eyes fixed on the road, I just drove. The farther and faster I went, the more my head cleared. Soon, I needed to take a leak, the multiple coffee's wearing out their welcome.

A few minutes later, I pulled into another gas bar, the parking lot empty save for a lone Harley. I parked near the bike as its owner came out of the shop with a large takeout coffee. I watched in awe as he strode toward his hog. He had to be the biggest biker I had ever seen. I mean, he was huge! There was nothing distinctive, he was big everywhere. How could anyone be that big? Where did they make clothing that big to fit him? He was dressed in black leather, his boots looking like what one would wear for landing on the moon, and he gave barrel-chested a whole new meaning. His sunglasses appeared custom-made. I thanked my lucky stars that the crazy bikers I had just encountered were not this guy. He stopped at the bike, shifted his helmet on the seat, then leaned back and opened the lid on his coffee. Taking a drink, he tilted his head up. What? Is he meditating?

I knew I had to approach him. I just didn't want to. Pulling the keys out of the ignition, I got out of the car, this time with no interest in pretending I was tired. I was tired. *Just get this over with.* Taking a deep breath, I shuffled towards the bike, my fingers crossed behind my back.

"Excuse me, sir. Good morning. Nice day. Sorry to interrupt, but I was wondering if I could ask you a question?"

They say your life can flash before your eyes in an instant. Bracing for that instant, fortunately, it never came. The biker-giant lowered his head, and in a voice so soft it would make Carlos sound like the devil himself, he said, "Morning. Beautiful day. So, what can I do for you?"

"My name's Pete."

"Hi Pete, I'm Alan."

Extending his hand I flinched, but his grip was warm and friendly, and yes, very firm.

"Well, Alan, I am looking for someone and maybe you could help me with that."

The next thirty minutes flew by, and by the time we were done, I had made a new best friend. I showed Alan the picture and he studied it thoroughly. He had not seen her and was surprised, as he travelled the lost highway corridor from early April to mid-November. He had seen similar bikes, just not her on one. He knew the Harley 883 well, it took a particular type of rider to handle it, and it was not for everyone. Still, he thought it strange their paths had not crossed; he knew all the regular bikers along this route, and they all knew him.

"I can only imagine," I said.

"I got my size from my grandfather. My dad used to say, I missed a gene somewhere along the line," he chuckled.

He took my number and promised to text if he saw Sara. Thanking him, he left me with an ominous warning. He had heard through the biker-grapevine that a group of Harleys had been cruising up and down the lost highway, harassing unsuspecting travellers. They liked fast cars, and looking over my shoulder at my Chevy, he said to be careful. Thanking him for the tip, I waved goodbye to another new best friend, thinking I liked this one a whole lot better. Alan hopped on his bike, and with an ear-splitting roar, headed north. I went inside, grabbed the washroom key, and hit the head, before getting back into the Chevy and continuing on.

Back on the highway, my oh my, where had the day gone? The Grateful Dead were right when they sang about what a long, strange trip it was. It had been, what, barely four hours? The highway stretched out in front of me, music thumping against my rear window; Otte earning his spot in my will for installing such a cool sound system. So apropos with the day so far, the Doobie Brothers were singing about having the highway blues and their motor running, or at least that's what it sounded like. The miles flew by, the perfect summer tonic for everything ailing me.

Humming along to the music, I started to find myself once more, thinking this better not become a habit of losing myself, as I hadn't packed the leash. Passing through a small town—one of many that were evenly spaced twenty minutes apart—I made a stop for gas and spotting parked bikes, made the rounds. All I got for my trouble was shaking heads; no longer surprised. Farther along, I stopped again, and it was rinse and repeat; parked bikes, no one knowing of Sara's whereabouts. It was coming up to noon and I had a brief flash of fear, that I'd be late for the drop at Havelock. Then I remembered Teddy said only to drop off the envelope when I passed through. *Whew!*

A few miles later Havelock came into view. Driving slowly through the sleepy town, it didn't take me long to find the Last Caboose. I pulled the tape out of the dash, the instant quiet a nice reprieve, and turned into the parking lot. I parked about halfway down, backing up against a maple tree for shade, and took a few minutes to collect myself.

Exhausted, I flipped the lever on my seat and pushed it back. The back of my shirt was sticky with sweat, and I felt clammy and dirty. Pushing away the uncomfortable feeling, I closed my eyes and tried to slow everything down. Breathing in and out slowly, inhale 1-2-3, exhale 1-2-3, clearing my head, I pulled the plug on my brain and let my mind empty. Suddenly, I jerked awake. Disoriented. I must have fallen asleep. The sun had shifted and now streamed in through the driver's window. I felt like I had been turned inside out.

I sat up, my shirt peeling away from the leather seat. I was groggy, and my head felt heavy. The heat was suffocating, and I was soaked in sweat. Squinting at the bright sunlight, I looked around. Where the fuck was I? I glanced at my watch. I had been asleep for almost two hours. Shaking my head, I heard a crack and grabbed for my neck. Fuck! I could barely turn my head. I was unraveling, more like melting. Where was that great vibe I felt when I started out this morning?

I tried to orient myself, breathing slowly, my head started to clear, and I saw the Last Caboose to my right. It's why I was here. Jimmy. The envelope. The drop. Looking around, my Chevy was the lone vehicle in the parking lot. Rubbing my hands along my bare thighs, I needed to get out of these sticky, sweaty clothes. Pulling the keys from the ignition, I moved around back and opened the trunk. Rummaging through my backpack, I found a dry T-shirt, peeled off my wet one, scrunched it in a ball, and fired it in the corner of the trunk. Shirtless, raising my head and arms to the sky, I stood back, letting the hot sun burn away the sticky, clammy feeling. I put on the clean T-shirt, reached for the toothpaste and quickly did a manual brushing with my finger. There, just like new, I was energized again. *I always was low maintenance.*

I pulled out the backpack and rested it on the edge of the trunk and unzipped the middle front pocket. I pulled out Teddy's thick manilla envelope, balancing the bag on the trunk, I tried to fold the envelope, but it was too thick. I guess twenty G's does that. I slipped the envelope in my back pocket, flipping the back of my T-shirt over to conceal it. Zipping up the pocket, I pushed my backpack in the trunk and pulled the lid down, the car keys jingling against the metal. At the sound, my eyes darted about, checking to see if anyone was watching. I leaned around and—squinting at my reflection in the side window—I mustered a weary smile, running my hand through my hair, pushing it back away from my face. I patted my pocket, feeling for the thick envelope, and reassured, I headed towards my rendezvous with Jimmy. I hoped I could get it over with quickly and get back on the road.

As I walked across paved paradise, I was feeling anxious, which surprised me. I had been in far worse places than this, so why was I feeling like this now? *I don't know, Pete, keep moving and don't think.*

I walked up the steps to the entrance, and on my left, facing the road, was the restaurant and to my right, facing the train tracks, was an outdoor patio. The outside ring of the deck had been designed like a waiting area at a train station, with picnic-style tables, umbrellas in their centers, scattered across the patio. The patio was empty due to the heat, so I went inside. Walking through the doorway, the cold a/c stung, and I shuddered, fueling my anxiety. To my left was the dining room—empty save for a table by the window, occupied by a family of four. To my right was a bar with TVs hanging overhead and empty backless bar stools lined up neatly along the front. Naturally, I moved towards them and plopped myself down on a stool in the middle, reaching behind and patting my pocket just to make sure.

There was no one behind the bar, and looking around, a server was finishing up with the family and noticing me, mouthed, "be right there." I waved and reached across the top of the bar for a newspaper.

"What can I get you?" the server asked drearily, now standing behind the bar across from me.

Looking up from the newspaper, I was face to face with Leia. Well, that's what it said in red script on her white golf shirt, an unsmiling Leia at that. Nervously, I reached around and felt again for the envelope. *What is wrong with me?*

Was this another red flag I casually waved off until it was too late?

"Uh ... hi!" I blurted out.

"Yeah, hi. What can I get you?" she asked impatiently.

"No, no it's Pete ... I'm not hi ... I'm Pete ..."

Leia, crossing her arms, glared at me. "Look hi or Pete, whoever you are. I haven't got—"

"My name's Pete."

She blinked and took a deep breath.

"Okay, *Pete*. Thanks just the same but I didn't need to learn your name. I haven't got all day. What will it be?"

I resisted the urge to look around at the all-but-empty dining room. Why had my boyish charm abandoned me? Pausing too long for Leia's liking, any moment would have been too long for her liking, I blurted, "Barking Squirrel, I'll have a Barking Squirrel please."

"A barking *squash what*?" Leia spit out. "We don't have barking stuff. We have beer! We have bottles and draft." She waved her hand at the taps lining the top of the bar, and the coolers behind her. "What'll it be? Pick something, pick anything from what you see here, okay? Tell you what? Take your time, have a gander, and I will be right back."

Sighing in disgust, Leia headed toward the swinging doors that led into the kitchen. With a forceful push, the doors flew back on their hinges, banging loudly as she entered the kitchen. The doors continued to swing back and forth, making loud squeaking sounds until they finally settled.

Five minutes later, the kitchen doors swung open, announcing Leia's return.

"And ..." she said, the doors still squeaking behind her.

I shifted forward on the stool. "Draft. I'll have your best house draft, please."

"Holy crap! All that for that?" she sighed, disgusted with me.

Moving behind the bar, she pulled out a mug and not bothering to tilt it, quickly drew the beer from the tap and slammed the mug down in front of me, the force so hard the foam jiggled and spilled out over the sides. I watched as a thick wet ring lazily formed around the base of the mug.

Amy, where are you? Carlos? Hell, even Teddy seemed an appealing companion right about now.

Mustering a weak thank you, I reached for the mug, dreading the ensuing foam bath. A menu splatted down in front of me, and I jumped back almost knocking over the beer.

"When you are capable of making a decision, let me know."

Leia returned to the kitchen, the sound of squeaking doors stuck in my head like when you can't get a song that you hate out of your mind. Rearranging myself on the bar stool, I leaned forward over the bar, so as not to wear it, I slurped my beer. Despite it mostly being foam, it found the spot.

With another big slurp, I finished it, placing the mug back in the giant puddle on the bar. I watched as it slowly slid six inches to the left.

Yep, that about sums up my day so far.

There was another thump-thump, I flinched and looked up to see Leia, carrying a large tray in her hands, pushing apart the swinging doors. Seeing the empty mug on the bar, she smirked.

"Well, what a good boy, you finished it. You want another?"

"Yes, please."

Be right back," she grunted over her shoulder, walking towards the dining room, carrying the tray.

"Well, I'm not going anywhere. I will be right here waiting," I flirted, rather badly.

"Too bad," she answered over her shoulder.

Leia returned, poured me another beer, placed it in front of me, though this time with less foam and more beer. Now that the ice had melted between us, I asked her if Jimmy was around.

"Jimmy *who*?" she said evasively.

"Jimmy, the owner. I was told he runs this place, and I'm supposed to meet him here. I have something for him."

"Sorry, there's no Jimmy here," Leia said, her eyes averted, and started towards the kitchen.

"*Bullshit*!" I hissed. I don't know who was caught more off guard, Leia or me.

Leia stopped dead in her tracks, slowly turned around, glaring at me. "Excuse me? What did you say?"

"You heard me. Bullshit! Stop playing games and get me Jimmy, please. I know he's here."

Leia quickly went on the defensive. "Hey, listen, buddy, I don't know what or who you are talking about." There was an air of finality to her voice. She crossed her arms and narrowed her eyes at me, trying to stare me down. "Like I said, there is no Jimmy here."

Slowly shaking my head, I met her stare. "*Jimmy*," I hissed. "Now! I'm not going to ask again."

She continued to glare at me. We were at an impasse. My mouth tight, eyes burning, leaning back on the stool, crossing my arms, "well, I'm not leaving until you get him."

Leia refused to budge, firmly entrenched behind her line in the sand. This wasn't going well, and the thick envelope was burning a serious hole in my back pocket. I wanted to get back on the road soon, but I couldn't leave yet.

Maybe he really isn't here ...

Just then, the universe intervened, and not a moment too soon, as Jimmy strolled out from the kitchen, the doors swinging behind him. Hand extended, a big smile spread across his face, Jimmy greeted me in a low, baritone, disc jockey voice. "Hello there! You must be Pete. I've been expecting you. How are you? Hot enough for you?"

A small man belying his voice, Jimmy appeared to be in his early fifties. He was maybe five nine, thick neck, marine style brush cut, with a middle-aged paunch that came from a lifetime of cooking. Colourful tattoos ran along his forearms, and he had a round, jolly face with big, friendly eyes. I could tell within lay a lovable character with many stories to tell. Jimmy pumped my hand vigorously, and once again, I was taken aback by the extremes this day kept revealing.

"Nice to meet you, Jimmy. I think you were the only one expecting me," I said, peeking over his shoulder at Leia, her head down, standing sheepishly behind the bar.

"Go easy on her, Pete. She's a good kid, just doing her job, following orders," Jimmy smiled.

"Following orders?"

"Yes, following orders. The last few months, we've been having trouble with some bikers roaming the roads around here. They come here and give my customers, and us, a hard time. Most bikers are pleasant and tip well. But this one group, they come in and harass the patrons, same for our servers. One time they even tried to go behind the bar and take our booze. I had to install cameras. So, it adds up, you know? Stressful too, as I'm losing customers. So, I told Leia, and by the way, did you know she's my best employee? Anyhow, I said to her, to be wary of any customer she thinks might be suspicious. I told her I would cover her lost tips, but at least we protect the bar."

Jimmy gave me a wink. "I'm guessing the two of you didn't get off on the right foot."

I glanced at Leia, whose head was still down, picking at her fingers.

"Something like that," I said, thinking my boyish charm needed fixing.

Jimmy smiled. "Go easy on her. Like I said, she's my best employee. She's a local girl, you know." Turning to her. "Tough times, tough town, tough kid."

Hearing Jimmy, Leia looked up and shrugged, a faint smile crossing her lips.

"So, Pete. You have something for me?"

"Yeah, yeah," I said, forgetting why I was there in the first place.

I reached behind and pulled out the thick envelope and immediately felt lighter. I handed it to Jimmy, who without even looking, slipped it in his back pocket. At this point, I was no longer questioning anything. Relieved, I got up.

"Well, that's a wrap. I gotta run. Nice meeting both of you. What do I owe for the beer?"

Jimmy laughed. "Whoa there, just a second, Pete. What? You didn't think you were going to get off that easy, did you?"

"Huh?"

"Here! Sit," he said, wearing a broad smile, motioning with his arm. "Have another beer, on the house. I will be right back with your stuff." Before I could speak, he turned to Leia. "Another beer for our friend here."

Leia, this time took care pouring the beer, expertly working the tap handle, and I could see why she was Jimmy's best employee.

But still, why all the attitude? Me? Suspicious? Stuff… what stuff?

Teddy had said it was a drop. He never mentioned any stuff. There is no stuff, is there? And, when did the drop become an exchange?

"Boss, I'm going to run over to the hardware store and get the supplies we need to fix the drain in the kitchen. I want to go before it closes, and besides—" Leia looked in my direction, "there's no one here, and it's a good time to go. Okay with you?"

"Of course, honey, go. I'm just getting Pete's stuff, and anyway, he seems okay to be left alone."

Leia left through the kitchen as Jimmy followed her, leaving me alone. I nursed my beer, the long day and random strangeness of it, catching up with me. It was only two forty-five. Today felt like it began three days ago. I played with my beer, leaning from side to side on the bar stool, watching and tilting the mug at different angles, swishing the beer around, trying to see if I could form white caps. Dr. Jayne thought I displayed adolescent tendencies at times, and she may have had a point.

Jimmy returned with my *stuff*, plopping it on the bar with a thud. My eyes flew open, as my stuff was in the shape of a brown cardboard banker's box. You know the ones, cut handles into each end and lid that slipped over the top. I stared at it, mesmerized.

The first thing that came to mind—crazily enough—was that old *Brady Bunch* episode. Remember when Bobby forgot the box of frogs in the back seat of Greg's car, and Greg headed to the drive-in with his girlfriend with the box in tow … the lid popping off and the frogs jumping out and landing on the girl's head and pizza …

What if there was something inside my box and the lid popped off?

Fortunately, Jimmy rescued me from my nightmare and secured the lid with packing tape.

"Okay, you are good to go there, Pete. Give this to Teddy next time you see him. No rush. Thanks a bunch. Listen, I've got tonight's dinner menu to prepare for whatever customers I have left. Beer's on me. Thanks again, nice to meet you, see you next time. And I promise Leia will be more friendly."

Next time? There is no next time. Is there?

At that moment, a very bright red flag went zooming up the pole. I shook Jimmy's hand, reached into my pocket, and pulled out my roll of bills. Thumbing through, finding a fifty, I pulled it out and placed it on the counter beside my beer. I said thanks for the beer and to tell Leia I was sorry for giving her a hard time.

Jimmy laughed heartily and looking at the fifty.

"That's the kind of apologies she likes." Then, in an eerie echo of Carlos: "Thanks again, Pete, take care. Be careful and stay safe."

Stay safe. I tried to remember if Alan had said something similar. Did they know something I didn't?

Nodding, I picked up the box. It was not as heavy as I expected, so I tucked it on my hip like a football and headed towards the door. The combination of the intense heat and blinding sun took my breath away as I stepped outside. The patio was still empty, and I placed the box on a table and stood on the deck, taking a second to orient myself. This seemed to be the only consistent thing I had done all day—pull myself together.

My eyes adjusted to the sun, and I felt familiar sweat starting to run down my back. I gathered the box of *stuff*, tucked it on my hip, and my hand outstretched, began to weave my way around the tables on the patio deck, pretending I was an NFL running back. Giving the last table my best head fake, I stiff-armed the chair, knocking it over in the process, and at the end of the patio, leaped through the air, out over the steps, and onto the pavement.

Yelling out, "Touchdown! and the crowd goes wild," I started to do a jig. Turning, I shifted the box from my hip, and as I began to spike it, sheepishly, I pulled it down and flipped it back on my hip, acting nonchalant. I turned towards the parking lot, where off in the distance, my Chevy was surrounded by a pair of Harleys and four riders.

Hello. What's this?

8

TEDDY POKED AT the last strip of bacon on his plate, then pitchforked it into his mouth. Chewing loudly, he tilted his head back, swallowed hard, gulping as the last bit slid down the back of his throat. He dropped the fork on his plate and reached for his water.

"Breakfast was great, sis! The best one yet, thank you. By the way, you look great today!"

Sara smiled as she cleared away his plate. She knew that happy tone all too well. Whenever Teddy was up to something, he was like a puppy dog, all smiles and affection. Everything was *great*, the weather was *great*, and she looked great (even when she looked like shit). It was always the same thing, a scheme of some kind. That was what drove her brother's world. This time, the scheme was Pete Humphries.

She liked Pete. There was something about him. He was cute, she reflected, maybe even handsome. He had that playful boyish charm that suggested he might be fun in bed. She quickly put on the brakes, starting to feel that familiar tingle. *No, don't go there,* she smiled to herself.

She could tell there was more to him than that. There was something dark and mysterious about him, like he was hiding or running from something. From something in his past, no doubt. *Isn't that where all our baggage comes from? The past. And aren't we all dark and mysterious in our own way?* She could relate, and maybe *that* was it.

Teddy interrupted her daydreaming. "Hey, sis! Beer and a whiskey chaser for your favourite big brother."

Even though she was older than Teddy—by three years—he always referred to himself as her big brother. This had always touched her, as she knew it was his way of protecting her. When he was little, he would follow her around everywhere, which was cute, but when she got into her teens and boys, he *still* followed her around everywhere; then it was no longer cute.

She learned to tolerate it, but it became a juggling act when it was a cute guy she was really into. And she had lost too many nice guys because of it. Nice guys didn't come along very often, but now, being older, the overprotective brother had its benefits. She could use Teddy to help weed out the bad guys, and when that nice guy did come along, he was that protective barrier. If the guy was that nice, he would have to prove it to Teddy first. Which, of course, explained why she was still waiting for that nice guy to come along. Pete? Possibly. She had noticed how he stood toe to toe to Teddy for the most part. Most guys wouldn't.

At the same time, she had been feeling trapped. Teddy being overprotective made her feel smothered, but there was more to it. The burden she was carrying because of what had happened that night with their parents. The weight of that night had grown heavier with time, and she didn't think she could carry it much longer. But how does one tell the truth in situations like that? That she was the one responsible for her parents' death, that they didn't perish as a result of the fire. Oh sure, there was a fire, and they did die, but that wasn't the real reason. Standing behind the bar, wiping glasses, she looked lovingly at her brother and allowed her mind to drift back to that night.

~

Teddy had been so excited when his father finally relented, letting him have the boat. A boat, a girl, a day on the water—it all added up to heaven on earth for her brother. Then, later that night, she watched in horror as it all unraveled, as Teddy and his father had a horrible fight over the boat. That stupid fucking boat! God, how she hated that boat.

Teddy and the girl slipped away just after sunrise that morning and were expected back sometime in the afternoon, but as dusk approached, they still hadn't returned. Their father had been pacing since noon that day, in anticipation of Teddy's return. Why? Because he couldn't bring himself to trust his son to handle a boat—*his* boat—on his own. He became worried, even angry, as the sun set, pacing in the living room, constantly checking his watch, looking out the window. She did think it was strange that Teddy would be so late, especially when they knew what he was like. She had tried to calm her father, and herself, saying if there was any trouble, Teddy knew what he was doing, and things would turn out fine, but that only made him more agitated and concerned about *that-stupid-fucking-boat.*

Finally, long after dark, Teddy returned, excited and proud. It had been quite a day. Teddy and his girl had come across a boat in distress, and he'd had gotten everyone back to shore safely. He had done the right thing. So, though they were late, he had rescued a boater, and he hoped his father would be proud of him.

Bursting through the front door, excitedly telling his father about rescuing the boat, his father, much to his shock, went into a rage, Sara watching helplessly from the kitchen, as he started yelling and screaming about the boat. Not the boat in distress, but his boat. He tore a strip off Teddy, admonishing him for towing the boat.

"Is my boat okay? Boating at night! What if you hit something? Did the boat get damaged during the tow? Are there marks on the boat from the towing?"

Teddy stood silent his head bowed.

"Don't you know you never tow a boat, you let someone else do that. You can get marks on the boat from towing."

That's all his father cared about, his boat. Not the people in the other boat and that they were safely back onshore. Not the girl, and certainly not Teddy and the good deed he had done. No. All he cared about was that fucking boat of his. Sara stood in the doorway listening, her brother's head bowed and either unable or unwilling to defend himself. Teddy tried to plead his case, but his father just yelled louder over him, shouting him down. He just wouldn't listen to reason. When his father tired of yelling and sat down, Teddy tried to calm him.

"I knew what I was doing, Dad. I protected the transom; I tied the other boat properly to the back. I wrapped beach towels around the rope at the back so the rope wouldn't rub and make marks. I centred the rope, so the pull weight was even. I watched my speed, never allowing the rope to slacken and tug on the transom. We came back up the lake right in the middle, the deepest part. I went very slow. I was cautious. I was careful. People on shore helped guide us in with flashlights the last part of the way. I did everything right."

That only seemed to breathe new life into his father's fury, and he stood up and started yelling again at him. Maybe, deep down, he couldn't handle that his son had done something he wouldn't, or perhaps couldn't, do. Or perhaps it was just that his father cared more about his boat than his son. So, doing the only thing he knew how to do, he kept yelling at him. Their mother, all this time, stood behind her husband supporting him, shaking her head in disgust at Teddy.

That part was pathetic. Sara tried to intervene, but they both turned on her

"Stay out of this, Sara! This has nothing to do with you."

It was horrible, awful, a nightmare.

Families shouldn't be like this, she thought.

Her father kept going on about his boat. "You should have just left them there and let someone else help them." That was the match that finally lit the fuse, and Teddy snapped.

In one swift movement, so fast no one could react, Teddy swung hard with a vicious uppercut, connecting flush under his father's chin, sending him ass over teakettle onto the rocker, his father flipping over the back of the chair and onto the floor, the chair then landing on top of him. Stunned, their mother screamed and moved toward Teddy, fists raised. Running in from the kitchen, Sara jumped between them, pushing Teddy away, her hand pressed against his chest, holding her mother back with the other.

"Leave! Now! Get out of here. Please, Teddy, just go. I will deal with this. Get out of here. Go! Please, just go."

Teddy stood in a daze, his eyes glassy. Sara pushed him again, her voice raised trying to get his attention, trying to get him to look at her. Finally, he looked down, their eyes locking. Blinking rapidly, he nodded, murmuring, "Sure, I'll go. Whatever you say sis …"

Sara turned him towards the front door, pushing him outside, then slammed the heavy oak door shut behind her. Then, she turned on her mother.

"Mom! How could you?" she hissed. "He's your son! Your flesh and blood, and you are defending that?" pointing to her father still lying motionless on the floor with the rocker on top of him. "I've had enough of watching this bullshit over the years. Neither of you appreciates Teddy for who he is, who he's trying to be. All you and Dad do is tear him down. You've never allowed him to grow. To grow up. To be a man the way he should be. Always the baby. You won't let him grow beyond on that."

Sara paused, her breath coming in short gasps, tears streaming down her cheeks, her voice cracking. "Why? Well, never again. This stops here. This stops now. Tonight. Never again."

Her mother refused to back down and—because she couldn't accept her faults and limitations either—tried to shout her daughter down, calling her all sorts of awful names. She couldn't believe what she was hearing, the anger now directed at her. Where was all this coming from? It seemed like her mother had been keeping a scorecard all these years, waiting for the right time to unleash. It all seemed so surreal.

They say there comes a moment in one's life when time slows down. Everything stops and you step *outside* of yourself and see yourself from above, like watching a movie. And that's what happened that night—Sara's moment in time came.

Silently, Sara turned away from the verbal onslaught, walking through the kitchen and out the back door toward the shed with her mother's words bouncing like rocks off her shoulders.

"Don't you dare turn your back on me. You come back here, you, you worthless—"

Reaching the shed, she opened the door, reached inside, and turned on the light. Adjusting her eyes, she gazed around the shed, looking for what, she didn't know. Then, along the back wall, she spied the gardening tools, lined neatly in a row. *There. Perfect.*

Stepping forward, she reached for the long-handled pitchfork and pulled it off its hook. Cradling it in her hands, feeling its heft, the bright shining metal gleaming, she held it out, twirling it in her hands, touching the razor-sharp forks, careful not to slice her finger. Nodding to herself, she exited the shed, switching off the light, pulling the door closed behind her. Barefoot, crossing the dew-soaked lawn, she left a wet trail of footprints on the sparkling clean kitchen floor. Walking into the living room, she saw her mother sitting on the floor beside her husband, cradling his head in her lap.

Strangely, she didn't feel any remorse, as she stood looking down at the two of them. She could feel the bile of disgust forming in the back of her throat and thought she might throw up. Her mother looked up to see her daughter standing over them, the pitchfork in her hands, the shiny tines glinting in the bright overhead living room lights. Eyes widening in surprise, her mother's mouth dropped open, but nothing came out. She stared up at her daughter, patting her husband's head, gently smoothing away his hair from his face. When her mother looked down again, gently kissing her husband's forehead, Sara struck.

The pitchfork made squishing sounds, as it hit home in her mother's chest. It felt weird, like sticking your fingers in Jell-O. Her mother never made a sound, only the squishing sound, as she pulled the pitchfork out and plunged it again. Thrust ... pull, thrust ... pull, her mother's body grotesquely pulling forward and falling back with each strike. Again, and again, how many times? She lost count, stopping only when her mother's lifeless body no longer responded to the jabs. Blood poured out of her mother's mouth, dripping down her jaw, onto the floor, forming a dark red pool. Reaching down, she pulled the pitchfork out of her mother's chest and with her foot, pushed the body to the floor. The pool of blood, a dark shade of red, spread in an ever-growing circle around her head. Emotionless, she stood over her mother, as tiny bubbles squirted in small circles around her cheek, which rested on the hardwood floor.

Kicking at her legs, Sara pushed them roughly to one side, stepping over the body. Reaching down, she pushed the rocker off her father, pushing it far enough away that she could step cleanly between his legs for a better angle. Raising the pitchfork over her head, she held it there, expecting him to react, but like her mother, he just stared at her with glassy, vacant eyes. With her free hand she reached out, pushed his head down so that the top of his head was fully exposed, grasping the handle firmly with both hands, she brought the pitchfork down on top of his head; the razor-sharp tines made squishing sounds as they penetrated his skull. It reminded her of when, as a family, they would carve pumpkins on the kitchen table at Halloween, the soft squishy feeling from the knife when cutting through the top. The tines got stuck halfway in the top of her father's head and embedded in his skull, and she had to turn and twist the handle, pulling hard, his head jerking up and down, stuck on the forks until they came free. He fell on his side, eyes open, staring straight ahead.

Standing over her parents, holding the pitchfork in her hands, blood dripping off the tines, she could feel her heart beating in rhythm with the gentle ticking of the cuckoo clock on the fireplace mantle. Looking down at her mother and father she felt nothing, absolutely nothing. That was the only thing that surprised her, that she felt absolutely nothing. She had just murdered her parents and didn't feel a thing. No, she wasn't a sociopath, far from it. She loved her brother, refusing to be manipulated any longer by her parents. That was it. She knew she had feelings, felt things, that a sociopath didn't. At least, that's what the doctor had said.

Quickly, Sara went about setting fire to cover everything up. That was the easy part. She just had to make sure the bodies were burned beyond recognition. Oh, and getting rid of the evidence. What did scare her, was Teddy finding out. That part shook her to her very core, and it was why she had spared her brother all this time. If he knew it was his big sister who killed their parents that night, the resulting fire a cover-up, she didn't know how he would feel. Would he hate her for it—or would he thank her for it? All a bit much to take in, don't you think?

Teddy, like her, hadn't been close to either parent and had never forged a genuine connection—though it was what he painfully longed for. Over time, Sara had come to accept what she'd done and hadn't allowed it to settle as baggage, or affect her relationships, or diminish her self-worth. No, her self-worth was perfectly fine, thank you very much. Relationship issues were simply that—it was about learning, experiencing, growing, finding the right connection and building something with the right person.

But not Teddy. He was good at hiding his emotions. He hadn't changed or grown as she had, still a man-child and fiercely protective of her.

She had come to learn his schemes were his way of coping—boyish fun, free entertainment at someone else's expense. No one ever got hurt, no laws were broken, well at least no laws that she knew of.

And on this beautiful, late summer morning, here he was, so playful, so happy. How could she ruin that? How could she tell him?

Sara decided that, for today, she wasn't going to be the bearer of bad news. Maybe tomorrow, or the next day, or the day after. Just not today. He deserved to be happy, even if it was just for today. She smiled as her mind drifted back to her early morning orgasm and that fleeting moment of forgetting.

She playfully tapped Teddy on the shoulder. "Beer and a whiskey chaser coming right up for my favourite big brother."

9

THE PAVEMENT SHIMMERED in the heat, squiggly lines rising from the cracks in the black asphalt, hot enough to fry an egg. Leia reached for her sunglasses, shielding her eyes from the glare, she moved between the parked cars until reaching the road, then quickly crossed, vehicles honking angrily as she passed. Safely on the other side, she put the bags down and placed her sunglasses on top of her head. Picking up the bags, off in the distance, she spotted two parked Harleys, its bikers surrounding a car, someone standing by the driver's door. She was too far away to make out anything more than that, but even from this distance, something didn't look right. Squinting against the sun, she pulled her shades down and looked again.

Hey, that guy looks familiar.

She increased her pace as she got closer and recognized who it was—that annoying but charming guy she had served earlier. He was surrounded by bikers who were closing in on him. She was still too far away and could only watch as two bikers sandwiched him, moving closer, narrowing the gap. She saw him turn, lashing out at the biker behind him who screamed out in pain, falling to the ground clutching his knee. Then he did a whirling one-eighty and facing the other biker, lashed out, taking out his knee as well. He followed with an uppercut, the biker falling to the pavement. Then she watched him get clobbered in the back of the head and drop to the ground like he had been shot.

"Hey! Leave him alone!" she shouted. Dropping her bags, she started running towards him.

The two female bikers turned to see where the voice was coming from, ignoring her, turned back to the body sprawled face down on the ground. One of the bikers leaned down and started going through the pockets.

"FUCK!" Leia exclaimed. "Hey, you motherfuckers, get the fuck away from him!"

The bikers ignored her, slowing, Leia reached in her shoulder bag, pulled out a .45 pistol, and flipped the safety off. Then she cocked it and aimed it towards them. Moving fast, arms outstretched, she yelled again. "One last time! Stop! Leave him alone!"

But neither biker moved, the larger female biker bent over, rummaging through the pockets.

"FINE!" Leia spit, taking a few more steps, she stopped. The loud bang of the .45 echoed through the parking lot, the bullet ricocheting off the pavement beside the Biker Mama. She slowly stood up, lifting her arms defensively, backed away. Her hands up, she tried to reason with her.

"Hey, hey, hey … we don't want any trouble. We were just having a little fun with your buddy here. He fell, and I was helping him up." Looking over at her biker companion. "Ain't that right, Bev? All in fun, right?"

Leia moved closer, the gun pointed at the Biker Mama's forehead.

"Bullshit. Now back off and leave him alone."

Calling her bluff, the Biker Mama didn't move. Now less than ten feet away, Leia lowered her aim to just between the biker's eyes. Finger on the trigger, she cocked the gun with her thumb. There was a metallic click.

"I will blow your fucking head off sure as I'm standing here. Back off and move away from him. *Now!* Bitch."

The Biker Mama slowly backed up as Leia motioned with her head. "You there, chickie-girl, drop that fucking helmet."

The red-haired biker did as she was told, lowering her hand, and letting the helmet fall to the pavement.

"Hey, Pete. Pete? Pete, you okay?"

～

Groaning, I tried to move my legs.

"Hey. Can you get up? Can you walk?"

I tried again, moving my legs a few inches, my body aching, I felt like I had been hit by a 10-pin bowling ball. My leg spasmed, twitched, then I felt a hard kick.

"Shit. Get up! Just like trying to decide on beer. You take forever. C'mon! I haven't got all day here, get your ass in gear, mister."

I shifted on my side and rolled into a ball. Even that was torture. I felt another hard kick and heard someone yelling at me in a shrill voice. I didn't know which was worse, my throbbing head or that voice.

"Atta boy! That's a start. You can do it."

I moved again, lifted myself painfully to one knee, rubbing the back of my head. Opening my eyes, I could see Leia holding a gun trained on the two biker chicks.

What the fuck?

Leia bent down, extending her free hand, reaching for mine, and started to help me to my feet. I guess that was the opening Red was waiting for. In a flash, she reached down, grabbed her helmet by the face bar, and in one motion, threw it in the direction of Leia. Leia ducked away, as the helmet whizzed by her shoulder, the hard plastic clacking on the pavement behind her. The Biker Mama quickly moved in, swinging her arm like a club, hitting Leia with her forearm. Leia fell forward, the gun coming out of her hand landing on the ground. I lunged, trying to reach for the gun and Red's leg at the same time, missing both, and falling back to the ground beside Leia.

Red helped her companion to his feet, limping over to his Harley, he swung his good leg over the seat, settled in and started the bike. He gave it some throttle, and the Harley made loud ear-splitting popping noises. Meanwhile, Biker Mama did the same—helping her burly companion to his feet, then helping him over to his Harley, starting the bike, the same ear-splitting popping sounds echoing across the empty parking lot.

The Biker Mama straddled her seat, then called out to Red, "Bev! Bev! The box! Get the box! Over there! Bring it!" pointing to the banker's box was on the hood of my Chevy.

I was unable to stop her. Still prone on the ground, I lunged futilely at her and could only watch as she snatched the box off the hood, running easily passed me, her eyes glued to me the whole time. Clutching the box under her arm, she swung her leg over the seat, straddling the bike. Holding her companion's waist with one hand, the box tucked beside her, he twisted the throttle and popped the clutch. The bike jerked forward, blasting out of the parking lot with the other bike on its tail. I could see Red on the bike, looking back over her shoulder at me. Though dazed, I sensed our paths would cross again.

Leia and I remained on the ground, licking our wounds, the sounds of the Harley growing fainter. Leia looked over at me, smiling weakly. "I guess I saved your ass. Does that happen often?"

"Does *what* happen often?" I asked, rubbing the back of my neck.

"Someone saving your ass."

"I had them you know."

"Yes, I could see that. I wasted a bullet for that?"

"Yeah, more or less …" I groaned, rubbing my shoulder, windmilling my arm.

Gingerly, moving to one knee, I held my hand out, holding Leia's hand we helped each other to our feet. Dusting ourselves off, Leia walked a few steps, reached down, retrieved her .45, uncocked it, flicked the safety on, and put it in her purse.

"Where did you learn to shoot like that?" I asked, and before she could answer, Jimmy interrupted, running up from behind.

"I taught her. Not bad, huh? Like I said, tough kid," he gasped, out of breath from his run across the parking lot. Leia smiled sheepishly, uncomfortable with the compliment.

"You both okay?" Jimmy asked, bent over, puffing hard.

"A .45 pistol? You got her a .45? It's almost as big as she is," I said, shaking my head in amazement.

Jimmy, still bent over, lifted his hand and waved. "Hold on, give me a second."

Leia moved over and stood next to me.

"See? That's what I was telling you about earlier. These … these … these gangs going around terrorizing innocent people—" Jimmy wheezed, upright now, waving his arms towards the highway. "Did they know you?"

"No. I don't know. Honestly, I don't. I ran into them earlier this morning near Sharbot Lake. They seemed friendly enough … but it was strange, when

I offered a simple good morning, that biker mama one got all pissy-like, and I picked up a weird vibe coming from them."

I purposely left out the part about my search for Sara and my brief flirtations with Red—based on my day so far, I was perfectly content to avoid all of that for the time being.

"Maybe your boyish charm needs work? You do have this way with people," Leia smiled.

Grimacing, I made a face at her.

"So, where did you learn to fight like that?" she said. "It was pretty impressive, until you got clobbered, that is."

"You wouldn't believe me if I told you," I said, reaching for the back of my head. "I had them."

"Yes, you said that already," Leia replied, amused.

Suddenly, it felt like everything was going to be okay, then, just as suddenly, everything wasn't. Looking over at the hood of my Chevy, the box was gone.

"Shit! The box! Shit! Shit! shit! The fucking box! Fuck! She took it!"

I turned to Jimmy, who had turned white. *Uh oh, something important was in that box.*

"Who is she? The biker who took it?" Jimmy nervously asked.

"Red ..."

Leia gave me a strange look.

"The red-headed biker-chick took it," I said, "I don't know her name."

I looked over at Jimmy. "Do you know why she would take it? I mean, it was just an old banker's box. Was there anything important inside? It didn't seem like much, as it wasn't heavy."

Jimmy, looking like he had seen a ghost, didn't answer.

"Do you suppose they were after the box, and that's why they were waiting for me?" I asked.

No answer.

"Jimmy? *Jimmy?*" I tried to get his attention.

Leia shifted her gaze to him. "Jimmy!"

Jimmy jumped. "Uh, er, uh, I don't think so," he answered haltingly.

I was growing impatient, and the back of my head was throbbing, a lump now forming, courtesy of Red's helmet.

"What, Jimmy? What? You don't think what? You don't you think they were waiting for me? Or was there something important inside the box? Which is it?"

Jimmy put his hands out in defence, "No, no-no. There wasn't anything important in the box. No reason for them be waiting for you. Maybe they just took it?" he said, looking at me in desperation.

Changing the subject, "Hey, guys, how about we all go inside and cool off? It's been quite a day, and Leia can pour you a nice cold beer, Pete, and some ice for that head of yours too. Maybe, some wings. We make great wings, don't we, Leia?"

Though Jimmy's offer sounded like the perfect tonic, a cold beer right about now would be heavenly, "I better go."

"No worries, Pete, I understand. And I will take care of that box too. Leave it with me. I'll let Teddy know." Jimmy tried to sound reassuring, but we both knew it was the opposite.

If there was something important in the box, then why so casual about it in the first place? There was no mention of it initially but giving someone twenty big ones should have been clue enough, and I was pissed at myself for missing the obvious here. Poor Jimmy, he was going to feel Teddy's wrath all right. Maybe, Leia could lend him her .45 or better yet, let her protect him.

"Take care, Pete. Be careful. I'll be in touch about the box."

"You coming?" Jimmy asked, looking at Leia.

"Yes, give me a sec," she said. "I will be right there. See you inside."

Jimmy nodded, waved, and started back through the parking lot towards the bar.

It was just me and Leia now. I had taken a liking to her. She was beautiful in that tomboyish, small-town girl way. She was just a kid. Maybe nineteen or twenty? But boy, she had spunk. She was tough. No one would ever walk on her, pity the poor guy who tried. She didn't need protecting, the others needed protecting from her.

I could tell she was a survivor. From what? Who knows? Small-town life? But that made her strong; she would be fine in this world. As Jimmy said, *tough times, tough town, tough kid*. Plus, she had her .45, just try and mess with that.

Breaking the awkward silence, a lump formed in my throat. "Listen, you take care, okay? And don't you be going around pointing that gun at every pissy customer."

"No, I won't. Promise. Only the ones that try and charm me and can't make up their minds."

"I'm guessing you keep it under your pillow at night?"

"Of course. I don't sleep without it."

In the late afternoon shadows, Leia was beautiful in her golf shirt, jean shorts, and dirty white sneakers. The summer breeze blew strands of her blonde hair across her face. Attracted to each other despite our age difference, we both knew it ended here. I reached out, pushing the strands of hair away from her face, leaned over, and kissed her on the cheek. Leia reached up, holding the tops of my shoulders, and pulled me in close. Her scent was fresh, small-town girl fresh, and I hoped it would a long time before I stopped smelling it. I squeezed her gently, she squeezed back, then pulling apart, I smiled.

"Bye, take care." Then I turned towards my Chevy, my heart in my throat.

"You too, Mr. Charming Indecision," she called out.

As I went to get in, I turned and saw Leia walking back to where she had dropped her bags. I watched, as she picked them up, then walked across the parking lot toward the Last Caboose. With her long hair blowing in the breeze and shoulder bag drooping at her hip, she didn't look back.

Whoever finds her, will be one lucky SOB. I got in my Chevy, oblivious to the hot leather seats, and barely flinched when my bare legs made contact. I was exhausted. What a day.

Our goodbyes said, the three of us headed in different directions: Jimmy to his dreaded phone call with Teddy; Leia, besides keeping a lock on the bar for Jimmy, sleeping with her .45, and hopefully dreaming about me. And me? I still hadn't found what I was looking for.

Now along with it, the banker's box with its mystery contents was no longer in my possession. Jimmy's reaction proved beyond all doubt that it contained something important, maybe, even life or death important. Jimmy said not to worry, he would take care of it, but I was pissed. No one steals anything from Pete Humphries and gets away with it. Those bikers were going to pay. When I caught up to them it wasn't going to be pretty.

10

THE CELL PHONE was lying face down on the bar when it started to buzz like an angry swarm of bees.

"Are you going to get that?" Sara asked after the third buzz.

"Maybe. When I'm ready."

As it buzzed, the phone slowly crept across the bar top, it having moved six inches already.

"It drives me crazy when you do this! You're such an ass—" Sara stopped herself.

"I know, it's why you love me, sis."

"No, it's not!" she sighed loudly, disgusted with her brother's childish behaviour. The angry buzzing continued, and Sara reached under the bar, bringing up a hammer. She raised it in the air. "Teddy, please!"

Teddy snatched the phone just as she was about to smash it. Smiling devilishly, Teddy put the phone up to his ear, as his sister glared at him. She put the hammer down and turned away, leaving Teddy to his phone call.

"Yup," he answered, sliding on a stool. Teddy listened intently, nodding and sipping on his drink, grunted a couple of times.

"Yeah, yeah … great!"

Pleased, he tapped the phone and placed it face down on the bar. He looked up at the TV overhead, CFL football. But today, he didn't care about that elusive missing down, something was more pressing.

Jimmy had called to confirm that Pete had dropped off the envelope, and in return, he had given him the box. *The box.* Inside that box was the answer to everything, the reason his parents died that night in the fire. Teddy had been after the answer for as long as he could remember. It had been a long, frustrating process, fraught with dead ends, false leads, and faint hopes. Costly too: $20,000 in cash under the table to Jimmy, courtesy of Pete.

After his parents died, Teddy was initially too distraught to think anything other than what it was, a wonderful day turned tragic. After striking his father, his sister had intervened, like loving big sisters do, pushing him out of the front door. He ran away, as fast and as far as he could, stumbling along the dark gravel road, badly scraping his hands and knees. It was only when he was out of breath, bent over, gasping, that he saw the glow on the horizon. Racing back, Sara was barely able to restrain him, shielding their faces from the roaring flames, as their home burned to the ground. Teddy wailed long into the night, as she held him tightly, big sister looking after baby brother, consoling him, trying to take away his pain. Afterward, he naively accepted what she said happened: their parents distraught, tried to calm themselves with their go-to fix—booze. After too much to drink, they passed out in their chairs, facing the fireplace and an unattended fire.

Then over time, cracks in the story began to appear. A few years later, he ran into one of their neighbours in a bar, and after too much to drink, the neighbour mentioned his parents being murdered and the fire used as a cover-up. That had shaken Teddy badly. Another time, arrested for public intoxication, the arresting officer recognized him as the guy whose parents were murdered in a fire. This had shaken him further. When pressed, the officer went quiet, confusing him with someone else. Whenever he asked Sara about that night, she said the same thing repeatedly, Mom and Dad were upset, got drunk, and passed out, the fire catching and burning them to death.

One night in Sharkees, Teddy had gotten drunk and started rambling on about his parents being murdered when Tony overheard. Tony had taken a keen interest in Teddy, noticing how much money he carried, and naturally, wanted a piece of whatever action there was. So he patiently bided his time until he discovered his own version of fortune meet opportunity.

Tony knew Jimmy, who owned the Last Caboose in Havelock. Jimmy knew a local cop, who knew a cop in Peterborough, who worked in the police administration building. Tony asked Jimmy to work his magic and do some digging around—money no object, eyeing Teddy's bankroll. Expecting nothing, months passed, then one day Jimmy contacted Tony, informing him there was a cold case file on Teddy's parent's death; the file locked away in the basement of the police station. Bingo. Overnight, armed with this information, Tony became Teddy's new and inseparable best friend. For the longest time things remained quiet, until one day, lady luck shone, bearing Teddy's name.

The administration building was closing due to an asbestos leak, the files were being transferred to a new location, in Lakefield. It was so easy. During the transit of the files to the new site, one of the boxes would mysteriously go missing, magically reappearing on the doorstep of the Last Caboose the next morning, part of the daily food delivery. All Teddy had to do was find an unsuspecting mule, pay Jimmy, and wait. Tony offered, but as much as Tony had put him on to Jimmy, he didn't trust Tony. He needed a complete outsider. Once more, fortune met opportunity, this time in the guise of one Pete Humphries. Pete was the final piece to the puzzle. Teddy couldn't believe the timing, running into Pete that day in Sharkees, right when everything was coming together. So apropos too. Pete fucking Humphries, of all people, was going to be his mule.

And now, Teddy was *this* close to finally knowing if his hunch was correct. He loved his sister deeply and would kill anyone that did her harm, but he sensed she was withholding the truth. Maybe his parents *were* murdered that night and Sara had witnessed something and was protecting him from it. Could the killers still be after her? She was so fragile, which was why he cut her so much slack, and why—much to his later chagrin—he bought her that bike. He'd done it to protect her, keep her preoccupied, to spare her. Though he was her little brother, he was her protector, wanting to be the big brother he wished he could have been.

Now that Pete had the box, everything had come full circle. It was only a matter of time—a couple of days tops—and Pete would deliver the box. Maybe Pete was on the way back right at this moment. That was the one thing he could tell about Pete; he was honourable, and if you gave him something to do, he'd do it. In that moment, Teddy suddenly felt at peace.

It was time to celebrate. He turned on his stool looking for his sister when his cell phone started buzzing again. He glanced down at the number.

Why is he calling?

•

11

WHAT A FUCKING day!

I drove, windows down, the wind howling and whipping my hair around my face, the temperature still warm as twilight fell. I tried piecing everything together, but I didn't know if that was possible, or where to start. And just now, I had starred in my first Hollywood movie, a B-movie at that. Did those bikers actually think I would hand over the keys to my Chevy, just like that? I couldn't wrap my head around their behaviour just now or earlier at the gas bar. Not that I expected to find Sara immediately, but I was surprised at the responses when I asked around, and I was pissed at myself for missing the telltale signs, that a simple drop was actually an exchange.

Really, Pete? Really? What the fuck is wrong with you?

Had Teddy set those bikers on me as some sort of perverse joke? Had the bikers been following me, or watching me all this time, or was it just a coincidence that we met in the parking lot like that? What was with all these people today? Leia, Jimmy, Red, Carlos, even Alan, the larger-than-life biker. What was up with all of this?

There had been a connection with everyone. It was no wonder I was fucking exhausted. I needed a scorecard to keep track. Was all this a sign? Who and where did all these people come from? And why was everyone telling me to be careful? None of it made any sense.

My head was jammed full, and it was all I could do to keep it from exploding. Entering the outskirts of Peterborough, my old summer stomping grounds, the no-vacancy sign in my head was blinking; no room to take a trip down memory lane. I needed a drink, a room, a shower, and a change of clothes, and I didn't care in what order.

What I loved about Peterborough had not changed. No matter the weather or time of year, it operated on permanent sunshine, everything appeared bright and cheery, and despite how I was feeling, it was nice to be back. Driving along Lansdowne, past the Memorial Centre, I turned onto George Street, and slowly made my way toward the downtown core. The streets were quiet, and up ahead, I could see Del Crary Park on my right and turned in. The parking lot was empty, so I parked across the painted lines not caring. Turning off the engine, I sighed and flipped the seat back.

I watched tourists leaving the park, returning to their hotels from after-dinner walks, as the sun set, the curtain closing on this stranger-than-fiction day.

How was your day, dear? Normal?

I needed that drink and shower, not to mention a room. The Holiday Inn was across the parking lot and hadn't changed a bit—I was hoping for a time warp, and they still had the Sunday-special, or better, my old room.

The Holiday Inn, from the outside, appeared to have gone through another makeover, and it was quite the place back in the day. I had spent many nights crashing there. Typical of many smaller Canadian cities—tourist traps—the hotel was a two-story, hockey stick-shaped, happening spot; ideally located on the main drag between the waterfront and George Street. I flipped my seat up and started my Chevy, pulled out of the parking lot, and made my way along to the next entrance. Turning in, my luck appeared good, the lot half empty. I found a space near the front and parked facing across the street.

I opened my trunk, reached in and retrieved my backpack, along with my special stash of rock band booze. Meaning Jack Daniels and a six-pack of tallboys. I never left home unprepared. Jack and I had been in a friends with benefits relationship for some time now. I called on him only when I was desperate, promising never to take him for granted, and Jack was always there for me. No strings attached, it worked, we fit, neither asking more than the other could handle.

The six-pack of tallboys was for insurance purposes only.

I strolled through the parking lot, coming up on a couple unpacking their bags from their leased, high-end, silver SUV. The jaded in me couldn't resist. The couple was probably checking in for one of those romantic escape weekends; the one where they will try to reconnect—despite life's daily push-pull struggle—with the life they created with the best of intentions. The one with their 2.5 kids, with their way beyond-cute names, something like Courtney and Madison. Their lives will consist of the around-the-clock, never-ending juggling of the kids' activities: hockey, piano, soccer; and their respective high-profile careers: hers in real estate, and his, doing accounting for some large firm. Their mortgage, currently the size of the gross national debt of some small African country, pays for all of this; ever-increasing instead of decreasing. This weekend, they will drink too much wine, have sex in the hot tub, he will still come too fast, and she won't period. Then, after checking out Sunday morning, they will pretend like everything's normal upon returning home.

    I trailed behind the couple through the sliding doors, and slowed my pace, fighting the urge to overtake them, run ahead to get that last room. Instead, I stood impatiently behind the snuggling couple, who were informing the front desk clerk, "Oh, it's our second honeymoon weekend without the kids." The front desk clerk, nodding like the toy dog in the rear window … "Uh-huh, yes, that's nice. I'm sure you'll both have a lovely time. The jacuzzi room with the fireplace is our most popular room."

    Upon hearing that, hubby gave his wife a playful pat on her butt and kissed the top of her head. *Oh, he's going to come fast all right*, I thought. Armed with their room key, happy-hubby and his bored, lonely, sexually frustrated wife, picked up their bags, walking down the hall of no return toward the elevators, and their date with destiny.

    Finally, it was my turn. The front desk clerk held in her hands my room key of fate. Where would I be sleeping tonight? A nice comfy hotel bed or the not-so comfy backseat of my Chevy in the hotel parking lot? Nervously, I stepped forward, her head was down, typing away on the computer console. She had long copper brown hair, tucked back behind each ear and spread evenly across her shoulders and was wearing a tan suit jacket opened at the front, white top underneath, and a name tag pinned to her jacket introducing her as Jackie.

    Shuffling my feet, I adjusted my shoulder bag, waited, then gently lowered my bag of rock band booze to the floor between my legs. She still hadn't noticed me. Or at least took no notice of me.

I cleared my throat. "Hello, Jackie," I said in my most hopeful voice, "How are you tonight?"

Her head remained down as she responded in a weary tone.

"Be right with you." She tapped the keys a few more times, reached over and closed a drawer on her right, then looked up. A friendly face appeared, bright white perfect teeth, thin face, round warm eyes, her demeanour changing instantly.

"Well, hello! Sorry about that. I was finishing up and didn't hear you arrive. How are you tonight? How can I help you?"

"Hi, um yes. I'm looking for a room."

"Do you have a reservation?"

Stammering, as visions of my Chevy's rear seat danced in my eyes, "No, uh, no, I don't. I was hoping you still had a room left."

"I just sold the last honeymoon suite, but I don't think that's what you were looking for," she winked.

Nodding, looking towards the elevators. "No, I'm good. Been there, done that, even have the T-shirt."

"Me too! And I do know what you mean. That's all I do on these weekend shifts is sell rooms to these middle-aged couples. One step from a midlife crisis, two steps from divorce, who hope that the two-day-weekend jacuzzi-fireplace room will save their marriage." She gave me a rueful smile. "Never has and never will."

Wow! I like her.

Jackie started typing, head down, staring at the screen and letting her fingers work their magic. After what felt like an eternity—the final *Jeopardy* song on a continuous loop in my mind—she looked up.

"Hmm, let's see ..." as she scrolled through the screen.

"I think you're the kind of guy that would go for a room in the far part of the hotel, away from those crazy mid-life crisis couples and other distractions. Maybe a balcony overlooking the river, and nothing but empty rooms all around you?"

She looked up. "Am I close?" she asked, already knowing the answer.

"Perfect!"

In my excitement, I wanted to hug her. Wisely, I didn't; however, I did make space for her in my will, squeezing her between Otte and Mary.

Jackie finished up on the console, motioned for my credit card, and ten minutes later, I was sitting on my room's balcony, feet up on the railing, listening to the frog and cricket symphony, a bottle of Jack open in my lap, a pizza on order. Between swallows, I gazed at the full moon, glowing on the perfectly still water. Heaven.

Sitting there, one thought wouldn't leave my mind. When Jackie gave me the cardkey to my room, and pointed me towards the elevators, she said something that disturbed me. Usually, I wouldn't think anything of it, but after today ... well, I don't know.

As I went to leave, she said (as if she knew me or had been expecting me), "Take care of yourself, Pete. Be careful, okay? Full moon tonight."

Carlos, Alan, Jimmy, even Leia. And now, Jackie?

It was time for that well-earned drink. There would be no even-buzz keeping tonight. Tonight was the pedal-to-the-metal, Pete Humphries special; drink till you're numb, or pass out, whichever came first. Pulling hard on the bottle of Jack, I tried to wash away the day and make sense of it. It all seemed too much. But nothing had made sense right from the start. This was only day one.

12

JIMMY WAS SITTING at the bar, the music off, doors locked, the Last Caboose neon sign dark. Wiping his forehead with a damp cloth, a tall glass of bourbon sat in front of him. Eyeballing it, hand shaking, he picked it up and took a long drink, gritting his teeth, as the potent liquor worked its way down through his system. Jimmy refilled the glass, took another drink, shuddering hard as he downed it, then pounded the glass on the bar. Holding onto the bar with both hands, he steadied himself, taking a few deep breaths, exhaling loudly on the last one. Staring at the phone, he wished he could wave a magic wand and make it disappear. Closing his eyes, he pretended the phone wasn't there, and when he opened his eyes, it would be gone. Keeping his eyes shut tight, he counted to ten, then opened them.

Fuck!

Resigned to his fate, sighing heavily, he picked up the phone, his hand shaking so hard, he had to rest it on the bar to dial. *Maybe he won't be there*, Jimmy thought hopefully, and he could leave him a message. Leia came out of the kitchen, walked behind the bar, spotting the bottle.

"Everything okay?"

Jimmy, ghastly white, sweat beads dripping off his brow gave her a thumbs up. "Yeah."

If his hand weren't shaking so badly, she'd have bought the lie. Maybe. As it was, she gave him an uncertain look and returned to the kitchen, pushing open the swinging doors, which loudly squeaked shut behind her.

I'm going to miss her.

Jimmy dialed and waited. One ring, two rings, as Jimmy's heart pounded, and on the third ring, Teddy picked up. The familiar 'Eeyuupp' on the other end.

For the next ten minutes Jimmy filled Teddy in on what happened out in the parking lot; the bikers surrounding Pete, and how he bravely fought them off; Leia, his best server, rescuing him. Then, his chest pounding, he told Teddy the dreaded news.

In the aftermath, the box had been taken by the bikers, and no, he didn't know who they were, or where they went, just that they had taken off down the highway. The subsequent silence on the other end turned Jimmy into a blubbering wreck, profusely apologizing, and promising Teddy, he would go to any lengths to get the box back, and soon. Of course, he had absolutely no idea how he was going to do that, but Teddy said not to worry about it, that he would take care of it.

Jimmy, visibly relieved, kept asking, *are you sure?* This amidst long earnest strings of sorry, sorry, and sorry. Teddy reassured Jimmy that everything was fine, not to worry. He would get in touch with Pete and sort things out.

"Gee, thanks, Teddy. I always knew you were one of the good guys, again I'm—" but there was only silence on the other end before the call abruptly disconnected.

Jimmy reached for the cloth on the bar, his hand still shaking. He wiped his brow and, leaning forward, rested his elbows on the bar, letting the damp cloth soak his forehead. Sighing heavily, he lifted his head, reached for the bourbon, looking at the glass, he put the bottle to his mouth and started sucking on it. The bitter liquor dribbled out of the corners of his mouth and down his chin as he chugged in large gulps. Putting the bottle down, he swiped the back of his hand across his mouth. Looking at his hands, they weren't shaking now.

"Okay, okay," he said, gripping the edge of the bar. Jimmy hopped off the stool and started humming to himself, entering the kitchen, he stopped, leaning on the doors, peering inside at Leia.

Leia looked up from the prep counter. "Everything okay, boss?"

"Never better," Jimmy answered.

13

SARA FINISHED RUBBING Teddy's shoulders and asked him if he wanted another drink.

"Sure, sis," he replied.

She moved behind the bar, poured him a scotch, and placed it in front of him.

"Listen, I have to get back and help Patty. Are you going to be okay?"

Reaching out, patting her hand, Teddy nodded.

"Are you sure?"

"Yes, I'm sure, sis." He smiled, angelically. "I'm sure."

Sara laughed, leaned over the bar, and kissed him on the cheek. "Love you," she said, tenderly, and turned toward the kitchen.

Teddy nursed his drink, trying to piece together the last few minutes. His phone rang, he picked it up and answered, and that's all he remembered. The next thing he knew, his sister was beside him, whispering his name and rubbing his shoulders, the customers staring at him.

Where's my phone?

Looking around, he didn't see it.

What the fuck?

He reached for his back pocket ... then he remembered. He had thrown it against the wall, the phone smashing into pieces, making one helluva racket.

That's why everyone was staring at him, and his sister was beside him, rubbing his shoulders. He'd had another blackout.

Strange, he thought. *Haven't had a blackout in years.*

What brought it on? he wondered. He tried to recall the last time, and then it hit like a lightning bolt. The night his parents died; he had blacked out in his sister's arms.

Why now, after all these years? He knocked back the scotch. The box! The fucking box! Jimmy had called to tell him Pete had lost the box. Then the next thing he knew, people were staring at him. Teddy finished his drink, let out a loud belch, and called out for Tony. When Tony didn't immediately appear he started bellowing his name.

"TONY! Tony … TONY? Tonnneeeee? Tony! TONN-YYY!"

Patty came storming in from the kitchen, waving her hand at him. "Keep it down! There are other customers."

Teddy casually waved her off with a flick of his wrist. "Now, don't go getting your panties in a knot there, sweet cheeks," he smirked.

Patty stopped dead and glared at Teddy. She stood silently, drumming her fingernails on the bar. She started to turn away, paused, and turned back. Sighing heavily, she slowly walked around to where Teddy was sitting. Stopping behind his stool, in a low voice, she ordered him to turn around. Turning his head, he shrugged and turned back. Not deterred, in a low growl, she forcefully grabbed his arm and yanked it.

"Turn around and stand up, asshole."

Teddy, realizing he had poked the wrong bear, slid off the stool and turned, facing her. Sheepishly, looking down, he towered over her, so tall Patty had to crane her neck to look up at him. Their eyes locking, Teddy gulped, blinking nervously. Moving closer, almost touching him, her left eye twitching, teeth bared, she reached up and placed her index finger on his chest.

"This is my bar, asshole, and you will not talk to me like that. Ever. You got it?"

Teddy, eyes transfixed, stared at her, not saying a word, not moving.

"And you will keep your voice down in here, mister. I don't care if you are Amy's brother, there are no special privileges with that." She tapped his chest hard three times, punctuating each of the next three words. "You. Got. That?"

Teddy, looking down at her, his body perfectly still, nodded. Swiftly, Patty reached out and grabbed him by the balls, clasping on tight. Teddy's eyes flew open, and he froze, not moving a muscle. Patty squeezed a little tighter, and Teddy's eyes bugged out further.

"Do I have your attention now?"

Teddy nodded, staring straight ahead, afraid to look anywhere but.

"Good! Because if you ever call me sweet cheeks again," as she squeezed his balls tighter, Teddy let out an inaudible gasp. "If you ever call me that again … if you ever … THIS IS MY BAR ASSHOLE, and don't you forget it!"

Squeezing harder for effect, Patty abruptly let go, turned, and rounded the corner of the bar, toward the kitchen, punching open the swinging doors.

"Tony! There's someone out front looking for you."

Teddy exhaled slowly and reached down to feel for his balls. Touching them, he sighed with relief and sat back down. He looked up to see Tony coming out of the kitchen, wiping his hands on a towel.

"What's up, boss?"

"Drop what you're doing. I've got a job for you. Oh, and I need a new phone."

"Sure thing, boss."

14

I AWOKE THE next morning to Jack's wrath. I showered and cleaned up the balcony littered with half-eaten pizza crusts and far too many dead soldiers. *Did I really eat and drink all that?* When I was ready to face the day, I decided to take a stroll along the waterfront, for I had missed that life. My life—at least it had been once, but then *that day* happened, and that was that. I never returned. I could feel storm clouds brewing in my head and forcibly pushed them away. My hangover was bad enough.

Walking through the hotel parking lot, I crossed the pedestrian bridge, entered the walkway, and strolled along the interlocking brick path. I passed the moored boats, tied up to the wooden docks protruding out like popsicle sticks. Their owners were gently padding about on the decks, coffee cups in hand.

Ahh, the boater's life …

Nodding hellos, I walked slowly past the boats, trying to catch a glimpse inside. The walkway ended, and I turned towards the bay and continued along. The gas pumps were up ahead, and I noticed the Lighthouse restaurant was still there with its ice cream stand on the main level and the winding staircase that led up to the bar and patio overlooking the marina.

It was a beautiful, peaceful morning, quiet and still, the water lapping gently against the boats; the click-clack, click-clack in the light breeze, the steady sound of water trickling out of the lower side of the bigger boats.

God, I miss all this.

Overhead, the morning sun was already burning bright in the clear blue sky, with light wispy clouds scattered across it. My favourite sky. I had not seen or felt like this in a long time. Either the universe was reaching out once more, or I was simply paying attention again.

Maybe there is hope for me.

Up ahead, there was an empty bench facing the water, so I stopped and had a seat. I leaned back against the bench, crossed one leg over the other, stretched my arms out along the top of the bench, closed my eyes, and let myself float—taking in everything around me.

I could hear the soft, gentle background noises of people talking, the clinking of cutlery as they ate breakfast, the scent of bacon wafting in the air, mixed in with the smell of diesel, coming from the pumps. The light sounds of traffic, the gas bar attendants chatting as they skittered back and forth from the office, getting everything ready for another day. Everything seemed so still, so peaceful. Birds were chirping in the trees behind me, a dog barked, and a boy shouted, "Hey, Dad! I've caught one."

Early mornings on the waterfront. No wonder it was my favourite place and time of day. It reminded me of the time in Key West, and the early morning on Duval Street where I ran into a woman, sitting on a bench outside the Margaritaville Store. I walked by, and she called out to me.

"Beautiful morning for a walk, isn't it?"

Wrapped up in my head, startled, I stammered, "Umm, yes, it is," and kept on walking, my head down.

But she called after me. "Stop. Here, sit a spell. Rest yourself."

I stopped, sat down beside her on the bench and we started chatting. It took me only a few seconds to realize she was blind, passing by, you would have never known. How did she know I was tired? That, I was exhausted and in an awful state? I guess maybe the universe knows. For the next most glorious hour of my life, I learned from that sweet, gentle blind woman about the universe, auras, the power of positive versus negative energy, and how all of it applied to the Law of Attraction.

She saved me that day. Maybe, she knew I needed saving. Maybe not. I will never know. I didn't get her name, but what stood out was that she couldn't see, but she could feel me coming down that street that morning. She told me as much. It was my aura and the negative energy I was projecting, she said. It was quite the education. For the longest time after, I saw everything in technicolour, becoming self-aware of my auras, and what they attracted, based on the energy I was emitting at the time. *The Law of Attraction: Code of the Universe.* It was wonderful.

The next morning, I went looking for her, but she wasn't there. I went inside the store and asked the clerk about the woman who sat outside on the bench.

"What woman?" she asked, puzzled.

I spent the rest of the day searching all over Key West for her, but there was no sign of her. It was like she had vanished. But, at that moment, she was there for a reason, to teach me—and teach me she did.

Then, like all things over time, seeing in technicolour and trying to manage my energy simply wore off. I allowed it to.

I needed to see and live in technicolour again or at least try to. I sat for a while watching the boats and the people go about their day, but soon the sun became too hot, and it was time to get moving. Besides, I was back here for a reason.

Don't forget that. You are back to find someone. You have a job, a purpose again.

I wandered farther along the concrete dock, my head down, then glancing to my right, I stopped dead in my tracks. Shit! The dreaded gas pumps. There they were. I started to feel light-headed, and immediately hit the play button on the VCR in my head.

Click, garble garble, rewind, garble garble, forward. Tina, fight, hot, circling, waiting, no gas, yelling, water everywhere, click, fast forward, garble garble, people running, gas spraying, more yelling, garble garble, click.

Standing there, transfixed, it felt like yesterday, and *that day* had come alive again, the sounds crystal clear in my head. And I swear, I could see the boats. My dad's boat, me driving my dad's boat, the others playing parts in the nightmare of *that day*. My eyes welled up, tears started to roll down my cheeks. That was so long ago, why did it feel like yesterday?

"Maybe it is because you haven't dealt with it."

"Huh? What? Who's that?"

I turned to the sound of the voice, and behind me, was a woman holding a little dog. The woman was wearing a sleeveless green and yellow floral sundress that flowed to the ground. A big white floppy sunhat shielded her face from the sun. Long brown hair stretched from underneath her hat and flowed down past her shoulders, almost to her waist. The little brown dog easily fit in her arms, quite content to be there—he looked up at me with his big round eyes, pink tongue out to one side panting, and our eyes locked, and he barked happily. His head lifting and tilting as he smacked his lips, curling his tongue over and around its mouth.

I quickly rubbed my hand over my eyes and face, brushing away the tears. "The sun makes my eyes water," I lied

"Mine too," she smiled knowingly, "that's why, I have *these*," she said, pointing to oversized sunglasses, perched on top of her sunhat. Embarrassed, I was at a loss for words. The woman didn't seem surprised.

"You haven't dealt with it, have you?"

I look at her, alarmed that she could see through me so easily.

"It's okay. It's your aura, I could feel it," she replied reassuringly.

I nodded.

"Oh, so you do know what that is," she said.

"Yes, I do," I said, recalling that morning on Duval Street.

"I'm not here to pry, I don't need to know. It doesn't matter to me what it is, it's not my business. It only matters to you. It only matters that you know what is haunting you and that you need to deal with it and let it go."

"Oh no, it's nothing like that," waving my hand trying to defend myself.

"They all say that and that's why the haunting continues. Denial. Whatever it is, you need to deal with it, accept it, let it go. You need to put it in its proper place and move on. And when you do, then, and only then, can you move on, be free, change your aura."

She reached out and lightly touched my arm, her touch sending shock waves up and down my body. "You deserve to live your life the way it was meant to be, for you. And until you let it go …"

Feeling a shiver run down my back, I surrendered, and admitted defeat. I knew she was right. I had always known. Whoever she was, she was right. Deep down, I had always known this. But hey, denial is such a sunny great place, isn't it? Feeling sheepish, I lifted my head and nodded at her.

"Yes, you are right. I haven't dealt with it, and I need to. Thank you."

"My pleasure," she smiled, warmly. "You take care of yourself. It will be okay. You will be okay."

A chill ran down my spine, I shuddered, feeling an immense sense of relief wash over me. There was a loud splash, and I turned to the sound—a boat's prop had come out of the water, dropping down with a bang. I turned back to the woman and her dog, but they were gone. I looked around, but there was no one in sight.

She was right, that woman, whoever she was, she was right. Just like that morning on Duval Street, I didn't question what had just happened and instead accept it for what it was; a message from the universe to pull myself together.

Looking around one last time, I forced myself to keep moving. I walked to the end of the concrete boardwalk, refusing to look at the gas pumps as I passed by, and stood at the railing, overlooking the water and the Centennial Fountain in the middle of the river. This morning, a couple of paddle boarders were paddling through the mist. It was one of the nicest things here, and I never got tired of looking at it.

One foot up on the railing, staring out at the colourful rainbow, I couldn't believe how much I had missed this place—mornings on the waterfront, boats, and the simple life. Why did I leave, and why hadn't I come back until now? Why was it so hard to let go? I wish I knew. Was it what happened *that* day, or was it the path travelled afterward?

Things happen for a reason, and I realized this was why I was back. I didn't connect the dots at first, I guess denial does that. But now the reason I was back—painful though it might be—was to deal with my past. That meant my dad, his boat, Tina, becoming a cop, my best friend Dale, Joanna …

That's a lot of past for anyone.

My search for Sara was the key that unlocked the door. The universe works like that—or perhaps subconsciously I brought myself back here. Maybe a bit of both. I don't know. I know I never dealt with what happened. I just ran and ran.

Enlightening as all this was, I forced myself to reconnect with the present. I needed to get moving forward again. I made a mental note to put a leash on my aura and reminded myself of my purpose here.

Sara, remember?

Sara. The one who was missing, and for whom I had been paid a whole shitload of money, upfront, to find. I had a job to do. I had a responsibility and a promise to keep, both to Teddy and myself.

With one last look at the fountain, I headed back along the dock toward my hotel; maybe not as purposeful as before, but at least I was moving forward. This time, I forced myself to look at the gas pumps as I passed by. A cabin cruiser was docked, and a bare-chested weekend warrior was leaning wearily against the pump, the click-click as he counted out loud, "350, 360, 375 …"

I smiled. *That, I don't miss.*

My next stop was a greasy spoon, a few blocks up from the Lucky 7evens, as good as place as any to start. And a greasy breakfast might help me out of that black hole that was always swallowing me.

It was the hole's fault, right? Are you listening, universe?

15

SARA WAS OUT on the patio, barefoot, with the hose, spraying away another day in the life that was Sharkees—summer patio style. The morning was steamy, the air heavy, the sun already burning hot overhead, and it was barely 9:00 a.m. The steam was rising from the patio where she had been spraying, and she could feel the sweat dripping down from her armpits, through the sides of her tank top. She was mentally drained from trying to make sense of it all, and why not?

Teddy. Tell him? Don't tell him?

The weight of it was becoming suffocating. *He* was suffocating. As much as she loved her brother, at times she literally couldn't breathe when around him.

Ahh, thank God for my bike, she thought. *I'll give him that.*

And what was with his blackout the night before? What was that all about? He hadn't had one in years, maybe not since that night?

Her mind drifted to that new guy Pete. *He is cute and everything, but there is …*

The patio speakers came on, the Eagles singing about someone new in town. Looking up at the speakers in disgust, she gave them the finger. "Seriously?" she yelled inside, "turn that fucking thing off!"

The patio was silent again.

I so need to get laid. She sighed, sitting down on one of the white plastic chairs, and continued to spray the deck. Getting laid. How long had it been?

She thought back to that last time in Peterborough. *Hmm ... heaven*, she sighed. That one was good. The release, and the best part, being left alone, for days, afterward. Looking down, she started to spray her legs and feet with the hose. She sprayed back and forth, enjoying the cold water. It was soothing, as she watched the water splash over and down her legs, running over her feet, between her toes. She tapped her feet on the wet wood of the patio, making small splashing sounds. Leaning over, admiring her recent pedicure, she wiggled her bright red toes, watching as they glistened and sparkled in the sun.

No wonder guys stare at my feet, she mused, *they're pretty.*

Making swishing motions with the hose, the cold water, the contrast between it, and the intense heat, felt sensual, and she started to feel better. Ahh, she sighed, feeling the familiar tingle; she closed her eyes and let herself fall back against the back of the chair, the water running over her legs and feet, gently tapping her toes in the puddles.

'BANG!'

Sara jumped, the hose flying out of her hands, spraying herself and the tables. She lunged, trying to catch it, and fighting its snake-like dance, she latched onto it and held it tight in her hands. Looking up, from the far end of the patio, Teddy's tank-top frame lumbered through the gate.

"Hey, sis," he cheerily waved.

"Shit! God dammit." Sara tried to blow her bangs out of her face, swiping at the water that had spilled all over the front of her tank top. Brushing the water away, pushing her bangs back. *Brothers!*

Oblivious, Teddy ambled over and plopped himself down at one of the tables.

"We aren't open yet," she said, exasperated.

"I know. Hey! How come you're all wet?"

She glared at her brother and fought the urge to turn the hose on him. "So, what are you doing here?"

"Came to see Tony."

"Why?"

"I've got a job for him."

Sara, returned to her chair, her head down, her bangs falling and covering her face, aimlessly sprayed the patio, washing the already washed parts. She remained silent and then out of nowhere, in a voice she didn't recognize … "Teddy, stop. Just stop! Stop this, please! I can't do this anymore."

She slumped back into the chair, the running hose falling from her hand and not caring, the hose snake-like swishing and spraying water along the wooden patio slats. "I can't. I can't. I can't do this anymore. I can't."

Hunched forward, she dissolved into tears, the hose spraying water over her legs and feet, as she buried her face in her hands. Teddy calmly lifted himself out of the chair, rescued the hose and turned it off. He coiled it and hung it on the hook on the fence. Then he turned and knelt beside his sister.

"Aw geez, I'm sorry, sis. I'm sorry to make you cry. It's nothing this time, I promise. No games, no setups, no nothing. I'm just asking Tony to go to Havelock and help Jimmy find something he misplaced. That's all, I promise."

He reached over, pulled her head into his shoulder, and hugged her. "Honest. There's nothing this time. It just came out wrong, that's all. It's nothing like that, I promise."

Teddy stroked her head, gently brushing her hair. Tilting her chin up toward his face, Sara looked tired, her eyes puffy and sad looking, not full of their usual life. Her cheeks were red and tear-stained, her bangs covering her face. He gently brushed them away and looking into her eyes, he lied. "Honest."

"Honest?" she answered back, looking up into his puppy dog eyes, searching, pleading, hoping. She tapped him on the chest. "Promise me. Promise me, no more. Promise me, Teddy."

"I promise, sis. I promise." Pulling her in close, he squeezed her tight.

At that moment, both gave each other only what supposedly close brothers and sisters can provide, telling each other what they wanted to hear. They sat a spell, holding each other, the sound of birds fluttering in the trees, beer pennants flapping in the light breeze, everything else perfectly still. If you closed your eyes, you wouldn't think you were sitting in paved-paradise, suburbia strip-mall style. Even it can have its own quiet, peaceful moments.

Teddy broke the silence. "Listen, sis, why don't you see if Patty can find someone to cover your shift, and you can jump on your bike and get away? You might feel better."

Ahh, getting laid.

A smile appeared, Sara pulled away from her brother's grasp, and turned to face him. Pushing her bangs away from her face, "That's not a bad idea. I'll probably just go tonight after my shift ends, okay? Working helps, thanks."

She got up from the chair, leaned over, kissed her brother on the top of his head, and went inside.

16

THE SUN WAS already burning hot as I made my way up George Street. I crossed the railroad tracks and found the same old barren stretch of wasteland—an empty parking lot that gave birth to cracking pavement and weeds, but now there was a No Frills tacked on at the far end.

Whoa, progress.

I continued along, and on the opposite side of the street, the used bookstore was still there along with that same guy sitting out front on the bench.

There, that's more like it. I thought. *Maybe he knows the woman and her little dog.*

Taking it all in, nothing had changed; then again, nothing ever really changes here, does it? I mean, it is Peterborough, after all.

Up ahead, I caught sight of a foot sticking out of the doorway, and as I approached, I slowed. A young guy wearing a black AC/DC T-shirt and tattered jeans with both knees ripped through was sitting in a doorway, holding out a black ball cap. He was wearing running shoes, the top of one shoe peeled back like a banana, exposing his foot and what was left of his sock. He looked up at me, mumbling an apology and tried to squirm back into the doorway. He was sitting on a pile of cardboard, and it kept shifting, and any movement only made the cardboard slide sideways even more.

I stopped and glanced down. "Hey, how's your day?"

"Today is better than yesterday," he said, looking up at me, answering in a tone that was somewhere between hopelessness and hopefulness.

Involuntarily shuddering, I could only imagine. Despite my years working undercover on streets just like this, it was a pair of shoes one had to walk in themselves to truly understand what it was like to be out here. Most people wouldn't last forty-five seconds out here; much like the SUV couple, their lives based solely on status.

"Hey, I'm Pete."

"Des," he answered hesitantly.

"Cool!"

"Nice to meet you ... Pete."

"Nice to meet you, Des."

A smile formed on his face, and my instincts said he was educated and had been something at some point. Maybe he lost it all, just like I did. The street becomes home easier than most people think. It happens all too often.

Reaching in my pocket, I pulled out a twenty-dollar bill, folded it in my hand, and dropped it in his hat. His eyes grew wide.

"Oh uh, hey, thanks, man. I mean, Pete."

Looking down at his feet, I pulled out two more twenties. "For socks and shoes, something to eat too."

He reached for the bills, his hand unsteady, and stuffed them in his pocket. Looking up, we made eye contact.

Just what is it about eye contact anyways?

"Thanks, Pete, I will."

I stared at him hard.

"Yes, I will. Promise."

Motioning with my head towards his pocket. "Okay Des. You have enough for both, right?"

He nodded in affirmation.

"You hang in there, Des. Take care of yourself. Tomorrow will be a better day," I said, trying to sound hopeful for him.

He smiled and laughed. "Yes."

Des had a nice smile, and I detected a hint of mischief in his eyes, and I wondered what his life used to be like? Did he have a job, a family, a home? Was there, or had there been, someone special in his life? My stomach grew tight, and I wished I could do more for him, but I couldn't. He knew that too. He had to do it himself, and he was not there, yet. And he may never get there. It was the least I could do and the best I could do.

I nodded. "Bye, take care, Des."

Looking both ways, I made my way across the street and up the other side, not looking back. I felt better, and the reason was not lost on me.

With a bit more purpose in my stride, up ahead, I saw the sign for the greasy spoon. It was almost noon, and I was starving. As I got to the storefront, things looked too quiet, and as I reached out and pulled on the door handle, it didn't give. The door was locked.

I yanked on the handle again, peered inside, but couldn't make out anything other than the fact the lights were off, and the place was empty. I glanced down and there was a note taped to the inside of the door window; something about a family emergency and being closed until further notice. My stomach rumbling, I shrugged and kept on walking.

As I walked along the sidewalk, I took a chance it might be safe enough to tie my aura to the dock, and let my mind wander some more. Yep, it was bound to hurt, but it was broad daylight, I was out in public, and the woman on the dock did say I needed to deal with this. I mean, what could go wrong?

My thoughts returned to those endless summers on my dad's boat. My dad, Randall, never Randy, moved us to Peterborough from Toronto, when I was five. My mom, Debbie, who I barely remember, left when I was three and Dad never talked about it. Why she left, what happened. But he wanted a fresh start and the small-town life on the water was what he wanted for the both of us. He bought a house on the Otonabee River, fronting on a small bay nestled in from the river, just up from the lift locks. The house came with a cartop boat and a 9.9 motor, then over time he worked his way up until he bought the Commodore 360, the summer I turned fifteen.

Tina Morrison was the love of my life, or so I thought. I'd never outgrown the schoolboy crush I had on her. She and I had attended the same public and high schools, were a part of the same circle of friends, and just like the change of seasons, frequently moving in and out of each other's lives. Our paths crossed again, the summer my dad let me take the 360 out on my own. My schoolboy crush instantly morphed into a head-over-heels in-love—with Tina falling in love with my dad's boat.

I was slow to catch on, enthralled to have Tina sitting on the bow. She was a natural, expertly handling the lines when docking or passing through the locks, and we made a great team.

Tina loved Chris Sage. Chris had been my competition growing up—school, sports, girls, you name it, he was better. He was a superior athlete, better looking, a sharper dresser, smoother dancer, and I was always the runner-up to him; second place, second fiddle, second everything. The harder I tried to compete, the worse I looked to everyone, myself included. I knew I shouldn't have been competing, and I just needed to learn to live with myself and accept who I was and all the good qualities I brought to the table. But I couldn't or perhaps just *wouldn't*—I honestly didn't know which. And I couldn't accept (or wouldn't) that Tina was with me for one reason only, my dad's boat.

The pattern started to emerge that Tina was happy to be with me so long as it was on the boat, and as long as Chris wasn't around. When Chris was available, that's where Tina wanted to be, boat or no boat. And I guess, that's where my proficiency with denial started.

Every summer weekend, I would call Tina up, asking her to cruise the river with me, and she always said yes. Unless, if Chris was around, then she would say no, or back out at the last minute, always with a flimsy excuse—and I *always* let her off the hook. I knew I was the second choice, the fallback, but denial had a firm grip on me. There is a song out there about a guy, who thought he had a place in someone's life, yearning to create something that could never be, and sadly, she never thought twice, or something like that. That was me.

Two summers later, when I was seventeen, the first summer without my dad, who had passed away tragically that spring, I had called Tina the night before, and she was to meet me at my place the next morning. It was a long weekend, the weather was beautiful, and I was hoping this time she would finally agree to go out with me. That morning, when she arrived, she told me her plans had changed, her aunt was sick, and Chris was taking her to see her. It was easier for him to pick her up there, and she hoped I would understand. Chris likes you, she said.

An ugly fight ensued, harsh words spoken between us, which is to say I flung harsh words at Tina. Standing on the front lawn, I tore into Tina, and it would be much later when I realized that the anger was directed not at her, but at myself. I was angry for deluding myself that Tina would finally come around.

After I had run out of hateful things to say Tina said, "Are you done?"

I nodded and slumped to the ground.

When I looked up, Tina was standing over me, arms crossed, shaking her head in disgust, then abruptly turned and left, not even saying goodbye. I watched her walk down the street, getting to the corner, as Chris's blue Camaro Z28 pulled up. The door flew open, and Tina got in. I watched Chris pull away in a cloud of dust and screeching rubber, Tina looking straight ahead.

I sat on the lawn, bawling like a baby, not caring if the neighbours saw or heard. Finally, I wiped my eyes, pulled myself up, and went into the house. I sat at the kitchen table as my dad's girlfriend, Lisa, poured me a glass of water. The tears started flooding back, and I fought them off with every ounce of strength I had. Deep down, I knew it was over between Tina and me. But how could there be an over, I thought, when there had been no beginning? Unwittingly, I had set himself up for all of this, and now I had a painful memory, and just as painful regret, that I would be forced to live with, or run from.

Lisa tried her best to console me. "Why don't you go anyways, honey. Get out. It will make you feel better. Take the boat, your dad would like that. Just you. It's your favourite place, Pete. You and the water. You don't need Tina or anyone for that."

Lisa was right, but I was too stubborn to listen. *Dad, I miss you*, my heart cried out. *You would know what to do.* I didn't need Tina or anyone else. I needed my dad. That's all I needed. But Dad was gone, and all I had was me. I kissed Lisa on the cheek, grabbed the boat keys off the hook, and headed out.

My gut was screaming as I untied the boat, *NO!* the little voice inside me booming, s*tay away today, Pete. Let yourself work through this. You will be okay. You knew this was eventually going to happen. Stay quiet today. Stay away. You will be okay.*

But I slammed the door on my gut instinct and, as time would dictate, I would pay for it. Ultimately, it would alter my life's path.

It was an absolute scorcher of a day, a clear blue sky as far as the eye could see, dripping humidity, the sun blazing down, baking the boat's fibreglass deck, burning the soles of my feet, as I cast off the lines. Any other time this would have been a picture-perfect postcard summer's day—my boat with Tina on the bow, but without Tina, it became a picture-perfect recipe for disaster.

The trouble started immediately, as I left the bay, passing under the railway bridge, guiding the boat around the swimmers and bridge jumpers. Uncharacteristically, I overreacted, barking at a couple of swimmers who got too close to the boat. That's when the hoots and howls started.

"Whoa! Hey, Pete! What no girl today? Where's Tina? She finally find a guy with a bigger boat?"

I tried to laugh them off, but I was seething inside, and I gunned the boat, creating a giant wake and coming dangerously close to the swimmers and other boaters. Everyone started yelling right away.

"Hey! Hey! Hey! Watch it! What are you doing, Pete?"

Losing control was something I never did. I swerved wildly, creating another giant wake on the narrow river; the boats bobbed violently in the water. Fishermen along the banks started yelling as the water came pouring over the edges, swamping their fishing gear. Slowing down, instead of apologizing, I flipped everyone the bird.

Fuck you! Fuck all of you! I snarled to myself.

As I approached the lift locks, the entrance was filled with boats idling, and it was going to be a full lock. In times like this, the lockmaster would cram everyone in, three-boats abreast, making for a very tight and uncomfortable fit. On a day like today, it would be merciless, and that's precisely what happened.

"Where's Tina? What no girl? Pete? Something wrong with you?" There was no place to hide. "Hey, big guy! You're missing something on the bow. You look like you lost your first mate. Hey, Pete! We have an extra girl. Want her?"

On and on it went, the entire twelve-minute trip down the lift lock, and since boats travelled in packs, it was rinse and repeat at the next lock. By the time I guided my boat into the bay, I was ready to blow. Normally, I would motor over to the beach, drop anchor fifty yards out, and go for a swim. Some days, I would swim to the beach and hang out for a while, catching up with all the beachgoers marveling at my boat—thus feeding my ego—then I would swim back out. But I didn't, and in hindsight, I should have. Dropping anchor and going for a swim would have cooled me off, settled me down.

I mean, what was the big deal after all? I had this big, beautiful boat, which was the envy of the locals. I was well-liked and respected by everyone. But I couldn't see that, and somehow, that didn't seem enough for me, especially with my dad gone. I wanted more, needed more, I wanted *everything*, which meant Tina. To me, Tina was everything. The final, missing piece, without her, everything else felt empty and didn't matter.

I headed straight for the waterfront, approaching the fountains, bathing everyone in a glowing rainbow mist. That's when I saw the line of boats slowly circling; driven by the hot, humid, enticing holiday weekend. I throttled back.

"Fuck! Shit – shit - SHIT!"

Now I was acting like I was in a hurry. But that was ridiculous; there was no rush, no urgency, no race; no reason to be anywhere other than, *here*. A beautiful, hot, cloudless, glorious day, on a long weekend, smack dab in the middle of summer. The perfect day. For everyone else but me, that is.

Without Tina, this was the last place I wanted to be, and I regretted taking the boat out. Entering the bay, slowing and getting in line with the other circling boats, I tried to lay low, feign indifference, as the catcalls continued.

"Hey, Pete. Where's your girl? Where's Tina? Boat not big enough for the both of you? Did she finally get wise?"

The wait was agonizingly slow, both gas pumps in use, the attendants being run ragged, soaked in sweat from running back and forth between the pumps and the office. The heat and humidity were oppressive, and the people on the boats were randomly diving into the water to cool off as the boats circled. This added more confusion, slowing things up even more, fearful of a swimmer getting too close to a boat's propeller. Around and around, the floating regatta from hell went, with me caught in the middle, and the comments getting under my skin, making me simultaneously angrier and sadder. Broken hearts will do that.

Forty-five minutes later, it was almost my turn, then some guy on the dock turned off one of the pumps.

"What?" I shouted. "Hey! Wait! Why are you turning them off? I'm fucking next, and I've been waiting like for-fucking-ever!" I squealed over the water. A young guy, just like myself, turned and shrugged, signaling there was no more gas. I snapped and lost it.

"What the fuck?" I yelled even louder. "Fuck you! Turn that fucking pump back on, you fucking-fuck! I know there's fucking gas still! I know there is."

But of course, I knew no such thing.

The other boaters, hearing the uproar, turned to look in my direction. Everything fell silent, the guy turned and called out.

"I'm very sorry, sir. We ran out of gas, and you will just have to wait your turn at the other pump." He pointed to the lone pump. "It won't be long, I really am sorry, sir, but there's nothing I can do." He shrugged and turned away, moving over to the lone working pump.

So, here I was, this bare-chested kid, with boaters and people onshore all staring at me now. Day or night, voices carry over the water, surprisingly well, crystal clear. I bet you didn't know that.

"Fuck you!" I yelled, and then I did something *really* stupid.

Everyone watched as my boat broke the line, and I hammered the throttle, racing straight for the dock. At the last second, I turned sharply, exposing the underside of the boat, and sprayed the dock with a giant wave of water, narrowly missing a docked boat by inches. The ensuing wave pounded the side of the docked boat, bouncing it wildly up against the concrete edge, scraping the fibreglass all along its starboard side. Another boat had just pulled away, caught in the wake, it bounced roughly, and a teenage girl on the bow fell overboard. Not content, I yanked on the throttle, pulling it back, then gunning it, stopped abruptly—the force of the water pushed the bow of my boat almost below the surface, then it bounced up heavily, as the wave passed underneath.

I turned and looking back, everyone on shore was scrambling, and it looked like a fire drill in one of those old movies. I put the boat in reverse and started backing up towards the dock. I inched the boat closer and closer to the gas pumps, aiming it directly for the guy in the white marina golf shirt. The guy who, in my world, was solely responsible for wrecking my day. Eyeballing him now, angling the boat just so, I raised the boat's prop to the edge of the waterline, and hammered the throttle, water sprayed up and over the dock, showering the guy and the other attendants. The water poured over the edge, toppling the metal carts that held boat supplies, the plastic bottles falling and rolling in every direction. The attendants were slipping and sliding, trying to chase down the dropped supplies before they slide into the water. The gas hose that was filling the lone boat, suddenly came loose, and one of the attendants, noticing, ran toward the hose and barely caught it in time, but was unable to stop it from pouring gasoline all over themself.

The water receded and the bay was completely still. No one said a word, everyone in shock at what just happened. The only sounds were the seagulls flapping and crying overhead and the sputtering of the other boats' engines. It was like time had come to a stop. I could hear the faint sounds of traffic from the street, but everything else was stock-still. I hammered the throttle forward.

"Fuck you! Fuck all of you!"

I zig-zagged through the circling vessels, creating another violent wake, as the boats bobbed and bounced roughly, boaters holding on tightly, cursing at me.

No one ever saw me or my boat again for the rest of that summer and, as things turned out, not the next summer, or the one after that. I never boated or returned to the waterfront again. The life I so dearly loved ended that day. My dad's boat remained in storage until I sold his house two years later and the boat along with it.

~

There was a loud honk, and I jumped. I was standing in the middle of an intersection, cars trying to move around me.

"Shit, sorry. Sorry—" I was waving my hands and ducking my head as I scrambled to the sidewalk. Mentally drained, I untied my aura.

Gee, that wasn't so bad, was it?

17

HAVE YOU EVER tried to push a rope? This whole Sara-easy-money-search wasn't going to be so easy after all. I was only on day two, and it felt like things were coming off the rails. Plus, I was now being forced to deal with my rather unpleasant past. Things could always be worse, right? At least I hadn't run into Tina. Now, that wouldn't be good.

I wondered what had happened to her, where she had ended up, and if she was still with Chris.

Why was I unable to leave well enough alone? Who cared whether she was still with Chris? It didn't matter now. It wasn't like I was going to run into her here. That was years ago. She was long gone. *Fini.* Time to let it go, as the nice lady with the little dog had said.

Shaken by my near-death experience in the intersection, I needed something to eat, and I made my way back toward my hotel. Up ahead, off in the distance, I saw someone come whizzing around the corner in an electric wheelchair, taking the corner sharply, not looking or caring who was in the way. The chair tipped, bounced hard, then swerved, the occupant's hand on the controls bringing it under control. I could make out the back of the head, the red ponytail bobbing in rhythm with the chair.

Are you fucking kidding me? No way!

That could be only one person, no one drove a chair like that.

Smiling, resisting the urge to call out, I broke into a jog, dodging an older couple window shopping, and a teenager on a skateboard. I ran hard trying to catch up to the red ponytail bobbing and bouncing along the sidewalk. Racing through an intersection, barely beating the red light, fighting off an angry honk, catching up ... I slowed to a walk.

I followed behind for a block, admiring the red ponytail, the chair click-clacking as it bounded along the sidewalk, the voice humming merrily away. I waited for my chance, and at the next block, there was a red light even that chair couldn't outrun. I stood behind the chair just watching. The red ponytail was singing happily out loud, head bobbing from side to side. "Dum-da-de-de-dum-dum ... Tra-la-la-la ... Tum-de-de-da-dum-dum-dee-dee ..."

I took in the moment and couldn't stop smiling. Just before the light turned green, I snuck up from behind, and reaching around, clasped my hands over her eyes. "Guess who?"

She jumped, surprised, then recognizing my voice, started to cry.

"Ah, I know that voice." She placed her hands over mine, rubbing them. She cried out, her body jerking, "Pete! Pete Humphries ... is that you? Yes, that's you ... I can tell. OH MY." She started to shake and cry harder, not letting go of my hands. My hands still over her eyes, I moved around in front of her, and pulled them away. She was bawling, and smiling, and laughing, all at the same time, her arms stretched out and pulled me in to hug me.

"Oh my! I've missed you so much!"

"I missed you too, Hanna."

"How are you? Where have you been? I've missed you. Oh my, oh my ... you still look the same."

I tried to pull away, but Hanna wouldn't let go, her hug a vice-like grip. She was holding me so tight I couldn't move. I tried to move my head, but she had me in a headlock. Finally, I bit her on the shoulder, she yipped and released her grip.

I pulled back, laughing. "I couldn't breathe."

"I don't care. I missed you." She pulled me down into her arms again. We hugged some more then I pulled back.

"You look great, Hanna! You haven't changed a bit. When was the last time you flipped your chair?" I teased.

"So do you! And no, I still haven't cuz you taught me how to take corners, remember?"

I laughed, recalling the last summer I was home. I was in the process of selling my dad's place and that September I was starting at the Police College in Barrie. Our paths crossed accidently one late night and the rest was history. We started spending the summer nights together, carousing in the bars along George Street, then terrorizing the streets after. After too much to drink, we would go experimenting with her chair, trying to see how far she could go on one wheel. There were a couple of honks from the street, as we were blocking the sidewalk and the road.

"Come on, kid! Let's walk, just like the old days, huh?"

"Yessir!" flicking the switch on her chair, off she went without looking, crossing the street, even though the light was now red, and cars were passing in both directions. There were more angry honks and loud screeches as she bobbed and bounced through the intersection, her chair gaining speed and oblivious to the oncoming traffic. I marveled at her—not a care in the world, she acted like she was invincible, or make that invisible; still thumbing her chair at authority. It was no wonder we connected.

I followed behind, trying to stay with her, gesturing to the cars that were swerving all around us. We made it to the other side, and she slowed down, allowing me to catch my breath.

"Getting old?" she asked devilishly.

I made a face at her and stuck out my tongue, and she did it back. Two peas in a pod. We started along the sidewalk again.

"I've missed you."

"I know, me too."

"You left and didn't say goodbye, you know."

"I know."

"Why?"

"I know, I'm sorry."

"Aww, it's okay."

I went quiet, my head down, and I struggled with what to say. We strolled along, just the sound of her chair bumping and clicking on the pavement. She broke the silence.

"You're back. I'm so glad you're back. It doesn't matter. Just you're back."

I snapped to. "Yes, I am. I didn't expect to run into you. You're still here?"

"Well, Pete," she said, "exactly where did you think I was going to go?"

"Yes, you're right. Sorry. I did think about you. Lots. I worried about you and if you were okay. But I had nothing to worry about because you still own these streets," I said, jerking a thumb back towards the last intersection.

She giggled, pointing to herself with her non-driving hand. "What, who me?" Turning serious she asked, "So, why are you really back, Pete?"

We stopped along the sidewalk, at a doorway, and pulled closer to the wall.

"I'm looking for someone."

"Yes, that's my Pete. You haven't changed."

"Uh huh."

"Wait! I bet it's a girl you're looking for."

I nodded.

"Same old Pete. You were always rescuing damsels in distress. How come you never rescued me then?"

"Because you were never in distress."

"Well, how about now?" And with that, she fell over sideways in her chair, her head rolling back, arms flung out over the arms of her chair, tongue sticking out to one side, eyes closed. She made gurgling noises, then with her head tilted, she opened one eye. "How about now? That distress enough for you?"

Laughing, I leaned in and hugged her. She reached up, latched on, and squeezed hard, not letting me go. I tried to pull away, but she wouldn't let go, and it was all I could do to breathe. I managed, in a muffled tone to say, "I will bite you again."

"Aw promises, promises," she said, and reluctantly let go.

We skipped along George Street just like old times, laughing at each other, and I reminisced. This for a change was a pleasant memory.

I met Hanna—which is to say almost got run over by Hanna—one drunken summer night, when I was nineteen, on George Street. Hanna was a child of the streets, and our paths collided on the sidewalk when I stumbled out of a bar late one night. In unison, we yelled "HEY! Watch out!" as she almost ran me over with her wheelchair. She swerved, almost taking out a light pole, wound up dazed, her chair tilted sideways, half on the curb and half out on the street. I helped her and we chatted for a bit, then wished each other good night, and off we went in separate directions. A couple of nights later, our paths crossed again. This time a couple of drunks were accosting Hanna, on a street corner and wouldn't let her pass by. Feisty as all get out, she refused to budge or be intimidated. But then, it took a serious turn, when one of the drunks put his hand on her breast. I jumped in and it was over pretty quick, and Hanna was free to go. I walked her home, and that night a connection was born.

We spent that summer on the streets together, an inseparable pair. It was only one summer, but we lived a lifetime's worth. I taught her how to take corners in her wheelchair, which was hilarious, as we would get liquored up first for courage, then off we went practicing trying to tip her chair. We were quite the pair, side-by-side, joking and teasing with her; telling her to hurry when crossing the street, the light turning red, she didn't know what the colour yellow or red meant, saying she was colour blind.

People would stare, not sure what to make of us. There was the time I called out to her, in the middle of the road, when she almost got hit by a car because she wasn't watching where she was going. It was a classic you-had-to-be-there moment if there ever was one. Ahh, all those good times. Then, at the end of that summer, I left, not even saying goodbye. It was just too hard. I didn't know how to say goodbye. I still don't know how to say goodbye.

We came up to another light, crossed over, and then crossed again and headed up the other side of the street. As we talked, Hanna told me that the streets were just not the same after I left. I knew I brightened her day, and she did the same for me; no matter how bad either of us was feeling that day, we made each other's day better. Her eyes would light up, when I came bounding across the street calling out, "Hey kid!" catching up, giving her a big hug; then off we went, the inseparable pair, two peas in a pod, cruising the streets of downtown Peterborough.

I could sense Hanna wanted to pry, but she let me be. Good ol' Hanna, smart as a whip. Finally, I broke the silence.

"Yes, I'm back. First time since—" but I quickly changed the subject. "Listen kid, as I said, I'm looking for someone."

We stopped again, and I pulled out the picture of Sara and handed it to her. She looked it over, thinking carefully. Shaking her head, looking up, she handed me back the picture.

"No, I haven't seen her. But I have seen someone like her. I don't know her name. You said Sara, right? I do know of someone who rides a bike and parks it in front of the Lucky 7evens. I've seen her playing pool at the table by the front window. Word is she's good. Word is also she's tough and to stay away.

Black cloud hanging over her. Eats guys up and spits them out. Just your kind of girl, Pete," Hanna winked. "I haven't seen her lately, but when she does come around, it's not until near midnight. She parks her bike right out front, and no one dares touch it."

I nodded, grateful for the information.

Hanna reached out for my arm. "Pete. Pete. Be careful. This girl. These streets. This town. It's not the same anymore, you know? Be careful. Please. Now that you're back, I don't want to lose you again."

I smiled and hugged her again. "I have to go. I'm so happy to see you. I want to do this again, but I've got stuff I gotta do first, okay?"

"I know," Hanna answered, frowning.

"I promise. We will do this again, okay? I promise," I said, trying to convince the both of us, neither of us sure our paths would cross again.

"Okay, Pete . . ." She reached out to hug me again. "Love you."

"Love you too, kid."

Hanna flicked the switch on her chair, turned and motored in the opposite direction, her ponytail bobbing and bouncing along. I watched her go, but she stopped, spun her chair around and came back, stopping in front of me.

"What is it?" I asked, concerned.

"Dave. There's this guy named Dave. He's been hanging around the Lucky 7evens. He's trouble."

"So?" I asked. "I'm not looking for a Dave. I'm looking for Sara."

Hanna turned serious. "Pete. That Dave guy is your kind of trouble. The kind of trouble, I'm sorry to say this, I really am, but the kind of trouble that you naturally attract."

Hanna eyes glistened. "Remember, I know you, too. Please be careful."

Stepping back, opening my eyes wide, feigning shock and indignation, I pointed to my chest and mouthed, "Who me?"

Hanna reached out to hit me, but I jumped away.

"I will, I promise," I said, trying to sound convincing, and yet again, someone was reminding me to be careful.

"Bye, love you," Hanna turned again, and off she went, the chair click-clacking loudly on the pavement. I waved and turned in the direction of my hotel and food.

18

THE BURNER PHONE buzzed. Fuck! Teddy, shit! I knew why he was calling. The box. I let it keep buzzing. He was pissed no doubt. Fuck this. I don't have time for this right now. I ignored it and let the phone finish buzzing. I leaned back against the wall, the pillows propped up behind me, and stretched my legs down the bed. The picture of Sara lay on the bed beside me. I ran my fingers over the image, trying to feel it. Feel Sara. Feel the vibe. It was an old trick of mine that had worked many times in the past. When I was stuck on something, I would sit, close my eyes and touch a picture, or an object, or whatever it was I was trying to connect with. Running my fingers over it, I found I could pull something from it. A vibe, a thought, a connection. Rarely, I did not discover anything, but now, I couldn't feel a thing. My head seemed clear, but was it really? Clouding my thoughts was what Hanna had said.

Who was this Dave guy she was so worried about? *Please be careful.* She was right about me attracting trouble. She knew me too well. Funny how all these people entering my life were telling me to be careful. Something was up here in universe-land, and I was going to have to start being more careful.

It dawned on me that the woman with the little dog at the waterfront was the only person who *hadn't* told me to be careful. She had said it would be okay. That I would be okay. Strange? I filed it away.

Hanna was correct, the streets had changed, I noticed it too. It was only four thirty, hours until Sara showed, if she did at all. I reached down on the floor and pulled up the Styrofoam takeout container. Opening the lid, I looked inside and then thought better of it—closing it up again, I put it back on the floor and stretched out on the bed, closing my eyes.

Suddenly, I jerked awake and was bathed in sweat. The room was pitch black, and I didn't know where I was. I was tangled up in damp sheets. I bicycle-kicked violently at the covers to untangle myself, then sat straight up in bed. I rubbed my eyes, shook my head, and tried to orient myself. *Where am I?* Looking around the dark room, I saw the red lights of the bedside clock: 10:38 p.m.

I rubbed my eyes and shook my head again. My T-shirt felt clammy and stuck to my wet skin. I tried to peel it off, but it got stuck around my head, and after a couple of hard tugs, I pulled it over my head, rolled it into a ball, and fired it in the corner. I moved to the edge of the bed and swung my legs over. I rubbed my eyes once more and stretched. Once again, I felt like I had been turned inside out and thought maybe I should just stay this way.

How long had I been sleeping? Six hours? Scratching myself, it was no wonder I felt like shit. I got up and padded over toward the sliver of light that separated the curtains. I pulled them apart to reveal the river below me. Looking around, there was a couple walking hand in hand through the courtyard. The soft lights along the walkway cast long shadows while the glow of the full moon shining on the river spilled over onto the freshly manicured lawn. Even through the window, I could hear the soft pfft-pfft of the sunken sprinklers strategically watering the lawn. Watching the couple, I felt a pang in my stomach.

Why did relationships have to be so fucking hard? Why couldn't it be that simple? Why did it always have to be so fucking complicated? Why couldn't it be just that!

Of course, maybe they weren't happy, I told myself. Maybe it only looked that way from a distance. Things are never as simple as they look from afar. Right?

I hate you, Hollywood!

I flung the curtains closed in disgust. Turning in the dark room, I shuffled forward, trying to find the light, and stepped on the takeout container—a loud crack followed by a squishing sound, my foot wet and sticky.

"Fuck!"

I looked down at my foot covered in congealed egg and fought back the urge to vomit. I hopped to the bathroom and stepped into the shower. I stood under the hot water for a long time, trying to burn away the heaviness that enveloped me. Finally, all pruney like, still feeling heavy, I got out and toweled off. I dressed in a clean red T-shirt, throwing on my best and only jean shorts, with the picture of Sara tucked in the back pocket. Taking a peek in the mirror, I appeared presentable enough for public—at least at night—and headed out.

Once outside, I felt better walking along George Street. It was a beautiful summer evening. The streets were filled with people: couples, groups of guys and girls, singles, pairs. Girls night out. Guys night out. Everyone laughing, joking, enjoying the perfect summer night. Up ahead, a pack of girls in their twenties came out of a bar and headed towards me. They were all talking excitedly at the same time, peering intently at their cell phones. Dressed in short summer skirts and heels, they clattered happily down the pavement towards me. I had to jump out of the way as they passed by, oblivious to anyone else. Trailing behind were a pack of guys, similar age, headed in the same direction.

I came upon the doorway that had held Des earlier, but he was gone now. His homemade sitting place was still there, so I stopped and reached down to try and rearrange it for him. The top layer of cardboard was wet and fell apart in my hands. I quickly looked around to see if anyone was watching and tried to reposition it, shifting the wet cardboard to the bottom and moving a dryer piece to the top, then I moved it deeper into the doorway and hopefully out of the weather. I made a mental note to come by tomorrow to check on it. On him.

Further ahead, the Lucky 7evens' neon sign was lighting up George Street with its whiteish-purplish glow. As I got closer, there were a couple of bouncers out front, and one of them looked cute. There was a small line that snaked along the wall, the bouncers checking ID's. I moved to the back of the line and waited, inching closer. Then it was my turn, a charming girl standing in front of me. *How can she be a bouncer?* She certainly didn't have that kind of build. Instead, she was tall, athletic, almost wiry.

In the light, I could see her toned arms and shoulders, matched perfectly with her white Lucky 7evens golf shirt. She was wearing black shorts and black Nikes, her legs long and tanned, with that cyclist's thickness. Her blonde hair was tied back in a ponytail. Hmm, a force to be reckoned with.

"ID, please," she asked, her head down.

"Sure," as I handed her my licence.

Her head remained down, as she inspected it, holding it up to the streetlight, she looked at me. Our eyes locked, that instant click, that instant connection. Hey, it happens.

Her bright blue eyes connected with mine, a big smile formed on both our faces, looking down, reading from my licence.

"It says here, Peter Humphries. That you?" she asked flirtatiously, looking me over with a mischievous grin.

"Guilty as charged, ma'am."

"Okay, you're good to go there, Peter Humphries. No wait. You seem more like a Pete kind of guy. Am I right?"

"Yes, ma'am."

Our eyes locked again.

"Okay Pete. And behave. I don't want to have to come in and drag you out if you cause trouble or have to come rescue you if you attract any."

She handed me back my licence, and as her hand touched mine, she let it linger just long enough, and the electric shock was palpable. I tried to focus and ignore the tweeting sounds circling my head.

"No trouble here, ma'am," I quipped. "But … that being said, if I *did* need rescuing who should I yell for?"

That made her laugh. "Sydney. My name is Sydney, but you can call me Syd. Now GO!"

Reaching out, Syd pushed me on the shoulder toward the entrance.

Can't I stay out here with you? I thought.

At the entrance, I turned and looked back—sure enough, Syd was looking at me. I smiled again, and Syd returned my smile then turned toward the next person in line. Shaking my head, I went inside.

The Lucky 7evens had changed since I had been there last. Gone was the dark paneling, the black and white checkerboard linoleum floor, the ratty pool tables with the ripped cloth and low flickering overhead lights. Gone too, were the cheap wooden chairs and tables, which came apart far too easily in a fight. The bar had gone through a complete makeover; redesigned like those new-age art deco warehouses. Thick painted concrete pillars, silver tube piping wrapping overhead, hardwood flooring throughout, and a polished bar stretched the entire length of the wall along the far left. There were standing areas strategically placed around the floor where patrons could stand and chat, play pool, or watch the dance floor. High tables and chairs covered the floor, and high-back chairs lined the long L-shaped bar from one end to the other.

A railing separated the bar from the pool tables, and flat-screen TVs were bolted to the ceiling, scattered throughout the bar. There were a half-dozen pool tables, in the center of the floor, all with low-hanging lamps over top. It was a happening place, but tonight it was half full, the loud thump-thump of the music, along with the flashing purple lights, made it feel more crowded than it was. Guys and girls were on the dance floor, dancing and mingling in groups, talking, laughing, drinks in one hand cell phones in the other.

I worked my way over to the bar and waited to order a beer. I gazed around and spied an empty pool table in the middle of the floor, and beside the empty one, was a table full of players. *This is my chance*, I thought. *Let's hope the pool gods cooperate.* Leaning over an unoccupied high-back chair, I waved my hand and caught the bartender's eye.

"Barking Squirrel? And a table if there's one free?"

Nodding yes to both, the bartender returned with my beer and a tray of balls. A few minutes later, I was playing pool, with an unobstructed view of the entire place. Perfect. I hadn't played pool in ages, and wondered, if I still had it. After carefully choosing a cue from the rack on the wall, racking the balls with my usual flourish, and after diligently chalking the tip, I proceeded to sink the cue ball straight off the break.

Yep, still got it.

Acting nonchalant, like it was the ball's fault, I retrieved the cue ball from the corner pocket, lined the balls back up, re-chalked my cue, taking extra care with my aim, sank the cue ball straight off the break again. I looked around to see if anyone was watching, shaking my head at the cue, I gave it a stern talking to. I walked over to the rack and carefully selected another. This time, I held each end up to the light and closing one eye, thoroughly inspected the length of the shaft in both directions. Not satisfied, I tried two more cues, until I found one to my liking—making certain it didn't have eyes for the cue ball.

I returned to the table, chalking the tip aggressively this time, re-racking the balls; I lined up the cue ball again. Bending over, and with a flair only Paul Newman could appreciate, I drained the cue ball once again. Cautiously looking around, hoping no one was watching, there was a couple seated nearby, trying to suppress their laughter. Catching their eyes, acting all serious-like, I pointed to the table and mouthed, *"Table's not level."*

Three Barking Squirrels later, my pool table mercifully devoid of any action, still holding the cue stick for support, I sipped on my beer, watching the front entrance. It was 1:15 a.m.

"Hey, buddy. Wanna play?"

I turned to see a wiry guy with thick muscular forearms standing beside the table. He was a little older than me and wore a black T-shirt, black jeans, black sneakers, black everything. I had to think fast. Did I want company or not? Had he been watching me play? That alone was worth a no. This wasn't the company I was expecting.

Think, Pete. Think.

Sara still hadn't shown, and who knows if she would now? Maybe this guy had seen her or knew her. Worst case, it would kill some time, and maybe he has trouble with the cue ball? It couldn't hurt. I looked at his face, he was wearing a sort of goofy grin.

Seems friendly enough, I thought. *Ah, fuck it.* "Sure. Rack 'em up."

I moved off to the side and placed my beer on the ledge. The guy placed a hard-backed case on the table, flicked open the two latches, and took out a cue. Screwing the two ends together, he closed the case and placed it on the floor underneath. He moved to the other side and reached underneath the table for the tray. Placing it on the table, he walked around to the pockets, gathering up the balls, then lined them in the tray, giving it a hard shake. He lifted it off with a flourish and slipped the tray back underneath.

"You want to shoot first?" he asked.

"No, go ahead." I waved my hand as visions of the cue ball slamming into all six pockets at once, danced in my head. And besides, if he cleared the table, I wouldn't have to shoot.

After rolling the cue on the table from side to side and seeming satisfied with the result, he picked it up, reached for the cue ball, and placed it on the table in front of him. He rolled it to a preferable spot. Bending over, he lined himself up and leaning in, as he was about to shoot, he looked up at me.

"My name's Dave, by the way. What's yours?"

19

PULLING UP IN front of the Lucky 7evens, Sara parked her bike in her usual reserved spot by the curb and got off.

"Evening, Miss Sara. How are you tonight?"

She unhooked her helmet and lifted it off. "Evening, Ronny. I'm good. Have you seen him? Is he here?"

"No, Miss Sara, I haven't, and I've been here since four this afternoon."

"Shit," she muttered, pissed he wasn't there. Tucking her gloves in her helmet, she debated whether to go in at all. *Don't feel like playing pool tonight*, she thought peering through the giant window. *I just want to get fucking laid. Why is that so fucking hard?*

She bit her lip and fingered the front zipper on her leather jacket, weighing her options. "Aw fuck it." She handed her helmet and bike key to Ronny. "Keep an eye on her, please."

"As always, Miss Sara."

Walking up the step, she looked inside and stopped dead in her tracks.

What the fuck is he doing here?

Angry, frustrated, and intrigued all at the same time, she stared inside.

"Excuse me?"

"Uh? What? Sorry," she apologized and shifted to one side to allow the couple behind to move past. Looking through the doorway, she was unsure what to do. *Fucking great*, she sighed. She stared at the pool table inside and shook her head.

"He's here!" pointing to the pool table and feeling the tingle below, "But he's not! Fuck!" *I can't do this tonight, not with him, at least not tonight.*

Sighing, Sara turned and went back down the steps towards Ronny. Retrieving her helmet and key, she straddled the bike, pulled her helmet down in disgust, and slammed down the visor. She goosed the throttle a few times, the ear-splitting popping caused the people standing out front to jump back in fright. She kicked off the kickstand, twisted the throttle, and without looking, roared away into the night.

20

IT WAS ANOTHER beautiful morning on the waterfront, but unlike yesterday, I was feeling alive, hopeful, and certain today was going to be a good day. No, make that today was going to be a *great* day, no matter what. I hadn't had that feeling since when, Duval Street?

The night was a bust, Sara a no-show, and my eight-ball prowess needed work. I made a note to speak with the manager about those tables not being level. Despite Hanna's misgivings, Dave was an interesting character. We had a blast playing pool until closing. He laughed out loud, pounding me on the back good-naturedly, when I sank the cue ball two more times off the break. And boy, Dave loved his beer! Quart-size Labatt 50. I didn't think they made quarts anymore. Talk about a time warp.

When 4:00 a.m. came along, Dave made me laugh out loud with his drunk puppy dog eyes as he tugged on my arm trying to coax me to head out for a bite, but I declined. I was pooped. I bid him adieu and, just like old times, staggered back to my hotel where, falling face-first into bed, I slept like a baby.

Waking around ten, with the sun streaming in, I pulled myself out of bed, feeling a spark I hadn't felt in years. I had life and jump in my step again. Quickly showering, I headed out, and passing through the lobby, gave hearty good mornings to everyone in sight; not caring if people thought I had forgotten to take my meds. These *were* my meds—the universe had shifted overnight and was now pleasantly in my favour.

That nice woman and her little dog yesterday was so bang on, I thought, *so easy!*

I had forgotten that all I had to do was pay attention … or was it move forward? Whatever. I didn't care, as long as it worked.

I strolled merrily along the boardwalk light-headed, feeling connected to everything—myself, the birds, the squirrels, even the sun way up overhead. In my head, I could hear a symphony of sounds, crystal clear, no longer jumbled and sounding like an orchestra warming up. Instead, each sound was harmonious, in perfect tune, with nature, me, the universe. So that's what letting go feels like. Neat.

Walking past the gas pumps, this time I purposely took in the scene, reading the dials on the pumps. The two attendants, nattily attired in dark red marina golf shirts and black shorts, scurried about helping tie up an incoming boat.

"Yes, sir. Fill it up? Anything else you need?"

The world seemed like a symphony, and I was its conductor. I stopped and stood transfixed, inhaling the glorious day that it was. It took a moment for me to realize that someone was calling out from the water.

"Hey there! Can you give us a hand?"

I turned to see a large cabin cruiser pulling alongside the dock. The sun's reflection was blocking my view, but I could see the shape of a petite woman with a boat line in her hands. She threw me the bowline.

"Can you tie us up?" and started to tell me how to tie the rope.

"It's okay. I've got it. I've tied a line or two in my—"

My world in that instant, shattered like broken glass, the symphony stopped, and I dropped my conductor's stick—it falling straight down through the sewer grate. Bullseye.

Standing on the bow, barefoot, wearing jean shorts, braless in a white tank top, was Tina.

"Excuse me? Um, when you are finished tying the line, could you give me a hand with the one on the stern please? Uh … Hello? Are you …"

Tina, shielding her eyes from the sun, stared for the longest time. "Pete?

Pete Humphries? Is that you? Oh my God! What are you doing here? I heard you were—"

"Hi Tina," I said, drearily. "As you can see, I'm alive and well. At least, I think this is me." At that moment, I wished I was anyone but me.

"Sorry Pete, you took me by surprise. You were the last person I was expecting to see."

Funny, so was I. "That's okay," I said, letting her off the hook—just like always, old habits hard to break.

"Give me a second to finish securing the boat, and we can catch up, okay?"

"Sure."

All I wanted to do was crawl into a hole and die. I couldn't fucking believe it. My head was swimming, and I tried to tell myself to hold on, take a breath, and see where this went. The universe, suddenly, was not my friend.

Tina finished securing the boat as I watched, bending over in my sightline, and no doubt on purpose. She always had that power over me, and she knew it too. Just like that, the song started playing in my head. *What a Fool Believes* or my version of it.

"She came from somewhere back in his long-ago ..."

Tina called out, the needle ripping across the grooves. "Chris? Chris? Guess who's here."

Oh Christ!

"Be right there, babe."

I heard rustling coming from the cockpit, and I could see partial movement, then Chris's legs appeared, followed by the rest of his body.

Not a hair out of place, he was wearing an Old Navy golf shirt that fit his muscular body perfectly.

Un-fucking-believable.

Chris came down from the cockpit, effortlessly moving across the deck, and extended his hand. I extended mine, and we shook firmly, just enough on my part to let him know that though Tina was now his, she was once mine, and I hadn't forgotten. BANG! (The sound of the door closing behind me, as I entered the room to denial.)

We both stepped back. Reflex? It was like a stalemate, and we warily eyed each other. Tina, noticing, shifted over to Chris, and put her arm around his waist.

"So, Pete, what have you been up to? Like I said, the last I heard—"

"Nice boat!" I said, looking at Chris and started talking about it, hoping the conversation wouldn't return to me answering where I had been, what I had been up to. I didn't want to go there, even on my best days, and certainly; not here, not now.

Ignoring me, Chris stepped ashore and was at the gas pump holding the nozzle in his hand. "Pete, uh, you're in the way. Could you shift a bit so I can fill the boat?"

Always in the way it seemed. The story of my life. On the outside, looking in. I always came up short when it came to Chris. He always was just a little bit better than me, just that tiny bit, maybe not noticeable to anyone else, but it was to me. I was always competing with Chris on something, and funny, he never seemed to be competing with me.

Tina had been forever linked to Chris, even when they broke up; it was only a matter of time until they got back together, destiny never had a truer meaning. That one summer, when they broke up yet again, I was *sure* it was for good, which is why I asked her out. I don't know if I was more surprised that she said yes, or that she barely paid attention to me when we went out. One night, walking home from the movies, we stopped in to see Chris's parents, Tina wanting to say hello. Yet, she was supposed to be with me. Sitting in Chris's parent's basement, listening to them talk about Chris, I felt like a third wheel. This was the choice I had made, and I paid for it, and was still paying, even now. Tina interrupted me from my head, or was she rescuing me?

"Listen, Pete, it was nice to see you, but we better get going. We have to gas up the boat, and others are waiting. Then we're heading up to Sturgeon Falls, and we need to make as many locks as we can today. Once Chris is done filling the boat can you help us cast off?"

"Sure, sure, no worries," I mumbled. Inside though I was screaming. *This should've been me, us, my boat, my Tina, ME! God! I hate those fucking Doobie Brothers!*

Chris finished gassing up the boat, paid the attendant, and with a quick leap, glided through the air, landing on the deck, striding toward the cockpit, stopping and giving Tina a long kiss on the mouth.

Asshole. As if.

I moved to the bow, reached down, and untied the line. Coiling it around my arm, I threw it, Tina catching it with ease. The kind of ease one acquires from years on the water, from the self-assurance and security of never having to worry about anything. They were the perfect couple, with a perfect happy ending. Life with a final destination, not a ripple, not a hair out place—too perfect even for Hollywood. Chris had started the boat's engines and was slowly backing away from the dock, no need for me to give a push off.

Tina was on the bow, finished securing the bowline, and leaned over and started to bring in the fender on the port side. Bent over like that, in the sun, she was stunning—her short brown hair, her perfectly formed breasts and hard nipples poking through her tank top; jean shorts with the fringes wiggling in the breeze, cheeks hanging out to show that underwear was optional, her bright red painted toes.

My God, so frigging hot.

I could feel the knot forming in my stomach. That pang, that sweet pang of regret, of loss, never having, always wanting, the longing. Too many times alone in the shower thinking of her.

She came from somewhere back in my long ago …

Tina, back on the bow, squinting in the sunlight, waved. "See you, Pete. Take care of yourself."

I couldn't tell if her tone was one of pity or concern, and I answered too enthusiastically. "You too, Tina. Take care."

I didn't bother with Chris as I didn't care. I watched as the boat slipped away from the dock and slide effortlessly out into the bay. Tina had moved beside Chris in the cockpit, her arm draped over his shoulder, nestled in behind, putting her arms around his stomach, kissing his shoulder and leaning her head into him. I could tell she was content, happy, fulfilled. She didn't look back.

Why would she? Was I expecting anything different? Seriously? Yes, I was dammit! That should've been me.

I turned away and started walking in the other direction. I looked up into the sky searching for the universe. Where are you? Where have you gone? Just a few short minutes ago, everything seemed possible, now, everything was impossible. I was numb, my legs weak and heavy, as I stumbled along the walkway like a drunk. A couple approached me, and the only reason I noticed, was because I walked right into them.

"Hey! Watch where you're going!"

I didn't react, forcing the couple to part, as I walked through them.

I had no idea where I was going, as I staggered along, oblivious to everything. I didn't even know if I was going in a straight line or not. I stumbled, almost falling into the murky green water below.

Keep moving, Pete. Keep moving.

My head was filled with noise, hyperkinetic energy that obliterated any technicolour thoughts. My head down, I felt like a pinball, as I lurched forward, bouncing off someone.

"Hey! Watch it, jackass," someone called out from behind.

The wooden bridge was up ahead, and directly on the other side was my hotel. I tripped on the raised step of the bridge and stumbled forward, falling to my knees, palms out, bracing my fall. I grunted and swore out loud, not caring if anyone was in earshot. I picked myself up, using my arm and the railing to steady myself. I could feel the hot sun beating down on the back of my neck, burning through my T-shirt. I felt heavy and sluggish, as sweat formed in my armpits, across my back, trickling down to the crack of my ass. I rubbed the back of my hand across my forehead, trying to wipe the sweat from my eyes, the salty sting causing me to blink rapidly.

I was hit by a wave of nausea and tried to push it away. Suddenly, my legs buckled and started to shake. The growling in the pit of my stomach increased, waiting for permission to erupt. I fought the urge by staring straight ahead at the flatline of the horizon, but it was too late.

With alarming rapidity, like an expressway to hell, my stomach exploded through the top of my mouth, spraying vile liquid and chunks onto the railing, and down into the water below. Three more big upchucks from the bottom of my toes, and I was done—my stomach empty but still reverberating, cold sweat enveloping my body. My T-shirt was soaked, and I was blinking rapidly, trying to whisk away the salty sweat that was stinging my eyes. My legs were weak and unsteady, and I continued to grip the rail tightly. I tried to breathe through my mouth, but the aftertaste almost made me start heaving. I ran the back of my hand across my mouth and, seeing the brown-coloured barf, threw up again, loud, heaving upchucks, but this time, only dry heaves, as my stomach had nothing left to throw.

The sun warmed my body, and the cold sweats subsided. Forcing myself to move, I held onto the wooden rail and unsteadily made my way across the bridge. I lurched through the parking lot to the side entrance of the hotel, pulled the room card from my back pocket, staggered into the hallway, and took the side stairs, hoping the maids wouldn't see me. I made it up to the third floor where it took two hands to insert the room card in the slot. Pushing the door open, I walked in and let it slam shut behind me. Then, with maybe the only real good thought I had today, I took the Do Not Disturb card off the handle, opened the door, and placed it on the outer handle, letting the door slam shut again.

I headed straight for the balcony and my cooler. Collapsing into the cheap plastic chair, I propped my feet up on the railing and reached in the cooler. I pulled out an unopened bottle of Jack, cracked the seal, twisted off the cap, and started drinking to numb the pain.

21

SARA STIRRED AND rolled onto her side, looking at the sleeping form beside her. A large butt extended out spoon-like toward her. Smiling, she lifted the blanket and moved closer, allowing herself to slide in and fit alongside the shape. Wiggling her hips, she reached out, pulling the cover over, creating a matching spoon set. Snuggling closer, reaching around, she ran her fingers along his bare chest, brushing across his nipples, lightly flicking each nipple with the tip of her finger. She could feel his body move, his hips grinding back into her, and she snuggled forward, moving her head to the back of his neck, nibbling gently on his ear, her tongue, warm and wet, slowly circled and licked his ear, gently biting the lobe.

She continued teasing his nipples, rolling each one between her thumb and forefinger, gently squeezing and tweaking. He stirred and pushed further into her crotch, and she could feel the tingle below, still wet from last night, coming three times, but she still hadn't gotten enough, yet. Moving from his nipples, she moved her hand down his smooth, hairless, chest, making half circles with her nails, dragging them lazily along the bare skin, feeling the slight tuft of hair just below his navel. Her fingers felt an involuntarily flinch, and reaching down, her hand slid over his now erect member, feeling for his balls, she started tracing her fingers lightly back and forth.

Emitting a groan, rolling over and facing her, while allowing her to continue, he reached out and started to caress her nipples lightly. Rock hard, they responded eagerly to his touch, and she started to moan, arching her chest up to meet his touch. He slid his hand across her breasts, flicking her nipples with his thumb, trailing his hand slowly down her stomach, until he felt her wetness. She turned over and eased herself back into him. Reaching around, she moaned and clasped her hand over his, pushing his hand down between her legs. His palm flat, her hips ground into his hand, pressing hard, her hand holding on to his, guiding him. Her breath coming in shorter gasps now, hips moving in rhythm, twisting and turning against his hand—he could tell she was close.

She gasped. "Don't stop! Don't stop ... don't ever stop," she panted, "don't everrrr——" as she exploded, coming hard against his hand. Grinding deeper, her hips violently pushed and twisted against his hand as he held on tight, trying not to move and break the rhythm, letting her finish herself off, as only she knew how.

Twenty minutes later, coming out of the shower, rubbing his head with the towel, Dale walked into the tiny kitchen with the small window overlooking the Peterborough Lift Locks. Sara was sitting at the table, her long brown hair spread across her shoulders, wearing nothing but his blue Police Academy T-shirt, legs stretched out on the kitchen table, bare feet locked, head down, she thumbed through her phone.

"So, what are you doing here?" he asked, irritated.

Sara looked up, surprised at his tone. "Looking for you. You weren't at the club last night, and I thought you liked fucking me?"

"I do. You know that."

"Well then, why the tone?"

"What tone?" he answered innocently, trying to deflect his annoyance.

"Seriously? Are we going to do this?" her voice cracked, tears forming. "I don't want to do this ... not anymore."

Putting his towel down, he padded over to her and reaching out, he put his hand on her shoulder, but she pulled away. "Aw, come on, baby. That's not what I meant, and you know that."

"Do I?" she answered angrily, staring up at him. "How do I know that?"

Dale shrugged and backed away, picking up the towel and returning to the bathroom; she could hear the water running and him rummaging around. Aimlessly scrolling through her phone, she wondered how things got this way.

The night of her parents' death, Dale arrived on the scene along with the many other first responders. It was chaotic, firemen and neighbours, all running in different directions at once, fire hoses snake-like laying in a tangled maze, her brother running away and returning, holding him back from entering the burning home.

Dale was a calming presence, steady, a take-charge guy. His voice reassuring as he asked her what happened. At that moment, she didn't know what to say, the truth or the lie? There was something about him that made her think, if she told the truth, she would be okay—that he would *make* it okay. Dale never wavered or cringed at the gruesome details, listening calmly, nodding, but strangely, as she realized later, he never took any notes, not jotting anything down in that policeman's little black notebook.

Finished, she expected he would nod in sympathy, cuff her, and read her rights, gently pushing her head down as he placed her in the backseat of his squad car. In hindsight, as much as she didn't feel anything, on another level, she was numb and in shock. I mean, if you watched your brother slug his father—though he had it long coming—then decided to murder your parents out of revenge, or spite, or both, wouldn't you feel something on some level? And maybe, that was why she blindly accepted what he told her next.

"It's going to be okay, miss. I will look after it. I am going to take care of this. Don't worry, everything will be okay. Do you have a place to stay, you and your brother? If not, I can get you one."

She said she was sure they could stay at the Hansen's, their neighbour nearby.

He nodded with a friendly, reassuring smile. "Okay, good. Now get some rest, and I will come by to see you in the morning. And this is important. I don't want you or your brother talking to anyone else about this, about what happened tonight. Not to the media, not to the Hansen's, not even amongst yourselves. Do you understand? This is important."

Sara, stunned, nodded zombie-like. Dale retrieved a blanket and wrapped it around her, then did the same with her brother, and drove them over to the neighbors. Sure enough, the next morning, he was at the Hansen's door bright and early. Mrs. Hansen had to wake Sara, and she groggily sat on the front porch as he went over the next steps.

During the night, she slept fitfully, coming to terms and making peace with what she had done, expecting to be arrested come morning. Instead, this cop was sitting across from her, explaining the next steps, and none of those steps involved having her rights being read, calling a lawyer, going to jail, and eventually a trial. All Dale talked about was how tragic it was that, upon returning home from a date, she found her parents' home burning out of control, with them trapped inside; her loving brother, gallantly trying to rescue his parents from the raging fire, and how she heroically held him back.

"The media will eat this up," Dale had said, "and you and your brother, just to need to lay low until things blow over. How does six months in the Caribbean sound? All expenses paid, and when you return home, you and your brother are free to start a new life. How does that sound?"

Blow over?

Sara's head swimming, she drunkenly nodded yes, and two days later, she and her brother were swimming in the Caribbean. It was only later, much later, after they had returned home and re-established their new lives, that the pied piper came a calling and the reason behind everything becoming clear.

⁓

Dale interrupted her thoughts. "Baby, I have to go. My shift starts in twenty. You're welcome to stay here, you always are, you know that. You know my shift isn't that long, and I can always take a break. Maybe you want to wait?" he asked, hopefully.

"No, it's okay. I have to get back."

Dale shrugged, disappointed as always.

"Can you do me a favour?" Sara asked.

"Sure baby. For you anything. What is it?" Dale walked into the kitchen and sat down beside her. Sara reached out and rubbed his thighs.

"I'm sorry, baby. It's, well, it's been a rough stretch. Teddy has been driving me crazy again, another one of his schemes ..." she sighed heavily.

"Want me to talk to him?"

"No, it's okay. But there's this new guy Teddy has latched on to with his latest scheme, and he's been coming around Sharkees. He's cute and everything, seems like a nice guy ..."

Dale frowned, Sara pulling his strings like only she could.

She ignored the frown. "Do you think you could check up on this guy for me? I don't know much about him. I'm sure he's harmless, but maybe, you could run one of your checks on him. For me. Please?"

She reached out and caressed his cheek, sending tiny electric shocks up and down his body, his member quickly becoming erect. He could never resist, despite her constantly trying to poke his bear with other guys.

"Sure, baby. What's his name?" He reached out to stroke her hair, and this time she let him.

"Pete. Pete Humphries."

Dale's eyes flew open, and he jerked his hand away, powerless to control his response.

"Baby, are you okay?" she asked, alarmed. "What is it?"

22

THERE WAS A faint knock on the door. "Go away!" I barked.

A pause, then another knock, this time a little harder. "No! Go away, will you! My room doesn't need cleaning!"

Another pause, I could hear shuffling and scratching, then the clicking of the lock; the door slowly opening. A dark-haired head cautiously poked their head through.

"Fuck! I told you the room doesn't need cleaning. Please go the fuck away!"

The head remained perfectly still, I could hear faint breathing, and softly someone spoke. "Mr. Humphries? It's me, Jackie. Remember me? I'm the front desk clerk who checked you in last Sunday."

Last Sunday? Sunday was only yesterday. "Last Sunday? What day is it? It's Monday ... okay, so maybe it's Tuesday. That was only a couple of days ago. I'm paid up, so what's the big deal?"

The head poked further through the door, and I could tell who it was. Softly, almost apologetic, "No, Mr. Humphries. Today is Saturday. Saturday night actually."

Saturday night? The Saturday that came after the Sunday that was six days ago?

It hit me, as I looked around my room. It looked like a war zone, half-eaten pizza boxes scattered on the floor, Styrofoam containers on the table, and the bottles; lots and lots of bottles, all of them empty. What was this? Vomit stains on the mattress? Is that pee stain on the carpet? Ugh! I almost threw up again. The bed covers were shredded, lying all over the floor, the top mattress was off propped upright against the wall in the corner beside the glass patio doors.

What was I doing? Pretending it was a blocking dummy? I did all this?

"May I come in?" Jackie asked, hesitantly.

"Are you insured?"

Poking her head around the door, Jackie slid the rest of her body through the opening and entered the room. She held the door with the back of her hand allowing it to close slowly without the loud bang. Stepping back closer to the wall, she started to gag and raised her arm to her nose and reaching out with her other hand touching the wall, she steadied herself.

"Good lord," she whispered. Then, removing her arm from her nose. "I just wanted to see if you were okay. I've been worried about you."

"Huh? Okay? Worried? Why?" I asked, surprised, thinking someone was dead and they had been trying to locate me.

Timidly, afraid of my response, she replied, "Well, Mr. Humphries, you have been on a bender for the past four or five days."

"Four or five days!" I blurted out.

At least no one is dead, I thought, though I wondered if I had telepathically murdered Chris, or even better, had done it for real?

"Yes, Mr. Humphries ... four almost five days ..." Jackie answered, cringing. "What happened?"

"Well, as you said, it seems I've been on a bender, for four, or was it, five days?"

"No, no ... I don't mean that. What I meant is what caused it?"

Pulling the stake out of my heart her question had driven straight through, the realization hit me. Tina. Suddenly, I was overcome by a wave of emotion.

"Um, uh, I saw someone on the docks the other day who I used to love. I still love, I mean, she is, um, I mean, she was from my past, and I hadn't seen her in years, since that day ... the day that everything happened, and why I haven't been back until now, I mean last Sunday, when I got here. It was my first time here, since I had left. I didn't know it was going to be like this, and I had forgotten about it, then I got here, and I saw her again with someone else, Chris. And it all came back, and I wasn't expecting any of that ... and ..."

Feeling lightheaded, I stopped and tried to catch my breath. Jackie was watching me with a concerned look, not sure what to do.

"I guess maybe, I've had a drink or two since cuz ... well, cuz it hurt, you know? And I don't know, I mean, I ... everything I had everything ... I had ... I had it all figured out this morning. I mean, uh, the other morning, whatever that morning was. The woman and her little dog, she said that I should go ... no, I should let go ... and I, uh, I thought I did let go, and then I was in this good place, and the universe was happy, so I was happy, then, then, all of a sudden there was this boat, and she was on it, and he was on it too ... and ..."

I could see Jackie had tears in her eyes. Why was *she* crying? Then I got it, she was crying because I was crying. Sniffling and wiping my nose with my arm, I rambled on. "So, I saw her, and I said goodbye again, and the song started playing in my head. I never made her think twice you know ... I don't think she even thought once ... no wait ... that's not true ... when she left that was when she thought ... you know I used to like those Doobie Brothers, but now, I fucking hate them, and I saw her hugging and kissing him, and that should've been me, and it wasn't, and then Dale said I should marry Joanna ... and I wasn't there ... I was supposed to be there, and I was, but I really wasn't ... and I, uh, I, uh ... and and—"

"Pete?"

"Pete? Pete."

"Uh? Yeah? What?"

"It's okay. It's okay, Pete."

I had moved backward and was now standing up against the wall.

"Come here. Come sit down, okay?" She made a place on the bed for me to sit. Reaching down, she grabbed one of the blankets on the bed and shook it out, chicken bones flew everywhere, I ducked as three of them hit the wall behind me and fell to the floor, the sauce leaving a brown stain on the wall. We looked at each other in disbelief.

"Okay," Jackie said, "how about we open the sliding doors and let in some fresh air. That will make you, and me, feel better."

Jackie gingerly stepped through the minefield of pizza crusts, chicken wings, and green French fries, picking up the empties along the way. Her hands full, she dumped the empties in the chair, spreading open the curtains. She slid open the balcony doors. A breeze blew in, and I wasn't sure if that made everything better or worse, the stench circulating, stirring the awful aromas.

"Phew!" Jackie exclaimed. "Have you been keeping a horse in here? Hotel guests aren't allowed to have livestock in their rooms. It's in the rules, you know."

Trying to keep from gagging, Jackie walked over and, holding my arms, led me over to the bed, and we sat down. Taking my hand and placing it in her lap, her other hand over top of mine, she patted it gently.

"It's going to be okay," Jackie reassured. "Sometimes—"

"But, but that's what the lady and her little dog said … that it was going to be okay. I was going to be okay. But it wasn't, you know. It wasn't okay …" I start crying again.

Jackie sat patiently, calmly rubbing my hand allowing me to get it out. "I know, Pete. I know. But it is going to be okay, I promise."

Latching on to that I said, "She didn't promise. You promised."

"Who didn't promise?"

"The pretty lady and her little dog. I think his name was Toto. He barked a lot, but he was friendly. She said it was going to be okay, but she didn't promise, you promised."

"Toto, huh? Barked?" Jackie looked at me like I had lost it.

"Never mind, forget it," I said, waving my hand.

Smiling, Jackie's eyes were soft and reassuring. "Pete. I promise. It's going to be okay. I promise."

"How do you know?" I demanded.

"That you're going to be okay?" She laughed out loud, still holding my hand and patting it tenderly. "What? Do you think you're the only one here who has had your heart shredded? Your heart broken so bad, a pain so harsh, it makes childbirth feel like the common cold? I'm guessing you did something foolish when that happened, and you are regretting that too, and you have been carrying all of it around for like what? A hundred years? Am I getting close?"

Sheepishly, I nodded.

She rubbed my hand again, and looking up, our eyes locked. "Pete, you're not the only one, honey, far from it. Been there, done that myself. Want to see my scars?" she asked, pulling her hand away, shifting, she unbuttoned her jacket and lifting her white top; showed me two parallel long and deep scars, each an inch wide, and about six inches long, that ran from just below her bra line and along towards her back.

"See these?" Jackie pointed.

I nodded, now intrigued.

"Well, there was this guy, Tim, and he was the love of my life, or so I thought. I would do anything, did anything, for him. We were planning on getting married, it was all laid out, the white picket fence. We had bought a house and just moved in, we were going to have six kids, we were going to have everything. We both had great jobs, great friends. We did everything together, went everywhere together. We were each other's best friend. We loved the same sports teams, and Sundays, we would watch football all day, having sex on the couch during the halftimes. I didn't think life could be better than that.

"All our friends were envious of me, Tim, us. My best friend, Janet, was the best friend, anyone could ever have, I was so lucky. Then, one day, I came home from work early. I wasn't feeling well. I thought I might be pregnant. I pulled in the driveway, and I think, *this is strange, why are Tim and Janet's cars in the driveway, at this time of day*? However, I thought nothing of it and walked in the house; it was eerily quiet. Rocky, our German shepherd, always greeted me. I looked down the hallway and I see him outside chained in the backyard. I started to get concerned, thinking, maybe he's been bad or something and Tim put him outside as punishment.

"I called out but there was no answer. That's strange, I thought. I walk up the stairs, and at the top of the landing, our bedroom door was closed, and at that point, my heart started to sink. I tried to push it away, thinking maybe Rocky had peed on the bedroom floor, and he wasn't allowed in. As I got closer, I could hear moaning. My stomach was in a giant knot, as it hit me, that I was not going to like what I saw on the other side when I turned the knob. But I needed to know, and I just couldn't walk away. So, I took a deep breath and turned the knob. There on the bed, our bed, was my best friend and soon-to-be husband Tim, and laying underneath him, was my other best friend, and soon-to-be-maid-of-honour, Janet, my best friend since we were seven. And what made it worse, Janet was tied up to the four posts, spreadeagled and naked, except for her black boots; tied up with my black stockings.

"Tim was eating her, and I could tell Janet was orgasming, and all I could think of was why wasn't that me? I had been bugging, begging actually, Tim for ages to do that to me. But he kept saying no, licking and kissing where you peed was gross, and the tying up was sadistic, and he wasn't into that kind of stuff. I would lay in bed at night fantasizing about it. So here were my best friends, doing to each other, what was supposed to be done to me."

I felt calmer now. "So, what did you do?"

"Nothing."

My eyebrows raised, I look at her, surprised.

"I did absolutely nothing. I quietly stepped back, reasonably sure they didn't hear or see me, and I slowly backed out of the room, closing the door. At that point, both were coming now. I guess he had gotten on top of her, they were coming together, something else I had begged Tim to try, and now they were having, loud mind-blowing orgasms together. All that should've been mine.

"I retraced my steps, tiptoeing down the stairs, back through the hallway, and out the front door. I never looked back, not at Rocky, not at our house, not at anything. I got in my car, which in all of this was the worst moment, and it's the moment I hope I never have to relive. I almost came unglued, the suddenness, the enormity of it, the impact. Everything that I loved, gone just like that, taken by the two people who I admired, and loved, more than anything in the world.

"I composed myself, I don't know to this day how I did, but I did. I started the car, backed out of the driveway, and pulled away. I never came back. I drove straight to work and quit my job right on the spot, then got in my car and started driving. I didn't stop until I could no longer drive—five o'clock the next morning. I turned off my phone, as the calls from Tim and Janet started pouring in, once they realized I was gone. I guess an upside is, I didn't have any family to worry about. My parents had long passed, and I had a brother out in BC whom I hadn't spoken with in years.

"The police tracked me down because Tim thought I had been kidnapped, and he'd filed a missing person report. When the cops found me, I told them what happened, and thankfully, they understood and let me go, and promised they would do their best to buy me more time. I had no idea where I was going, or what I was going to do for money. I had no job and left all my possessions behind. All I had, was my car, and my credit card, and that was close to the max already. But I didn't care, and I wasn't scared. All I knew was, I needed to get away. Get away from that, the ultimate betrayal. That was all I knew.

"So, over time, I tried different cities and towns until I found a place that fit, that felt like home, that felt like the fresh start I needed. And here I am. Once I got settled, I contacted a lawyer who contacted Tim, and I said to keep it all, I didn't want my half. For me, all of it was tainted now, and it didn't matter to me anymore.

"Over the ensuing months and next couple of years, Tim kept trying to contact me, especially during the holidays and around my birthday. He was frantic, so was Janet, and I can see their side. They didn't know what I had seen, I'm pretty sure of it, and I decided I was going to keep that pain to myself. I mean, what good would it have done to confront them with it? Was it going to change anything? Were things magically going to go back to the way they were? And seeing what I saw, painful as it was, meant I'd seen Tim and Janet for who they were. And what? If I hadn't seen them that day, I would have gone through the rest of my life, thinking they were the two most beautiful people on earth and counted myself lucky, when all the while they would have continued fucking each other behind my back, until the inevitable day they slipped up and I caught them.

"So, painful as it was, and trust me, it was painful, leaving everything and everyone behind, leaving behind every single thing that was your life, and being forced, and not by choice mind you, to start over entirely from scratch. Think about it. I ignored their every attempt to contact me, and there were times, when I was feeling especially lonely and vulnerable that I almost answered. But I'm so glad now I didn't, and the strength I got from not answering, I realized over time empowered me in a way I never thought possible. Finally, the calls stopped.

"The phone rang one day, and not recognizing the number, I answered, and it was a former co-worker who had been concerned about me and decided to reach out. I let my guard down for the only time, and we caught up. She had heard that Janet eventually moved in with Tim, taking my place, but then it blew up on both of them. Karma's funny that way. Once all that sex settled down, I mean, I guess you can only be tied up so many times, they found they weren't attracted to each other after all, and it was just the sex. So, they split up, and from there, both their lives went downhill. Tim lost his job twice, then finally, with it, the house. Janet moved from guy to guy, but then she had found this charming, great guy, and they moved in together. Then one day she comes home from work and yup, the guy's left her a note, leaving her for someone else. So, like I said, Karma's funny that way, it works its own magic. I thanked the co-worker for calling, but told her, never to contact me again. I appreciated her telling me, but I didn't want to know anymore; I didn't care anymore. She sounded disappointed but respected my wishes.

"And you know what? I didn't care. I stopped caring. I don't feel anything now for either one of them. The two people whom I loved more than anything in life, a love I didn't think could be any stronger, and here now, I no longer feel anything for either of them. Go figure. It took me a long time to figure out why, and then one day, it hit me. All I needed was myself. I realized that as long as I had myself, I would be okay, and never again would I get hurt. I could never get hurt anymore, because I had me, and that's all I needed. I would never leave myself, I would never cheat on myself, and I would always be faithful to myself. I would be my best friend, and I would lean on myself during difficult times. It was all internal, and I realized I could trust myself a hundred per cent. And can you say that about anyone else? That's an external trust. Can you trust anyone else to love you and care for you, as you can? I had and look what it got me.

"So, through all of this, the absolute worst thing to ever happen to me in my entire life, well, something good, no make that, something wonderfully pure and emboldening came from it. I found Me. I reconnected with me, and it's so strong it will never let go. No amount of money can buy this. I can't describe it. It wasn't overnight, and it wasn't a quick fix. It took time, lots of time, and it was painful. Boy was it painful, and I have the scars to prove it, as I showed you. But it was all worth it, you know, because all I needed was me, and no one else mattered anymore. It was me who made me whole. Wait, no, that's not true. People matter to me, you matter to me, but the people who hurt me like that, who tried to take away my soul, in the end, they didn't, as I didn't let them. Suppose I had stayed that day and confronted them right then and there. Well, they would have won and stolen everything from me, even if we had reconciled. I would have never got it back."

I stared at Jackie, my mouth open and felt chills run up and down my spine. Jackie shifted on the bed, getting comfortable, and still holding my hand, she continued.

"As for Tina, this Chris, you speak of. Well, it sounds like they did something awful to you, and I'm sorry honey, but you allowed it. It's okay. It really is. It's all part of the learning. You can do this. If I can, anyone can. That's how I know you will be okay. As much as, on the surface, my life doesn't look like much, it's the happiest I've ever been. Sure, I work in a hotel, but it's the people. I love the people and especially people like you. I can see you're special. There's something about you. But, until you let all this shit go, you will remain stuck right here, never moving, never living, and the really beautiful doors to your life, to the life that can be yours, will always be closed to you.

"You can have that life, anyone can, if you let go of the past. My life here is good. I walk home each day to my tiny two-bedroom apartment, it's small, but it's cozy and warm. Everyone knows me, and everyone greets me; the older men protect me, I have it all. And none of it has to do with money or material things or status. Instead, it all comes from the heart. And in case you're wondering, I am happily single. I go out on dates when I feel like it and when I miss that human connection and conversation. And I have this amazing little purple friend that keeps me happy, if you know what I mean. But one day, one day, I know the right person will be out there for me, our paths will cross, and we will connect when it's time. I know it, I can feel it. So, for now, I'm just enjoying the ride."

"Do you ever regret turning that knob and not, I dunno, just backing down the stairs or something?"

"Letting sleeping dogs lie, you mean? Hell no! Because my life would have always been that, with it eventually happening. I'm much happier here. I'm reconnected with me, the ultimate gift."

Taking all this in, I didn't know what to say. I felt a sense of shame. I thought I was the only one, and what Tina and Chris had done was the worst thing anyone could do to anyone. Boy was I wrong. Sitting on the bed, I slumped down, feeling the shame wash over me.

How could I be so stupid? So selfish?

"I can tell what you are thinking, Pete. You are feeling stupid, that you thought you were the only one, and that you didn't see this sooner. Am I right?"

I nodded.

"Well, I haven't told you yet, how I got those scars, have I?"

"No."

"So, you think you are feeling stupid for going on a four-day bender and feeling all sorry for yourself and trashing your hotel room—which by the way, you've got some explaining to do here, mister."

I nodded, as I looked around the room, mentally calculating the damage.

"Remember the scars I showed you? Well, about three weeks after leaving, something happened. Driving all day, I'm exhausted, and I land in some small town out in the middle of God-knows-where. I've barely eaten in days, but all I'm craving is a drink. Going through the main drag, it's about 10:00 p.m. pouring rain, and I pass by this neon BUD sign. A bar! So, I turn around and head back. Parking, there were three pickup trucks in front. That should have been the first sign. Looking through the front windows, it's near empty, and I think it seemed friendly enough, so I went inside.

"Opening the door and walking in, right away, I realize I had made a mistake, and unlike what happened with Tim and Janet, I didn't step back and leave this time. I was stubborn. I wasn't backing away again, no siree, not this time. *Fuck you,* I thought. Fuck you, Tim, fuck you, Janet. I'll show you. This time I'm going to be brave and strong, and besides, there was hardly anyone in there, it's late at night, what's the big deal? All of that should have been a sign of trouble, any one of them, or all together.

"The vibe was strange, and I could feel it right away: heavy, negative, eerie. But I pushed on and sauntered up to the bar. The bartender, a guy in his forties, asked me what I wanted. I ordered a beer and a whiskey chaser. He served them to me, and I dropped the whiskey chaser in my beer, waited for a second, then downed them both. It was orgasmic-like, as the booze washed over me. I had been feeling so bad, and I was so tired.

"Suddenly, there was loud metal click of a bolt snapping shut. Turning, I saw this big guy, with a bushy grey beard, wearing a lumberjack shirt and matching toque with black rubber fishing boots, and he had locked the heavy wooden door shut behind him. I think, *What the hell?*

"Looking around, the bartender had disappeared, and there were two more burly guys, coming out from the kitchen, about the same ages, lumberjack shirts, bushy beards ... they were brothers maybe? But they had different colour lumberjack shirts. One was black and green plaid, and the other was black and blue plaid. Crazy, what you remember in stressful situations like that? Yet later, when I was in the hospital, I couldn't remember how I got there. Anyhow, I look over and there was a pool table, and I quickly did the math; this was my chance to be Janet.

"I had to think fast, I had seconds, and I knew what happened with Tim and Janet would be a cakewalk, compared to what came next. I reached in my purse and feeling for my car keys, I pulled them out and put them in my pocket. I casually rolled my purse under my arm and slid around on the bar stool. The guy that locked the door was blocking it, so there was no way I was getting past him. The other two guys were slowly walking toward me, and to my horror, one of them had rope coiled in his hand."

"So, what did you do?" I asked.

"There were these big windows on both sides of the entrance. That was how I could see in so easily when I pulled in. Despite the rain and dampness of the night, I noticed that just to the left of the guy guarding the door, two of the windows, were partially open. If I got a good jump, I figured, I could run and barrel roll through them. Worst case, the sound of breaking glass would get the attention of someone outside. And that's what I did. Taking a deep breath, I counted to three and ran towards those windows and jumped. But I misjudged my jump, and instead of barrel rolling, I fell through, falling awkwardly into the parking lot, glass everywhere. I landed hard and some shards of glass pierced my side.

"The pain was beyond anything I had ever experienced, and the blood started flowing immediately. I could feel it pouring down my side. I was in shock now and running on pure adrenaline. I forced myself to get up, and strangely, I could hear the guy trying to unlock the bolt from inside. I stumbled to my car, and miraculously, I was able to open the door. My hands were shaking so bad, I could barely get the key in the ignition, but finally I did, and unlike the movies, my car started on the first try. Backing up, I plowed into one of the trucks, my trunk turning into an accordion. I got turned around and floored it out of the parking lot and down the highway."

"So, you got away then?"

"Yes and no."

"Yes and no?"

"Correct—" Jackie paused and took a deep breath. She pushed her hair back, and I could see her fighting off the emotion of it. I let her be and we sat for a moment quietly. Gathering herself, she continued. "Yes and no. Yes, I got away, but I nearly died."

"But you didn't."

"That was lucky. Going through the window, I lost my purse, I must have dropped it. It had my cellphone, my money, credit cards, ID, driver's licence, everything. And I left it behind in the parking lot. But that wasn't even the worst part. I'm bleeding so bad, I can feel myself getting weaker, and I'm going deeper into shock. I'm tearing down this two-lane highway, late at night, pouring rain, no idea where I am, and I think, if I don't find help soon, I'm going to die. I start looking for farmhouses or lights, but there's nothing. Pitch black, I'm driving and thinking, what am I going to do? I'm going to die out here, and all because I didn't confront Tim and Janet. If I had, then none of this would have happened, and I wouldn't be in this spot now. I'm thinking, I'm just going to pull over and let myself go. They'll find me in the morning, and I hope Tim and Janet will feel like shit from this. But just as I started to slow down, I came over a rise, and there was this big blue 'H' up ahead. I thought it was a mirage. I turned in at the sign and pulled up to the entrance, collapsing on the steering wheel, the horn blaring, and everyone came running at the sound.

"I spent two weeks in that hospital. The police came by asking me questions about what happened. I told them what I could remember. What was chilling, and this made my blood run cold, was when the one cop asked me, where I came from that night, and why had I gone in the direction I did? I said I had no idea. I had jumped from the window, and I was in shock from the fall. I had gotten in the car and backed into one of the pickup trucks, the force of the collision turning my car in the direction that I ended up going. The officer said that if I had gone in the other direction, whether by choice, or by circumstance, I most certainly would have died, as there wasn't a town within a hundred miles. By fate, I had gone in the direction of the local hospital, barely five minutes down the road."

I looked at Jackie and she could tell I didn't get her point to this.

"Pete. I was still living in the past, and I wasn't paying attention. I was so focused on proving Tim and Janet wrong, that I ignored the *now*. I wasn't living in the now when I pulled into the parking lot that night. Oh, maybe I was in a way, craving a drink, but as soon as I thought about entering that bar, I reverted to the past. And that almost cost me my life. If I was paying attention, and living in the present, listening to and trusting myself, then my intuition would have told me this place was dangerous, and not for me, no matter how bad I wanted that drink. Instead, look what happened? I lost everything again. I almost died, and only by the grace of who knows what, I went in the right direction.

"*That* close," she said, placing her thumb and finger together. She put her hand back on mine and squeezed it tight. "And that, my friend, is how I know you are going to be okay."

Looking down, I nodded sheepishly.

She patted my hand. "Pete honey, you *are* going to be okay."

Jackie paused, allowing it to sink in, then she leaned over and kissed me tenderly on the cheek, and dropping my hand, she stood up. She smiled down at me and looked around the room.

"So, can you get this place cleaned up, and get up, and get on, with your life? Please? I can't hide this, and you, or your horse, forever, you know."

She winked, then opened the door and left.

23

SITTING ON THE edge of the bed, I took a moment to let everything sink in. Jackie was right, and she was also right in that there was no shame in this. It is what it is, as they say. I was starting to see that now. I felt a burst of energy and a renewed faith, and for the next two hours, ignoring the steady buzz-buzz of the burner phone, I tore around the room and balcony, sweeping the stable from top and bottom until it looked as good as new: the empties, pizza boxes, food containers all piled neatly outside, stretching down the hall to the next room. A shower and shave, and after finding the cleanest of the dirty clothes, I was good to go.

Coming out of the elevator, passing through the lobby, I glanced over at Jackie behind the counter. Her head was down, typing away, so I didn't want to bother her and kept going. As I got to the doorway, I looked back, and she looked up and smiled. It was a smile of understanding and reassurance that it was going to be okay. A chill ran down my back, goosebumps forming on my arms and legs.

Out in the parking lot, I gently patted my Chevy on the hood and whispered, "Daddy's back." She needed a run. Just as I put the key in the ignition, the burner phone buzzed. I knew I should answer it; Teddy was going to be pissed if I didn't. But I still needed more time to figure things out, so I powered it off and tossed it in the back seat. Time for a cruise.

I reached for a new tape, Blue Oyster Cult, slapped it in the dash, windows down, music thumping; all crunchy guitars and more cowbell—the mandatory cruising ingredients—and pulled out.

It was another beautiful summer night, warm breeze, twinkling stars above, the street filled with people. I did the loop—or circuit, depending on who you talked to—cruising up George, a right on Sherbrooke, following the bend onto Water, up towards the top, turning left at Brock, back across, and down again. Just for fun, I drove the loop three more times, and on the fourth trip down, I spotted Hanna bouncing along the sidewalk. Slowing, I honked and waved as I drove past, feeling guilty, promising myself I would catch up with her another time.

Up ahead, I spotted a street bike parked along the curb. I booted it through the intersection, cutting off a car, braked sharply, and with a loud screech, bounced into the parking lot across from the Lucky 7evens. I pulled around until I was facing the bar and killed the engine. The bike was parked out front, and I could see Syd was on the door.

This could work to my advantage, as busy meant inconspicuous. And maybe I could find Sara and put all this nonsense to bed. I hopped out of my Chevy, headed across the street, and walked towards the bike parked out in front, walking around it, pretending to admire it. By the way, did I tell you I never liked bikes? No metal, or glass, to protect you from the elements, no eight-track either. Studying the bike, it was black and purple, and it was a Harley 883 all right; said so right on the side.

Hmm, maybe Sara's not a myth.

Looking at the line to get in, it was much longer than the other night, and wait? When was the other night? How many nights ago again? Maybe Syd wouldn't even remember me? The line snaked down and around the block, maybe forty or fifty deep, and I did some quick math.

"Hey, Syd. How are you tonight? Busy huh? I'm just gonna head in and grab a beer. You look great tonight," as I casually strolled past. Reaching out and stopping me, Syd grabbed my arm firmly.

"Hold it right there, mister! You're not going anywhere. Wait here a second."

Syd finished checking a young girl's ID, letting her through, and then turned to me.

"Hey, stranger, I haven't seen you around. Thought you might be just one of those one-off types, but no, look? Here you are again. And trying to jump my line no less." She shot me a playful frown. "There's a penalty for that."

"And what that might be?" as I held my wrists out waiting to be cuffed.

Circling her tongue along her lips and across her teeth, she chuckled, "Oh, that's for later … definitely later."

"Just don't lose the key," I winked.

Syd was wearing a black golf shirt bearing the Lucky 7evens logo on the left breast pocket, tan shorts, black Nikes, her blonde hair tied back again in a ponytail. Her eyes as usual, sparkled, full of life. She had an attractive dimple on her left cheek when she smiled, which was a lot. It was no wonder I was playing beach blanket bingo in my head.

"Your penalty is, and I'm sure you can afford it, and me; is you have to buy me a beer when my shift ends at midnight."

"That's it?"

"Yep, I'm easy," she said. Then, serious enough, to keep me on my toes. "Just not the easy you might think."

Breaking into a salute, "Yes, ma'am! Understood. Beer it is. See you at midnight."

Syd slapped at my hand playfully.

"So, I'm free to go in, then?"

Syd stepped aside. "Yes, you're free to go, mister." She waved me past, purposely letting our bodies touch ever so lightly, the subsequent 'ZING!' palpable.

Unable to resist, I stopped and turned. "Hey, if you don't find me by midnight, I might turn into a pumpkin, so don't be late."

"*Go!*" Syd exclaimed, laughing and shaking her head, as she pointed towards the door.

Inside, the bar was packed, everyone trying to shout over the pounding beat and each other. I weaved my way through the crowd, dodging bodies and drinks, all the while trying to catch a glimpse of the floor and Sara. Fighting my way to the front of the bar, I was able to catch the bartender's eye, the same guy as last time, and ordered a beer. When he placed it in front of me, I pulled out Sara's picture and yelled over the noise.

"Have you seen her in here tonight?"

He eyed it, looking at me suspiciously, but I was prepared, and pulled out a fifty, passing it over to him. Stuffing it in his pocket, he looked at the picture again, and shouting over the din.

"No. I've never seen her. Nice bike though. It looks like the one always parked out front."

Handing the picture back to me, as I lamented the loss of my fifty, he spoke again.

"Maybe the person you are looking for is over in the corner."

"Where?"

"Over there. A chick in biker leathers ordered a glass of wine from me, and the last I saw her, she was over in the far corner at one of the tables. She was sitting with some big guy. He had a brush cut and looked like a cop."

I tried to see over the crowd but couldn't make out anyone.

"Are *you* a cop?" he asked, looking at me hard.

Ignoring his question. "Where again?" I asked.

"Over there, behind you," he pointed over my shoulder.

I followed the direction of his hand then grabbed my beer and started to work my way in that direction. But it was too crowded, I couldn't see, or move, beyond the people who were blocking the bar. I wiggled my way through the crowd and made it to the center of the floor and tried to see over to the far corner. My view was still blocked, the crowd too thick, so I weaved my way around the maze of pool tables, sidestepping outstretched cues and people, gingerly stepping around a protruding butt bent over in mid-shot. Winding my way around a group of women holding cues, talking, not interested in playing, I spotted the table in the far corner that the bartender had been pointing at. Sure enough, after all that, empty glasses were on the table, and by the way the chairs were turned, the occupants weren't returning anytime soon.

I spun around, and hastily worked my way back through the maze of pool tables towards the front entrance. I spotted a female figure in a black and purple leather jacket walking out the front entrance.

Shit!

I dropped my beer on a nearby table and made a beeline for the front entrance, my hands out, pushing bodies away until I finally made it to the doorway. A couple jostled me as I was blocking them from entering. I shifted to one side, craning my neck, all the while trying to keep my eye on the leather jacket. When I was able to see clearly, I looked out into the street and saw the bike slowly backing up, the helmeted figure straddling it. There was an ear-splitting pop, the bike lurched forward, and it took off down George Street. The visor was down, and I was too late to catch a glimpse of the face, but I was certain it was Sara.

Naturally, I did what anyone would in a situation like this, I cut my losses and went after her. I jumped off the step, skirting around the people coming inside, and raced across the street. There were angry honks and a near miss, followed by tire screeching and cursing. I had my keys out by the time I got to the car. I went straight across the curb, bouncing hard, swerving to avoid oncoming traffic.

Luck was on my side, as up ahead, the bike was stuck in the Saturday night traffic. Gunning it, blowing a red light at the next intersection, I passed the waterfront, and two blocks later, I was nestled in behind a Dodge Caravan, the bike in front. I followed leisurely behind for a couple of more blocks, as the bike appeared to be in no hurry. Getting to the end of George Street, we were in a line at the light: the bike, the Caravan, and me. Waiting for the light to turn green, I wasn't sure where this would lead, but this was the closest I had gotten to Sara, if indeed that was her. At least I would be able to tell Teddy the truth, that I had actually seen her. Patting myself on the back, for a job well done, I wasn't paying attention, and just as the light was changing to yellow in the other direction, the bike tore through the intersection, making a sharp left onto Lansdowne. A quick look in my mirrors, I pulled around the family van, and blew through the intersection also. Shifting through the gears, I caught up quicker than I expected, or maybe she was letting me.

I was right on her tail as we crossed over the river. Traffic was lighter here, and coming to the next intersection, neither of us slowed. Then abruptly, she hung a hard left, a loud roar as the bike accelerated. Jamming on the brakes, I started to turn but was forced to the right to avoid an oncoming car going through the intersection. I made the turn and through the swirling dust, I could see the bike in the distance. I debated whether to try and catch her. I wasn't sure if it made sense to try, as there was just enough traffic that I couldn't safely keep pace with her bike. On a flat straight yes, but here, no. When she reached the Lift Locks and cut sharply to her right, I called it a night.

Slowing, turning left, I made my way back to the Lucky 7evens, and my midnight rendezvous with Syd. Pulling into the parking lot, I glanced at my watch, and it was twelve fifteen. Shit! I was the one who was late.

I parked and ran across the street, and by now, there was no line to get in. I jumped the step and bolted through the front entrance. The crowd had thinned considerably, but the music was still thumping, and I made a beeline for the bar. The stools along the bar were empty, my heart sank, then I spotted Syd, by herself in the far corner. A beer was in front of her, her head was down, as she scrolled through her phone. *Shit! Nicely done big guy*, I muttered to myself.

I walked over and sat down on the seat beside her. I knew she heard me, but she didn't move or acknowledge me, thumbing through her phone. Looking straight ahead, she reached for her beer, took a drink, and put it back down, then returned to thumbing through her phone. I didn't know what to say or do, feeling like a jerk, and if that was her intention, it was working. Feeling sheepish, I caught the bartender's eye and ordered a beer. He brought it over and placed it in front of me and, looking toward Syd, raised a questioning eyebrow at me.

I shrugged and thanked him. Staring at my beer, then over at Syd, I sighed, took a drink, and thought about calling it a night one more time. I had blown it. But had I really? What was the reason I was here? I asked myself. That was easy. Sara.

"I don't do late."

"Huh?"

"You heard me. I don't do late."

Syd hadn't moved, still buried in her phone, but it certainly sounded like her.

"I'm sorry."

Her head still down, not looking at me. "If you say you are going to be here at twelve, then you better damn well be here at twelve. And unless there is a death, yours, or your cat got lost, or your car got stolen, then when you say to meet me at twelve, then twelve it better be. Not 11:59, not 12:01, and certainly not, 12:15."

Point taken, as I remained silent, my head down, fiddling with my beer.

"And if you are going to be late, then you find me and let me know. And that, mister, is the one, and only time, I do late."

There was no point in trying to explain, she was right. I took a long drink for courage. "Understood, you are right. Do you want to shoot some pool?"

"Can you say that again?"

"Say what, *shoot pool?*"

"No, *you're right.*" Syd put her phone down and turned toward me, smiling.

"I'm right?" I asked, innocently.

Syd reached over and punched me hard on the arm.

"OW! What did you do that for?" I whined, wincing, I rubbed my arm.

"I'll do it again," she warned, cocking her fist.

"You are right, Syd. I'm sorry." And maybe for the first time in a long time, I genuinely meant it. I hoped she could tell.

Syd reached for her beer and phone, tugged at my arm, and pushed me toward the pool tables. "Okay there, mister Pool Shark, show me what you got."

24

"SOME GUY WAS following me tonight, but I think I lost him. It scared me, I don't know who he was, but he had a fast car. I couldn't shake him, and I was pretty sure he could have caught me if he wanted to, but he backed off."

"Did you get a look at him?"

"No, just his car."

"Are you sure?" Dale asked, not believing her.

"Yes, I'm sure."

"What did he look like?"

Sara hated this side of him, interrogating her like she was one of his perps.

"What kind of car did he drive?"

"I don't know! I, well ... I don't know. Some red something."

Sara, flustered, sat slumped in the chair, fighting back the tears. Taking a couple of deep breaths, wiping her eyes, she sat up. Her voice calm again. "It looked like one of those old muscle cars. You know the ones, fat tires, raised back end, hood scoop. That thing was fast. That guy could drive too, I could tell. I gave him my best moves, but he hung right with me. When I got near the Lift Locks, he backed off, and that was that."

"So, you did see who it was," Dale said, suspiciously.

It was always the same, whenever Sara mentioned it was a guy, any guy, no matter how innocently, he would become defensive and sulk, or act like the cop he was—treat everyone like a suspect, guilty until proven innocent.

"No, I didn't. I couldn't get a good look at him, just his car. Why don't you believe me?" Sara looked at Dale who was wearing the same expression when she asked him to check out Pete Humphries.

Was that who that was, she wondered. Pete? Cute, fun Pete from Sharkees? Now things were starting to make sense. What would he be doing here? And why would he be chasing her?

Fuck! Teddy! I knew it! What the fuck is going on?

Something was wrong here. When she had said Pete's name, she had never seen Dale react like that, not in all the time she had known him. He didn't have any reaction when she'd told him about her parents, yet he reacted like he had seen the devil himself when she mentioned Pete by name.

Sara could feel the noose slip around her neck and the loop slowly tightening. *I don't like this.*

Looking across the table, her eyes met his. "Dale, I'm scared."

25

"YOU SUCK."

"No, I don't."

"Yes, you do."

"No, I don't."

"Seriously?"

"Okay, maybe just a little."

"Did you ever think of practicing or something? Though I'm not sure that would even make a difference. Sometimes you just can't fix suck."

"Anything else you want to comment on?"

"Hmm … let me think. Besides the fact that you suck at pool? So many choices and so little time. And how many times was it that you sank that white ball? Six? Or was it eight? I lost count."

I punched Syd hard on the arm. I waited, I watched, nothing, no reaction of any kind. She didn't move, didn't flinch, not even rubbing her arm.

Do my punches suck also?

Syd pondered for a moment, and I braced myself.

"You suck—"

"We've already done that round, remember? Just now, in fact."

Smiling devilishly, she said, "Well, you didn't give me a chance to finish. Just like last night, you jumped right in."

"I was anticipating, that's all. I was—"

"Can I have a turn please? Can you park your tongue for just one second? If you let me finish, you may like what you hear."

"Well, I didn't like the other stuff. That I suck and all."

"Truth hurts, huh?" She smiled good-naturedly, ruffling my hair. "So, are you going to let me finish?"

"Sure … go ahead, nuthin' can hurt me anymore; I'm too far damaged now," I pouted, my bottom lip hanging out, looking up at Syd with sad puppy dog eyes.

Trying not to laugh, she asked, "Are you sure? I don't want you interrupting me again and spoiling the surprise."

"You were going to surprise me with another insult?"

"Oh, good heavens—"

Lying on my side, facing Syd, I was halfway down the bed and the view was terrific, more like breathtaking. A room with a view of the ocean, as they say.

"Okay, mister, this is your last chance. Are you going to let me finish what I was going to tell you, as with all this waiting, I might just forget."

"Oh, okay," as I started to curl myself in a ball and bring my arms over my head, protecting myself from the next volley. Syd playfully slapped my arms away and turned me towards her. She reached over and held the back of my head with her hand.

"What I was going to say after I said you suck was that, well, you suck great!"

She abruptly opened her legs wide and pulled my head down into her crotch, forcing me to move onto her. She lifted and wrapped her legs around my head, locking her feet and ground her hips up into my mouth. And just like that, another round of submarine races commenced.

~

What a night! What a morning! Syd and I certainly clicked. We played pool until after 3:00 a.m., going toe-to-toe in the beer department, and the more we drank, the better the pool we played. Well, except for that minor white ball issue, and now that it happened again, I was certain the tables were not level. Anyhow, we drank and played, and drank and played, until giggling like teenagers, we staggered back to Syd's place. Not content to call it a night, we decided some beach blanket bingo was in order, and during the warm-up, Syd found out I liked giving, and I found out Syd liked receiving. And so, I gave, and she received. When the sun started to peek through the curtains, we thought it might be a good idea to rest for a bit. So, we switched ends, and Syd gave, while I received, until we passed out.

Waking a few hours later, legs and arms intertwined, we had another round just because we could. After showering, we moved outside to the small balcony in her art deco walk-up apartment, two blocks from the Lucky 7evens, and directly across from the waterfront. Sort of like finding another pot at the end of the rainbow.

Sitting at the table, letting the sun wash over us, we nursed large steaming mugs of black coffee.

"Better than booster cables," Syd said.

We sat in silence, staring at the water fountain, mentally replaying last night's submarine races.

"So, where were you headed last night?" she asked. "What made you late?" Then it was as if she caught herself. "I'm sorry. I mean, if you want to tell me, that is. I don't want to pry. It is your business."

Sighing heavily, I reached over, taking her hand in mine, and looked deep into her eyes,

"You mean what made me late? Well, if you must know, I had rushed out to buy you flowers for our midnight beer. But I was too late, and the florist had closed. I tried a few other places, but they were closed also. Then I got stuck in traffic, as there was an accident with a semi and a pickup truck, and all the elephants got loose, so I stopped to help round them up, and before you know it was twelve fifteen. I was going to call you and tell you, 'Honey I'm going to be late and don't wait up for me,' but my phone was out of juice, so I started driving around looking for a payphone to call you, but I gave up and decided to drive back."

Sitting with her feet up, legs crossed on the chair, Syd looked at me with a blank expression.

"You want to kill me, don't you?"

"Too late, I already have, I gutted you right when you started talking," Syd said, rolling her eyes.

We looked at each other, a Mexican standoff of sorts; who was going to blink first?

"OW!"

I guess I blinked first. I leaned in and we hugged, both laughing at how juvenile we were, realizing this was what made us tick. We kissed and hugged some more, enjoying the new sensations, inhaling the intoxicating scents of sex and each other. Leaning back in our chairs again, turning serious, I told Syd about looking for Sara. Retrieving her picture, I showed it to Syd, telling her I had been hired by her brother to find her.

"What? You're a cop or something?" she asked.

"I used to be. A long time ago," I answered without thinking, and though I felt a slight pang, it didn't bother me like earlier. I wisely left out all the other stuff, telling Syd I was good at finding people, that it paid well, and leaving it at that.

Syd stared at the picture for the longest time, shaking her head.

"No, I haven't seen her," and handed it back to me. "But there is this girl, who comes in later in the night, around eleven or twelve. She parks her bike out front, which you're not allowed to do. But Ronny, the head bouncer, fell for her like a rock, so *presto*, free parking out front. She plays pool mostly, and there is this big guy, he looks like a cop, who is always around when she's there. Much too old for her, but hey, who knows, her Sugar Daddy?"

This was pretty much what the bartender had said. Hanna too. Sara existed all right, just not the girl in the picture that Teddy gave me. I was certain now that it was her last night. All I needed was to see her. And it was the second time I had heard about a big cop. Once again, nothing was as it seemed.

"You know, I might be able to help you find her," Syd offered, interrupting my thoughts.

"How?"

"Hungry?"

"Huh? What's that got to do with it?"

"There's this guy I want you to meet. I think he can help you find her, or maybe, give you a lead or something. Isn't that what you TV detectives are always looking for? Leads?" Syd reached over and pulled me off the chair, "Come on, DiNozzo, I'm starving."

I tried to punch her, but she was too quick, giggling, dancing away easily.

"Okay, where?"

"You'll see."

26

TEDDY WAS SITTING at the bar, nursing a beer, and scrolling through his phone. Sharkees hadn't opened yet, but that was a minor inconvenience. He had entered through the unlocked back door, sneaking through the kitchen and out to the bar, along the way helping himself to a beer. Of course, all this was done, with his heart pounding and his head on a swivel, on the lookout for Patty.

He tried calling Pete again and once again got no answer. "Fuck!" He slammed the phone on the bar then covered it with his hands. He took a deep breath then peered up at the sports highlights on the TVs above him.

Nothing had gone right from the start. He couldn't recall a scheme not ever going right, they always worked. Yet, this scheme had gone wrong right from the moment it started. Now, his mule was dodging his calls. Rattled, he sent Tony to Peterborough to keep an eye on him and have a chat with Jimmy about the missing box. Jimmy had promised he would get it back, but exactly how was he going to do that? Jimmy said he didn't know where the bikers had gone, or what their intentions were. He wondered if he should call Dale. Maybe he could help? But what would he say? Besides, the call would just give Dale an excuse to find fault with him. He didn't need an excuse for that.

Dale, just like his father, had no trouble making Teddy feel small, inadequate, and incapable of looking after himself. And just like with his father, he kept trying to prove himself worthy to Dale. Around and around it went, so what was the use? Plus, the last time they had spoken, Dale hadn't seemed himself. His fuse was shorter. He was on edge, volatile. Teddy wondered why, and come to think of it, Sara seemed more on edge of late too. She was getting on her bike, leaving immediately after her shift ended, and not returning until her next shift, and he guessed where. To add to his uneasiness, he had started second-guessing himself—something he never did.

I fucked up using Pete. I can't trust him.

He'd never liked him, ever since that day, twenty-some years ago, on the waterfront. He still didn't like him. He was always so smooth, charming, always flirting, that goofy grin the girls go crazy for. Even Sara fell under his spell. Then he went and screwed up the one thing Teddy had needed him for. How hard could that be? The box was gone, and the fucker wasn't answering his calls.

Patty poked her head in the bar and asked if he was okay. Startled, Teddy jumped straight up and stood at attention, trying to distance himself from the bottle on the bar. Patty shook her head and smiled and returned to the kitchen. Teddy sat down and reached for his beer. He noticed his hand was shaking and placed it on the bar, trying to steady it.

Maybe I should have Tony lean on Pete?

He guessed now it wasn't such a good idea letting Tony talk him into getting the box. But there hadn't seem to be any other way, nothing but dead ends until Tony brought up that he knew Jimmy, who knew someone, who knew someone. Those things never worked. But that's what made desperation tick, proving once again, desperate choices were rarely good choices. And now it was too late to fix it, end it, or start over. Things were already too deep.

If Dale ever found out what I was up to ... He shuddered hard at the thought.

Teddy went to take another drink, but his beer was empty. He quickly looked around the bar, listening if anyone was coming or within earshot. With one last glance around to be sure, and with the agility and quickness of someone much smaller and leaner, Teddy hoisted himself onto the bar, leaned over and stretched his arm down the other side. Arm fully extended, he flicked the latch on the cooler, and in one motion reached in and pulled out a beer and closed the door, flicking down the latch.

Sliding off the bar, he parked himself back on the stool. Another check to be sure no one was watching, and he bunched his shirt at the front, pulled the bottle down into his lap, and wrapped the cloth around the top—twisting until he felt the cap loosen and pressed tighter to muffle the *poof*. He brought the bottle up and snuck a quick drink. Then checking again to make sure no one was watching, he put the bottle down softly on the bar. He took the empty, leaned up and over the counter again, and dropped it into the empties box on the floor beside the cooler. Sliding back on his stool, he glanced around one last time, satisfied, he started thumbing through his phone, acting as if nothing happened.

Remember when the teacher wasn't looking? But she was, of course. Nothing got by her, they just let you think you did. There were three entrances to Sharkees: the back door in the kitchen and the double set of doors at the front. And there was the side door beside the piano, that led out to the patio, which if you were sitting at the bar, was behind you.

Teddy never bothered to look behind him, for if he had, he would have noticed Patty outside on the deck, fixing the pennants on the wooden patio fence right near the door, watching him the whole time. Smiling and shaking her head, she muttered with disdain, "Boys …"

27

SYD STOPPED AT the doorway beside the Lucky 7evens. "Here we are."

"It looks closed."

"It is."

"You have a key, and you're going to make me breakfast?" I asked, confused.

"No, silly."

"You have a key, and I'm going to make you breakfast?"

"Oh geez! Come on." Syd grabbed my arm and pulled me towards the door.

We stepped inside, our eyes going black, and it took us a moment to adjust, tiny black dots filling our eyes.

Syd had a hold of my hand and led me through the narrow hallway, then we were out in the open. It was like a vast warehouse, the floor empty with soft yellowish lights overhead. I noticed a light over in the far corner and a stairway that led up to an even brighter light at the top. Syd pulled me in the direction of the light, and climbing to the top of the stairs, I followed Syd through the doorway, and we were back out in the bright sunshine, our eyes once again filled with tiny black dots.

Syd reached for my hand and led me across the rooftop patio toward the opposite side. My eyes started to adjust, and I could see a picnic table with a large umbrella, with an even larger figure seated behind it. I was still rubbing my eyes, Syd chattering away excitedly to the figure seated under the umbrella. I couldn't make out the person, but I recognized the voice. A giant knot formed in my stomach, goosebumps started popping out all over my arms and legs, and I could feel tingling at the base of my neck.

"Hey Pete, come over here. This is who I want you to meet."

But what if I don't want to, and I'm perfectly okay with staying right here? I told Syd telepathically.

"Pete, Pete … come … I want you to meet—"

"Tony," I said, reluctantly stepping forward. I moved around to the side of the table and stood beside Syd. "Fancy meeting you here, the last time I saw you, you were pointing your finger at me."

Syd, mouth open, was looking at me in bewilderment. "You know each other?"

"We know *of* each other," I said. "There's a difference."

Syd, her mouth still open, looked at me, then over at Tony, then eyed the server standing off to the side. "A Bloody Mary, please. In the largest glass you've got, hold the celery. I think I need to sit down."

Syd sat down on the bench facing Tony. Patting the empty spot beside her, she looked up at me. "Want to sit? I think I need someone to hold me up."

I sat beside Syd and snuggled up close. Her hand moved over on my thigh, and she rubbed my leg lightly. Her touch felt warm and safe, and most importantly, calming.

Tony was stuffing his face from a heaping plate of pancakes, beans, hash browns, bacon, sausage, eggs, and a pile of toast at least twelve slices high. Watching him eat, I was no longer hungry. The server arrived with Syd's Bloody Mary, *sans* celery, and holding it with two hands, gently placed it in front of her.

I looked at the glass. "You might need a ladder to get up the side to take a drink. Maybe a life jacket in case you fall in." Then I turned to Tony. "Hey Tony, you have any ladders and life jackets?"

Tony, his fork in his mouth, mumbled, spraying food everywhere. "Aww, no wonder Teddy calls you Pistol. You're a funny guy there, Pete Humphries."

At least, I think that sounded like what he said. I flicked away a bean that landed on the table in front of me, and hoping Syd hadn't noticed, carefully flicked away the one that had landed on the side of her Bloody Mary glass.

"Funny, I heard you—" but I was rescued by Syd when she pinched my leg hard keeping me from committing verbal suicide, possibly actual suicide.

"So, how do you two know each other?" Syd asked, warily.

No one answered, only the sounds of banners flapping in the breeze, the muffled sounds of traffic coming from the street below. Syd, becoming ner-vous, pinched my leg again, and I pinched her back. Neither of us reacted. She reached for my hand under the table and squeezed it tight. I took that as a cue. If at first you don't succeed, try, try, again.

"Tony and I go way back," I said. "Though I wouldn't say we were exactly friends, right, big guy?"

Tony looked up, stuffed another piece of sausage in his mouth, chomping down on the meat, dropped his fork on the plate. Still chewing, his lips smacking loudly, he pushed himself away from the trough. Wiping his mouth with his sleeve, he finished chewing and took a slurp from his coffee mug. Licking his lips, tapping himself on the chest, he burped, grunted, and then for good measure, burped again.

Lovely.

"Aw, Pistol, stop! You crack me up. I can see why Teddy likes you." Then, he burped once more. Patting himself on the chest. "Teddy has been trying to reach you, and he's getting worried. He thinks you might not be taking his calls. Is everything okay with the phone he gave you?"

Ahh, an oldie but goodie, it's cat and mouse time.

"Yup, it's fine. Battery all charged. I've been busy."

Tony eyed Syd and winked. "Seems you have."

Syd, getting more nervous by the minute, and trying to be of help, inadvertently poured gasoline on the fire.

"Tony, Pete is looking for someone, and I wondered if maybe you could help? It's a girl. Her name is Sara, I think. He's been looking for her." She turned to me. "Babe, do you have that picture? You could show Tony."

I remained silent, staring straight ahead. And just why exactly was I so unnerved over Tony? Afraid? Afraid of what? And if so, why? There had been guys way worse than him over the years, and it certainly wasn't Tony's body-builder size and tattoos. The bigger they were, the harder they fell. Then what was it? What was it about Tony that was making me come unglued so easily?

"Pete baby," she said, "you have that picture?"

"Uh? What? Oh yeah …" I reached behind and pulled out the picture of Sara and grudgingly handed it across the table.

Tony had bellied up to the trough again and, with his free hand, took the picture. Looking at it, his mouth full, chewing, he studied it. Shaking his head, Tony looked up at Syd and handed the picture to her.

"No … nope. No sir, I don't recognize her," he said. "What's she to you?"

I sat expressionless, trying to figure out his game. Syd looked surprised.

"Are you sure?" she said. "There is this girl who's been coming in later at night. She's almost a regular. I've only seen her from a distance. Do you think that could be her? Are you sure, Tony? I mean, you—"

"Yeah, I'm sure." Tony had resumed eating, stuffing a slice of toast in his mouth, smiling as he chewed. "I haven't seen her, but I'm sure your new friend here will find her, won't you, Prince Charming? I heard you were good at finding people."

He jammed the last remnants of the toast in his mouth. Then he slyly winked at me, just like he had at Sharkees, and I was expecting him to cock his hand again, instead, he swallowed hard, his Adam's apple bulging grotesquely.

A chill ran down my spine, a chill unlike I had ever felt before, and I shuddered so hard, Syd reacted, reaching for my hand under the table, squeezing it tight. Tired of playing charades, I abruptly let go of her hand and got up from the table.

"Okay, that's a wrap. I'm out of here. I've lost my appetite. Thanks for breakfast."

Tony, still chewing, wiped his hands on his thighs and looked up. "Anytime Pistol. I'm up here every morning. Come for breakfast when you've got an appetite. I'm sure our paths will cross again. After all, you are charming and all the women like that, right Syd?"

My back turned, I didn't respond, and Tony purposely left me one last nugget.

"I heard you stopped in Havelock last weekend. It's a nice place. Cute young things packing heat."

I stopped dead in my tracks and bit down hard on my tongue, but I refused to go for the bait and started towards the exit.

"Wait! I'm coming too," Syd yelped. Syd stood up from the table and moved closer to Tony, and I turned and watched as she leaned in.

"What the fuck was that? What the fuck is this all about, Tony? He's my friend, you know. You could have been nicer. And that's bullshit about this Sara person, and you know it."

Tony looked up, his eyes dark. "You watch yourself there, sweet cheeks."

"Fuck you, Tony!" Syd growled, raising her fist.

"C'mon, let's go," I said. "It's not worth it." I placed my hand on Syd's arm and gently pulled her towards me. "C'mon."

On the second tug, Syd turned, and I motioned with my head toward the door. We walked hand in hand until we got to the exit; letting Syd go in front of me, I stopped at the doorway and turned back to where Tony was sitting.

I, Pete Humphries, have just up and walked away from trouble.

"Pete?" I felt Syd's warm hand wrap around mine. "Are you coming?"

"Yeah, yeah," I responded, in a daze. We went down the dark stairs and out to the street. The contrast from light to dark and back to light affected us both; we stood outside on the sidewalk, taking a moment to adjust.

"Mister, are you going to tell me what all that was about?"

"No."

"Why?"

"Because I don't want to."

"That's no reason."

"To me, it is." But the truth was I had no clue where to begin.

"That's not good enough, mister." Syd tugged my arm, forcing me to turn toward her, her touch no longer gentle, and I could feel the tension.

"Tony's my friend," she said, "despite him being an asshole. I'm not sure I like this side of Pete."

I didn't blame her. I couldn't just blurt out everything, expecting her to listen and make sense of it all, especially in public. I paused for a second and looked at Syd. In the bright sun, she was beautiful, the light breeze blowing her hair across her face, bright blue eyes sparkling, wearing all at once, the looks of confusion, uncertainty, concern, and anger.

Taking a deep breath, I offered, "Listen, I'm sorry, Syd. There is some stuff going on here, and you're right, not everything is as it seems. Tony and I crossed paths recently back in Ottawa, and he was the last person I was expecting to see this morning. You had no way of knowing that, and I appreciate you wanting to help, I really do." I reached out and took her hands in mine. She looked at me, this time with understanding in her eyes.

"Can you trust me?" I asked. "I just need a bit of time to process this myself, and then we can talk about it, okay? I promise. It's complicated, this missing people stuff always is. This is what I do, what I'm good at, I just need you to trust me, okay? Please?"

There was a long pause and I let Syd be. Then she broke into a wide grin. "Sure, mister." She reached over to hug me, then kissed me deeply. "Just don't shut me out, okay? I will be here when you're ready."

I leaned in to kiss Syd again when, from behind us, the *whup-whup* of a siren made us jump in fright.

28

NO MATTER WHAT side of the WHUP-WHUP you were on, it still left one with the impression of guilt. *Who me? What did I do?* Holding onto each other, we looked to the street, and slowly pulling up alongside the curb was an unmarked car. There was another WHUP-WHUP for effect, and we jumped again.

"Shit!"

Syd grabbed my arm, worried I was going to piss off the cop.

"Fucker!" I snarled.

Syd squeezed my arm tight. "Pete, stop!"

The window rolled down on the passenger side, and through it, I recognized that familiar brush cut, the thick head on top of the square hanger-like shoulders. Letting go of Syd's hand, I walked over to the car and, placing my hand on the door, peered inside. I started to laugh then turned back to Syd, who was now in shock.

"It's okay, Syd," I said. "I know him. We're old friends. Come over here. My turn, I want you to meet someone."

Timidly, Syd approached, unsure what to make of this. I reached out and pulled her the rest of the way toward the car and forced her to lean in the window along with me.

"Syd, this is Dale. Dale, this is Syd."

"Hi," she said.

I couldn't stop smiling. How long had it been?

"Hi, Syd, nice to meet you. I pulled you over, miss, because of the company you are keeping," Dale said, causing Syd to crack up.

"Yes, please arrest him, Officer, and take him away. He's bothering me." Syd, looked at me with that mischievous glint in her eyes.

"Dale, give me a sec, okay?"

I stepped away from the window and pulled Syd up with me.

"He's an old friend. I want to go catch up with him. Okay, if we connect later?"

"Sure, go."

"Okay, thanks. I will see you later tonight, okay? Promise. And I won't be late this time."

"Better not, mister."

Syd gave me a warm, wet, and very passionate reminder of what I would lose if I was not careful. Point taken, as Syd flicked her tongue across my lips, dangling her fingers in mine just long enough. Distracted, I watched Syd walk down the street. Dale laughed and hit the siren.

I jumped again.

"You fucker!" Laughing, I opened the door and slipped in beside him. Instantly, it was like old times, and I realized how much I missed it, him. Amazing, how well blocking out things worked.

Beside me, sat Dale Simpson, my best friend. I hadn't seen him in a very long time. We originally met at the Police Academy and were partnered together in Barrie, then, a few years later, Dale had requested a transfer back home to the Peterborough area, at the same time I abruptly left the force. Dale had tried to stay in touch after, but if someone doesn't respond, you stop trying, right?

"Nicely done there, Pete-boy. She certainly is your type. She must be new, she's still all shiny and happy. No doubt, she hasn't met the real you yet."

Ouch! I knew he was right and was only saying it out of concern. "Yeah, she's new, just off the showroom floor. I like her, she's fun."

"I heard you were in town," he said and then, in his fatherly tone. "Just what in the name of gosh darn peanuts are you doing here, Pete?"

A smile came to my face. That was Dale to a T, and why we were so different. For as long as I had known him, I had never heard him cuss, say an actual swear word of any kind. Oh, I tried. A bunch of us got him drunk one time, and try as we might, we couldn't get him to swear. Not even a 'damn'. All we ended up doing was making him very sick and very hungover the next day. He wouldn't speak to me for a week.

Dale was everything I wasn't and what I thought I wanted to be, but wrapped up in my own inner turmoil, I could never see it. Back then, I couldn't even see me never mind Dale or anything else. Dale always had a soft spot for me, no matter how much I screwed up, pissed people off, crossed the line, thumbed my nose at authority. With my dad gone, Dale was the constant, the only one, as it turned out, who could keep me in line. We were the exact opposites in every way—attitude, dress, choice of drink—with one exception, we made a great team on the street. I wondered many times if it was simply a case of opposites attracting.

He kept me in line, he wanted me to be like him, and I guess that's why he tried to buy me that white picket fence. Dale had this beautiful family, a loving, doting wife Karen, two little girls, and a large home on Pigeon Lake. Since it worked so well for him and Karen, he thought it would work for me too.

My white picket fence was Dale's idea, an attempt to help me get over the loss of my dad and Tina. Karen had this co-worker, Joanna, who was nice and all, and she was on the hunt for that white picket fence. The problem was, I wasn't on any such hunt, as much as Dale wanted me to be, with the best of intentions of course. Karen set us up on a blind date hoping we would connect. They felt that was what I needed, someone to replace my dad and Tina. Ever since Tina, I had bounced from girl to girl, staying long enough to endure the honeymoon phase, moving on once the glow started to dim.

I loved being a cop, it was all I ever wanted. The problem was, as hard as I tried, I couldn't be a cop 24/7/365. I couldn't be out on the streets all the time. That was where I was happiest, where I felt grounded, where I could just be *me*.

So, I caved and built a white picket fence exactly the same as Dale's, marrying Joanna and buying a house in Barrie, two streets over from Dale's, wanting to please my best friend, as he seemed to know what was best for me. God knows I didn't have a clue. Did I say I missed my dad?

Life for me became about pushing a rope and trying to make everyone else happy, and in the end, Dale's purchase of my white picket fence—for others a good thing—was the thing that ended up driving us apart. Go figure.

We drove slowly through the late morning traffic, Dale looking over periodically. I turned and made eye contact with Dale, and I could see the fatherly look of concern in his eyes, but I looked away, too much time had passed, and pain does that.

"Funny Dale, I've been asking myself the same question. What the fuck am I doing here?"

Dale smiled at my use of *fuck*, my go-to word.

It dawned on me how much I had missed him, leaning on him, talking, throwing at him all my thoughts, worries, concerns, and questions; Dale catching them all, every single time. Here, now, side-by-side, it was like no time had passed. Me and him. Him and me. Just the two of us. I missed all this, the feeling of being grounded by him, and I wanted to recount my recent events to him, only.

Maybe, he could tell me why I was back, as I honestly didn't know. And maybe, he could tell me why I had just walked away from trouble. It certainly wasn't because I had grown up, and became all sage-like: older, wiser, smarter? Or was I? This was what Dale was good at, helping me answer my own questions.

We turned into Del Crary Park, Dale parked the car and reached for the radio. He called in to let dispatch know he was going for lunch.

Gawd! I miss this, I screamed inside.

I felt that all too familiar pang in my stomach, the knot twisting and turning, tighter and tighter. Dale rescued me from my head, just like old times.

"Come on Pete, let's take a walk."

How many times over the years did he do that?

He always knew—he could sense it—how to bring me back. He said many times he tried to figure out how and why he could do this because he could never do that with anyone else, not his wife, not his kids, but he could with me. I kept him up at night trying to figure out why. Finally, he gave up and just accepted it. Which probably explained why he used his credit card on my white picket fence.

We got out and started walking. We were quite the pair.

Dale Simpson, six foot five, two hundred and thirty-five pounds, except at Christmas. He was the 1960's prototype football lineman: tall, lean, barrel-chested, hulking forearms, brush cut, rugged features, soft eyes, with a quick, friendly smile. The classic teddy bear, but when crossed, watch out.

I stood at an even six feet and weighed a buck seventy-five, even at Christmas: wiry, dark hair, agile, athletic. I had to rely on guile, instinct, and speed in everything I did. And I was fast, very fast. I could catch anyone.

Every spring, Dale would suggest a race between us to see who was faster. And every spring, halfway down the line, I would be laughing and giggling, running backward, waving to him. Dale had stamina and could run forever, just not fast like me. Dale and I were the perfect match, that's where the opposites meshed very well.

We strolled along the concrete walkway, gazing at the boats. It was a busy morning, boats idling at the entrance to the marina, waiting for a slip to open up. Up ahead at the gas dock, a few more boats were lined up, waiting their turn. We walked in silence, the crackle of Dale's portable radio giving us the excuse not to talk. Passersby nodded hello to Dale and ignored me.

"Pete, let's see what the Lighthouse looks from above for old times' sake, shall we? We can get a coffee and catch up."

At the entrance, we walked up the circular metal stairs and went inside. Nothing had changed, time warp city. I involuntarily shuddered, and Dale looked at me.

"You okay?"

"Yeah, just need a drink is all," I lied.

Dale ordered a coffee, black, and I ordered a beer. Shocking. No matter what time of day or night, our orders were always the same, except when on duty. We took our drinks out to the patio overlooking the water. It was such a peaceful place. We settled in the white plastic chairs, squinting and shielding our eyes against the bright sun and glare coming off the water. Dale sipped on his coffee, and in two quick gulps, I downed my beer. I licked my lips and sighed, the alcohol washing over me. I got up and went inside to get another one, Dale knowing this all too well.

Returning, I slumped in the chair, my legs stretched out, crossed, on the chair opposite me, staring out at the water. Twisting the bottle in my hands, poking at the label, Dale broke the uncomfortable silence that had been building.

"So, Pete, how are you? How've you been?"

"Which moment?"

"Huh?"

"You asked how I am. Which moment? Because, honestly, it's been nothing but moments."

"Which moment then?" Dale chuckled.

Spinning the wheel in my head, I tried to find a moment to pick, but that was pointless, so I started at the beginning.

"Things haven't been great for a long time now, that much you know. Recently, everything just up and changed, for the better. At least, it seemed like it at first. It was so random, completely out of the blue, almost like I won the lottery, you know? But now, I'm not so sure.

"I took this job, a missing person case, which was a big chance, and ever since I've taken it, it's been beyond strange, even for me. Nothing added up right from the start. Then, I've got all these people now, people I've never met until I meet them, and they are all telling me to be careful. Careful of what? No one would say. Just be careful is all. There was a bunch of close calls along the way, and that rattled me, and you know me, I am always careful no matter what."

Pausing, I looked at Dale, who was watching me, and it was what I loved about him the most— listening intently, concerned, interested.

"One Saturday afternoon, back in Ottawa, I'm in this bar called Sharkees, and I meet this guy, Teddy, Teddy Polson. We get to talking and he offered me fifty grand to find his sister, who he said had gone missing back in May. Her name is Sara Polson. But I don't think she is missing. It just didn't add up. And there's this server, Amy, a sort of femme-fatale, who works in Sharkees. She's really cute and all, and though they say they don't know each other, I'm pretty sure they do."

"Who?"

"Amy."

"Oh. I thought you meant Sara."

"No, Sara's the one who's missing, and Amy's the one who works at the bar. Anyhow, there's this really creepy guy, Tony, I don't know his last name, who works at the bar also. Do you remember that guy Dickie years ago? The undercover operation we ran, and the stuff we found when we raided his place? How crazy he was that day when we tried to arrest him? How hard he was to take down? How absolutely insane he went, and after, we said never again, and of course we did. Well, this guy Tony, for whatever reason, makes Dickie look like a saint. I mean, you know me and everything, but this Tony guy just unglues me."

Dale nodded, recalling that time, taking a sip on his coffee, letting me continue.

"Anyhow, I ran into Tony just before we ran into you, up on the Rooftop patio beside the Lucky 7evens. I came unglued at the sight of him, even Syd noticed. And I walked away when he gave her a hard time. Normally, that would have been fist city, and you, or anyone else, would be pulling me off him. Like I said, everything is strange."

Dale was listening intently, watching me—the beer taking hold, winding me up, I started speaking rapidly and a wee bit less coherently.

"Anyhow, I start out on my search for this Sara early one morning from Ottawa and head out on the lost highway. Everything seems fine, but then I stop for gas and meet these crazy bikers. Then there's this Carlos guy who warns me that there is trouble out there. Where? I don't know. Then I drive farther, and I meet this massive biker Alan who meditates, and he warns me of impending trouble. But he doesn't say from where either. Then I drive some more, and I meet this guy Jimmy in Havelock and I give him the twenty grand that Teddy gave me to give him, and he gives me this box, which I lose right after I get it. The bikers from earlier that morning showed up and Red, this biker-chick, takes it and then there's Leia, and she carries a .45 and almost shoots the bikers with it. Then I finally make it here and I meet this woman and her little dog right down *there*."

I pointed down at the gas pumps.

"And she tells me to be careful, then Jackie at the hotel tells me all this stuff I'm supposed to be doing instead of hanging out with Jack, and oh … and oh yeah, you'll never guess who I ran into the other day? Hanna. Remember Hot Rod Hanna? Anyhow, then I meet Syd who I really like, but then there's this guy Dave, who Hanna warns me about, but he's harmless and then this whole missing person case seems a sure dead end, or a snow job maybe, but I don't know for sure, but then I think I see her the other night and chase after her but lose her, then I go back and hook up with Syd. Did I tell you Syd's a lot of fun? Anyhow, I think that's about it."

It was funny, but Dale had exactly the same expression as Jackie.

"Okay slow down. Who's *her*?"

"What?"

"You said you saw her the other night and chased after her."

"Sara," I said. "She's the one who I think I saw the other night."

Mentally drained, I took a long swig from the bottle, letting it settle inside. I took a breath and started again a little more coherently this time.

"I have a picture to go on, and that's it. I'm pretty sure that was her leaving the Lucky 7evens on her bike, and I went after her, but I couldn't catch her, and I never did see her face up close. She knows how to ride a bike, and I gave up chasing her because it got too dangerous, and I didn't want to attract attention either."

"Can I see it?" Dale asked.

"Sure." I pulled it out of my back pocket and handed it over to him.

Dale studied the picture and took a sip of his coffee. Still holding the picture, he looked up at me.

"So, tell me again, *who* hired you?"

"This guy Teddy. The guy I was telling you about. Teddy Polson. He's a really strange guy. As I said, he just showed up that day in the bar. He was persistent, and now that I look back, it's like he planned it. But at the time, I thought it was just one of those things you know, meet a stranger, do some shots."

Shaking his head. "I thought you'd sworn off shots."

"Yeah, yeah I know … I know … I think I lost the pact moving or something. Sorry," I replied sheepishly.

"How bad was the damage this time?"

"Oh, the usual, two or three days. Anyhow, we did these shots, and we both kinda got bent a little sideways from them. Amy was there, she was bartending, and it was strange too because I think the two of them know each other but they weren't copping to it for some reason. I tailed them a few days later, and they sure knew each other all right. Sorry, I'm getting ahead of myself. Now uh—"

"Ahh, Pete, I've always loved your stories. Can you hold it here? I want to get another coffee. Another beer?"

"Sure."

Dale put Sara's picture on the table and went inside. I sat up and looked out over the water at the boats, but I didn't feel that pleasant waterfront vibe, as I couldn't fight off the nagging feeling that something wasn't right with all of this. Dale just rolling up on me and Syd like that. Almost like he knew where to find me. He said he'd heard I was in town. How would he know?

Was Dale the guy the bartender had seen with Sara, the guy Syd said looked like a cop? If so, she hadn't recognized him at the car. Or if she did, she didn't say anything. Plus, the whole Tony and Syd connection was strange, wasn't it? Was Syd in on something? No way, that much I was sure of; it was maybe the *only* thing I was sure of.

"Here you go," said Dale. "Barking Squirrel. I don't know how you can drink that stuff."

Grinning, I lifted the bottle. "It's easy! Watch." I took a long pull, then punched my chest for effect, emitting a loud burp.

Dale laughed. "Pete, you haven't changed a bit." He leaned over and affectionally ruffled my hair. Sitting back in his chair, he glanced down at the picture on the table then up at me. "I see you've got your car back on the road again. Looks good as always. Still fast as ever?"

That was the only contact I had with Dale. I had sent him a picture of my Chevy when I purchased it. I was so proud and wanted to show it off to him, but when I lost it to hock, I lied and said it had been an accident, and after, I ignored his attempts to contact me until he finally stopped. Shame does that.

"She flies all right. As I said the other night, I had no problem catching up to Sara on her bike. I backed off only because it didn't feel safe. And hey, did you know that my eight-tracks still play as good as new?

Dale knew all about the connection with my dad. That's all I would talk about when we were stuck on stakeouts and having to kill time.

"So, this Teddy guy, what do you know about him?"

I took another drink. "Not much, really. I had never met him until that day in the bar. I never laid eyes on him before. But he had lots of money. He peeled off ten grand in bills like it was nothing."

Dale wore a blank expression, the kind he wore when I was up to something he didn't approve of.

"Dale, I know I shouldn't have, but I took that job just for the money, and I'm realizing now that wasn't my smartest decision. All I could see was the dollar signs and my Chevy back on the road. But now, how things have played out, well, it's not that I regret it, but I just jumped right in, you know?"

"Yes, Pete. I do know. Because that is who you are."

I frowned, his comment stinging, and looked down.

"Look Pete, I'm not saying that's a bad thing, but it is who you are. Sometimes you can't change that. Change certain aspects of who you are. It's so deeply ingrained, and all you can do is recognize it for what it is and work with it. Maybe I wish ... well, heck, I wish we were closer, and maybe you could have called me first with this and we talked it over. Just like we used to."

I looked over at Dale who now was staring out at the water. We sat in silence. A few minutes later, Dale changed the subject.

"Have you seen her yet?"

"Who?"

"You know who. Tina."

"Yeah, I did. The other day."

"Where?"

"There," I said, pointing down at the gas pumps.

"And she saw you?"

"Yep. Asked me to help tie up her boat," I said. "Well, *Chris's* boat I guess."

"*Oh boy.* How did *that* go?"

"About as well as could be expected. I only went on a four-day bender this time."

Dale nodded, knowing what my benders were like. "Well, you seem to be holding up better than I'd have expected. And now here you are parading around town with this year's model."

Dale looked into my eyes, forcing me to connect, "Pete. Syd is not Tina, and Tina is not Syd."

"I know that," I said, as I slumped forward, looking away.

Dale suddenly irritated, his voice sharp, "But do you? Do you honestly know the difference? Because I don't think you do."

I refused to look at him, and we remained silent, with only the clanging of the sailboat lanyards off in the distance.

"For fudge sakes, Pete! When are you going to stop running?"

"Maybe never?" I answered flippantly. "It's something I'm good at. I could always run fast, faster than you."

"Atta boy, Pete. Just keep doing what you do best—being a smart ass and running."

"Denial's a great place. You should try it," I growled.

"When are you going to stop? When?"

Tired of our tennis match, I knew he was right. I was running. I was lost. I wasn't grounded. Despite the past few days, I wasn't anywhere close to being there yet. I got it. Dale grounded me. The job grounded me. My dad grounded me. All the things that grounded me for some inexplicable reason I had lost. And that was the real problem. Though I knew what happened—and it was becoming more apparent each minute since my return—I still didn't understand why it all happened. A coincidence? Maybe? Possibly?

Dale jerked me back to reality.

"Pete, you have to stop running, stop … *chasing*. Because you are still doing both. Stop running from what happened and stop chasing whatever it is you are looking for."

All I could do was nod. I heard him. But I was not hearing him, if that made sense. Because I didn't know what I was looking for in either direction.

Dale's radio crackled, and the voice informed him he was wanted at the other end of town. We finished our drinks, and he handed me back the picture of Sara, saying he had never seen her before, but he would keep an eye out and let me know if anything came up and would run a check on her just the same. We exchanged numbers and promised to stay in touch. As we walked back to his car, Dale turned to me.

"So, Pete, what's next?"

"Well, I need to catch up with Teddy back in Ottawa, and I think, later tonight, I was going to hang out again at the Lucky 7evens in case Sara showed … and submarine races with Syd later," I grinned.

Dale shook his head at me and laughed. "Only you, Pete, only you."

We shook hands, a quick hug, and Dale got into his car. I walked over to my hotel as it was time to return Teddy's calls.

29

ENTERING MY HOTEL room, the burner phone on the bed was buzzing. Teddy had beaten me to it; after letting it ring six more times for effect, I picked up.

"I have her."

"What?"

"I have her."

"Who's this?"

"It's Pete. That you, Teddy?"

There was silence on the other end, and I could hear breathing. 'Click,' and the phone went dead. I tossed the phone on the bed and walked over to the cooler, reaching in, I pulled out a beer, opened it, took a big gulp, then moved out onto the balcony that overlooked the river. I plopped down into the plastic chair and propped my feet up on the railing. I took another big gulp of beer, finishing it, crushing the can in my hand I counted out loud to ten and when I got to ten, the phone on my bed buzzed again.

"Perfect."

I went back into my room, tossing the crushed can into the corner, and reached in the cooler again, pulling out another beer, and on the eleventh ring this time, I picked up.

"City Morgue. You stab 'em, and we slab 'em. How can I help you?"

"Fuck you!"

"Why Teddy, you don't seem too pleased, considering I found Sara and all."

"What do you mean?"

"I thought you would be happy now that I've found your sister. I mean, that's what you hired me for, right?"

"You found Sara? Where?"

"Neat, huh? Yep. I found her all right, tucked away in beautiful downtown Peterborough. Easy peasy too. I just walked into the Lucky 7evens, and there she was playing pool all by herself. I bought her a beer, poured on my boyish charm, and voilà! She's coming back with me. I figured you would be pleased as punch over this. Don't tell me you're not?"

I could hear deep breathing on the other end, and was that the faint smell of wood burning?

"Um, yeah. I am. You caught me off guard. I, well, I wasn't expecting you to find her so quickly. When I hadn't heard from you, I figured you had run into a dead-end or something, or maybe you hadn't found her yet and needed more time."

Teddy, trying to sound a little more friendly. "So, I was calling just trying to see where things were at, that's all."

"Well, Teddy, you did ask me to find your sister, and there was no timeline for it, remember? I was doing my job, the one you hired me for. Gee, I don't know. Maybe there should be a reward in it for me, considering how easily I found her? What do you think?"

Silence, more breathing then … "Can I speak to her?"

"Aw sorry, Teddy, she's in the shower. You know long women take. I'll get her to call you when she gets out. Promise. Now about that reward…"

"No, no need to call. And yes, a reward works. You name it, Pistol. When did you say you were coming back with my sister?"

"Oh, I was thinking sometime tomorrow night. We will meet you at Sharkees around ten? That work for you?"

"That works. I missed her. You did a great job! And you're right, you deserve extra for this. I'll have it ready for you tomorrow night when you get back. Sound good?"

"Sounds great, Teddy, see you tomorrow night."

"Oh, and Pete, drive safely. I wouldn't want anything to happen to my sister now that you've found her."

"No worries, Teddy. I'll treat her like she's my very own."

I hung up and lay back on the bed.

Well, gee, that was fun.

I laughed to myself, rocking Teddy's world like that. The problem was, I had completely rocked mine also. I mean, what? I was going to hang at the Lucky 7evens tonight, with no guarantee that Sara would even show. And if she did, then what? I was going to walk up to her and tell her this wild story, about her brother looking for her, and now that I had found her, politely ask her if she wouldn't mind coming back to Ottawa with me the next night. Sure, that'll work all right.

I leaned over the bed, flicked open the cooler lid with my foot, reached in, took out two more beers, and moved back out on the balcony. This was at least a two-beer plan.

I sat out on the balcony chastising myself. *Nicely done, Pete.* As I sipped on my beer, it hit me, Teddy never even asked about the box.

30

TEDDY PUT THE phone down on the bar, picked up his drink, and downed it. The liquor burned as it slid down the back of his throat. He picked up his other phone and started thumbing through it. The Texas football game was on overhead, a replay mind you, but he took no notice.

Patty walked in. "How are things, Teddy?"

Teddy grunted, and Patty asked him again, as she noticed the football game, but his head remained down, buried in his phone. "Teddy? Everything okay?"

He didn't bother looking up. "Huh? Yeah, sure … sure … yeah sure I'm okay. Just got stuff on my mind is all."

Patty nodded and turned away, but Teddy suddenly looked up, now alert. "Sorry, Ms. Patty. Do you need anything?" He started to stand up.

"No, it's okay." Patty laughed and gestured with her hands for him to sit, realizing she now totally owned him. She turned to leave, but then stopped. "Have you seen your sister? She was supposed to be here two hours ago, and I haven't heard from her."

Teddy's eyes started blinking rapidly, "No, sorry, I haven't seen or spoken to her in the past few days."

Patty knew Teddy was lying since she had seen the two of them out on the patio the other morning deep in discussion. Still, she decided to let it be, as much as she owned him, she had been there when it came to covering up for family.

"Hmm okay … oh, you haven't seen Tony, have you? He's not in either and was supposed to do a double today."

Teddy lied once more, unable to look Patty in the eyes, and pretended to be distracted by his phone. Patty sensed something was up. Maybe Amy and Tony were seeing each other or just screwing? Opposites attracted, so who knew? It was so common in places like this, and she figured it was not worth pressing over.

Patty looked down and noticed the bare spot on the shelf under the bar. *That's strange?* she thought. *It's gone again. One day it's here, and then it's not. I wonder whose it is?* Turning to Teddy, "Teddy? Do you know who … aw, forget it."

You know what? I don't want to know. Patty went into the kitchen, pushing open the swinging doors and barking, "Okay! Who wants to work a double?"

Teddy, alone again at the bar, reached over and helped himself to the bottle of Scotch, and poured himself another drink, this time not even bothering to look or listen for Patty; too concerned about his call just now with Pete. That he wasn't expecting. He said he had found Sara. Sara wasn't supposed to be found. And he hadn't seen or heard from her since the other morning. *Had Pete really found her? Did he have her? Was he holding her against her will?*

None of it was making sense. He thought he was leading Pete on a wild goose chase with the intent to be his mule and pick up the box in Havelock and bring it back. At least that was the plan. Somewhere along the way, things got screwed up.

There was a strong gust of wind followed by a loud bang from outside, and startled, Teddy turned toward the patio and watched as one of the table umbrellas bounced across the deck. He jumped off the stool and raced outside, grabbing the umbrella pole just as it was about to fly off the patio. The wind pulled the umbrella and his arm, the force pinning his back to the fence. He held on tight, then just as quickly, the wind subsided, the pole went limp in his hand, and he let it fall to the ground. Breathing a sigh of relief, another strong gust of wind came through and picked the umbrella up again. The pole started to lift, and Teddy held tight once more, the wind so strong it was jerking his outstretched arm, his back now pressed against the patio fence.

Snap! Snap! Crack! Another umbrella came loose from its hole in the table and came flying across the patio directly at Teddy. Still holding the pole, ducking and reaching out with his free hand, he caught the pole as it flew past. He was now pinned starfish-like against the fence, arms outstretched, holding on to the two flying umbrellas. The fabric was flapping loudly and jerking his arms with each gust.

Patty came rushing out. "Here let me help!"

She lunged for the pole nearest her and grabbed on just as another strong gust swept across the patio. Patty was off balance as she held on to the pole, her back to the wind and deck, the force pushing her up against the fence. She started to come up off the ground, looking like Mary Poppins, as the umbrella lifted away from the fence, her arms jerking her forward, as she and Teddy held on to the poles. In Teddy's other hand, the umbrella was also trying to lift off now, and the substantial size of Teddy was the only thing keeping them and the umbrellas from flying away.

In all the chaos, Teddy and Patty, staring at each other wide-eyed, laughed out loud at the absurdity of it. Just as fast, the wind stopped, and the umbrellas went limp, and Patty's feet touched down again on the deck. They took a minute to gather themselves, then Patty looked up at Teddy, and thanked him.

"You're welcome, Ms. Patty," Teddy said, as he folded up the two umbrellas, and rearranged the chairs and table, beside the entrance. Then it hit him.

Shit, shit, shit! It was my idea! What was I fucking thinking? He slapped his forehead. *I did this. I had it all planned out, and then I went and fucked it all up.*

Panicking now, his hands shaking, he went inside and picked up his phone, and dialed Sara's number. There was no answer, so he tried the other number, and on the third ring, the phone picked up.

"Hello?" the voice answered, groggily.

"Is she there with you?"

"I told you never to call me here."

"She's not answering, and I was worried."

"So? That's not my problem, that's yours."

"Is she there with you?" Teddy asked again.

"Yes, she's here."

Teddy collapsed forward on the bar, breathing a huge sigh of relief.

"Is she okay?" he asked shakily.

"Of course, she is. She is always okay with me."

"And what were you thinking sending Pete out this way? You sent them both this way! You stupid fucking idiot! Sara always comes here, and you sent him in the same direction. What were you thinking? No wait, you weren't as usual—"

Wound up now. "And what's this having Tony rough up Jimmy and a server in Havelock. Are you fucking nuts?"

There was a pause then Teddy said, "I was only doing it to protect you."

"Protect me? Protect me from what? I don't need protecting. You've gone and screwed everything up. If you had just left well enough alone but … but you couldn't, could you? Did you know Tony's here, holding court in the mornings again on the Rooftop?"

Teddy could hear heavy breathing on the other end and waited for the inevitable.

"Dammit! You fucking moron! And as usual, I'm going to have to fix this, clean all this up, just like always."

Teddy tried to control his breathing. "I'm … I'm sorry Dale … what do you want me to do?"

"Do nothing! Do nothing … do absolutely nothing! Please!" There was a loud click as Dale hung up.

Teddy put the phone down and slumped on his stool, feeling defeated. Just like his father used to do to him, Dale treating him like a child and putting him down, making him feel useless and devalued.

He could still remember the night of the incident at the waterfront. He had gotten home late that night, as he had trouble hitching a ride back. It was almost midnight when he walked in the front door, his father was still up, waiting for him. Teddy had hoped to avoid his father for fear of being grilled about his day. He couldn't hide how disheveled he looked, nor mask the pain and humiliation on his face, and he was hoping his father wouldn't be up. His clothes were still damp and wrinkled, and his hair was all matted. He was still feeling embarrassed, and out of sorts, even though everyone on the docks—even some of the boaters—had helped clean everything up. They were all so helpful and encouraging.

Everyone told him how well he handled the incident, how composed he remained, while that maniac made a complete jackass of himself. The problem was, he believed them, but his father wouldn't. So, he was forced to tell him what happened with his mother standing behind his father and nodding, both taking turns going up one side and down the other, disappointed that a Polson had backed away like that.

What were the people at the golf club going to think? asked his mother. And she had the audacity to ask Teddy if he would write a note for her, explaining that he was sick that day with the flu, and that was why he hadn't stood up for himself.

But he had stood up for himself. Everyone there on the waterfront that day saw and commended him for how mature he was. But his parents saw things through the distorted lens of what they feared the neighbours might think.

The words seem to bounce off his body like rubber bullets. "You didn't do *anything*? You just let this guy make a fool out of you. A complete fool. I'm going to hear about this for sure the next time at the club, how my kid, my boy didn't stand up to that jerk and just stood there like a coward and took it, while everyone watched."

On and on it went, Teddy standing in the hallway, taking it until his father tired and his parents turned away in disgust and retreated to the liquor cabinet and their chairs in front of the fire. Sara, powerless, had watched it all unfold from the top of the stairs and later did her best to console him, but to little effect.

Teddy finished his drink and gently placed the glass down on the bar. *Fuck this! Fuck them!* Teddy spoke silently to himself. Angry now, he tried calling Tony, who answered on the first ring.

"Where are you?"

"Where you told me to go, boss. Peterborough."

"Have you seen him?"

"Who, boss?"

"Pete Humphries."

"Yes, boss. I ran into him this morning on the Rooftop. Syd, the Lucky 7evens bouncer, is screwing him and she brought him up to show off her new toy."

"Perfect."

"Have you seen my sister?"

"Yes, boss. She's here also."

There was a long pause, and Tony could hear Teddy breathing through the phone.

"Boss?"

"I'm here, just thinking,"

"Can Syd be bought?" Teddy asked.

"No, boss. No way. I tried once, but she's like Humphries with that fucking honour thing."

"Shit. I want to hurt him. Do you know of anyone?"

Another pause, as Tony was spinning the rolodex in his head.

"Yeah, boss. I know of someone. He's been hanging around the Lucky 7evens playing pool. He can't pick up a chick for his life, but he would be perfect. I heard he likes this stuff, he enjoys it."

"Good. Give him the usual rate. Rough him up enough to put him out of the game for a while, but no killing, just rough him up. Got it?"

"Got it," he said. "Uh, boss?"

"What?"

"I can do it. Why not let me do it? I don't like the guy. Never have, ever since I first met him. All that boyish charm bullshit and hitting on the women. Why don't you let me take care of it?"

"Ahh, sorry, Tony. I know you would enjoy it. I would love to do it myself. But we're just too close to home on this one and need an outsider and no trace. So go with this new guy, okay?"

"You're right, boss. That makes sense. I guess that's why you're the boss. When do you want this done?"

"Can you make it happen tonight?"

"No problem, boss. Tonight it is. This guy is always there, and he will lap this up like giving a dog a big fat juicy bone."

"Good. Keep me posted. What's his name?"

"Dave. I don't know his last name, but his first name is Dave. Tough as nails and built like a fire hydrant. I heard he put two guys in the hospital in a bar fight recently in Sudbury. You know how tough that town is. The one guy lost an eye, and the other guy may never walk again. I think we're good on this, boss."

"That's good. Text me when it's done."

"Yes, boss."

Feeling much better, Teddy called it a night. His scotch empty, he needed a traveler for the road. He looked around and Patty wasn't in sight. All clear.

Fuck it. You deserve this for fixing things for Dale, he thought, patting himself on the back.

Teddy got off the stool, checking again to see if anyone was watching. Satisfied, he placed both hands on the edge of the bar, braced, and then hopped over to the other side. Landing like a cat, in one motion, he moved to the cooler door on the floor, opened it, and grabbed two travellers. He slipped the bottles under his shirt, gingerly stepped to the opening on the other side and tip-toed towards the front entrance. Just as he started to open the door, he heard a voice behind him, and he froze in his tracks.

"Be here for eight sharp tomorrow morning and not a minute later. You've got some dishwashing to do."

Teddy's back remained turned. "Yes, Ms. Patty. See you then." Still covering his beers, he pulled on the handle and started to leave.

"Good night, Teddy. You don't need to bring the empties back. You can keep them."

"Yes, Ms. Patty. Thank you, Ms. Patty."

31

I SHOWERED, CHANGED, and managed to find an actual clean shirt. When I unfolded it, a note slipped out and fell to the floor. I picked it up and started laughing.

> Clothes are much happier washed, and you have a much better chance with the opposite sex wearing them.
>
> You're welcome, Jackie.

After giving Jackie the window seat in my will, I had a couple of things to take care of first, before my attempted peaceful kidnapping of Sara, if she showed, that is.

Big IF.

I ignored my Chevy and walked the couple of blocks up to the Lucky 7evens. It was another warm, starry night, and looking across from the other side, it was busy. Syd was in fine form, chatting with everyone out front. I fought the urge to cross over, and instead, I walked quickly up the few blocks to the doorway where I saw Des the other day, but the doorway was empty; no cardboard home, no Des. I looked around, but there was no one else hanging about in the area.

Oh well, one down.

I crossed the street and headed back down the way I came. I stopped and turned when I heard the loud click-clack thump-thump coming from behind me, and I waited for the noise to catch up.

"Hiya, Pete! Fancy meeting you here. Miss me?" Hanna cheerily greeted me.

"Always," I said, a knot forming in my stomach, as we hugged.

"Where you've been? I thought you had left again." She noticed my frown. "Sorry. I shouldn't have said that."

"No, it's okay." My eyes started to well up. *Shit! I hate this.*

"What is it, Pete? Is everything okay?" Hanna asked, sensing something was wrong.

"Um, uh … um … aww shit I'm sorry Hanna, I really am."

"You're leaving again, aren't you? This time for good."

"Nothing ever got by you, did it?" I said, as my eyes filled with tears. "I'm not good at this," I sniffled, my head down, kicking at the sidewalk.

Hanna began to cry as well. "I know. It's okay."

"Why are you leaving, Pete?" Then, before I could answer. "I'm sorry. I don't mean to pry."

"It's okay." I reached for her hand. "Tonight, maybe tomorrow? Sometime tomorrow, I think. I don't know exactly when or what time. I just know. And you're right, I don't think I am coming back. I can just feel it, you know? I can't describe it. I just know. I'm sorry, Hanna."

Hanna let go of my hand and wiped her eyes with her sleeve. Her body shook. I leaned over and hugged her, her hand coming up and patting me on the shoulder. Just like old times. We held each other tight, not wanting to let go. All those times together came flashing back, as we hugged on the sidewalk. I pulled myself away from her embrace and wiped my eyes.

"Listen kid, can you do me a favour?"

"Sure! Anything for you, you know that."

"See the greenish doorway over there?"

"Yes. Des is usually there."

"You know Des?" I asked.

"Yes, why?"

"I met him last week and gave him money for shoes and food, and I was looking for him again. I haven't seen him since. I hope he's doing okay."

Hanna started to laugh. "Oh boy, Pete, you certainly don't get around much, do you?"

"Huh?"

"Des. He's off the streets because of you. That's why he's not in the doorway. Hasn't been since you gave him the money that day."

"What?"

Hanna looked at me in admiration. "Oh, Pete. So you. Whatever you said to him that day worked. He pulled himself together and is back in the halfway house. There's no guarantee, but whatever you said, worked. At least for now."

"But I didn't do much. I really didn't. I just gave him some money, that's all. But wow! That's great!" As I looked over at the empty doorway.

"Yes, everyone is happy for him."

I reached into my pocket, pulled out my roll of bills, peeled off five twenties, folded them in my hand and handed them to her.

"What's this for?" Hanna asked, her eyes bugging out at the sight of the money.

"Des. You. Just in case."

"Oh, Pete," Hanna blubbered, taking the money from my hand, she started crying again.

We hugged some more, but it was time, stepping back, I looked down at Hanna for the last time. Hanna reached out and patted my hand, then sighing, and wiping her eyes.

"Bye Pete, take care, I love you."

Flicking the switch on her chair, she swiftly turned and sped off into the night, her ponytail bouncing and her head bobbing, but this time she wasn't singing, and all I could hear was the chair, bumping and clicking on the pavement. I stood watching until she got to the next corner, then abruptly turned and was gone.

"Bye kid. Love you more than you know."

Choking on the huge lump in my throat, I turned and retraced my steps back down the sidewalk toward the Lucky7evens. Syd was out front, I snuck up from behind, placing my hands on her hips, and gave her a gentle squeeze.

"Ooohhh, I know that touch. Hmm there, mister, you better be careful."

Squeezing a little harder. "Or what?"

"Or, I'm going to be the one who ties you up instead," she cooed, as she turned towards me and gave me a quick hug. Laughing, I pulled back, and instead of her usual mischievous glint, there was a look of concern in her eyes.

"What's up, Sparky?"

"Do you really need to go in tonight? I can beg off, and we can go back to my place and take turns tying each other up. I'll even let you do me first." She held her wrists out and playfully twisted them.

"Almost too hard to resist," I teased. "Almost …"

Any other night, any other time … man oh man … My David Cassidy hook immediately awoke from its slumber and came into view. Casually, I placed my arm over my crotch.

"… Later, later," I said. "I *so promise*, later."

Syd, wearing the look of concern, frowned.

"Everything okay? Not like you. What's up?"

I leaned in to kiss her, but she pulled back, and now I knew something wasn't right.

Syd shook her head. "I don't know, but something doesn't feel right. I don't know. I just … I just … don't feel good about tonight, about you, and in there."

Syd moved toward me, and reaching out, held my hands. "C'mon baby, let's just go. We don't need this. You don't need this. Not tonight, please baby." Her eyes pleaded, searching mine, trying to connect.

Touched—and caught a little off guard—I held her, caressing her hair, and whispered in her ear.

"I have to, Syd, I have to go in. There's something I have to do. Remember this morning and Tony? It's to do with that. I'm still trying to sort this out, and I can't explain it yet." I tried to sound reassuring. "Things will be fine. I promise. I'm just going to shoot some pool for a bit and maybe that girl Sara will show." I looked at my watch. "Tell you what? If she doesn't show by eleven, we'll call it a night, go home and fuck each other's brains out. Sound like a plan?"

Wisely, I left out the part where I had this strong sense of foreboding ever since I had gotten off the phone with Teddy earlier. Ending the call, throwing the phone on the bed, I was enveloped by an icy chill. For a second, I thought I was coming down with something, but it left as quickly as it came. But when I saw Syd, I felt that same icy chill again.

Syd laughed, and that broke the spell. Smiling again, she kissed me and playfully pushed me toward the entrance. "Go!"

As I was walking in, I heard her call out, and turning.

"Babe. You know you suck at pool, right?"

I nodded and shrugged.

"Good," she called out, "then neither of us has anything to worry about."

I winced, making a face, and went inside.

The music was pounding, and the purple and yellow lights were especially blinding, as I scooted through the groups of people mingling on the dance floor, checking out the pool tables in the middle of the floor.

Good, I thought. *Not too many in use tonight.*

I made my way to the bar, and when I went to order a Barking Squirrel and a table, the bartender shook his head.

"Someone's already done it for you."

"Huh?"

The bartender pointed over my shoulder, and I turned to see Dave in the middle of the floor waving.

Dave! Shit! I had forgotten all about Dave. Though that was a fun night, it seemed like ages ago. Shit, tonight of all nights, shit, shit. Dave was waving and pointing at the full beer on the table. As much as I wanted to, I couldn't blow him off easily, and I had no patience for drama.

Shit.

"Hey, Dave. How you've been?"

"Hiya, Pete! I was hoping you would be here tonight. I've been looking for you, so glad you're here. I got you a beer, and they're all racked and ready to go," making a sweeping gesture to the table.

With one eye on the door, I took a swig of beer.

"Thanks for this," I said distractedly. "Want to shoot first?"

Suddenly, I shivered hard, so hard the bottle almost fell out of my hand. Startled, I put the beer down on the table and grabbed for my wrist. I rubbed it, and that same icy chill ran through me. I was on high alert now. Everything seemed to slow down in that instant—the pounding music now a garbled half speed, the swirling lights and people moving in the same slow rhythmic motion. The sounds around me were heavy, voices low, in a deep baritone. I sensed something bad was about to happen. I looked around and couldn't see

Dave. Where was Dave? I quickly spun all the way around, but I still didn't see him. My senses were screaming now, fists clenched at my side, I spread my legs further apart.

Just as I went to turn again –BAM– I was rocketed forward, my arms catching the edge of the pool table, and I landed hard on the floor. My head was spinning, and I felt a sharp pain at the base of my neck. Stunned –BAM– as I was hit from behind again, felt another sharp pain, this time from my shoulder. I was hit once more, and my shoulder went numb, and tingles were running down my arm. I tried to roll away, but I wasn't fast enough, and something was kicking me in the hips and stomach. I lost my breath briefly but recovering, I made another attempt to roll away.

Whoever was doing this, was doing a good job, because it was relentless. Now on my side, I raised my arms to protect myself, and there was a stabbing pain as my forearm took a direct hit. I screamed out and, covering my face and head with my arms, managed to get a peek at whoever was doing this.

Dave. *What the fuck?*

BANG! BAM! The pool cue came crashing down again. My forearm and hip were throbbing, the pain excruciating, and bombs were going off in my head. Despite this, I knew I had to keep moving and find a way to get up. I kicked wildly in the direction of Dave, who was swinging the pool cue like a baseball bat. He swung down, and I rolled away, forcing him to miss, losing his balance; I kicked at him, and he fell off to one side. I inched my body across the floor, backing away. Dave recovered quickly, retrieved the cue, and bringing it up over his head, brought it down on my shins. I screamed out in pain, but somehow, I was able to keep twisting and turning, squirming away. He swung the cue yet again, I blocked it with my good arm and grabbed onto it. He tried to pull back, but I wouldn't let go, and with the cue in mid-air, we stopped.

Holding the thick end of the cue, I screamed, "What the fuck are you doing?"

The music was still pounding, I could see a crowd forming, everyone looking on in shock.

"Fuck you," he snarled and yanked the cue from my hand. I scurried backward as he swung again, hitting me on the thigh with a loud thwack.

"FUCK!" I screamed out and tried to move farther away. Dave, winded from laying a beating on me, lowered the cue and was breathing heavily. Despite the intense pain, I had to find a way to get off the floor before I passed out or worse. I frantically looked around, and on the table near me, was a beer bottle. Looking again at Dave, still hunched over, using every ounce of strength I had, I forced myself up to my feet, the pain screaming through my insides. I lunged toward the table and grabbed the bottle, turning, I threw it in the direction of Dave.

My aim wasn't exactly true, the bottle grazing the side of his head knocked him off balance, and he slipped backward. Taking two excruciating steps forward, I jumped with both feet, and turning my hips, landed on Dave's outer leg; hitting the outside of his knee dead on, the sound of crunching and the crack of the bone, as his leg bent inwards and buckled. He screamed out in pain, the cue falling from his hand and sagged to the floor. Landing on my side, I crawled on all fours, and using his body as leverage, I pulled myself up and stood up over him.

"Get up," I hissed.

"Fuck you," he whispered, moaning.

"Get up!" I hissed again.

"Fuck you."

"Get up!" I yelled, kicking at his legs. "GET UP!"

Then, I stepped hard down on his shattered knee. He screamed, and someone gasped out, "Oh my God." I reached down and pulled him up by his T-shirt, stretching it, as his body fell back; dead weight with his leg shattered. I leaned over farther, and yanking him up by his shirt again, hissed at him.

"Who did this? Who set me up? Who put you up to this?"

Our faces inches apart, Dave's eyes were wild, spittle hanging from the corners of his mouth, snot running from his nose. He spit in my face, disgusted, I shook my head hard and wiped away the gob. I let go of his shirt, and he dropped limply to the floor.

I shakily made it to my feet, reached out to the table to balance myself, and as I turned away; I felt a stabbing pain in the back of my leg and screamed out once more, falling to my knees. I instinctively reached for the back of my leg, and I could feel the warm sticky blood. Dave was now upright and holding a knife.

Throwing myself forward, I hit him flush in the face with my fist, his nose shattering, making a horrible crunching sound; the force of my motion dragging me across his body. His head snapped back at the impact, and the knife slipped out of his hand clanging on the wooden floor. I lifted myself off him, bent down, grabbed his shirt, and pulled him up, holding him, I slammed my fist into his face, again and again, blood spurting everywhere.

I brought my fist back and slammed it into his face once more, this time between his cheek and just under his eye. There was another crunching sound, this time louder, and I heard someone gasp behind me. His head snapped back, blood pouring out of his nose, and as I pulled him up to hit him again, something grabbed my arm from behind, locking it, so I couldn't move. I tried to shake free, but the grip was too firm. From behind, I heard a soft voice that sounded far away in a warm, safe world; somewhere, anywhere, other than here.

"Stop. It's okay, mister. I'm here to rescue you just like I promised I would."

Turning my head, eyes ablaze, my arm shaking, I tried to break free from Syd's firm grip.

"Remember the first time we met? And how you said to come and rescue you? Well, here I am." Her voice quivering, Syd squeezed my arm gently. "C'mon, this is not you. This not the Pete I know."

"I think he's the one that needs rescuing," I said, motioning at what was left of Dave's face.

Syd looked into my eyes.

"I don't care about him. I'm rescuing you from you. I'm here just like I promised. Come on, mister."

She gave my arm a couple of quick tugs, and I looked back at her, making eye contact; her eyes flickering, wet, hopeful, searching for mine. I lowered my arm and Syd released her grip, I let go of Dave's shirt, and he fell back to the floor with a thunk. Syd reached down and helped me to my feet. My leg was bleeding, and I was afraid to put any pressure on it; shaking from adrenaline and shock, I leaned on Syd for support. She wrapped her arm around my waist and under my armpit and whispered, "C'mon mister let's get you home and cleaned up. We've got some fucking to do, remember?" smiling at me.

"Right about now, that would be lovely," I grinned weakly. Syd positioned me, taking most of my weight, and I hobbled along, as she led me away from the pool tables and toward the front entrance.

We stopped and she spoke quickly to the other bouncers. "Guys, get this cleaned up before the cops get here, you know the drill. And get that piece of shit out here, have Ronny call a cab and drop him at Emerg as a John Doe. I will check back later, okay?"

The other bouncers nodded dutifully and immediately got to work. Syd felt warm and safe, and I could feel myself coming down. The back of my neck and shoulders ached, and I sensed the knife wound in the back of my leg might only be a flesh wound; a few stitches, but otherwise, I had survived. I guess I was lucky. As we slowly shuffled across the floor, my head was spinning both from the pain and the why.

The crowd parted, allowing us to pass by, and they were mostly silent with the odd murmurs … "What happened? Does anyone know? I wonder what he did?"

At the front entrance, Syd shifted, and still holding on to me, we squeezed our bodies through the doorway. As we hobbled out into the street, I sensed someone watching. I looked up, and over on my left, I could make out someone standing in the background, peering over the onlookers, wearing a perplexed look. I could just make out the head and face.

Amy? Why would she be here?

32

WE WERE QUITE the pair, hobbling back to Syd's apartment, passersby gave us a wide berth on the sidewalk, as Syd was carrying most of the load. My shirt was ripped, and covered in blood, and the back of my leg was leaking and throbbing, the blood leaving a long scraggly line down the back of my leg. Luckily for me, it looked worse than it was. Syd struggled to get me up the stairs, but I gainfully made it, throwing in some exaggerated groans along the way, hoping to elicit sympathy.

"Don't be such a girl!" she said, punching me in the arm and making me laugh out loud.

Once inside, I slumped down on the chair at the kitchen table. Syd peeled off what was left of my shirt and went into the bathroom, returning with a paramedic size medical kit. My eyes flew open at the size of the bag.

"Life of a bouncer," she shrugged.

I didn't require stitches, and Syd expertly cleaned and bandaged my leg. She washed the blood off my face and then, just for fun, washed my chest and arms with a warm cloth, thoroughly enjoying herself. With each movement, she brushed against me a little more, increasing the sexual tension between us—the violence of the night and our mutual connection, its own aphrodisiac. Her hair fell over my face as she leaned in, her breasts, barely covered by her tank top, her nipples rubbing against my bare chest, her breath warm across my face and neck, as she washed away the fight.

Facing me, she straddled my leg and rubbed her crotch along my thigh as she wiped the dried blood from my face with the warm cloth. Finished, she stood back, admiring her work.

"I should've been a med," she sighed wistfully.

"Why didn't you?" I asked, thinking that was her calling.

"Money. It's always about money. I didn't have it … well, I don't have it *yet*," she said, trying to sound hopeful. "But I will. It is just taking longer than I thought. Then, I can get out of here and that place," she sighed ruefully, pointing in the direction of the Lucky 7evens, "and this town."

"Where would you go?"

"East, home. I'm from Cole Harbour, and yes," she said, finishing my thought for me, "I'm named after Sydney Crosby. My dad …" rolling her eyes, as she returned the supplies to the medical bag.

"How did you end up here then?"

Syd frowned, and her eyes went dark. Reaching over, I touched her arm.

"Sorry. It's okay." I searched her eyes. "Really." I smiled and despite the pain, leaned forward and gave her a warm kiss on the cheek. I remembered what Carlos had said: *We are all coming and going from somewhere.*

Leaning forward, our heads touched, and we sat quietly, enjoying the peace of the moment.

"Hey!" she said, "I got you something. I almost forgot."

Her mood bright again, she jumped up from the table, padded over to the cupboard and brought out a large bottle of Jack. She held it out in front of her, turning like a game show model displaying today's prize.

"Huh? Huh? I was thinking of you the other day," twisting her hips, one foot on top of the other, turning the bottle, she smiled devilishly.

"It's Christmas!" I exclaimed, and we both laughed.

"I'll get the glasses, and you take the chairs out on the balcony, okay?" She hurriedly closed the medical bag and threw the blood-stained cloth in the sink.

We adjourned to the balcony, and Syd poured us a drink. Clinking glasses, we toasted the warm summer night, then we toasted the moon, the stars, the shimmering river across the street, even a couple below, who were walking past. Giggling like teenagers, we called out and when they looked up, we quickly slipped back, hiding in the dark. We could hear the thump-thump coming from the Lucky 7evens, and it was hard to believe what had transpired only an hour ago.

Syd had turned her chair toward me, her foot in my lap, reaching, she poured us another glass, finishing off Jack. She tossed the empty plastic bottle off the balcony, waving bye to the best Christmas present ever. Holding my glass, with my other hand I played with her toes, gently rubbing and caressing them, running my fingers slowly around and through each toe. My David Cassidy hook made a not-so-surprising appearance. Syd, eyeing his entrance, brought her other foot up and pressed it against my erection, immediately bringing it straight to attention. She giggled, running her tongue across her mouth, as she started rubbing my erection up and down with her foot, thoroughly enjoying my uncontrollable reaction. I jerked, twitched, and moaned, with each caress, still all the while playing with her toes. We both sipped on our drinks, eyes locked and glassy, drinking each other in, smiling, as lust reached its boiling point. When Syd managed to pull my shorts down with her toes—exposing David Cassidy—it was time.

Putting down our glasses, we stood up, giggling and hugging on the balcony, and we almost came right there. Her hand stroking my erection, now outside the top of my shorts, and me with my hand down the front of her shorts.

"Put your finger here," she whispered, placing her hand on my wrist and guiding my hand to her very wet opening. My finger slid easily in and out with gentle movements, and she started breathing heavily and moaning. I had to hold on to her, to keep us both from collapsing from pleasure; her knees bending and buckling, my finger holding her up.

She licked my ear. "Let's go inside."

She released her grip on me, and I pulled my hand out of her shorts. Hobbling behind, she reached back for my hand and led me inside. Despite the pain, I was more than ready to go, and we barely made it on the bed, and well … you can guess the rest.

Waking early the next morning, I untangled myself from Syd and slid out of bed. I looked over and she was fast asleep. Trying not to disturb her, I pulled the covers up and kissed her lightly on her head. Throwing on my shorts, I snuck out shirtless and walked the two blocks up to my hotel. The cool morning air was the perfect tonic for my bruised and battered body. Stopping at my Chevy, I opened the trunk and pulled out a clean T-shirt. I ran my hands quickly through my hair, pushing it down and back, then I reached for the toothpaste, dabbed some on my finger, and rubbed it on my teeth.

Reaching in the trunk, I unhooked the nut on the spare tire, flicking and spinning the oversized screw until it came off. I lifted the jack and feeling around until I found the latch and gave it a tug, I reached inside and pulled out a cloth bag. I balanced the bag on the spare tire, unzipped it, and peered inside. I pulled out a tan-coloured rag and unwrapped it, and pulled out my .45, feeling the coolness of the metal and the heft in my hands.

Turning the pistol over, I inspected it, looking inside the barrel, and up and down both sides, then I ejected the clip, checked it and snapped it back in place with another loud click. I pulled on the hammer, heard the click, and slid it back. I checked the chamber and satisfied, I snapped it back, flipping on the safety, I reached around and tucked the gun in the back of my shorts, flicking my T-shirt over to conceal it. I put the bag back, closed the lid, and turned in the direction of the Lucky 7evens.

Oh, and in case you were wondering, putting a gun down, the front or back, of your pants is not as glamorous as Hollywood makes it out to be. First of all, it's heavier than you think, and when walking, you feel like your pants will fall down, never mind the fear it may go off, with your private parts the first point of entry. And think about it, watching those movies or TV shows, when the guy placed the gun in his pants, how long do you actually see him walking for, huh? And running? Good luck. Also, the barrel is cold if you place it against your bare skin, especially if you are going commando. It's not as manly as you think with the cold barrel of the gun stuck in your crotch, or down the crack of your ass. And yes, now that you're curious, this morning, I was going commando.

The streets were quiet, joggers and an older couple in matching tracksuits walking hand in hand, the odd car passing by. The sun was starting to make an appearance, its orangey reflection on the windows of the taller buildings, bouncing off and fighting with the shadows that protruded along the sidewalks. It was my favourite time of day, except for today that is. If I was correct,

Tony would already be on the Rooftop, bellied up to the trough for his morning feeding.

I stopped outside of the entrance and thought for a moment about the best way to approach this. I quickly ran all the options through my head.

How much did he know? How much did *I* know? I sighed.

Fuck it. Time for the Pete Humphries Special.

What's that, you ask? What I did best. Winging it, and flying by the seat of my pants.

Taking the long stairway two steps at a time, I stepped outside on the rooftop patio, and since it was not as bright yet, my eyes quickly adjusted. Looking around, the place was empty except for a sole body seated at a picnic table, over in the far corner. It was eerily quiet, and I could hear the sound of slurping coming from behind the umbrella. I stood for a moment, then reaching around for my gun, I pulled it out of my shorts, and flicked the safety off. I hesitated, unsure of my next step—when the decision was made for me. A server came through the doorway, carrying a tray, and almost bumped into me.

"Oh, excuse me, sir. Sorry, I didn't see you. We're not open yet. We don't open until ten. If you can come back then, I will gladly seat you ... anywhere you like."

Ignoring her, I started toward the picnic table, the server trailing behind. "Hey! we're not open yet. If you can come back later—" then, noticing the gun, she backed away.

Tony, hearing the commotion, looked up and casually waved her off. Holding my gun at my side, I cautiously approached, moved around the giant umbrella until Tony came into view. Still eating, he looked up, grunted, ignoring the gun.

"Morning, Pistol. Just in time for breakfast. What'll you have?"

Standing over him, I hissed, "No, I'm good."

Tony smiled. "Aww, Pistol. It looks like you've lost your sense of humour. What's wrong?"

His eyes wandered over me, seeing the bruises on my face and the bandage on my leg.

"You look like shit. What happened? Run into something, or did your cute little girlfriend do that? Sit and take a load off. Coffee?"

I stood where I was, glaring down at Tony.

"Why?" I asked.

"Why what?" Tony said.

"You know what. Did you do it?"

"Do what?" Tony looked at me curiously.

Tired of playing cat and mouse, I stepped closer, holding the gun out with both hands, the barrel of the .45 pointed straight at Tony's forehead.

"I'll ask again. Why?"

"Aww, Pistol, settle down. Come on. You and I both know you aren't going to do anything. Not here. Not now. Not like this. This much I know about you. You need to be provoked, you and that honour bullshit. But this? Nope."

Tony resumed eating, ignoring the gun inches from his head. I was seething, fighting off the rage that threatened to overtake me.

"I heard someone got busted up bad last night," he said, looking up at me. "You wouldn't happen to know anything about that, would you?"

I cocked the hammer, the metallic click echoing across the roof, my finger now on the trigger.

"Why?" I demanded.

"Pete! PETE!"

I turned my head toward the sound, ignoring Syd, I turned back, staring down the barrel, straight at the spot between Tony's eyes.

"One ... last ... time ... why?"

"NO!" Syd screamed, "No ... mister, please."

Syd had me at mister, and grudgingly, I lowered my gun and backed away. She walked over, reached around, and pushed my hand and the gun against my side. She moved around in front of me, standing between Tony and me, and fighting back tears.

"I can't keep rescuing you. I can't. I can't do this ... not anymore. Please, can we just go? Please, Pete."

Looking into her pleading eyes, she was right, this was not for her. It wasn't for me either, but this was my doing. I nodded and, lifting my hand, uncocked the gun, slid the safety on, and slipped it back in my shorts.

"Rescued by a girl once again. Aww, ain't that sweet. Bawk! Bawk!" Tony crowed.

Syd whirled on him. "Fuck you, Tony."

I reached out, touched Syd on the shoulder.

"Come on let's go. You lead." Still glaring at Tony, Syd turned away and started walking toward the stairs.

Just as I got to the exit, Tony called after me.

"Talked to Leia lately?"

I froze in my tracks. Syd pulled my arm, and I followed behind zombie-like. By the time we got outside, I was somehow able to push away Leia, for now.

Standing on the sidewalk, in the same spot as the other day when we encountered Dale, Syd was trembling despite the warm sun. We stood, silent, trying to gather ourselves from what had just transpired. Syd broke the uneasy silence between us.

"I can't keep rescuing you, I can't. As much as I like the sex after, there's more than that, we're way more than that, anyone could see that. We could have so much, and I could so easily love you, and I know you would love me. But I can't keep doing this. I can't keep rescuing you."

Syd's eyes were filled with tears, and I knew she was right. I stood silent, not sure what to say.

"You're chasing something, or you're running from something, or maybe, it's a bit of both, I don't know. But we all are, in our own way. I know I am."

Syd paused, fighting off a wave of emotion, pushed her hair back from her face and wiped her eyes.

"I'm chasing too," she said, "so I know how exhausting all this is. I get so tired sometimes. But what I'm chasing is different, I'm chasing my dreams, to be a para-med and go back east. But baby, what you're chasing … I don't know, it's different somehow. It's not … it's not tangible, you know? Though, I've only known you a short time, you're this amazing guy, I can see that. There's so much good in you. But I know absolutely nothing about you, your hopes, your dreams, what you want. All I can see is you are troubled. And I get that because I'm troubled too. But it's different, and I can't explain it, but it's just different. And it's scary because I can't help you. I want to, I really wish I could."

Syd was right, the truth hurt, so what does one say?

"Looking at you here, right now, I know you know I'm right. I can see it in your eyes. And what I'm hoping with that, is you will understand and hopefully, find yourself from all this. Only you can stop this chasing, this running, no one else can. You can't keep running, keep hiding. You can't because, either it will catch you and kill you, or you will run for so long that when you stop, it will be too late then. You need to stop and face it, whatever it is. And unless you do, you'll never be more than this, and there's so much more that you can, and deserve to be."

Syd reached over and touched my face, stroking my cheek, her hand soft and warm, her touch heavenly.

I am so going to miss her, miss this.

My eyes filled with tears, but I remained silent. We stood looking at each other, two people who fit perfectly together.

It was another glorious day, the sun shining bright and hot, a gentle summer breeze that filled one with warmth and hope. Any other time, this would be a perfect moment to a perfect day, and off we would go, doing what ordinary happy people do—living a normal day. But it was not, and we both knew a normal day was not in the cards for us. At least not today, or anytime soon, and it was time to disconnect, here, now.

My head down, I kept my eyes averted. "Everything you said is true," I whispered, biting my lip. Syd looked at me with understanding eyes, as both of us were painfully aware this erotic, fun-filled connection was about to break, permanently. Tears started running down her cheeks.

"Another time, another place ..." I lamented softly.

She sniffled, running her fingers across my lips, and I fought back the lump building in my throat, and swallowed hard. I bit my lip again to fight off the wave of emotion that threatened to overwhelm me.

Life was all about timing. I didn't want to say goodbye—and was terrible at goodbyes in general—and looking at Syd was almost too much. Recognizing this, Syd rescued me one last time.

"Listen, mister," she said through her tears. "You take care of yourself, okay? And that tongue of yours ..." as she ran her fingers across my mouth, and sticking her finger inside, searching for my tongue. I gently kissed her finger.

"Who's gonna rescue me now, huh?"

"Well, I hope one day you do. That's the only rescuing you will ever need, mister."

"I'm going to miss you," I sniffled.

"I'm going to miss you too. No one sucks at pool like you do. That I won't miss, but I promise to always rescue you from that."

Syd managed a weak smile, stepped forward, and wrapped herself around me. I held on tight, not wanting to let go. Her head nestled under my chin, the smell of her hair intoxicating, we squeezed as much from each other as we could.

Knowing we had to let go, neither wanting to, we hugged each other tighter, prolonging the inevitable. Finally releasing, we stepped back, still holding each other hands and kissed one last time.

"Bye, mister," she whispered, turned and started down the sidewalk. She stopped, turned back, and walked toward me.

"I forgot to tell you. That friend of yours, Dale? When I saw him the other day, I recognized him, but I couldn't figure out from where. But now I remember. He's the one that was with this Sara. They would sit in the back corner together, always late at night. I could never get a good look at her, she was always wearing that bike helmet, or I could never see her up close. I never tried because I had no reason to. But then, when I saw Dale the other day, things started to click. I would see them leave together, she would get on her bike, and he would walk to his car. Not a police car of course, but a black BMW sedan, and they would head off in the same direction, and I swear they were going back to whoever's place. I hope this helps." She smiled and, waving bye, quickly turned away.

I nodded, and watched as Syd walked out of my life, my stomach twisted in a tight knot, and hoped I would never feel this way again. I wiped my eyes and crossed the street, making my way to the hotel and to checkout. Walking through the lobby, trying to hide my red eyes, I waved to Jackie and mouthed "checking out" and she nodded.

In the room, I gathered up my stuff, throwing my clothes haphazardly into my backpack, not caring that Jackie's nicely folded clean clothes were scrunched in with the dirty ones. I drained the water from my cooler over the side of the balcony, leaving a half-empty bottle of Jack and three beers for the next victims. Then throwing my bag over my shoulder and slinging my cooler on my hip, I opened the door and let it slam loudly behind me.

Back down in the lobby, Jackie was checking in another middle-aged couple and this time I let them be. I dropped my bag and cooler over by the window and stood looking out. I was numb, and could you blame me? Syd. And Tony's comment about Leia had sent shock waves through me, and I needed to get to Havelock to see for myself. I was afraid of what I might find and shuddered at the thought.

"Pete," Jackie called out, "I have your bill ready."

I shuffled over to Jackie, embarrassed by my appearance, but as usual, she was way ahead.

"It wasn't meant to be, that's all. Look at what you did for each other in that short of time, how much fun you both had, and don't think for a second that you didn't give something back to her, not for one second."

Dumbfounded, I asked, "How did you know?"

"I just did, that's all, especially that your room no longer smelled like a barn and that you weren't coming home at night." Sighing dramatically, she placed the back of her hand on her forehead, sighing and tilting her head back. "And I left a light on for you and everything."

I laughed, and it felt good. *Would I ever feel like that again?*

Jackie folded my bill and handed it across the counter. "Listen, you take care of yourself, Pete Humphries. I've enjoyed getting to know you, and I am so happy our paths crossed. Despite this morning, you are still going to be okay. Don't lose sight of that."

I nodded, thanked her for everything she had done for me, and told her that her laundry note was tucked safely in my wallet.

I walked over to the window and picked up my bag and cooler, and turning, I went to say goodbye, but Jackie was on the phone. I tried to catch her eye, but her head was down. I felt this warm sensation run through me as I walked outside, and with it a feeling that, in spite of everything, things were going to be okay.

33

TONY WAS RIGHT, I couldn't kill him, or anyone else, unprovoked, but if he had touched Leia? That was provocation enough for me. I zipped along Highway 7, trying to remain inconspicuous to the cops, at the same time zigzagging around the slower cars, pushing my Chevy hard on the straight stretches, constantly checking my rear-view mirror. The feeling of dread threatened to overwhelm me, and I tried to block out what I might find; Tony's ominous words echoed like sonic booms in my head.

Talked to Leia lately?

The Last Caboose parking lot was empty when I pulled in, and I started breathing rapidly, choking and coughing, almost hyperventilating, my stomach twisted in a tight knot. I parked near the steps to the front entrance. There wasn't a soul in sight. Fighting off the dread, I reached for my gun and got out, letting the driver's door close quietly. I sidestepped up the wooden steps and placed my back against the wall. Breathing heavily, chest pounding, I had to force myself to slow down. I slid along the red brick wall until I got to the big windows, and cautiously peered inside.

The dining room was empty, the tables and chairs overturned, and no sign of life. I brought my gun up and shuffled past the windows farther along the wall. At the entrance, I noticed the window panel on the door had been smashed and the door ajar. I looked behind me, but there was no one in sight. My hand shaking, I reached for the door handle, holding it, pushed the door open, the frame making a crunching sound from the shattered glass underneath. Cautiously, I stepped inside.

The bar was in shambles, its contents smashed, the tall bar stools lying on their sides, the beer taps ripped out of their moorings and lying in pieces on the floor. Stepping carefully over the debris, I moved past the bar and peered into the kitchen. The swinging doors had been ripped off their hinges and were lying on the floor. Feeling the panic rising in the back of my throat, I started hollering, "Leia! Jimmy? Leia? LEIA … JIMMEEE!"

Nothing, dead silence except the sound of dripping coming from behind the bar. Frantic, my gun raised, I tiptoed forward, stepping over the broken glass, walked in the kitchen calling out their names. The kitchen had been turned into a war zone: pots and pans, broken dishes everywhere, a large garbage can overturned, the stainless steel fridge doors open, the contents spilling out on the floor. I was beyond frantic, all I could think about was Leia.

Where was she?

My hands were shaking so badly I stopped for a moment. Leaning over, I took a deep breath, holding it in as long as I could, then exhaled loudly. Standing up, I breathed in again deeply and exhaled once more. I wiped my forehead. Fighting back the fear, I went back out into the bar. I stood listening, hoping, praying, when I heard a soft bang, and I started running toward the sound, the broken glass crunching loudly under my feet. My gun out, I tried to keep my hand steady, as I ran toward the dining room.

I looked down the hallway toward the two small his-and-hers washrooms and tip-toed toward them. Standing in front of the first door, I kicked open the door, but it was empty. I slid two steps to my right and kicked open the second door. Nothing. Fuck! Sweat was running down my forehead and into my eyes, causing me to blink rapidly. I slowly walked back into the dining room.

"Leia! Jimmy!"

I listened, then in a barely audible whisper, I heard "what." I turned toward the sound, and Leia was standing in the doorway, her .45 hanging limply at her side. I stared at her, frozen, thinking I was dreaming, too afraid to believe it was her. I remained motionless, staring at her.

"What?" she said, annoyed, staring back, her body trembling.

Hearing that wonderfully, annoying, monotone, I felt a wave of relief but remained glued to the floor. Leia, still trembling, shook her head.

"Good lord! You're still undecided. What am I going to do with you?"

The spell broken, I broke into a wide grin, walked over, and stood in front of her.

"You're okay? You're all right? Did anyone touch you?" I asked, my eyes running up and down her arms. Leia looked at me, eyes dark, full of fear, lifted her hand and showed me her .45.

"Why wouldn't I be? And no, no one touched me," she said, smiling weakly. Visibly relieved, I moved forward and wrapped my arms around her, pulling her into my chest, holding her tight. Her arms remained limply at her sides, I squeezed hard, running my arms across her back, trying to hug away every bad thing that had ever happened to her.

"You're smothering me."

"Sorry."

I let go and stood back.

"I didn't say stop holding me, I just said you were smothering me," she said, looking up, her eyes searching and connecting with mine. I leaned in again, taking her in my arms, a little more loosely this time. I hugged her, and closed my eyes, wishing we could be anywhere but here.

"Matching .45s. I should've known," as Jimmy's unmistakable voice interrupted our moment.

Leia gave me a gentle squeeze, I unhooked my arms and stepped back. I uncocked my .45, flicked the safety on, and tucked it in my shorts. Leia, her gun still in her hand cocked and ready, I motioned with my head towards her hand. "Leia, honey …"

Looking down, she smiled and did the same, tucking her .45 in the back of her jeans.

"You okay, Jimmy?" I asked, looking at Leia, my back turned to him.

"I'm okay. Been better, but I'm all right."

Jimmy rubbed the side of his face, his eye an ugly shade of green, his cheek red and swollen. Wrapped around his forearm was a white towel, stained red with blood. I suggested we clean the place up, and an hour later, the tables and chairs in the dining room area were upright, the broken ones stacked in the corner. We moved over to the bar side, and another hour later, things looked manageable: bar stools upright, the broken beer taps piled in the corner, the swinging doors placed on each side of the entrance to the kitchen like a memorial.

Jimmy leaned on the bar, Leia behind it, and she pulled a rabbit out of her apron, finding a glass that wasn't broken, poured me a beer from the only working tap.

"Here you go, just like I promised, Mr. Charming Indecision," she smiled as she placed it in front of me.

I downed the beer in one long gulp and plunked it back on the bar. Leia reached for it, but I shook my head no. Nodding, she leaned back against the wall. I turned to Jimmy.

"So, what happened? Tony do this?" I asked.

Jimmy looked suspiciously at Leia.

"Guys! Guys, I'm not the enemy here, I want to help," I pleaded, frustrated that my efforts were going unrewarded.

Leia nodded at Jimmy, but he ignored her.

"You work for Teddy, and Tony works for Teddy, so—"

"Oh shit! Yes and no. Yes, I'm working for Teddy, but no, I'm not on their side."

Jimmy was still looking at me warily.

"Look," I said, "would I have come busting in here just now if I was on their side? I mean, come on, guys." I was about ready to call it a day.

Jimmy looked over at Leia, who nodded toward me.

"Look Pete, I'm sorry. You have to understand I don't know who to trust right now. You seem different than the others. Leia said you were a good guy, she could tell right away, and she told me that you could be trusted."

I looked over at Leia who shrugged her shoulders. Jimmy continued, "I'm sorry, it was me who wasn't sure. And yes, I should have listened to her and trusted what she said, after all, she is my best employee."

"Your only employee," I winked at Leia, who stuck her tongue out at me. "So, what happened, Jimmy? I want to help if I can. I have a stake in this too."

Jimmy looked at me, still uncertain.

"Jesus Christ, Jimmy!" Leia, snapped.

"All right, all right. Well, after you left and they took the box, I called Teddy. I told him that I would get the box back, but honestly, I had no idea how. I was just scared, you know."

I nodded, understanding all about the scared part.

"Teddy seemed okay with that, leaving it to me to get it back. But then, a couple of days later, Tony showed up here, and he wasn't happy, going on about how I screwed Teddy over and took the twenty grand for myself. He wanted the money back, but I had already paid the cop in Peterborough. That was the original plan. The cop gets the box and drops it here. Teddy sends someone, you, with the twenty grand to pick it up. You give me the money, I give you the box, and you take it back to Teddy."

I started to connect the dots, the why to all of this beginning to take shape. I was Teddy's mule. Sighing at the realization, I looked at Leia. "Another beer, please."

Jimmy continued, "And now, Tony thinks I'm lying, and no amount of convincing would change it, so he started busting me up, and he only stopped because Leia came out of the kitchen holding her .45, pointing it straight between his eyes. He backed off then and left, and I thought that was that."

I looked over at Leia, who was pouring my beer, she looked back at me but remained expressionless.

"But what about all this? Who did all this then?" I asked, puzzled, looking around at the busted-up bar.

Jimmy looked at Leia and sighed. "Those bikers. The ones that jumped you and took the box. They came back. I heard this light tapping on the glass at the entrance. I thought it might be Tony again, or the morning delivery guy. But I had Leia grab her .45 and hide in the kitchen, while I went to have a look. I couldn't see anyone, so stupidly, I unlocked the door, and as soon as I turned the knob, they busted in, breaking the glass and grabbing my arm. A hand tried to pull my arm through, but I managed to break their grasp, but the door flew open, and in they came; that heavy biker chick and the tall redhead, along with their two companions. Leia came running out, her gun pointed at them, and they backed off. Then, that redhead did to Leia what she did to you that day. She managed to move off to the side, and when Leia wasn't looking, she threw her helmet, catching Leia in the shoulder. She jumped Leia, pinning her on the floor, and the other three started busting the place up. I tried to stop them, but the tall one got me pretty good."

I looked from Leia to Jimmy. "But you're both here, and you seem okay considering. Did they stop? What made them stop?"

"I guess they got tired of busting the place up and left. We are both still pretty rattled, though, as you can see."

"Do you think they'll come back?" I asked.

"I hope not, but I honestly don't know," Jimmy said, sounding fearful.

"When they left, did they give any indication about coming back? People like that usually leave a warning."

Jimmy waved his hand. "No, no … they left without saying a word. And that's why we are so scared because we don't know what's next, and when you came busting in, we thought it was them returning. When we heard your voice, we thought it might be a trap."

"How long ago did they leave?"

Jimmy looked over at Leia and shrugged his shoulders. "About an hour before you got here, I guess."

"Which way did they head? Did you see which direction?" I asked, perking up.

"Sure," said Leia, "they turned right out of the parking lot, heading east on 7, but from there, I wouldn't know. There are so many side roads off the highway, they could have turned anywhere, and you'd never find them."

I remembered what Alan, my giant biker friend, said about them travelling up and down the highway, which made me think they were staying relatively local.

"Maybe. Maybe not. I don't think they're far," I answered confidently, "I'll find them. How about a quick one for the road?"

Leia moved behind the bar and poured me another beer. Staring at her the whole time, I downed it in two long gulps, looking for the quick buzz and courage hit. I was going to need all I could get, as I knew if I found them, it would get messy. I plopped the mug down on the bar, and my stomach tightened at the thought.

Goodbye again, how many was that now?

Leia and I both knew we couldn't do another parking lot goodbye.

"Bye, Leia," I said. "Take care of yourself."

Leia returned my smile, and we disconnected just like that.

From behind, I heard Jimmy call out, "See you, Pete, take care."

I stepped over the remnants of broken glass and walked out. With a couple of quick strides, I leaped over the patio steps, landing with both feet on the pavement and broke into a run toward my Chevy.

Forward Pete … forward … keep moving forward.

34

THE PHONE BUZZED on the seat beside me. Teddy. Fuck! Just as I went to tap ignore, on a whim, I tapped connect instead.

"Hi, Teddy."

"How ya, pawdner!"

I shuddered at Teddy's fake Texas drawl.

"What have you been up to?" he asked. "You never return my calls."

"Oh, a little of this, a little of that, you know," I answered hesitantly.

"Where are you? It sounds like you're in a tunnel."

"Oh, just driving."

"Well, if you remember our last phone conversation, you should be on your way back now with my sister."

Shit! Sara. I forgot. Quick! Think Pete, think.

"Pawdner ... you still there?"

"Yeah, yeah, I'm still here. Just passing a semi, gimme a sec."

There wasn't a car in sight, but I revved the engine and sped up to make it sound like I was passing. I needed to buy myself time, even if it was only seconds, so I made what might be the longest fake passing of a semi in history.

"I'm still here, how many trucks are you passing? A convoy?"

"Almost there, big guy." I threw on my turn signal, hoping Teddy could hear the loud tinking. "Almost there ... one more semi, and I'm almost there ... hold on."

Nothing came to me. *Great.* Slowing, I flicked off my blinker and had no choice but to fall back on what I did best.

"Okay, I'm back. Whew! Four semis, that was a convoy all right, nice long stretch to pass. Now, where were we?"

"You were telling me you were on the way back with Sara. Can I speak to her?" Teddy asked, agitated.

"Uh, um, I would love to put her on Teddy, but uh, um, she's sleeping in the back seat."

"Sleeping? In all that racket?"

"What can I say? It seems your sister is quite the drinker and tied one on last night. I had to pour her in my car this morning, and she's been passed out ever since. Tell you what, I will have her call you the minute she surfaces. Sound good?" I replied, hoping he was as stupid as I hoped he was.

"What time should I expect you both?" Teddy asked, and no, he wasn't that stupid. Though, I understood his frustration, I didn't blame him, but I didn't care.

"Oh, a little after ten, I guess." A response we both knew was an outright lie.

"Okay, pawdner, see you then. And pawdner?"

"Yes, Teddy?"

"You wouldn't be trying to screw me over, would you?"

I purposely waited before answering, counting out—one steamboat, two steamboats, three steamboats.

"Who me? Not me Teddy. I mean, I'm your Pistol after all. I would never do anything like that, especially after all you've done for me. A promise is a promise, I said I would find your sister, and I did."

It was silent on the other end, and I sensed Teddy wondering what I was up to. That alone had to count for something. "See you in a few hours pawdner, bye," and I tapped disconnect before he had a chance to respond. As I drove along, I cursed out loud at what an idiot I was. How exactly was I going to get out of this one?

I scanned each side road, slowing enough to have a look, but there was nothing, no one in sight, and the panic started to rise. Looking at my watch, it was now after seven, and the sun was fading in my rear-view mirror.

Passing through a small town, I stopped at a fast-food joint, slowly cruising through the parking lot, but it was a wash. Back on the highway, thirty minutes later, I came upon a sign for another side road, I slowed and turned on it. It was a hilly gravel road, and I drove along for about ten minutes, but gave up, as it was nothing but trees and long grass; no farms or dwellings in sight. I turned around and when I got to the highway, I stopped. The road was empty, so I sat, drumming my fingers on the steering wheel, looking up and down the highway in both directions. I fought off the panic, slowed my breathing, and counted out loud to ten. My head started to clear.

Checking the road again, I pulled the tape out of the deck, reached behind for my eight-track case, flipped open the lid, closing my eyes, I played the game my dad and I would play on road trips—pick-surprise. I ran my finger along the tapes, tapping the plastic edges, and pulled one out, opening my eyes to *Dark Side of the Moon*. So apropos, exactly where I had been living. Holding the tape in my hand I looked up and down the highway.

Don't give up, wait, be patient, just wait.

A car whizzed by, then a couple of semis passed, in opposite directions, in front of me, the loud roar making the hood of my Chevy shake. It was quiet again, and I could hear crowing off in the distance. It was such a peaceful summer night, and I could picture sitting on the front porch as the sun set. Feeling better about things, even though nothing had changed, I heard an unmistakable roar to my right. Turning, two Harleys were coming toward me, and I watched as they passed by. The bikers! Red on the back of the bike closest to me, the biker mama and her trusty sidekick parallel to her.

"Yahoo!" I yelled out, tossing the tape in the back seat. I waited, checked for oncoming traffic, then pulled onto the highway and followed them. I quickly closed the gap, then held back enough to keep them in view. *Ha! I knew it!*

I followed the bikers, riding in tandem, blissfully unaware I was behind them. I had no clue what I would do, so I kept a safe distance, and let things unfold. We passed through another small town, and about twenty minutes later, the bikes slowed and turned. Following, I did the same, but the road immediately twisted snake-like, there was a steep incline, and the bikes had disappeared. I gunned it up the hill, coming across the top, the road stretched out, but there was nothing but pavement.

"Shit! Shit! Fuck!"

Moving down the hill, the road twisted again, and my instinct was to look left, and as I did, there was a farmhouse sitting back in the trees, the bikes parked out front. Not wanting to attract attention, I drove farther up the road, killing the lights, pulled a U-turn and parked on the shoulder. I shut off the engine and took stock.

Dusk was quickly changing into night, everything was perfectly still, only the sounds of crickets and frogs croaking. I looked up through the tree canopy and could make out a full moon, which was going to be both a blessing and a curse. Grabbing my gun and jean jacket off the seat, I slid cautiously out of my Chevy and silently closed the door. I looked around, listening, my heart beating rapidly, but it was just me and my pals, the crickets, and frogs. I slipped on my jacket and tucked my .45 in the back of my shorts, started along the shoulder toward the farmhouse. Hunched down, I stopped and looked behind me every few seconds.

The bushes rustled to my left, startled, I dropped, reaching behind for my gun and turned toward the sound, but it stopped as soon as I turned. I slipped my gun back in my shorts and noticed my hand was shaking. Up ahead, I could see a clearing and the entrance to the farmhouse. Hunched over, I cautiously approached the clearing, and stopped beside some thick brush along the shoulder. Crouching down, I peered through it, there was a long gravel driveway that led down a hill to the farmhouse. There was a greyish barn-like shed on the left and in front was a gravel clearing where the bikes were parked.

The two male bikers were moving around the bikes, covering them up with tarps. Lights were on in the farmhouse and through the curtainless windows, I could see Red and the biker mama moving about. The bikers finished covering the bikes and went inside, then a light came on in one of the upstairs windows. I made a quick check of my surroundings, turning my head in every direction, nothing but forest, the farmhouse being the only dwelling of any kind.

Alan was right, staying near the highway made the bikers less conspicuous, easy-on, easy-off access, the farmhouse tucked back from the road. If I hadn't driven by when I did, I would have never found them. I looked up at the sky full of twinkling stars and mouthed a silent 'thank you.'

In the large front window of the farmhouse, I could make out a table and a kitchen in the background. Red and the biker mama were moving around the table, setting it, and a male biker was standing behind them. The light turned off in the upstairs window, and a few seconds later, the taller male biker passed through the dining area.

All present and accounted for.

Red came into view, carrying something and placed it on the table. I did a double-take, shaking my head and rubbing my eyes. No way! The box! That fucking box! I started to let out a whoop and slammed my hand against my mouth just in time. I looked skyward again, thanking those lucky stars for the second time tonight. Two birds with one stone was the next thing that came to mind. Looking down at the bikes, parked under their protective tarps, I had an idea, as piled along the side of the shed were several red gas cans.

Really? This easy?

There was only one way to find out.

"BEEP! BEEP!" The sound of the horn made me jump in fright, and I almost fell into the road and under the wheels of the vehicle that came out of nowhere. The headlights blinding me, my eyes filled with tiny black dots, I managed to pull myself back in time as a black pickup roared past, spraying me with gravel, red taillights flying over the crest of the hill toward the highway. My heart pounding, I swiped away the gravel from my face and hair, and looked toward the farmhouse, expecting to hear voices and the bikers come running out at any moment. But there was nothing, the cricket and frog symphony picking up where it left off.

I lay back in the grass, my chest on fire, and took a moment to gather myself. Then I leaned over on my side and looked down at the farmhouse. The window was partially blocked now by the box, and the four were seated around the table eating. I stood up, hunched over, moved slowly, the gravel crunching beneath my feet, and worked my way toward the tree line on the other side of the driveway, scampering the last few yards through the tall grass to the other side. I stopped, crouched down, and listened for a minute. I high stepped my way along the treeline, guided by the light of the moon, until I reached the side of the shed. I peeked through the narrow opening of the barnboard slats, and I could make out a tractor and a trailer parked side by side. I tiptoed along the outside wall, reached the gas cans, lifted each one, and gave them a quick shake. I looked skyward once more and thanked each and every one of those lucky stars for the hat trick they had bestowed upon me, promising I would never shake my fist, or curse them out loud, ever again.

I cautiously moved to the front of the shed and tried the door, but it was padlocked. I had a clear view of the farmhouse; there was a small three-step porch leading up to a screen door with a heavier inside door open behind it. The lights from inside streamed out the screen door and onto the gravel, I shifted a bit, trying to get a better look inside when suddenly, a dark figure appeared in the doorway. The figure stopped at the door, their back to me, speaking to someone inside. I looked left and right only to find I was stuck in the middle of the shed; any sudden movement would give me away. I stood, frozen, like when you were kids playing freeze-tag, not moving a muscle, I couldn't even pinch myself. Lifting my eyes skyward, I tried to reach my lucky stars telepathically.

Fellas, anyone there?

Remember when I said about time standing still and everything slowing down? Well, this time, it was at a dead stop—my back up against the shed, hands at my sides, even my gun was out of reach. I bit my lip to keep my breathing as shallow as possible. The dark figure still had their back to me, and they were leaning on the screen door now. I pressed tighter against the shed, hoping it would open and swallow me whole, just like in the movies. I was afraid to move; even the rustling of my jean jacket against the barnboard could give me away. My heart was pounding, sweat forming on my brow, and a bead dropped down into my eye. I tried to blink it away but only managed to make it worse.

The figure was still standing with their back to the screen, and through my sweaty, blinking eyes, I could make out that it was Red. She started to push harder on the door with her hip, and slowly pushed it open, her body turning towards the outside. I could hear her speaking, then she stopped, half-in, half-out the door. I couldn't make out what she was saying or who she was talking to, only that the conversation was animated, and she wasn't happy. My heart was pounding so hard, I swear my jean jacket was pulsating in time. I remained frozen against the shed door, and I thought about trying to make a run for it, but then what? I get away but lose any element of surprise, and they would just catch me again, this time no Leia and her trusty .45 to bail me out. All I could do was wait. I looked skyward again.

Red pushed the door open a little farther, more out than in now. If she shifted her gaze to her right, we could make eye contact, the one and truly only time in my life when I didn't want any part of eye contact. I telepathically texted an SOS to the universe to see if anyone was free and could create a distraction. Abruptly, Red walked inside and slammed the heavy inside door shut behind her. I glanced up at the sky, but I remained firmly glued to the shed door just in case. I waited for a bit, then slid myself along the front of the shed and back around the side where the gas cans were.

I still needed something to light the gas with, so I retraced my steps to the back of the shed. Looking around, I saw the remnants of a gas BBQ. I walked over, and on the metal shelf was one of those cheap plastic lighters. I shook it a few times but didn't feel any fluid. Leaning over and holding the lighter against my leg, I gave the trigger a couple of quick presses, and on the fourth attempt, I got a spark. One more click and I had a flame. Perfect. I had everything I needed for a bonfire, all except the marshmallows, of course.

I walked back to where the gas cans were piled, screwed off the top of the first can, looking over at the parked bikes, I felt a brief tinge of sadness—such a waste of gas. I moved over and gently pulled the tarps back, poured the gas over the bikes, trying to avoid any splashing sounds. I finished emptying the can and quickly went back and retrieved the second one. Two more cans later, the bikes had been thoroughly doused in gasoline.

With the last can, I created a small trail of gas leading away from the bikes back to the shed. Crouching down, I pulled out the lighter, and just as I went to press the trigger, it dawned on me.

I needed to get that box.

The box was on the table by the large window in the dining room. Running into the house was too risky, but what if I worked my way around behind the farmhouse and came out the other side? I could break the window, reach in and take it. That could work, as the bikers would be focused on the bikes and not me.

Suddenly, the heavy wooden inside door opened, and the porch light came on.

SHIT! I thought. *They'll smell the gas.*

I crouched lower and waited. Maybe, they just wanted air? The problem was, they would smell the gas in no time, so it was now or never, and I was going to have to trust that I could get to the other side unseen, and get the box through the window.

Taking one last look at the farmhouse and a quick check of my exit plan, I pressed the trigger. Nothing, no spark, nothing. I pressed the trigger again, nothing. Looking up at the front door, terrified someone was going to notice, I looked down and pressed the trigger again—click, click.

Looking skyward: *fellas, can you help me here? One last time ... promise.*

I clicked again, and this time a pretty blue flame appeared. Shielding it with my hand, I bent down, placed it against the gas trail on the gravel, and swung the flame back and forth. A spark, but then it went out, and I realized, I was going to have to light the bikes directly. On all fours, I crawled over to the nearest bike. The smell of the gas was overpowering.

How have they not smelled this yet?

I pressed the trigger again, but nothing. Seriously? I kept looking up at the front doorway, my hands shaking as I pressed the trigger once more. Nothing. I had no choice now and I start pressing the trigger rapidly until there were sparks then finally a blue flame. This time not waiting, shielding the flame, I tossed it under the bike, and it instantly connected.

Flames started immediately, and I was surprised at how quickly I could feel the heat. I jumped, turning my back, and there was a loud 'BANG!' and I was thrown forward. I landed hard on my stomach, but got up quickly, dazed, I stumbled to the side of the shed and waited. I could smell the gas, and the shadows on the trees were dancing in the moonlight, already smoke mixing with the flames, swirling up into the night sky.

Two smaller bangs, followed by another loud bang, and the second bike caught fire. Both bikes were engulfed in flames now, the smoke rising past the tree line and the haze blocking the moonlight. I could hear voices coming from the entrance, and there was a bright flash and more loud bangs, as the screen door squeaked open. I could see dark figures running outside, their voices indistinguishable, yelling, cursing, barking instructions.

I ducked back and ran down the side of the shed, then into the back field, crouching down, I ran along the tree line that wound along the back of the property. I moved to my left, keeping the farmhouse in sight, and worked my way to the far side. The smoke blocking the moon made it difficult to see, and I could hear the bangs, loud voices, and cursing; all the while, the smoke got thicker. The shooting flames were creating eerie shadow puppet-like figures in the trees above, colliding with the smoke, turning everything greyish-white.

I had lucked out, the land around the back of the farmhouse had been cleared, only tall grass and short bushes remained. Getting to the other side of the farmhouse, I quickly moved alongside the large front window. I looked inside, and there amongst the bowls and plates of food was the box. So near yet so far, as the window was sealed shut. Banging on the window with my fist, the glass was too thick, and if I really wanted that box, I was going to have to go inside to retrieve it. Pissed, I retraced my steps back behind the farmhouse, cautiously peeked around the corner, and watched the bikers losing their battle with the now raging fire.

Taking a deep breath, I leapt onto the porch and darted straight through the open doorway. Electric shocks ran up and down my spine as I hurried down the hall and into the dining room. In one motion, I grabbed the box off the table, turned around, and started running back towards the entrance, following the glow of the flames outside. Holding the box out in front of me, I burst out the door, head down, I ran off the porch, stumbling and regaining my balance, towards the safety of the back of the farmhouse. I turned the corner and stopped, leaning against the frame, my chest heaving. Breathing heavily, I listened, but all I could hear was the sound of the bikes burning.

Shifting the box to my hip, I broke into a run across the open field and into the forest about twenty yards away. I stopped and crouching down, looked back. Nothing. I looked up at the sky, the moon covered by the smoke, but I could see well enough. I moved through the trees, looking for a path, coming across one, it wound up a hill on an angle towards the road. I followed the path, stumbling in the darkness. A few minutes later, I came to a clearing at the edge of the trees, and I could see the road. I gingerly worked my way down the embankment, and just like that, I was out on the road. To my left was my beloved Chevy, still parked where I left it. I turned and looked back at the orange glow of the sky, the smoke swirling around the tops of the trees. There were a couple of loud pops, I ducked from instinct, and I could hear muffled voices. Looking at the box, I broke into a grin.

I jumped in the front seat, plopping the box beside me, and curiosity winning handily, quickly peeled back the tape, lifted the lid and looked inside. All it contained was a bunch of file folders filled with papers.

That's it? I just went through all that for this?

I started the car and pulled out slowly, coasting down the road, as I got to the clearing, I slowed, then stopped, and looked over at the farmhouse. Both bikes were ablaze, smoke billowing high up into the sky, I could make out the two male bikers, racing around, trying to put out the flames with small hand extinguishers, but it was too little too late. The biker mama was standing off to one side barking instructions, and I could see Red come running out the door with another hand extinguisher. I shuddered at the thought of how close our paths came to crossing again.

I smiled to myself, this was worthy of a front row seat, even if they did see me. I got out, moved around to the passenger side, and leaned against the door, legs crossed, arms folded across my chest, smiling like a Cheshire cat. I looked back inside at the box on the front seat and smiled. There was a loud bang and I flinched, as the bikes exploded into pieces, creating a huge fireball, sparks and flame shooting high in the sky, orangey cinders sparking and swirling up into the trees.

The two male bikers stood farther back, shoulders slumped in defeat, the biker mama behind them, shielding her face and still bellowing. Then, I spotted Red.

Thrown to the ground by the force of the blast, she was sitting on her hip. Her hand came up and she brushed her hair away from her face. She appeared dazed, shaking her head, she looked up. Our eyes met, leaning back against my Chevy, I nodded, "So we meet again, huh?"

Red nodded in agreement, I reached inside the window and pulled out the box, holding it up for her to see. I smiled and nodded once more. Red, wiped at her forehead and pushing her hair back, nodded once. We stared at each other for the longest time, then I pushed the box back inside and walked around to the driver's door. I stood, looking over the roof, taking one last look down at the burning bikes, and Red—who was still on the gravel. I got in, slamming up on the gearshift; I let the clutch out and roared off, gravel and stones flying, tires squealing, the bright oranges and yellows filling my rearview mirror.

The sky aglow behind me, I barrelled along the highway as two fire trucks, their flashing lights long preceding their appearance, blazed past in the opposite direction, shortly followed by the flashing lights of an ambulance and an

OPP cruiser. Not concerned about my speed, I came flying over a hill, and on my left were the bright lights of Carlos General Store. I braked sharply, skidding and sliding, pulled a U-turn and entered the parking lot, bouncing roughly over the curb. Parking, I got out of my Chevy and looked up at the burnt orange glow in the distance.

Neat! I did all that.

I reached inside for my phone and dialed Teddy. After numerous rings, I was about to disconnect, when Teddy answered.

"Yup."

"Hey, Teddy, it's your pawdner, Pistol."

"Where are you?" he growled.

"Listen, about that, there's been a change in plans."

Nothing but dead silence on the other end.

"Don't you want to know what they are?" I asked. "Not even a little bit curious?"

Still dead silence.

"Teddy? Teddy? You there?"

"Yes, I'm here." Another long pause. "What are your plans? You better have my sister."

"Oh that, yeah, well, um … that's part of the change in plans, see? When I stopped for gas, Sara was still asleep in the back seat, and by the time I paid and came back, she was gone. She just up and left. Maybe, she hopped on the Greyhound, and who knows where she's headed now?"

There was another long pause.

"Teddy? You still there?"

"Yes."

"Good. I'm not so sure I would be, losing my sister and all again. Just when you thought you found her too. You're a better man than me, that's for sure."

"Fuck you, Humphries! You're a dead man!"

"I *thought* that's what you'd say." Proving I had not gotten enough of starting fires tonight. "Okay, do you want to hear the rest of the change in plans? Might be of interest to you *before* you kill me."

I could hear Teddy breathing through the phone.

"Teddy? Come on, play with me. Just like in the sandbox, remember?"

"You are so fucking dead! I am personally going to rip you apart. I am going to cut your cock off and stuff it down your throat and watch you gag on it. I am going to—"

"I have the box," I interrupted.

"What?"

"You heard me. I have the box."

"How?"

"It doesn't matter how, but I have it. It's sitting right beside me, all pretty and brown. Never seen a nicer banker's box in all my life. So sturdy, yet so fragile, all at the same time, you know? And the stuff inside, wow! All those papers with neat handwriting. They mean something all right. Going to be some great bedtime reading tonight, that's for sure. Lots and lots of fairy tales, or is it, nursery rhymes? Happy endings? Or more like dead men tell no tales? And I'm guessing even more important than your sister, huh?"

"What do you want?"

Hmm, I hadn't thought of that.

"I need some time for that, and maybe reading through all these papers will give me the answer."

"How much?"

"How much what?"

"How much money do you want for the box?"

"Ha! I thought so! This box is important. Teddy, Teddy, tsk, tsk, I would have thought blood was thicker than water, to you of all people. Tsk, tsk."

"You're an asshole. A dead asshole at that."

"Takes one to know one, and maybe next time you will choose your mules more carefully, huh? I really didn't take kindly to that."

"Fine. Now what?"

"I will be in touch. A burner phone will be arriving at Sharkees with your name on it. So, Teddy? Are we good?"

"Yeah, we're good."

"That's my boy. Oh, and Teddy, one last thing." I paused again.

"Yes."

"That sister of yours, she fucks like a mink," I said and quickly tapped disconnect.

Well, that was easy. Now, where to?

I jumped inside and drummed my hands on the steering wheel. Then, it hit me. Timmins. My dad's favourite hockey player was from there and he used to go on about him all the time. He promised me we would take a road trip there one day, but that one day never came.

I miss you, Dad. And now, in a way, that one day was here. *Timmins, why not?*

I turned the key, and a soothing rumble of the engine responded. I slapped in Frampton Comes Alive and turned the volume on the tape deck up, way past eleven.

35

FUCK!

The roar of the semi made me jump back in fright, the wind buffeting me against the concrete barrier. I knew I was up in the north because, even though it was summer, I was freezing, standing on the side of the highway, in shorts and a jean jacket. Dawn was breaking on the horizon, the sun still sleeping, and I was hoping its alarm clock would go off soon. And it didn't help that the only sleep I had in the past forty-eight hours, was the two-hour catnap in the back seat at some weigh station around 4:00 a.m. Shivering on the side of the highway, stranded on some nondescript concrete bridge, I looked over at the sign:

The Frederick House River Bridge

I wondered, if he was someone important, like maybe he built a railroad or discovered gold? Perhaps he was a famous hockey player. *Wonder what number he wore?*

I looked back at my Chevy, stopped dead on the side of the bridge, hood up, naked, defenceless. I rubbed my hands on the front of my shorts then did a couple of quick jumping jacks to get my blood circulating again. Another semi roared past, I jumped as the driver hit the horn, probably because he could. I shuddered and shivered and felt like I had been turned inside out. I walked back along the concrete barrier and stopped at the passenger window and looked inside, on the seat was the banker's box.

I forced myself to return to the task at hand—changing the spark plugs. I popped the trunk and rummaged around inside for something warm. *What were you thinking, Pete? A three-hour tour?* Sighing, buttoning my jean jacket up under my chin, I pulled out the metal toolbox, and moved to the front of my Chevy. I wasn't paying attention and walked on the highway side, when a green and white flash went whizzing past, I jumped back heart pounding.

"Fuck! Watch it, asshole!" I yelled, my futile response dying in the wind twenty feet later. I saw the bike slow, the rider shift and flash me the finger. Shrugging it off, I checked for traffic, then quickly shuffled to the front of my Chevy. I placed the toolbox on the ground, opened it, located the spark plug wrench and, leaning over the front fender, on the passenger side, started ratcheting.

The clicking sound was soothing. Loosening the plug, I started on the next one. I was lost in thought when I heard a voice.

"Hey!"

I jerked up, banging my head on the hood, dropping the wrench. A dull clunk as it hit the pavement under the engine. Seeing stars, I cursed and reached for the top of my head, hunched over, I gingerly backed out from under the hood, rubbing the top of my head, I stood up, checking my hand for blood.

Someone was standing in front of me wearing a lime green and black leather jacket, matching helmet, the visor flipped up. Underneath, I could see a pair of eyes. The muffled voice was barely audible.

"Hey, sorry, I didn't mean to scare you, but it looked like you need some help."

Rubbing my head, annoyed at being surprised along with being told I needed help, I glared at the leather-clad figure.

"No, I'm good. I always stop on the side of the highway, at the break of dawn, to change my spark plugs. Doesn't everyone?"

"Are you sure? Good thing I stopped because it looked like you needed help."

"And what? Giving me the finger is the universal signal for help?"

"Er, yeah, sorry."

"Brat," I muttered.

"Huh? Did you say something?" she asked, just as another transport went roaring past, shaking the bridge, the breeze blasting us, and we instinctively stepped towards the safety of the concrete barrier.

She reached under her helmet and flicked open the strap, twisting her head, pulling her helmet off. She shook her head quickly and ran her gloved hand over the top of her forehead, pushing her hair away from her face. Another quick shake, she flipped the helmet onto her hip, balancing it under her arm. She pulled off the black leather riding gloves and folded them together in her hand. I tried not to stare.

She was tall, maybe five seven, and lean with long dirty blonde hair and a dimple in her left cheek—her face more squarish than round. She had dark green eyes that shone full of life. She stood packaged together on long legs, her hips cocked in an attitude of self-assuredness.

I, meanwhile, was shivering in my shorts with tweety birds circling around my head.

"So, are you *sure* you don't need my help?" she asked, mischievously.

Our eyes locked, the clicking sound so loud, I'm sure it was heard over in the next county.

"Well, you could just stand here, hold the spark plugs, and hand them to me when I ask, but I think that's a little below your pay grade."

"Only if you're not doing it right," she said with a grin—turning me inwardly, and outwardly, into a powerless puddle of love, lust, and mush. "Well, I will leave you to it then, and I will have to trust this isn't your first time holding a spark plug wrench."

I bent down, crawled under the hood, retrieved the wrench and was back up in a jiffy, wiping the wrench on my shorts. "My wrench and I are joined at the hip much like you and your helmet there. We're so close I sleep with mine. You?" I flirted.

"Replaced by a wrench, who knew? Whatever floats your Chevy, I guess."

"Yeah, my wrench is perfect. It never argues, doesn't give me grief when I stay out late or when I drink too much. It just does what it's told."

"Yes, I can see the two of you make a lovely couple. Well, I will be on my way as you and your wrench appear to have things well in hand. I don't want to hold the two of you up any longer."

Our eyes remain locked, me with a goofy grin, and her, wearing a bright smile. She tucked her gloves under her arm and started to put on her helmet.

"Hey, um," I said trying to hold her up a bit, "do you know any place around here to get something to eat or where to stay?"

"I thought as much," she said. "You don't look from around here, you're certainly not dressed for the part, that's for sure."

She looked at my bare legs and could see I was shivering in my buttoned-to-the-chin jean jacket. I looked down at my front. *Just who buttons jean jackets anyways?*

"Sorry," she said, "I'm not really from around here either, so I can't help you." She pointed down the highway past the bridge. "But I'm sure there's something up ahead."

"Okay, thanks," I said, unable to hide my disappointment.

We stood, silent, but it wasn't one of those uncomfortable silences, and it was easy to see that there was that instant, and hopefully not fatal, attraction. Neither of us was sure what to say next, maybe not wanting to break the moment, but just then another semi roared past, the pavement shaking under our feet, the decision made for us.

"I better be going, and you better get off this bridge because I don't think even your wrench could save you."

Nodding reluctantly, I moved around to the fender and leaned over. "Bye, nice meeting you," I said, trying hard to hide my disappointment, and not waiting for a response. I started ratcheting again. When I heard the sound of her bike starting, a quick rev of the throttle, I looked up and watched, as she spun the bike around with a loud squeal and took off down the bridge.

Thirty minutes later, after changing the plugs, I was back on the road cruising through South Porcupine, wondering if I missed the turn for Timmins. Up ahead, there was a billboard with Bill Barilko's picture on it, and I recall my dad telling me the story about him scoring the cup-winning goal then disappearing later that summer on a fishing trip; his body not being found until ten years later, and coincidently, the same year Leafs won their next cup. Strange stuff. Bob Nevin's from here too, my dad's favourite player. But wait for it, not with the Leafs or Rangers but when he was with the LA Kings. The Kings? Go figure. And I guess it explains my dad—purple and gold uniforms and eight-tracks.

I rolled through South Porcupine, and was back on the highway again, a nice long stretch, and just for fun, I punched my Chevy. When I hit 110 miles an hour, I backed off and let it wind down, as I rolled around a bend to find I was entering Schumacher.

Where was Timmins?

I did a double-take in my rear-view mirror, then noticed a red brick building with its arena-style sloped roof on my right, the Timmins Rock logo on the brick wall. The streets were still sleepy as the sun poked its way through last night's leftover clouds, and I rolled past a typical strip of fast-food joints, cheap motels, and pawn shops.

Home away from home.

I passed under a rail bridge, and cresting over a hill, I could see in the distance a distinguished-looking building, approximately seven stories, and above it a fancy sign in bright red and black block letters. AMBASSADOR. I knew right away I had found my next home. Slowing, as I drove past, there was a parking garage under the sign. At the light, I turned left, another quick left in the entrance, I parked, taking my keys and not waiting for the valet to come running out.

I was stiff and sore from the all-night drive and took a minute to stretch out the kinks. Glancing around, I could see all the amenities I needed within walking distance—gas station, convenience store, pizza place, and a do-it-yourself car wash. Smiling at my luck, I went inside to find the lobby was deserted, except for a tiny figure behind the front check-in counter. I ambled over and, when I looked down, she was staring at a screen typing quickly.

"Just a sec," she responded without looking up.

I stepped back and waited, turning around, and taking in the lobby. In the corner near the entrance, was a small walk-in convenience cubby hole, a cooler for drinks and one for ice cream and frozen snacks, along with a matching pair of slanted trays filled with nothing but late-night calories. There were a couple of black faux leather couches and matching coffee tables along the walls, unread magazines and newspapers strategically scattered across them.

"Yes, can I help you?"

I turned, I know I heard a voice, but I didn't see anyone. Then I heard the voice again.

"Yes, can I help you?"

"Hello?"

"Yes, I'm here. Can I help you?" But all I heard was the voice. Then, I saw the top of her head over the counter, and I moved closer and leaned over. I was met by two giant eyes behind bicycle wheel size glasses, and we both jerked back in surprise.

"Oh, sorry, sir." She pushed her glasses back on her face, the huge eyes behind them blinking at me. Her head and body, which were attached to them, were at least two sizes too small.

"No, excuse me, sorry," I stammered.

"No, it's okay. It always happens. Sorry about that."

I stepped back, and on my tiptoes, leaned forward, trying to see her safely from a distance. I checked the name tag on her jacket. Rebecca. Good lord, her name was longer than she was tall.

"Yes, I'm looking for a room."

"Do you have a reservation?"

"No, sorry, I don't."

"That's okay, I think I have one for you," she replied cheerfully.

"Great." I let out a sigh of weary relief thinking of a hot shower and freshly made bed.

Rebecca typed away on her keyboard, and in mid-stroke, her hand flashed out, and without looking up, "Credit card, please."

I handed her my card, and she scanned it with her giant eyes.

"Just a few moments more, Mr ... Mr. Humphries. Now how many nights will you be staying with us?"

I hadn't thought that far ahead.

"That's a good question. How about three nights, and we go from there? Does that work?"

"Yes, it does, Mr. Humphries. We have plenty of rooms, which is strange for this time of year, as usually we are booked full. Your lucky day."

She looked up, smiling like a game show host. I waited, as she finished up, rocking back and forth on my heels, staring out the window. A large truck roared by, with the glass on the hotel windows rattling and the floor trembling under my feet. Jumping in fright, I turned toward the counter.

"You uh, have any rooms away from that?" I gestured at the window.

"Away from what?" she asked, looking up from her screen. "Oh, silly me.

I'm so used to them, I don't even notice them anymore. Sure, I can place you somewhere quiet away from the street and out back."

Finished, she stood up—she was scarcely taller standing up—and handed me an envelope containing the room key along with a breakfast voucher. She leaned forward and pitched her voice low.

"I shouldn't be saying this, but the best place to eat is the diner just behind the hotel. It's on the corner, can't miss it. All the locals eat there. I have to give you the vouchers, it's my job, but if you care about your stomach ..." she winked, as she patted hers.

"Duly noted, ma'am," I said and gave her a smile.

"The elevator's just around the corner," she said, pointing over my shoulder. "If you park on the second level near the stairs, your vehicle will be perfectly safe. You can get to the diner from the parking lot. Walk down the ramp to the street, turn right, and it's the next block over."

"Duly noted again, Rebecca." I gave her a salute. "My Chevy thanks you, and no doubt my stomach will too."

"You're welcome, Mr. Humphries." She pushed her glasses back and sat down, disappearing from view, and I could hear pecking on the keyboard.

I went outside and was met by the roar of another large hauler, the ground shaking, the glass on the hotel windows vibrating and rattling. Flinching, I expected the glass to break and come falling out. There was another roar and the sound of engine brakes, a tandem trailer filled to the brim with large boulders, came to a sudden stop at the light.

So, this is Timmins. Now I know why Dad never brought me here.

I drove around to the back of the hotel to the parking garage entrance and parked on the second level by the stairs, as Rebecca recommended. Mine was the only car on the level, and I wasn't sure if that was a good or bad thing. Locking it and giving it a gentle tap on the hood, I took the elevator to the seventh floor and easily found my room. Entering, throwing my backpack on the bed, and pulling open the curtains, I was met with a killer view of the roof, eye-level with a tangle of oversized a/c ducts scattered across the roof. Rebecca was right, it was quiet. Two men were standing near the ledge, at the far end of the roof carrying walkie-talkies. I couldn't tell if they were jumpers or talking someone off the ledge, I wouldn't blame them either way. Jaded already.

I stepped away from the window, letting the curtains fall shut, and prepared myself for a swan dive onto the bed, ready to sleep for the entire duration of my stay, but then my stomach growled, and thinking death was better on a full stomach, I rummaged through my bag for a change of clothes. Five minutes later, after double-checking on my Chevy, I was walking along the street behind the hotel, the diner up ahead.

The street was full of pickup trucks, and I debated going in, but my stomach—probably aware of my uncertainty—decided for me. I crossed the street and went in, struck by how comforting the diner felt. It reminded me of Sharkees and my first time there. The front cash was on my left, straight ahead was the kitchen, its swinging doors reminding me of Leia. My stomach tightened but I quickly pushed the thought away.

Like Sharkees, the diner was larger than it appeared from the outside. There were booths lining the walls in a large rectangle, with two rows of tables down the middle. It was busy, and I could feel the hustle and bustle. I was forced to stand to one side, as the kitchen doors swung open, and out came one of the servers. She was carrying a large tray filled with plates, the steam rising as she brushed past.

"Make way! Excuse me, plates are hot."

Another server came out, right on her heels, balancing a tray on each arm. I jumped back against the counter and scrunched up, trying not to get stampeded.

"Sit anywhere you like, honey," the second server called out. "Someone will be right with you."

As she blew past with the trays, one of them almost clipped my nose. I reached for a newspaper, tucked it under my arm, and made my way down the aisle, looking for an empty table. The restaurant was packed, filled with all shapes and sizes that meant only one thing—locals. I spotted an empty booth in the corner, gingerly stepped between a table trying not to bother the seated patrons and took a seat with my back to the wall.

Old habits are hard to break.

I flipped open the newspaper, and started reading up on the local gossip.

"Hello, good morning! My name is Mandy, and I will be your server. Coffee?"

I reached for my cup and held it out. As she filled it, Mandy handed me a flimsy one-page menu.

"Trust me," she said as though reading my mind. "It's all you need. Have a look, and I will be right back."

I scanned the menu, giving both sides a quick once over, and returned to the newspaper. I didn't hear Mandy return, so caught up was I in a story about a local man caught stealing fish from someone's garage freezer.

"So, what will it be?" she asked.

"So many choices," I sighed, flipping the menu over, "so little time, and these prices!" I teased.

"Ha, I'm with you. But wait until you see the portions."

I looked at the menu again, flipping it over and back. "Mandy, I think I need your help."

"Hmm, let's see …" She leaned to one side and looked up and down my legs. "I think you're a number four kind of guy."

"I've never been a number four before," I said, flirting out of reflex. "Will I like it?"

"Oh definitely, and you will probably come back for seconds." She smiled and wrote down '#4' on her pad. She reached over, her top falling open, and lingered longer than necessary, picking up the menu from the table.

No harm, no foul, I thought, as she walked up the aisle, and I returned to my paper. Tired of the fish tale, I couldn't concentrate and put the paper down.

I spotted a family across from me, a hubby, wife, and their 2.5 kids. I looked under the table to see if the family dog was there. It wasn't. Over in the opposite corner, by the window near the entrance, there were four old guys, probably retired miners, who undoubtedly congregated in that very spot, every day without fail. One was wearing a Timmins Rock ball cap and matching satin jacket. He probably ran the 50/50 draw at the game. The other three were in various shades of similar satin jackets. You know the ones—shiny, snap buttons, two-tone cloth collar, pockets that wouldn't hold anything bigger than a matchbook, embroidered crest on the front. I looked down and checked the paper for today's date, fearing during the night, I had driven through a time portal, losing twenty or thirty years in the process. Mandy returned with breakfast, placing the sizzling hot plate in front of me. My eyes grew wide as it was a meal fit for at least three kings.

"Guess I should have ordered the kid's plate, huh?"

"There are doggie bags, don't worry."

"Is there a free T-shirt, and my name goes up on the wall if I finish this?"

Mandy laughed and turned, hearing her name called. "Enjoy."

She moved over to another table as I waded into the number four special. I was hungrier than I thought, finishing it off quickly, leaving behind some orangey stuff. She returned and squealed in delight at the empty plate. I sat, slumped in the chair, rubbing my stomach.

"I think I need a nap." I groaned. "Like maybe all through winter."

Mandy laughed as she scribbled out the check, and placed it face down on the table.

"You can pay up there," she said, motioning to the front. She took the empty plate. "Come again, don't be a stranger."

"I promise," I said, "like maybe six months from now when I'm hungry again."

I finished my coffee and pushed back from the table, giving my swollen stomach room to escape. I got up and started to make my way between tables toward the cash. My head down, I squeezed past an occupied chair, and collided with a server, her back to me, carrying two trays.

"Hey, watch it!"

Lifting my head, I was face to face with the biker chick I had met just a few hours ago on the bridge. Catching us both off guard, we stood frozen in silence—one glaring and the other lusting.

"Well, fancy meeting you here. That was quick. I didn't know anyone could find a job that fast. I almost didn't recognize you without your helmet. Still passing through once your shift is done?" I asked, grinning.

She continued glaring at me, her bottom lip started to tremble, eyes twitching, as that very attractive mischievous grin was now replaced by a rather stern frown.

"Excuse me," she said, and roughly pushed by.

I raised my hands in surrender and squished myself up against the chair, allowing her to pass. I watched as she carried the trays down the aisle, her ponytail bouncing in rhythm as she walked. Shaking my head, I slid past the tables and made my way to the front counter.

Women!

I paid and the woman on the cash said, "Thank you, please come again."

I nodded and started out of the door, then stopped and turned. "Who's that?"

"Who's who?"

I motioned with my arm toward the entrance to the kitchen. "The blonde with the ponytail that just went through those doors carrying the trays. Does she work here?"

The woman turned her head toward the kitchen and then back at me. "She doesn't date the customers."

Waving my hand. "Oh, no, not that. No reason, just curious. Thanks."

Stepping outside, I squinted in the morning sun. Then, like a hammer, I was hit by a wave of exhaustion, and all I wanted to do was sleep. I trudged back to my hotel, passing the locals out for their morning walk, and grunted at their hellos. I was too tired to care about the box on the front seat of my Chevy and trusted the parking garage gods would keep watch over it.

Entering my room, the clock on the nightstand read 9:31 a.m. Sighing heavily, I faceplanted, clothes and all, into bed and fell fast asleep.

36

I WAS JERKED awake by the sound of running and children's voices outside my door, followed by laughing and giggling. The thumping stopped abruptly. I could hear banging, followed by a door opening and a booming voice, then the door slamming shut. I reached out for the night table, stretched, felt for the clock radio, and turned it: 9:47 p.m.

I groaned. Rolling over, I could see the lights from the roof streaming in through the open curtains. I wondered if anyone jumped today. I felt like I had been run over by one of those giant rock haulers, and that for good measure, it then backed up and did it again. I had been asleep for twelve hours. I was surprised it hadn't been longer. Twenty minutes later, I was standing under the shower, and another ten minutes later, I was coming out of the elevator and into the lobby. I needed fresh air, but more importantly, I needed to escape from the walls of my room that had been talking to me as I slept. I passed the front desk and there was a different person on duty.

"Hi, good evening."

"Well, hello there! Enjoying your stay so far, Mr. Humphries?" she asked, pleasantly.

"So far so good," I said, glancing at her name tag. "So, Abby, where can a guy get a drink around here?"

She sized me up with a look. "Do you dance?"

"Good gosh, no!" I stammered, taken by surprise at her question, lying just the same. Dancing was the last thing I needed up here.

"Well, there is a place just up the street that is open late. Pool, dancing, beer, youngish crowd, but you could fit," she smiled, eyeing my jean jacket. "It's called The Club. When you go out the door, turn left and go up to the next block. It's across the street above the Chinese food place. Bright neon sign overhead, can't miss it. Go up the stairs, and it's on the second floor."

Thanking her, I went outside, but turned right instead, and headed around the corner to the parking garage. I wanted to make sure the box was safe, and my Chevy untouched. The parking level contained one other vehicle, a dark blue Ford F-150 parked two spots over. Moving the box to the trunk and covering it as best I could, I decided to go for a spin and have a look around.

Abby said The Club was open late, and I hoped open late meant later than 10:00 p.m. in Northern Ontario. After filling the tank and lovingly washing my car, I took a trip along Algonquin Blvd., which appeared to be the main drag, and it was like any other smaller town—car dealerships, hunting and fishing stores, snowmobile/off-road dealers, and a big box store flanked by a strip mall at the end. When I was driving in darkness, I knew it was time to turn around, so I went back in the direction of my hotel. Turning on Mountjoy, I found The Club right where Abby said it was.

Pulling into the gravel parking lot—it was maybe half-full—I found a spot near the front towards the street. *Easy getaway,* I thought with a smirk. I locked my Chevy, patted the hood and walked around to the front, following the loud thumping and unmistakable sound of disco.

I walked through the double doors, the music thumping louder now, there was a staircase on each side, and I fought myself for a second over which side to take. Fighting off the urge to flip a coin, two couples came barrelling down the left side stairs, and I moved to my right, allowing them to pass. I hoped they weren't trying to escape. I took the stairwell to my right, and at the top of the stairs, there was another set of double doors, and guarding them was an enormous bouncer sitting on a chair two sizes too small.

"Good evening," I yelled, trying to be heard over the thumping music.

"Five bucks," he grunted.

"Huh?"

"Five bucks," he grunted again, holding out his hand.

"Huh? I can't hear you."

"Five bucks," he mouthed, holding up his hand flashing five fingers.

"For what?" I stammered, just as the music stopped, my ears ringing.

"This is how we count the bodies," he spoke in a deep voice.

"Huh?" I asked again, tilting my head, holding my hand to my ear, thinking I heard something about bodies. The music started up again, the bouncer's palm opened, and he flicked his fingers impatiently.

"Come on, haven't got all night! Either five bucks or leave. No loitering!"

I thought back to Abby who said this was a nice, friendly place to go. I reached in my jeans pocket, pulled out a ten, and handed it to him, fighting the urge to add, "keep the change you filthy animal." He tucked the ten into the fist-size roll of bills in his hand flipped through them, found a five, and handed it back to me.

The music stopped again as his thumb came up, he pointed over his shoulder inside. "Behave in there! I'm comfortable here, and I don't want to have to get up."

"Yes, sir." I nodded solemnly. "Ever seen those Maytag commercials?" I asked, rubbing my hand on my chin and grinning.

"Huh? What?"

"You remind me of someone, that's all," and quickly turned sideways, holding my stomach in, I slid past the heavily bearded three-storey condo acting as the bouncer. Moving inside, I stood at the landing and looked down at the floor. The music had started up again, the lights dim, the disco ball in the center of the room spinning slowly overhead, multi-coloured lights slashing across the walls and floor. The dance floor was filled with sweaty bodies, everyone dressed in some form of lumberjack attire, all bouncing and gyrating to the thumping backbeat.

Over in the corner, to my left, was a long bar, a large mirror on the wall behind it, flanked on either side by glass shelves holding bottles of all shapes and sizes, the front of the bar was occupied by backless stools.

The bartender was petite with dark hair tied back, a thin bang hanging down the right side of her face. She was busily pouring drinks, serving three customers at once: turning, twisting, juggling, flicking open the cooler doors with her feet. *Coyote Ugly* came to mind, minus all the theatrics.

I looked back to the dance floor, and on the other side of it were three pool tables neatly aligned along the back wall. Pool cues hung on racks behind every table. The pool table in the middle was in use, two women playing, and the other two were empty. To the right of the dance floor, were unoccupied tables and chairs, all except the one in the corner. A lone woman was sitting at a table nursing a drink, a motorcycle helmet keeping her company while she watched the crowd on the dance floor.

Wait! I know her. It was the biker chick I ran into earlier. Twice. *Well, I'll be. Still passing through, huh?*

I made my way over to the bar where a lone couple were buried in each other at the far end of the bar. I slid onto an empty stool at the opposite end, faced the dance floor, and waited.

"Hey, what will it be?"

At the sound of a lovely voice, I turned my head. "Beer … um, Barking Squirrel if you have it."

"Coming right up." She smiled and turned to the cooler behind her. I watched as she, and her hourglass figure, kicked the latch on the door, stooped down, pulled out a bottle, twisted the top and flipped the cap in the garbage all in one motion. Swinging the door closed with her foot, she placed it on the bar in front of me.

"You're not from around here," she said matter-of-factly.

"Gee, does it show?" I said, disappointed and reached for the bottle.

"Barely."

"I guess I didn't dress for the occasion," looking down at my jean jacket.

"No, you're dressed fine. Nice to see someone not in a lumberjack uniform for a change."

"My anti-social disposition then?"

"Yes, that's it," she smiled. "So, what are you doing here? Just passing through?"

"Waiting for the dance contest to start."

"Yes, I can see that." She stood up on her tiptoes, leaned over the bar, trying to get a glimpse of my legs.

Taken by her charm, I sensed something profound about her, and my gut instinct told me to lay off and just be me, I mean, the other 'me.'

"I just arrived today. I'm staying over at the Ambassador."

She rubbed her hands together in glee and giggled, "Oh, I bet they gave you the presidential suite too. The one with the panoramic view of the rooftop and the a/c vents."

"Gee, how did you guess?"

"Oh, it's not rocket science." She smiled, shaking her head. "Everyone from out-of-town stays there. Who sent you here? Wait! I bet it was Abby on the front desk."

"Two for two."

"Okay, now that we've established you're not a local—yet, what's your pleasure tonight? I'm guessing you dance but would prefer not to. Am I right?"

"Three for three." I lifted my beer, tipping it toward her. "Keep going. Do you want to read my palm too?"

"Later maybe." Looking me up and down again. "Oh wait! You're not a billiards guy, are you?"

"Why yes," I said, leaning forward and puffing my chest out. "I'm quite handy with a stick if I do say so myself."

"Hmm, I bet," her eyes twinkled as she reached under the bar and pulled out a tray of balls, then pointed with her head over to the tables along the back wall. "Take any free table you like. The one on the far end is perfectly level," she said, as if reading my mind. "The cues are hanging beside the table, and the rack is underneath, but I bet you already know that."

I nodded. "Thanks. What's your name?"

"Bree."

"I'm Pete," extending my hand across the bar.

"Nice to meet you, Pete."

Her hand felt warm and delicate in mine. My heart started to go pitter-patter, and I hoped she wouldn't notice.

"I better take another beer, just in case, y'know, for courage," I flirted, forgetting that the two of me still collided at times.

"Sure, coming right up."

Bree returned with my beer.

"One last thing."

"Sure, Pete, what is it?" Then playfully frowning, "please don't tell me you need me to show you how to hold the cue."

"Oh no, nothing like that," I lied, motioning with my head over to the other side of the dance floor. "The woman over in the far corner at the table sitting by herself, is she from around here?"

"Yes, she's here most nights. That's her spot, why?" She looked at me. "I don't think she's your type though."

"Sure, just curious. Thought I had seen her somewhere before."

Bree tilted her head and looked at me funny, and I thanked her and told her to keep an eye on me in case I ran into trouble.

"Yes," she laughed, "I will keep you on my radar, promise."

Carefully holding the tray of balls and juggling the two beers, I walked over to the pool table at the far end of the floor and took up residence. I searched for a cue stick, found one to my liking, gave it a roll on the table, and realized it was just as warped as all the others. Satisfied I had my built-in excuse, I racked the balls with my usual flourish and loud clicks while eyeballing the biker chick over in the far corner. I gave the cue tip a thorough polishing, set up on the dot, leaned forward, took aim, and drained the white ball.

I looked up to see if anyone was watching, then looked over in the far corner, but *her* attention was on the dance floor. *Whew!* I racked the balls, retrieved the cue ball from the side pocket, placed it back on the dot, leaned in once more, when a dark shadow covered the table.

"Hey buddy, wanna play?"

37

MO SAT IN her usual spot, over in the corner, far enough away from the action, still close enough to watch. She had been coming to The Club by herself, after she stopped coming here with someone else.

It's nicer like this, she thought.

She looked out at the dance floor. The next contest underway—for the life of her she never understood what the fuss was about. Dancing was fun, and she'd been told many times she had natural rhythm, more than most, and if she wanted to, she could have danced professionally. Recently, she had been toying again with the idea of opening her own dance studio, after seeing the For Lease sign, in the storefront window on Third Street. But she struggled with letting herself go, something she would have to get over, and preferred to dance alone, behind closed doors, where she could turn up the music and let herself be. She watched from a distance, judging the others, deep down envious, wishing she could be more like them.

Bored, she was ready to call it a night. She downed the last bit of her wine and stood up to leave when she saw the guy she had run into twice earlier that day, standing beside one of the pool tables. Slowly, she sat down. A knot, more like butterflies, formed in her stomach, the same feeling she had earlier that morning on the bridge when she stopped to see if he was okay. Of course he was okay, who was she kidding? She knew exactly why she stopped. She watched from across the floor, her view clear, and she thought he looked good in a jean jacket, so used to nothing but lumberjack wear up here.

She watched him play pool by himself, smiled when he drained the white ball and laughed at his reaction that it was the table's fault. She debated about going over but stopped herself, thinking back to her reaction at the diner—even on the bridge, she had given him no indication of even the slightest interest, so she just couldn't walk over now and introduce herself—*Hey, I think you're cute. Want to play?*—so she watched from afar, just like always, her *normal*, which she knew all too well, and long ago had given up on it being anything but.

Then, three young punks, dressed in lumberjack, approached his table. He didn't notice them right away—he was leaning in to take a shot—but she sensed this was not a social call. She recognized them, they were troublemakers, always lurking around the pool tables, trying to hustle the other players. They blocked her view so she stood up trying to see over the throng on the floor but couldn't, concerned, she reached for her helmet, grasped it by the face bar, and made her way across the floor toward the pool tables.

Mo wound her way around the dancing throng, skirting the edges of the dance floor, until she came into clear view of the table, moved forward, and stood directly behind the three young punks. She tried to listen in, but with the thumping music, she could barely make anything out. She shifted to her right to get a better angle, and she could see *him* now. He was gesturing with his hands and didn't appear happy. Instinctively, her grip on the face bar tightened, and she twisted her hand bringing the helmet back against her hip. She widened her stance and turned with her left hip facing out. She knew what was coming next and was ready.

38

"NO, I DON'T wanna play," I snarled, not looking up or caring who was behind the dark shadow.

A strong sense of foreboding came over me and I knew why. *Dave.* This was the last thing I needed right now. Angrily, I struck the cue ball, with a loud clack it broke the spread, sending the coloured balls flying in every direction. I watched as the cue ball spun crazily off the side of the table, bounced on the floor, and rolled to a stop under a bar stool.

"Fuck," I spat, shaking my head in disgust at the three punks standing at the end of the table. I roughly brushed between them. "Be gone by the time I get back," I said and stooped to retrieve the ball from under the stool. I turned and they were still standing there. "And what part of what I just said did you not get?" I said to the one in the middle.

"We want to play you," he said.

"That's nice, but I don't want to play you," I snapped.

They stepped back, allowing me to move between them, I returned to the table and reached underneath for the tray.

"What? Are you still here? Run along now, shoo! Don't you have homework or a prom to get ready for?"

"Hey buddy, we don't want any trouble, we just want to play you."

"Good! We agree on something, none of us want any trouble."

I guess Hanna was right, I just naturally attract this stuff.

I gathered the balls and moved to the end of the table and reset the cue ball. I started chalking my cue, all the while glaring at the three punks, who were still standing at the other end of the table.

"Guys, there's an empty table." I angrily pointed, waving my hand at the vacant pool table. Just then the two girls finished playing on the other one. "No, wait, make that two empty tables. There see? Look at that. You can go play by yourselves. I'm sure you're still learning how good that feels."

I finished chalking my cue and leaned down. The punk in the middle moved closer, his dark shadow hovering over the table, and sighing, I stood up. The music had picked up in intensity, the thump-thump heavy under our feet, the DJ eagerly promoting the next dance contest, and that it was time to grab your partner and get out on that floor.

"Guys, look, the prom has started. Why don't you find your little Susies and go shake a leg or whatever you call it up here? But fuck off and leave me alone!"

I noticed Bree watching from behind the bar and looked over to the far corner, the table empty, the bike helmet gone. *Where did she go? Shit!* Then I spotted her, helmet at her side, looming in the background, standing behind the three punks.

Holding the cue, I stepped around the table, and walked over and stood in front of the leader. He looked at me, eyes blinking, and when I noticed his fists were clenched at his sides, I swung my cue, connecting to the side of his head, sending him falling to the floor. I spun around, butt-ended the second punk in the stomach, then connected with an uppercut to his chin, he groaned and slumped forward.

I heard "Hey!" and spinning around, I saw *her* fling her helmet at the third punk, nailing him square in the face. She stepped forward, her leg flashed out, kicking him square in the balls. He fell to the ground groaning, blood pouring from his nose.

Turning, she reached down and grabbed a pool cue off the floor.

"Look out!" she yelled.

I ducked just in time, as she swung wildly over my head, connecting to the leader's shoulder, sending him sprawling to the floor. We whirled around, twirling the sticks in our hands, on guard at the ready. Suddenly, everything stopped, the music pounding but everything else was still. No one moved, no one said a word, everyone just staring at each other.

Then just like that, the fuse was lit.

~

The battle-royale raged on, a free-for-all, fists, kicks, and objects flying in all directions, mixed in with the screams, yells, and cries in pain. Everyone fighting everyone else—no sides, no battle lines drawn. Standing back-to-back, his body up against hers, they fought off the attacks coming from all angles. Strangely, they were in sync, each knowing what the other would do. Then she grabbed his arm, yanking it and pulling him towards her.

"Hey! We've got to get out of here now!"

"Huh? What did you say?" he yelled, ducking as a bottle whizzed past.

"Look out!" she barked.

Ducking, she tomahawked a punk in a lumberjack shirt sneaking up from behind.

"Watch it!" as he pushed her roughly out of the way and batted away a bottle, slumping down, groaning, holding his arm.

"Hey, you okay?" as she pulled him up by the scruff of his jacket.

"Yeah," rubbing his arm, "sorry about that."

She grinned. "It's okay, I won't break, but we gotta go. The cops! We gotta go now!"

Dropping the pool cue, she ripped his out of his hands, tossing it aside, and yanked him forward. Racing up the stairs, she stopped abruptly at the landing.

"My helmet."

"Your what?"

"My helmet, I threw it protecting your ass."

"My ass doesn't need protecting," he snapped.

Tilting her head, she smiled. "Funny, it looked like you needed it."

"I had them, you know."

"Sure, sure."

"So, are we going to stand here arguing, or are we leaving?"

"As soon as I get my helmet."

"Where is it?"

"I think it's somewhere in there," she said pointing to the dance floor. "Can you get it? I will stand guard here."

"Down there?" he gulped. "People are fighting."

"Yes, please."

"But you threw away my stick," he pleaded.

"You don't need it to get my helmet, and besides, I will be right here if you need me. You'll be fine," patting him on the chest, "better hurry."

"Brat," he grumbled, looking down at the floor.

"What did you say?"

"Nothing," as he stood glumly watching the pier-six brawl he no longer wanted any part of, even if he was the one who started it.

She gave him a hard shove and he stumbled down the steps, losing his balance, he lunged at the railing to keep from falling. Recovering, keeping to the fringe, he gingerly stepped over the bodies, sidestepping an overturned table. Body checked from behind, he fell forward, instinctively tucked his head down and scampered on all fours in the other direction. Then cautiously looking up he could see her standing at the top of the railing pointing.

"Hey! Hey! You're going the wrong way! It's over *there*."

Following her hand he spotted the table in the corner, the same table she was sitting at when he first saw her earlier, and lying underneath, was a lime-green motorcycle helmet.

"That it?" He pointed.

She nodded, and checking to see if the coast was clear, he ran hunched over to the table and reached down for the helmet, but as he stood up, he was face to face with the punk he had started the brawl with.

"There you are, motherfucker," he snarled, grabbing his jacket, his face inches from his. He could see the drool hanging at the corners of his mouth, mixing with the blood streaming down the side of his face.

He was stronger than he looked, pinning him against the table. The punk cocked his fist, and wincing, he shut his eyes and braced himself.

There was a loud crack, a whoosh, then everything went quiet.

Opening his eyes, the punk lay crumpled at his feet, and she was standing in front of him holding a cue stick.

"As I said, it looks like you need protecting. Come on, let's go! Let's get out of here!"

Dropping the stick and grabbing his arm, she pulled him forward, and they ran toward the exit, taking the steps two at a time, roughly pushing people out of the way. Pausing at the top of the steps, he looked back to see the bouncer wading into the fray tossing people aside like stuffed toys. Then he caught a glimpse of the punk, lying sprawled on the floor, and could see a dark red patch at the back of his head. She did that he marveled?

She gave his arm another hard yank and pulled him sideways through the doors. They raced down the stairs, stumbling out onto the sidewalk, gasping for air. Leaning over and breathing heavily, they took a second to catch their breaths. There was a wail of sirens in the distance.

He handed over her helmet.

"Where's your car?" she asked.

"It's parked around on the side. Where did you park your broom?"

She laughed, stood upright and brushed her hair back from her face.

"That's about right. Just make sure you can keep up. Come on!" grabbing his arm again and pulling him towards the parking lot.

They turned the corner, and under the lights sat a lime green-and-white Suzuki street bike, and two spaces over a bright red, souped up, Chevy Nova SS.

"Is that really yours? Not used to seeing it without the hood up," she teased.

He muttered 'Brat" for the umpteenth time.

"What did you say?"

"Nothing … where to?"

"Follow me, that is if you can keep up," she said, straddling her bike as she pulled on her helmet.

"Ha!"

He ran over to his Chevy, jumped in, turned the key, and pressed on the accelerator, revving the engine. He slammed it into reverse, hit the gas and backed up, kicking up dust and gravel, then jammed on the brakes, shifted into first, foot on the clutch, revving the engine, and waited.

Except the bike wasn't moving. Peering through the windshield, he could see her fumbling on the front panel, making pushing and twisting motions with her hand, her head frantically moving up and down. She twisted the throttle, turned her head, and looked behind, then leaned over and looked underneath. Shaking her head, she looked up and tried pushing the button on the front panel again. Nothing. The sirens were getting closer, and he watched her kicking at the bike trying to get it started. Despite their predicament, he couldn't resist, kicking on the emergency brake.

He got out and calmly walked over.

"Excuse me, Ma'am. May I be of assistance? Do you need a tow? Want me to call the auto club for—"

"Fuck."

Her visor was up, and she glared at him. They turned their heads at the sound of squealing tires and could see the silhouette of flashing lights bouncing off the side of the buildings.

"Well brat …?"

She looked down under the bike again and growled, "Fuck!" her head bobbing. She kicked up the kickstand holding the clutch in, tried to start the bike again. But it still wouldn't start. He was going to suggest to take his car, when it hit her that the bike was already in gear. She put it in neutral, pushed the button, and the bike finally started, its low rumble turning into an ear-splitting roar as she spun the throttle.

Snapping her visor down, she twisted the throttle, the front wheel coming up off the ground, the bike leaping forward with a jerk, bolted out onto the boulevard. He ran back and got in, tires spinning, gravel flying, and followed her tire trail under the streetlight, across the curb, hitting the edge and bouncing roughly onto the street. Tires squealing, he punched the gas, fishtailing wildly on the rain-slicked street, corrected and made a hard right, across from The Club, passing by the now parked cop cars.

She was waiting for him at the next block, and as soon as she saw him, took off the wrong way down the one-way street. He followed, quickly catching up, and they flew through the next intersection, blowing the stop sign. She slowed briefly, then accelerated and pulled ahead, taking a left, then a right, then another left, winding their way through the sleepy side streets. Wisely, he stayed back just enough to give her space. At the top of a hill, she turned right and accelerated again. Right behind her, he caught up, and they raced side by side along the glistening street, the whoosh-whoosh as they flew past parked cars. He looked over and, despite the visor, he swore she was wearing a maniacal grin.

Backing off, she pulled ahead, and he slipped in behind as they wound through an S-turn, and up ahead there was a cemetery on his right—glancing over—the biked braked suddenly, the green-and-white metal twisting and turning on the slick pavement. He slammed on the brakes, tires screeching and narrowly avoided hitting her.

She turned off onto an unlit street, and he followed, the road full of potholes, and he cursed out loud as she weaved effortlessly around them while he plowed through. Gripping the steering wheel hard with both hands, it was all he could do to hold on, as the Chevy bounced, jerked, and bottomed out, water splashing up over the hood—wondering all the while how much a new front end was going to cost.

She slowed and turned into a gravel driveway on her left. Through the mist, he could see her motioning him to wait as she parked her bike and got off. She walked over to a tall, white, wooden slated gate, reached over the top, and unhooked the latch. Stepping back, she swung the gate open and waved him in. He pulled in over to one side, turned off the engine and got out, as she retrieved her bike and wheeled it in beside the Chevy, then swung the gate shut behind them.

It was deathly quiet. His ears were ringing, and the sudden stillness added to the surreal feeling. It had started to rain, more like a drizzle, and he could hear sirens in the distance and wondered if they were from The Club or somewhere else? There was a roar of a car, and he turned his head toward the sound, and heard it go whizzing by from the top of the street, the silhouette of flashing lights dancing eerily above the houses in the foggy mist. She took off her helmet and shook her head, her long blonde hair falling back over her shoulders.

"We're fine," she said. "They won't find us now. Want a beer? Come on in."

Before he could answer, she had turned away and was heading toward the front door.

"Sure. Why not?" he said to the empty spot and followed the leather jacket inside.

39

"EXCUSE THE MESS," she hollered over her shoulder as I came face to face with a blanket fort in the middle of her living room.

"Oh man, cool!" Unable to control myself, I headed straight for it. I circled the fort, admiring the blankets covering the chairs placed in a square. "This is so cool! You made this?"

"Oh that …" She blushed, trying to hide her embarrassment.

"Now I don't feel so guilty," I said, staring at the blankets draped over the chairs, the entrance closed over with a plastic clothes peg.

"What can I say? It's my go-to. Be lost without it, and sadly, I spend more time in there than I should."

I nodded, envious.

"Beer?" she asked, holding out two cans.

"Huh? Oh yeah, sure."

"Cheers!" I popped the top. The beer fizzing out quickly, I leaned forward and gulped it, trying to catch the beer before it dripped on the carpet.

"Nicely done," she said with a wry smile. "Your first time? Here, let me move some stuff so we can sit down. Unless, of course, you want to hang out in the blanket fort?"

I smiled. "Maybe next time, okay?"

She shrugged and shoved the blankets, pillows, and laundry on the floor and motioned for me to sit down.

"There, sorry, I'm not the best housekeeper. That domestic woman stuff is not my best suit."

"Well, besides your blanket fort, what is your best suit?"

Ignoring my question, she changed the subject. "I guess we should introduce ourselves. I mean, it's late at night, and here you are in my place, and I don't even know your name. For all I know, you could be a serial rapist or something ... no wait, I think I'm safe after watching you struggle with those punks."

She took a sip of her beer, eyeing me curiously.

"I had them you know."

She shook her head. "Yeah, sure, sure. You had them all right, so there was no reason for me to jump in then, was there?"

"No, but thanks anyway."

I raised my beer, she leaned over and tapped mine with hers.

"I'm Pete."

"Nice to meet you, Pete. I'm Mo."

"So, is this your home, or is it like everything else I've seen of you so far today, and you are just passing through?" I teased.

Mo frowned at my question, and I could hear the loud click, as her walls went up, and I thought, *Well, that's something else we have in common.*

"It keeps the jerks away. Are you?" she asked abruptly, turning serious, her eyes narrowing, searching mine, trying to read my intentions.

"Am I what?" I asked.

"A jerk."

"All depends on which day."

The temperature suddenly dropped in the room, and we returned to our respective corners, sipped our beer, warily eyeing each other. I felt that familiar pang in my stomach with the uneasy silence between us. Was I blowing this, whatever *this* was?

Fortunately, Mo started round two by changing the subject. Turning toward me, in a friendlier tone. "So, what happened back at the bar? What started all that?"

"Oh that. Yeah, um, that…" I smiled weakly and drained the beer.

"Another?" Mo asked, sensing I didn't want to talk about it.

"Sure," I said, thankful that, for the moment, I didn't have to explain myself further.

She pointed to the fridge. "Help yourself, bottom shelf."

"You?" I asked, walking into the kitchen.

"No, thanks," she shook her can. "I'm good."

I pulled out a beer from the bottom shelf, closed the fridge door, only to see a dark figure coming toward me. A white and blackish-grey cat trotted out of the dark hallway, headed straight for me. I bent down and held out my hand.

"Aww ... he's cute. What's his name?"

The cat went straight to my hand rubbed his face on it, then flopped to the floor, rolled over, and exposed his furry belly. Stretching its legs out, I playfully rubbed its stomach, the cat purring loudly, twisted and turned his body like a slinky toy. I looked over at Mo, her mouth open, looking like she had seen a ghost.

"What's wrong?"

"You."

"Me? Huh?"

"You," she said, shaking her head in amazement. "He never goes to anyone but me, never ..."

I continued to rub the cat's stomach, then shifted to scratching and kneading his ears. Lowering his head, he pushed against my hand as I gently scratched the top of it.

"Neat, huh?" I said, knowing it bugged her. "I think he likes me."

"How did you know he's a *he*?"

"Lucky guess," I smirked.

Mo frowned, disgusted that her cat liked someone else other than her.

I moved back to the couch, the cat in tow, and when I sat down, he waited then jumped up on my lap and settled himself in. Mo fidgeted with her beer, and I fought hard to keep a straight face, as I stroked the cat's head, it softly purring, eyes shut, content.

"Here, can you open this for me? I'm kinda busy here ..." I leaned across handing her my beer.

"Open it yourself," she snapped.

Laughing, I shifted my hand from the cat's head, and carefully holding my beer, popped the top, took a long drink, then resumed rubbing its head.

"You're not going to tell me his name, are you?"

"Nope."

Mo reached down for a blanket, lifted it, wrapped it around her legs and feet, and stared at me and the cat, with mock—or was it *genuine*—disgust?

I took another drink, and looked around the living room, then over at the small bay window, and through the entrance to the kitchen. She had a nice place, and despite her earlier comment, she had that domestic thing down pat. Her home felt comfy and warm, and I could feel a positive vibe emanating throughout. I looked down at the cat, softly purring in my lap, Mo beside me, wrapped in a blanket, her feet curled under her, and it hit me like a bolt of lightning.

That feeling of 'we fit'.

The white-picket-fence feeling of comfort and familiarity, safe and secure, the ultimate blanket fort. It was a feeling no amount of money could buy. The feeling Dale had tried to purchase for me many years ago. And, of course, as things played out, it proved a feeling that could not be bought, no matter how much room was on his credit card. Now, up in Timmins, with a person I had only just met, that feeling instantly and naturally clicked. I shivered involuntarily.

"You cold? Want a blanket?" Mo asked, reaching for the floor.

"No thanks, I'm good," I said. "Your cat, whatever his name is, is keeping me warm."

"Bandit."

"Huh?"

"His name is Bandit," Mo said, her guard dropping.

We sat quietly on our respective ends of the couch, the gentle tick-tock of the clock coming from the dark hallway, content to just be. I was exhausted, coming down from the high of the fight and our escape from the law, the adrenaline rush running its course. All I wanted was a nice warm bed—preferably with Mo beside me—but I pushed that thought away quickly. Looking over at her, it was clear the night had caught up to her also. Her beer was at an angle in her lap, head nodding, eyes blinking, she was fighting a losing battle to stay awake. She had brought the blanket up over her shoulder and tucked it under her chin and had turned on her side facing me, her head drooping against the couch.

She was beautiful, snuggled in with her blanket, her blonde hair spread across her shoulders, the bangs covering the front of her eyes and along her cheeks. An angel in disguise—delicate, fragile, a soft interior covered by life's hard shell. It was no wonder there was this instant connection between us. This was something deeper though, this bordered on something completely different, and it scared the life out of me.

Normally, I would have run as fast and far as possible in the opposite direction from this, yet, strangely, I had no desire to run away. Instead, I wanted to run as fast as I could towards the feeling, and her. Mo's body twitched and jerked, and her eyes flew open as she realized she had fallen asleep. Seeing my goofy grin, Bandit still in my lap, she smiled.

"Sorry. I must have dozed off."

"It's okay, I was enjoying the free show."

"What? Watching me sleep? You're sick." She abruptly sat up, the blanket falling to the floor, pushing her hair back.

"I better go." I leaned forward, put my beer down, lifted the cat, and gently dropped him to the floor. I took the beer over to the kitchen and put it on the counter.

"You're welcome to stay," she called out from the living room. "This couch is quite comfortable, and Bandit has obviously taken a liking to you …"

"Are you sure?" I answered, trying not to sound too eager. "I promise not to snore."

"Good thing because I do, or at least that's what I'm told. But you should be safe out here."

Mo got up and quickly made a bed for me on the couch with the pillows and blankets. Then she said good night and headed down the dark hallway, Bandit chasing after her.

"Good night, and thanks for the beer … and couch," I called out.

"Don't mention it. Sweet dreams," Mo said over her shoulder, the sound of the bedroom door closing. The perfect ending to the extreme of everything that this day and night had been.

Just another normal day, right, big guy?

Mo had stirred something in me. A feeling I had all but given up on. Mo was different.

Where the fuck did that come from? I asked myself. Maybe this wasn't just a normal day after all.

I took off my jean jacket, shirt, and shoes, leaving my jeans on, I slipped under the blanket on the couch. I lay there, head spinning, but not from the beer, or the fight and getaway after. All I could think of was Mo and that moment on the couch. My brain was in overdrive, and I couldn't find the switch to turn it off.

Oh, sure Pete, you're in this strange woman's home, and just because the two of you happen to be sitting on the couch, her cat on your lap, you are getting all domesticated? And you're certainly not the first guy she's brought home. How many times with how many other guys?

I tried to convince myself that I was just another notch, this time on the couch. I shifted, got comfortable, and started counting eight-tracks in hopes of falling asleep. I felt something jump up, then burrow in the curl of my legs. Looking down, Bandit had his head on my hip, staring at me, purring softly.

"You are going to get me in trouble, buddy boy," I whispered to him, then leaned back and fell asleep.

40

MO LAY IN bed, restlessly tossing and turning, unable to get Pete off her mind. What had happened just now out on that couch? Where did that come from?

The feeling was so unexpected and powerful it took all her strength to hide it. She had just met the guy, and it was like they had been together forever. He was charming and handsome, but she had met other guys like that. He was different and felt so comfortable to be around. She felt a calmness, a sense of security—a feeling that she could just be herself.

And she couldn't help but laugh at the irony. Didn't things come in three's? She had run into him three times that day. The sign couldn't have been bigger. Her walls had come down much too easily, catching her completely off guard, and she was beside herself for it. Then, when he saw the blanket fort and started raving about it, thinking it was cool; it was completely the opposite of Rick, who had shown disdain the first time he saw it, and immediately took it apart. On the couch, wrapped in her favourite blanket, looking over at Pete with Bandit on his lap, she saw and felt what she had been missing and longing for all her life. And then, surprisingly, she couldn't stop herself and offered him the couch, unable to hide the hopeful tone in her voice. She hadn't felt like that in … what? Ever? *Had* she ever felt like that? She certainly didn't feel that way with Rick, even during their honeymoon phase.

Rick had been her first real love, meeting him when she was seventeen, dating for years, and because they didn't know any better, eventually marrying. They moved to Timmins from Sudbury so he could start up his construction business. Then three years ago, Rick up and left one day, leaving her for a hot little nineteen-year-old who had started working that summer in his construction trailer. Mo, sitting at the kitchen table, stunned, wiped away the tears as, unable to hide his excitement, he told her how he was moving in with Gina and her two dogs. A two-bedroom townhouse out near the airport. He hated dogs, never wanted pets, he said—too much work, constantly cleaning up after them. Rick went on about how Gina didn't make him feel small. How he had found his true soul mate. He was at least gracious about it—letting her keep the house and everything in it, only wanting his truck and his tools.

The thought of it all again made her gag, and she sat up in bed coughing hard, her throat constricted. She felt like she was going to throw up and put one foot on the floor, and when her stomach settled, lay back down. Reaching for Bandit, she patted the covers.

"Bandit?" she called softly, sitting up, she switched on the light and saw Bandit's spot on the bed empty, then noticed the bedroom door slightly ajar, the light from the hallway peeking through. She groaned, knowing where he was, and fell back into bed, reaching over, she pounded the pillow with her fist.

I hate him already.

After Rick left, and she had gotten over the shock of it, she realized that she was happier on her own. She decided to keep the house, there were no couple's memories associated with it, so there was no point in a fresh start. Rick never liked having their photo taken, so there were none framed and hung as reminders of their love. Rick had been too focused on his construction company to do anything else, at least that's what he told her. He had wanted to retire by the time he was forty. Then they would do *all that stuff*—take all those trips, frame all those photos, and make a family in the log cabin he was going to build on the twenty acres of property that they had been saving for.

Then, poof, just like that, it was all gone. Though at times it still felt like yesterday. It did help to learn that a year later, she heard that Gina was pregnant, possibly with twins, and Rick had found a townhouse closer to town.

So much for that log cabin out in the woods, huh Rick?

Bandit had become her companion and sole source of comfort. She found him the following spring, one wet day out on the back roads. She had bought herself a lime green 2002 Suzuki 650VS street bike that first Christmas on her own. Thanks to her father, she had grown up on dirt bikes back in Sudbury but had stopped riding when she met Rick. He said that girls—well, at least the good girls—shouldn't ride bikes, and so, wanting to please him, she stopped.

Out for a spin, she passed a cardboard box on the side of the road and thought it was strange to be left there like that. Curious, she turned back, straddling her bike, leaned over, and looked down into the box. She burst into tears at the tiny face with its big round eyes staring up at her, shivering and meowing. She scooped up the sopping wet kitten, wrapped it in her scarf, placed him inside her leather jacket against her warm body, his head burrowed in her chest, and raced home. They had been inseparable ever since.

That was the only room in her heart that she had opened up; she was, by choice, otherwise closed off. She could never trust again and vowed to herself one night, after having too much wine, that she would never allow anyone to get close to her ever again. Bandit was her one true companion. But maybe Bandit didn't get the memo, for while she was sitting in bed, he was out on the couch with Pete, a cute guy whom she had only just met but felt an instant undeniable connection with.

Unable to sleep, she reached under the covers and touched herself—and discovered she was soaking wet. Surprised, she pulled her hand away and rolled over on her side, pushing a pillow between her thighs, pulling the other pillow in close as though snuggling a partner. She chuckled at the irony. Finally falling asleep, she woke the next morning late, no Bandit to wake her at dawn like he always did by nuzzling her face, his rough tongue tickling her nose and eyelids, meowing and leading her out to the kitchen for his breakfast.

Padding out to the living room, she found Bandit snuggled in the curl of Pete's legs, his head resting on his hip, staring back as if to say, *he's here for the both of us now*. Smiling and shaking her head, she went to make coffee and fill his bowl, yet Bandit still didn't move, watching her from the couch.

Just who the hell is this guy?

She showered and readied for work, and as she was leaving, paused by the door, looking over at the body sleeping on her couch. The blanket askew, his arms crossed over his stomach and tucked under his armpits, and his dark hair bed-head messy—she thought about adjusting his blanket but, instead, let him be, sleeping peacefully. Bandit lifted his head, looked up at her.

"Take good care of him for me," she whispered and slipped out the front door, quietly pulling the door shut.

Mo opened the gate and walked the bike out, closing the gate gently. She walked her bike to the top of the road, before starting it, and even then, she rode off slowly in low gear. As she rode into town that damp, cool morning, the road still slick from last night's rain, she felt as light as a feather, and to her, the dark grey ominous clouds overhead looked like a beautiful summer's day.

41

I SWIPED WILDLY with my arms, trying to push away whatever was crawling around my head, then I felt something sticking into me on my shoulders and side. Something was walking on me. I tried to brush it away again, my arm hitting something furry. There was a meow, and I realized where I was. Opening my eyes, I was face to face with Bandit, who was sitting on my chest. He leaned in and rubbed my nose, purring. He licked the tip of my nose, his tongue rough, and I smelled cat breath.

"Morning, buddy," I smiled, playfully rubbing his head.

I stretched to get the kinks out, kicked the blanket off, and shifted Bandit, who dropped to the floor and went off in search of food. I sat up and swung my legs on the floor, shivering. It took a few minutes to adjust. I scratched myself, then rubbed my hands through my hair; I needed a shower.

"Hello?" I tentatively called out. "Mo? Mo, are you there? Hello?"

I expected at any moment to hear her voice. But the house was quiet, just the sound of Bandit chowing down and the soft tick-tock of the clock coming from the hallway. I chuckled at the irony, usually, it was me who left first, not the other way around.

There were no shower sounds coming from the hallway, no padding of feet. I walked over to the window and looked outside, and Mo's bike was gone. I returned to the couch, fighting off the sinking feeling in my stomach, embracing the reality that this wasn't a Hollywood movie, and she wasn't coming back with bagels and coffee. My inner voice was now wide awake and begging for attention.

Look! Enough! You've been down this road a thousand times, and this is just like all the others; a typical night followed by the usual nightcap. And, okay, so you didn't have sex this time, but everything else was the same. And this morning, instead of you bailing, she bailed. That's it. Yes, she's nice, and all and certainly different from the others, but so what? The result is always the same, so get up and get on with things.

I nodded to myself, knowing I was right, and forcefully pulled myself up, folded the blankets, and piled them and the pillows neatly on the end of the couch. I headed down the hallway in search of the bathroom, eyes straight ahead, I refused to let myself look anywhere but the bathroom.

Her bathroom was on the small side, the counter space filled with all the things that women need, and all things that being a guy meant I didn't need. Peeking behind the shower curtain, starting the water, my eyes remained glued to the faucet, afraid of the things I couldn't unsee. Finished, I stepped out, looked in the mirror, and did a double-take. Whoa! I had a shiner. My left eye was a pretty rainbow mix of purple and black and yellow and green. I hadn't had one of those in like … well, since my last bar fight.

I went back into the living room and gathered up my keys and phone, and as I turned to leave, the least I could do was check out her blanket fort. Getting down on my hands and knees, I unclipped the clothes peg, peeled back the blanket, and peered inside. There were a couple of pillows and another blanket, a box of tissues and crumpled ones lying beside it. A cell phone charger, a well-worn romance novel, and an empty wine bottle turned on its side, completed the décor. Smiling, and not feeling even the slightest bit of guilt, I backed out and closed the blanket over, clipping the clothes peg, careful to leave everything exactly as it was. Bandit was beside me, rubbing against my legs, and I reached back and petted him.

"Our secret, okay?"

I stood up, fighting off the pangs in my stomach, and walked toward the door, Bandit trailing at my feet. I looked down.

"Gonna miss you, buddy," I said softly.

I closed the door carefully behind me, making sure Bandit remained inside. The coolness of the morning was biting. I shivered, pulling my jean jacket tighter. Everything was still wet, and the sky overhead was filled with dark grey stormy clouds, matching my mood. I walked over to the gate, reached up, flicked the latch, and swung it open. My Chevy was sitting just as I left it, now covered in dew, the water droplets rolling down the windows and spilling over onto the frame, then running down the sides.

I got in and started it up, the throaty rumble, normally soothing, made me feel uneasy.

What the fuck is wrong with you? I wish I knew.

I slowly backed out, stopped and got out, swung the gate shut then got back in. Looking at the eight-track player, I had no interest in music, and sighing heavily, I backed out into the road. As I pulled away, I took one last look at the house. Then I carefully steered my way through the water-filled potholes until I got to the top of the street. Another look back through the rear-view mirror, then I punched the Chevy, and with a loud squeal, I was out on the paved road, heading back into town, frowning in the rear-view mirror.

Back at my hotel, I parked in the same spot on the second level and took the freight elevator to the seventh floor. I changed into some clean clothes. Though feeling better, I was restless and forced myself to sit down on the bed. My stomach rumbled, and I knew where I wanted to go but decided against it.

I can't. I won't. It is what it is. Move on, Pete. If things are meant to be, then your paths will cross naturally. Let it be.

I needed to stay busy. Noticing the breakfast vouchers by the TV was a start. I had promised to send Teddy the burner phone, plus I needed to check out the contents of the box more thoroughly. And maybe drop by and apologize to Bree for breaking up her bar.

42

"HEY, WHAT'S UP?" Mandy asked, concerned.

"Nothing. Why?" Mo said.

"You haven't said a word since you got here. Is everything okay? And why do you keep checking the front entrance?"

"No reason. Just looking at the weather and if it's going to rain. I wanted to take a run on my bike later." Mo's lie sounded unconvincing even to herself. "Honest ... I'm fine. Everything's good."

"If you say so," Mandy said, not buying it for a second. All the same, she let the issue be. There was no point in pushing, that much she knew. Mo hadn't said a word or taken her eyes off the front door since she arrived at the diner, twenty minutes late, the breakfast rush already underway. She was never late.

But that had been Bandit's fault, as he hadn't wakened her at dawn like he did every morning. So, this morning, she was late for the first time. She wouldn't get in trouble—that didn't bother her—she was always early for work, so being late this morning would undoubtedly raise eyebrows, but not in the way that would leave cause for concern.

Mo couldn't get her mind off Pete. The image of him lingering in her head. And the butterflies still hadn't stopped fluttering in her stomach.

What am I, fifteen?

Though she knew it was stupid, she kept watching the front door, afraid

Pete was going to come through it at any moment—and she didn't know what she would do if he did. Part of her hoped he wouldn't and that she would never see him again. That he was passing through and maybe, right now, was on his way to wherever the next stop was for him. But the other part of her hoped he would come through those doors and take a seat. She would serve him, bringing him everything he wanted, and then he would get up to leave.

"Bye," she would say. "See you when I get home."

And that was why she was so frightened. She was more frightened of herself and what she would do because that was what she wanted and hoped for—to have that same feeling as on the couch last night. To have that feeling over and over ... forever and ever.

Mo tried to keep herself busy, but the morning's breakfast crowd thinned out quicker than usual, and she had too much free time. She refilled the saltshakers and all the other condiments. She swept the floors twice, then washed them with the big bucket and mop. She recounted the cutlery and then did inventory in the large walk-in freezer, the cold not bothering her in the least. At three o'clock, her shift done, she went out back, got on her bike and took off, racing through the side streets, then out on the back roads, where she tore up and down them until well after dark, trying to outrun herself.

When she got home, walking through the front door, the first thing she looked at was the couch. She saw the pillows and blankets piled neatly on the end and felt a sharp pang in her stomach, squeezing her insides tight. She went straight to the cupboard and pulled down her biggest wine glass, grabbed the bottle off the counter, tucked it under her arm, retreated to her blanket fort, and didn't come out until morning.

43

PASSING ON THE breakfast voucher, breakfast at the local drive-thru was quick and easy, providing me with lots of time to explore Timmins. I drove up and down Algonquin Blvd. several times, pulling over and giving a wide berth to the giant haulers as they roared past, afraid one of those giant rocks was going to fly off and land on my baby. I killed time, people watching, and wandering in and out of the maybe two dozen stores that made up the local mall at the far end of the strip. I bought a coffee and sat amongst the locals in the food court, sticking out like a sore thumb. I found an electronics store and bought a burner phone, then finding a post office inside the drugstore, dropped it in the mail, care of Sharkees, figuring Teddy would have it in a month or two.

With my errand done, I thought I would take a drive by The Club and see if Bree was there. I felt guilty about starting the fight, plus I liked Bree and wanted to apologize. I would leave out the reasons behind what happened and hope that a little grovelling and an offer to help pay for damages would suffice.

As I cruised along the boulevard, what struck me was the permanent gloom that permeated from above. The sun was doing its best to break through the grey cloud cover, but there wasn't that permanent sunshine feeling, unlike Peterborough on a similar day. Of course, maybe it was because of the previous night's extracurricular activities. I had endured worse things recently, and even with all that, Peterborough never lost its sunny disposition. At least not in my eyes. Maybe it was *the north*'s fault?

I turned onto Mountjoy, in front of my hotel, and a block later turned into The Club. The parking lot was empty except for a green Pontiac Sunfire, a hole in the roof where the sunroof cover used to be. I pulled in beside it and got out. Walking around to the front, the doors were locked, so I backtracked and saw a black metal staircase that led up to a set of double doors. One side was propped open, so in I went, and wandered through the kitchen until I came to another set of double doors with round porthole windows. Standing on my toes, I peeked through the window, and I could see the bar on the left. I cautiously pushed open the door, and Bree was behind the bar. The place was empty and overhead, Journey was singing about a small-town girl living in a lonely world. The chairs were upright on the tables, and over in the opposite corner the broken tables and chairs were stacked neatly against the wall.

Hmm, not as bad as I thought.

Bree's back was to me, taking inventory and stocking the coolers, so I slowly approached the bar, and then from about twenty feet away, I cleared my throat. She turned and noticing it was me, instantly glared and threw the clipboard onto the bar.

"You got some nerve showing up here," she scowled.

"Yeah, I figured."

"Well, what do you want? And how did you get in here?"

"Through the kitchen," I pointed over my shoulder with my thumb.

"That's for employees only, but you can leave the way you came, bye," she turned back to the coolers.

Sheepishly, I stood there, embarrassed.

She glanced up and saw me in the mirror. "Look! I'm closed, and I don't think you should come back even when I open. So, please just go," Bree sighed, over her shoulder.

"If you give me a minute, I want to explain. I want to pay for the damages, then I promise I will leave."

"What's to explain? You tore up my bar," Bree said, facing me now. "I don't want your money. You're all alike, same shit."

"What do you mean all alike? You don't really know me."

"The hell I don't. You're like all the others that come through here. Same shit. Play pool, chase women, start fights, break stuff, wreck my bar."

"Well, no, look … that's not me," I pleaded, trying to defend myself.

"Really?" Bree's eyes narrowed, her laser-like stare going through me like melted butter.

"If you just give me a chance. Please, two minutes, then I'm gone."

Bree looked at me disbelievingly.

"Yes. Okay, I'm a guy, and I play pool, but the fight thing … I don't—"

"Oh please, don't take me for an idiot. I know your kind, and watching you last night, you're no stranger to barroom brawls."

"Correct, on that part you are right. That wasn't my first rodeo. But I don't go around starting shit."

"Until last night, you mean? Remember? I was watching."

"Yes, no, uh sort of."

"Which is it? Yes, you start them or no, you don't start them?" Bree asked, frustrated. "I find either one hard to believe."

"If you will just let me explain."

Bree was standing behind the bar, her arms folded. It didn't take a rocket scientist to figure out that coming here was a mistake. What did I hope to accomplish? She had every right to be pissed, but this wasn't the first brawl in a place like this. So, why was she so angry at me then?

If I called it a day and left—which my gut instinct was screaming at me to do—it would just be like all the other times and places, Peterborough coming straight to mind.

I had run from that. Despite being worried about Leia and chasing the box. I could have gone back after blowing up the bikes that night. Just returned to Peterborough that night or the following day. Gone back to Syd, Hanna, and maybe even Dale. I had conquered my demons with Tina, thanks to Jackie. Nothing had stopped me from returning, except I didn't. I ran instead. Hightailed it to Timmins of all places, using the excuse my dad would have wanted me to. Lame.

So, why was I now trying to explain myself rather than running away? What was happening here? This wasn't me. I mean who apologizes for starting a barroom brawl?

"Look, Bree, I can explain, I *want* to explain, please. Then I promise I will leave."

She looked at me, uncertain, but sensing the sincerity in my tone, her guard dropped slightly. "Okay. Make it snappy. I open at four, so I don't have time for your life story."

Nodding, I slid on the bar stool, expecting she would offer me a beer, but Bree leaned against the back ledge, her arms folded again, legs crossed over, her mouth tight.

"I'm waiting."

Gathering myself, I told Bree I had come from Peterborough after an incident at the Lucky 7evens. I wisely left out Syd, Dave, and what really occurred, and the morning after, when I almost shot Tony in cold blood. I wasn't sure whether she needed to know about my search for Sara and how her brother had given me all this money to go on a wild goose chase—which of course, was the reason I was standing here—so I left all that stuff out. Imagine trying to read a book with every other page ripped out.

"Well, that's a nice story and everything, Pete. So, you got into a bar fight in Peterborough, big deal. What's that got to do with starting the fight here last night? The Lucky7evens can be a rough place, Peterborough can be a rough town. But I heard things took a turn for the better when they hired a girl bouncer, the fights stopped. Well, except for the one recently. I heard that one was bad."

"How did you hear—"

"News travel fast huh?"

My head dropped, wishing I had that beer, I started picking at my fingers. Bree looked at me curiously, and then slowly started putting two and two together. Her head remained still, but her eyes moved up and down, and she stood for the longest time studying me. A sly grin formed across her mouth, her eyes narrowing into a squint, then her face lit up.

"That was you," she said. "Jesus Christ."

Bree turned and flicked the cooler door open with her foot, leaned over, and pulled out a Barking Squirrel; twisting off the top, she placed it on the bar in front of me. Not a moment too soon, and thanking her, I finished it in one long gulp, placing the bottle on the bar. Bree reached down for another.

"Yes, guilty as charged," I answered sheepishly.

"Why be embarrassed? I heard about the guy. Dave something or other. You did all of us a favour."

"Huh?"

"Pool tables, beer, fights, people talk, bars talk, word gets around, even up here."

"Wow," I replied, stunned.

"I still don't understand about last night. You said you never started fights, so I'm assuming, down in Peterborough, that Dave guy, started it first, correct?"

"Yeah, he did. Someone put him up to it."

"But those three last night. Just obnoxious punks, trying to stir up shit and not the first time either, I mean—"

"I was afraid," I said, my head down.

"Afraid of what, them? Sure, there were three of them, but Shane, the first guy you hit, he's the only one of the three of them to even think twice about."

"I was afraid of me."

"I don't get it. Afraid of yourself? Why would you be afraid of yourself?"

"Because of what I might do to them."

"But you did beat them up. They were all bloody, thanks to you. You had no problem with them." Bree was trying to make sense of what I was trying my very best to avoid telling her.

My head still down, I fiddled with the label on the bottle, peeling it off in thin strips.

"Hey," she said, "it's okay if you don't want to talk about it. I don't want to force you. I'm not a shrink, though gawd knows, I should be, working here. But it may help to talk about it."

I knew she was right. I was the king of keeping things in (and looked where that had got me). I looked over at Bree, who was wearing a look of concern. I took a deep breath.

"I was afraid I would do to them what I did down in Peterborough."

"What do you mean?"

"I was attacked from behind by that guy Dave, and something about that set me off. A rage maybe. I don't know. And if Syd … if, if I hadn't been stopped, who knows? Maybe I'm in the Peterborough jail and they've thrown away the key."

"I still don't get it," Bree said, hopelessly lost now.

"Starting a fight, I'm pissed, angry, you name it, but I'm not in a rage. And there's a difference. Even if I'm provoked, I get mad, but I don't feel that rage. But what happened in Peterborough … it was too recent." I shuddered hard at the thought of it and took another long drink, then continued. "Those punks pissed me off all right. They wouldn't take no for an answer. And I got scared that if I let things continue, at some point they would have jumped me. And if that happened, I was afraid I would do to them what I did to that guy Dave. I nearly killed him you know, and if that bouncer hadn't pulled me off him, I probably would have killed a man with my bare fists. And I was afraid of that happening last night."

I shuddered again at the thought of Syd.

"So, by starting the fight, even if it was three on one, you felt more in control," Bree said, now starting to understand.

"Bingo. Give the girl a prize. Even if I got my ass kicked, at least I'm not in jail or worse."

Bree smiled warmly, reaching out, placed her hand on my arm. "I was wrong about you. You are different, sorry."

"Then why were you angry at me when I came in just now? If I am different, as you say, then why all the attitude?"

Bree pulled her hand away and stepped back. "Oh boy, my turn, busted," she smiled, sheepishly.

"Well, you know I'm not a shrink, and gawd knows drinking here I should be one, but—"

"Oh, shut up!" Leaning forward she playfully slapped me on the hand, then quickly pulled it back. "You. Because of you. I'm pissed because of you."

"You've made that abundantly clear."

"No, not that. I wasn't mad about you starting the fight. Gawd, it's a good night here when there isn't one. And just in case you were worried, the cops aren't looking for you. They don't care, all they care about is restoring the peace."

"So, why don't you want me coming here anymore?" Bree paused, uncomfortable. "Seriously, if you don't want to talk, I can go."

"No, stay." Sighing, taking a breath, Bree continued. "You left last night."

"Yes, I did."

"With someone. You left with someone else."

"Yes, I did. The woman sitting by herself in the corner. The one I was asking you about. Mo."

"Yes, Mo."

I looked at Bree, confused about her obvious concern about the two of us leaving together.

"She jumped in to help, then kept grabbing my arm and dragged me out of here. She packs a mean punch."

"Yes, I had a front row view, remember?"

"I had them, you know."

Ignoring me, "So, where did the two of you go?"

"Back to her place. Well, after we dodged the cops that is. Then I had to catch her, but eventually, we ended up back at her place."

"And?"

"And what?"

"What happened?"

"Nothing happened."

Bree looked at me. "Really? Nothing happened. You expect me to believe that?"

"We had a couple of beers. We sat on the couch and talked."

"And that was it?"

"Yep ... I'm afraid so. I ended up sleeping on her couch."

Bree almost fainted in shock. "You what?"

"I slept on her couch."

"You slept on her couch?"

"I just told you I did."

"No one sleeps on her couch. No one stays over. Ever."

"Tell me you aren't serious?"

"Very."

"I'm confused. She's an adult, you know, has needs and stuff."

"Oh boy, does she ever. She's just like you and me. But ... but ever since Rick left."

"Rick?" I asked, suddenly worried she had a boyfriend.

"Yes, her ex."

I felt a wave of relief—and hope—wash over me.

"Rick is her ex. She and Rick came here from Sudbury about three years ago. They had just gotten married and bought the place you stayed at last night. They had been off and on since high school and had finally gotten married. To me, they were more like brother and sister. Anyhow, Rick started up a construction company, and Mo was going to open her own dance/yoga studio here in town. That had been a dream of hers since she was ten, owning a dance studio. They would come in here on the weekends to dance, play pool, hang out. On the outside, they looked like the perfect couple.

"Then Mo started coming here by herself, as Rick started working late. He told her he wanted to retire by forty and buy some property just outside of town and build a log cabin in the woods. He said they could have it all, log home, kids, her studio. Though, I could never understand that part. How can you have kids and run a dance studio at the same time, especially from a log cabin in the woods? But Mo seemed to buy into it, or maybe she didn't have a choice. Anyhow, she was coming in here more and more, and it was like a safe place for her. I got to know her. She would sit in the corner, play pool occasionally, but mostly kept to herself. Over time, I started to become protective of her. She has this tough outer shell but soft on the inside."

I nodded as those little tiny dots started to come together.

"Then one day, Rick comes home from work and tells her he's leaving, and he's taken up with some young bimbo who had started working in his construction trailer that summer. Gina something, barely legal. He moved out that night. Just up and left. Poor Mo. And now she's a regular here. Plays a mean game of pool. Takes on all these guys and toys with them. Some nights she lets them win but most nights, she owns the table. Then if she's feeling lonely, she'll take one home as a prize. We all have needs, right? But they never stay over. No one stays over, in her bed or like you, on the couch. Congratulations! You're the first."

It all made sense. I could see why she had the blanket fort. I was more surprised she wasn't fortifying it with something heavier.

"And she has this cat. A stray she found on the side of the road."

"Bandit," I said.

"What? You know its name?"

"Yup. Slept with me too. All night."

"Holy fuck," shaking her head, "I guess I was wrong. Maybe she is your type."

"Well, that's a nice story and everything, but you still haven't told me why you were mad at me," I giggled. Bree reached for a rag on the counter and threw it in my direction. I ducked as it flew over my shoulder, landing on the floor with a splat. Looking up at the clock, it was almost three thirty.

"Look, I have to get ready to open. I was mad at you because I don't want to see Mo get hurt, that's all. And I thought you were just like all the others." Leaning forward, Bree placed her hand on my arm again, her touch warm and gentle. "Take it slow, ok?" she said, her eyes searching out mine.

"I promise."

I finished my beer, then slid off the stool and started toward the kitchen doors.

"See you later?" Bree asked.

Sighing dramatically, I raised my hand to my forehead, "Aw, if I have to," and giggling, ducked through the kitchen doors as a wet rag smacked the door behind me.

44

BREE GLANCED AT the clock and saw she had twenty minutes to spare until The Club opened. It was more like an hour as there wouldn't be a stampede to get in, and besides, who lines up at four in the afternoon to get in a dump like this? She quickly moved around the floor, taking the chairs off the tables and aligning them just so, the damage from last night's brawl barely visible, the bloodstains on the carpet blending in with the beer and bloodstains from all the other times. Shifting to the pool tables, she took the covers off, folding and dropping them in a heap in the corner. She gave the top of the bar another quick wipe down then crab-walked behind the bar double-checking the coolers. Finished, she went into the kitchen and wheeled out two grey metal tubs filled with ice and cheap beer—the Two-for-Tuesday Special—placing them at each end of the bar. And all the while, she kept thinking about Pete and Mo.

If there was ever a tragic love affair, this was going to be it. A Hollywood blockbuster and she was going to have a front-row seat. There would be no in-between as they would either fall hard and fast for each other, crashing and burning into flames, or they would live happily ever after, riding off into the sunset.

Of course, it all depended on which script they followed. And she was going to do her best to help with that because she loved Mo and had taken a liking to Pete. But she knew it was going to be difficult because, well, have *you* ever tried to drive a car from the backseat? Bree took another glance at the clock, took her keys from behind the bar, and started toward the front doors when her phone rang.

Stopping, she pulled her phone from her back pocket and looked at it, "Fuck … no …" she sighed heavily.

She debated whether to answer it, but she knew if she didn't, he was going to keep calling until she did. Gawd, how she hated him. He was a pig, mean, crass, rude, and he treated women like sex objects. The sight of him made her skin crawl, and after being in his presence, she would go home and stand in the shower, under the burning hot water, trying to wash him off. The phone continued to ring.

"Hello?" she answered.

"Hey, sweet cheeks."

"What do you want?"

"That's no way to talk to your boss."

"Yes, it is. You're a despicable creep. What do you want?" Bree snarled, disgusted at the thought of him.

"I can fire you, you know."

"Good! I accept. Is that why you called? I'll leave the keys behind the bar. Bye."

The voice on the other end cackled, and Bree shuddered at the sound.

"Always with the jokes. You crack me up. It's no wonder you're my favorite sweet cheeks."

"Fuck you, Tony," Bree hissed. "What do you want? I'm just about to open."

"I'm coming up soon. I wanted to give you a heads up."

"Thanks for the warning. Should I bake a cake, put some nails in it? Or maybe rat poison in your drink?"

"Ah, sweet cheeks, you're hurting my feelings."

"Feelings? How can you have any feelings? You're not human!" Bree spit, her hand trembling in anger, as she held the phone. Bree lowered her phone, and slowly breathed in and out. Gathering herself, she put the phone back up to her ear.

"Look, Tony, I have to go. Is there anything else?"

"Nope. I just wanted to let you know I was coming up."

"Wonderful. Bye."

"Bree? Wait! Bree? You still there?"

"Yes Tony, for fuck's sake, I'm still here. Where else would I be?" Bree looked around the bar, hating everyone and everything about the place. "What is it?"

"Say hi to Mo for me, will you? I can hardly wait to see her and maybe this time the two of you will kiss for me," Tony cackled loudly.

"Fuck you, Tony!"

Bree threw the phone on the floor, but it didn't break, landing on the carpet, amidst last night's blood and beer. She picked it up, slipped it back in her pocket, and walked up the stairs to the front doors. She fumbled with the keys then finally fit the key in the lock, the keys jangling against the metal handle as she twisted it. Pushing open the door, someone was standing in front of her.

"Aw fuck! I don't have time for this," she said, her heart sinking. "What do you want, Rick?"

45

RETURNING TO MY hotel, I flopped on the bed, feeling much better after the unexpectedly pleasant encounter with Bree. I must admit I didn't see that coming. And I could see why I took an immediate liking to her. She was right, too, in taking it slow with Mo. And hadn't I done just that by not going to the diner this morning and not purposely running into her? Still, I was restless, and though Bree said to come back—and I would—it wouldn't be tonight. I needed a break from beer, pool, and to rest my sore knuckles. I pulled out my phone and caught up on things back down Ottawa-way.

I texted Mary to see how my place was, and she responded right away, saying everything was fine and that she hoped it was okay that Cat had moved in with her. I knew it was for the best, as she could give him what I couldn't, which is to say constant attention and food. I replied that I was happy and that he would be good company for her, and maybe help manage her love life. She got a chuckle out of that and asked when did I think I would be back? I said I honestly didn't know, and she said not to worry. She had things under control there. Grateful for neighbours like Mary, I moved her off the waiting list and back into my will.

It was too soon to contact Teddy, as the burner phone wouldn't have arrived yet. So, that meant one thing—time to tackle that box. I went down to the garage, and after retrieving the box from the trunk, I decided to take the freight elevator up, wanting to avoid being asked what was in the box. I don't know about you, but every time I see a banker's box, I wonder what's inside. And since I still didn't know what was inside, I didn't want to try and explain that I didn't know.

Stepping into the freight elevator, I punched the seventh floor, and just as the door was closing, a leg appeared, stopping the door, and in came the front desk clerk, Abby.

"Well, hello there, Mr. Humphries. I hope you are enjoying your stay so far. It's a beautiful day, and I hope you got out to visit the area. Such a lovely time of year to visit Timmins," she said cheerfully, looking down at the box.

I bet even if it was forty below and ten feet of snow was on the ground, she would be saying it was a lovely time of the year to visit.

"Did you visit The Club as I suggested?"

"Why yes, I did, and I even got a souvenir," I said, shifting the box in my hand and pointing to my eye.

"Oh, dear! Dear oh me, I am so sorry. I hope you are all right. The locals can be overzealous at times," she said.

"Yes, I'm fine, thank you for asking," I said, thinking she knew beforehand what I eventually found out afterward.

The elevator dinged, we stopped at the lobby level, and she got off, then turned, holding the door open. "Have a nice evening, Mr. Humphries, and do take care of that eye. A cold compress will make it as good as new in a jiffy. I can get you one if you like and have sent it to your room."

"Oh no, it's fine, thank you. I've been icing it," I lied.

"Very well then. Have a pleasant night, sweet dreams," she said, as the door shut.

Funny, she never said a word about the box. Go figure.

Back in my room, I dropped the box on the bed, then grabbed the ice bucket and went off in search of ice. Back again, I flopped on the bed, holding a towel wrapped in ice over my eye, while with the other hand I flipped the lid and peered inside.

There were about a half-dozen or so manilla folders, old police files, some stapled or paper-clipped, and still others, just loose pages. That was it. I took the folders out and spread them over the bed. Leaning back against the headboard, I picked up a folder and started reading.

The folders contained information pertaining to a case some years ago near Lakefield. As I flipped through the pages, what stood out was how meticulous and detailed the notes were, the sign of a good cop—something I didn't have the patience for, the paperwork itself. Which, of course, was why I had never made detective.

The case was a sad, tragic tale of a house that burned down in the middle of the night, trapping the husband and wife inside. The couple had burned to death, leaving a teenage son and daughter—who had escaped—orphaned. Initially, it appeared to be a simple open and shut case as stuff like that happened far too often; it was the thing I missed the least. So, what was the big deal, then? Why was Teddy so interested?

I went back through the papers a few more times, but nothing jumped out, then as I started to put them away, something caught my eye. Reading carefully, my eyes moving slowly up and down the pages.

"What the fuck?"

My mouth dropped open. *What in the fuck? No fucking way!*

I stared incredulously at the two names on the page: Sara and Edward Polson.

46

"WHAT ARE YOU doing here?" Bree asked, disgusted at the sight of Rick.

"How is she?"

"How is *who*?" Bree deflected, knowing full well who he was asking about.

Rick's eyes blinked rapidly, he was fidgeting with his hands, head down, reluctant to look Bree in the eyes. Sighing heavily, Bree finished unlocking the other door, and pushed it open.

"You've got two minutes," she said, very much annoyed. "That's it!"

He shuffled past her, "Thank you."

"Come on," she barked, motioning Rick to follow her.

They walked down the stairs and over to the bar, Bree stopping along the way to adjust a chair and stooping, picked up an earring off the floor. Rick sat down on a stool at the corner of the bar as Bree moved behind. Turning toward him, she could see he had lost weight and appeared almost frail. He was disheveled, his hair was long and unkempt, his five o'clock shadow looking like it was way past closing. He placed his hands on the bar, and she detected a slight tremor.

Biting her lip, fighting off the urge to lean over and hug him, Bree steeled herself. "Want something to drink?"

Rick shook his head no and looked like he was going to break down at any moment.

"How about something to eat? I can make you something quick. How about some soup?"

"No, no, I'm good. Thanks though."

He looked up into her eyes, searching, pleading for her to tell him that everything would be okay, and he could go home again. But she didn't, she couldn't, because it wasn't.

The bar was still empty, yet to be filled with the incoming Two-for-Tuesday crowd, and it was just the two of them. They stared at each other, waiting to see who would speak first. Finally, annoyed again, Bree sighed and broke the silence.

"Rick. Why are you here?"

He looked down, playing with his hands, trying to stop them from shaking, then biting his lip hard. "I've got no place to go," he whimpered, sniffling like a five-year-old.

Bree didn't react, the urge to hug him, replaced by disgust, and pity.

"I'm sorry, I'm sorry," he sniffled, wiping his eyes, he straightened up on the stool and composed himself. "How is she? Is she okay? Does she need anything? I have money—" he said, reaching into his pocket.

"She doesn't need anything. Not from you. Especially your money. Save it, you're going to need it, Rick."

"Has she moved on?" Rick asked, hopeful she hadn't.

Bree sighed, unsure what to say, because she didn't know, and she doubted Mo even knew herself. But what she did know was that she was done with Rick. Then she asked a question that she was pretty sure she already knew the answer to.

"How's Gina?"

With that, Rick slumped forward and started crying. Big heaving sobs engulfed him, his body shaking, back heaving, as he gasped loudly. There was nothing she could do, or say, that would comfort him. Instead, she watched the pathetic sight play out in her bar.

Christ, this shit usually happens at closing.

"Rick ... Rick ... Rick!" she pleaded, trying to get his attention. "You've got to stop this. Rick. Please!" Bree reached out, shaking his arm hard. "RICK!"

Nodding, Rick stopped crying and lifted his head, his eyes red and wet. He wiped them, his hands shaking harder now, and tried to sound convincing.

"Yeah, okay. Okay … I'm good," he said, sliding shakily off the stool. He reached out to the ledge to steady himself as Bree looked on, alternating between anger and indifference.

"Are the twins okay?" she asked, suddenly worried.

"Yes, they're fine," Rick waved his hand. "Gina kicked me out." He sighed heavily.

Relieved to hear about the twins, Bree bit her tongue. *Couldn't see that coming.*

Rick turned to leave, and in a moment of compassion, Bree called him back.

"Rick, sit down for a second, okay? Just sit. And I need you to listen to me. Can you do that for me, please?"

Nodding, Rick sat down, and leaning across the bar, Bree reached out and took his hands in hers, and looked forcefully into his eyes.

She told him that Mo had moved on, at least from him, but the hurt from what he did would never go away. She told him that he couldn't come around here anymore, that Mo didn't want to see him again, and he had to get on with his life. Her harsh words pierced his body like bullets, breaking through the skin, burrowing deep inside, shattering his already broken heart. He twisted and turned, trying to break free from her grip, but her grip was firm, and she refused to let go.

She told him he had a responsibility now to the twins and that they needed a father growing up. She said things happen for a reason and that he must move on with his life without Mo, and that it would be up to him to find acceptance with that; no one could help him but himself.

Bree didn't know if her words were sinking in or not, but it was the least she could do. Looking up, people had started to come in.

"Time for you to go, Rick."

She squeezed his hands once more for reassurance and was hopeful he would figure it out. Letting go of her hands, Rick slid off the stool, then trudged up the stairs, his head down, hunched over, and exited through the double doors.

Bree grasped the edge of the bar, taking a couple of deep breaths; she reached down and pulled up a shot glass and the bottle of tequila. Her hands shaking, she twisted off the cap and filled the glass to the brim. Holding the glass out in front of her, she stared at it, contemplating, then abruptly tilted her head back and swallowed the liquor, her eyes shut tight as it burned the back of her throat. Swallowing hard, she poured herself another and downed it; then, pounded the glass on the bar.

Fuck my life! Why am I always the one driving this fucking bus from the back seat? Fuck!

Bree resealed the bottle, leaving it out on the bar, turned toward the kitchen, and pushing open the double doors, bellowed, "Adrian! Are you there? ADDRRIIIAANN!"

47

THERE WAS A loud knock. I stirred, careful not to disturb the pile of folders and paper strewn over the bed. The hotel security guard was at the door, under the mistaken belief that the loud voices and running up and down the halls had been coming from my room. Someone had called the front desk and complained, and the room number and floor were transposed. It was the floor below. Lovely.

The nosey guard tried to force his way into my room when he noticed the covers askew and the box and papers spread out on the bed. I shooed him away, and I guess it was a good thing after all that my gun was in the trunk. Could you picture tomorrow's headline in the local paper? Hotel shooting in Timmins. I mean, that never happens in the north, right?

After the guard left, I was a bit rattled, and hastily threw the folders and papers back in the box and dropped it on the chair in the corner. I swan-dived into bed and slept through the night.

The next morning, I was awakened by the sounds clomping on the roof outside my window.

I wasn't going to let that, or the nosey security guard from the night before, ruin my day. My mind was on Mo. What I had discovered in the files could wait, and the roof jumpers would just have to fend for themselves. I showered and shaved, and after hanging my best T-shirt and shorts on the shower rod, steam pressing them for twenty minutes, I made a beeline for the diner.

You owe it yourself, big fella.

I hated wasting yesterday avoiding her—but not today. Nope, today's the day. As I walked along the street behind my hotel, I realized I was almost running, so I forced myself to slow down. The diner was crowded this morning, at least from the outside, and my heart sank; how could I get her to serve me? Standing in front, peering through the door, a couple came up from behind and attempted to get by. I apologized, letting them pass, then trailed inside and waited. Peeking over the man's shoulder, the diner was packed. Worse still, I didn't see her.

Shit! My heart sank further.

"Be with you in a minute, honey," a server breezed by, talking to me.

"Oh, I'm not with them," I stammered.

"Doesn't matter. Be right there," she cheerfully hollered. The server returned a few minutes later, seated the couple, then returned once more for me. A family of four departed, and as they exited, I peered over them, searching for Mo.

"What'll it be, honey?"

I stopped my search and looked at the server's name tag. Ginny.

"Window or booth?" she asked. "Oops, no, wait, sorry, no window or booths today. Busy, huh?"

But I hadn't really registered what she'd said as I had resumed my search for Mo.

"So, what will it be?" Ginny asked, in a less friendly tone, noticing that I was looking everywhere but at her.

"Um uh er uh, Ginny, I'm … I have a question."

"Yes, what is it?"

"I was in here the other day, and as I was leaving, I saw a server working here. She was sort of tall, blonde hair in a ponytail."

"You mean Maureen?"

Maureen. Mo.

"Yes, that's her. Mo. I don't see her." I searched for her, looking over Ginny's head. "Is she working today?"

Ginny eyed me suspiciously. "Listen, what do you want? It's busy today, so are you going to eat or not?"

"Look, I'm sorry I don't mean to creep you out, honest. I was looking for her. We met at the club down the street the other night, and well—"

"Let me guess, you're Pete, right?" Her temporary hard look had softened around the edges.

"She, uh, told you my name?"

"Yes, she did. She tells us everything, me and the other gals that work here. We like to keep an eye on her, look after her. She's been through a lot."

I smiled at how all those nice pretty dots finished connecting so easily.

"Right," I said.

"So, you're the one that started that fight. She was telling us about you. You drive a fast car she said. She also said you were cute." Ginny gave me an appraising look.

"Ginny, I was hoping if I could see her—"

"She's not in today. It's her day off."

"Shit."

Ginny leaned closer. "Maureen would kill me if I told you this, but on her days off, she works in the afternoon over at the Village Mart behind the Canadian Tire Gas Bar. Know where it is?"

"No," I said, perking up.

"It's not far from here. You're staying at the Ambassador, right?"

"Does it show?"

"If you're not a local, or from here originally, you stay at the Ambassador, and honey, you ain't either," Ginny laughed. "So, from your hotel, you can either drive or walk, and since Maureen says you have a fast car, it might be a good idea to drive, as otherwise, I don't know how you will ever catch her on that bike of hers."

I nodded, thinking back to a few nights ago.

"Head down Algonquin from the hotel one block and at the light turn right and the Village Mart is right beside the gas bar. Can't miss it."

"Got it!" I reached out and pumped her hand in appreciation, forgetting that I wasn't twelve and shaking the hand of my Grade 8 crush's father. I started out of the door when Ginny grabbed me by the arm.

"And where do you think you are going?" Ginny asked sternly.

"To go find Mo. I mean Maureen."

She looked at the clock behind the counter. "Not on an empty stomach you're not. It's only nine thirty, and you're going to need all the strength you can get." She laughed huskily, and I wasn't sure if she was serious. "Plus, I told you she works afternoons over there."

She reached for a menu, and I followed her down the aisle to a table in the middle. I wisely skipped the number four for something a little less filling and hopefully healthier.

When I was finished, I went to the front to pay and bumped into Mandy who gave me a smile. Ginny was at the till, and I left her a large tip, grateful for providing the lowdown on Mo. She smiled and said to keep it our secret. I ran my finger across my mouth, in a zipping motion.

Back outside, squinting in the bright sun, I walked briskly back to the hotel. Though there was no rush, I thought I should shower and shave again, and see if the front desk could send up an iron.

48

MO GROANED AS her phone buzzed, and she fumbled trying to find it, but it was not in reach. Thankfully, it stopped buzzing. She groaned again and pulled the blanket over her shoulder and tucked it under her chin. Shifting on her side, her legs curled in, she could feel Bandit as he shifted along with her. Snuggled in, her phone buzzed again, and she knew it wouldn't stop this time until she answered it. She hated Bree for it, she always did this. It was a game to her. She would call, let it buzz a few times, hang up, wait a few minutes, then call back waiting for her to answer.

Gawd! I hate her. She's so bloody persistent.

Except Mo *didn't* hate her, far from it. It was the opposite, she loved her, she was her best friend. She wouldn't know what she would do without her. She remembered that night three years ago, the first time she went to The Club alone—finding that table in the corner, away from everything and everyone. She'd sat alone and drank her wine. Later, when she was up to it, she shot some pool, alone, then returned to the table and her wine. Alone.

Bree always seemed to be the one who served her, but most importantly, Bree just let her be, respecting her privacy. She never asked any questions, and it was just a polite hello and small talk. Once Bree recognized the pattern, she placed a reserved sign on the table and would have her glass of wine waiting for her. Even better, Bree was adept at steering the guys away, protecting her, just letting her be.

One night, Mo asked Bree to sit with her. When Bree's shift ended, she came over, bringing with her a carafe of wine to share. They bonded over that carafe, and Mo felt comfortable enough to tell her story. After that, Bree asked her to start helping out behind the bar, suggesting it would be good for her to stay busy. It gave her a feeling of belonging and a sense of control.

Mo's phone buzzed again, throwing off the blanket, she banged her head on the table—she had slept in the blanket fort ever since Pete stayed over.

"OW!"

Bandit jumped up and went out the opening, meowing loudly, in search of the food that she forgot to put in his bowl. Kicking at the empty wine bottle by her feet, Mo swept her hands across the blankets searching for the phone, but all she could hear was buzzing. Finally, reaching around behind her, she felt for it and pulled it into her lap, touched the screen, swiping, she answered, groaning.

"I hate you."

"No, you don't."

"Yes, I do."

Mo could hear giggling on the other end. "What's so funny?" she asked.

"You."

"Me?"

Mo could still hear giggling, and a smile came to her face, despite the pounding in her head.

"You say this every time, you know."

"What?"

"You hate me," Bree giggled.

"This time, I mean it!" Mo pushed her hair back from her face. Looking down at her feet, she saw the empty wine bottle that was unopened last night.

"Mmm hmm. So, you okay?"

"Yes. Why?"

"Because I know you, and you've taken up residence in your blanket fort again, haven't you?"

"Maybe …" she said drawing out the word. "It's no wonder why I hate you. How did you know?"

"What? That you've been sleeping in your blanket fort again?"

Mo made a face, sticking out her tongue.

"Stop!"

"Stop what?"

"Stop making faces at me."

"Oh, gawd! I surrender. Go away! I hate you," as they both broke out laughing.

"Honey, you know today is Wednesday, and you work at twelve thirty, right?"

"Yes, Mom."

"Well, your shift starts in fifteen. Just saying."

"Shit!" Mo ran her hand through her hair again. It was dirty but she wouldn't have time to wash it now.

"You're welcome," said Bree.

"Exactly why I hate you!" With her free hand she started to crawl toward the opening

"Listen," said Bree, "I need to tell you something quick, okay?"

"Sure, what is it?" Mo said, as she crawled out the opening and stood up. She looked over at the couch and felt a sharp pang.

"I had a visitor yesterday."

"Oh yeah?"

There was a pause, and Mo could hear Bree breathing.

"Someone you know."

Mo's stomach tightened, and she moved over to the couch and sat down. "You still there?"

Mo took a deep breath. "Yes, Bree, I'm here. Who was it?" she said, dreading what was coming next.

"The guy from the other night, the one who started the fight."

"Oh!" Mo looked at the other end of the couch, and a smile came to her face. "Oh yeah? Pete?"

"Yeah, he showed up about an hour before I opened. Came in the back through the kitchen. Strangest thing, he wanted to pay for the damages from the fight he started."

"He what?"

"This guy is something all right. He started a fight then returns the next day wanting to pay for the damages."

Mo smiled at the spot on the end of the couch. "What did you say?"

"I wouldn't take his money. He apologized for starting it and even explained why. We ended up talking for a while. He seems like a real stand-up guy. I can't describe it, but he has this whole honour thing going."

Hmm, my instincts were right.

"You there, Mo?"

"Yes."

"Take this one slow, okay? Promise?"

"I will, I promise."

"Pinky swear?"

"Yes, pinky swear." Mo looked at her watch. "Aw shit, I better go, Bree."

"Okay. But look, one more thing." Bree's tone changed.

"What?"

"After Pete left, I did have another visitor."

Mo sighed. *Oh for fuck's sake.*

"What did he want?"

"Oh, same ol', same ol'."

"What did you tell him?"

"The same thing I always tell him. To leave you alone. To not show up at The Club anymore. To move on, that you have moved on."

Mo wondered, had she? Had she moved on? She didn't know either. She just knew she could never see or speak to him again. That much she knew.

"Thanks, Bree, I owe you."

"Nah you don't. Oh, and one more thing. Fuck, sorry."

Mo got up and padded down the hallway toward the bathroom, juggling the phone as she tied her hair back.

"Go ahead, I'm listening"

"I had a phone call."

"Busy girl."

"Yeah, lucky me," Bree sighed, "Living the dream. Guess who's coming up?"

Mo felt her skin begin to crawl. "When?"

"Didn't say but sometime soon. And you know with him, he always seems to show at the worst possible time."

"Thanks for the warning. Good thing I'm getting in the shower."

"Give a scrub for me, make that two."

"Will do."

"Oh, and bonus!"

"There's a bonus to all this?"

"He wants to watch us kiss this time," Bree giggled.

"Lovely, tongue, I bet."

"Naturally."

"Honey, I gotta run, you better get going too. You don't want to keep those customers waiting. Isn't it Green Stamp Day?" Bree teased.

"I hate you; I really hate you."

More giggling, "Neat, huh? Just another day up here in paradise."

Mo shook her head, laughing at Bree, and showered quickly. It was 12:35 when she rushed out the door, looking and feeling like shit.

49

I CAME OUT of the shower, and sitting on the bed was an iron, beside it a note from Abby with instructions on how to iron denim.

Really?

I crumpled the note and tossed it on the floor, plugged in the iron, and set it on the table. I unballed a T-shirt lying in the corner, turned my jean shorts right-side out, and started ironing. After a few strokes, I put the iron down and crawled on the floor, searching for the note. Ten minutes later, my T-shirt and shorts freshly pressed, I was standing in front of the mirror. Mo was going to be one lucky girl.

There was the sound of buzzing coming from my backpack, and reaching in, rummaged around, pulled out the burner phone, and on it were three missed calls from Teddy. I didn't want to deal with this now as I had far more important things to do. I hastily took the stairs, two at a time, down to the parking garage, unwilling to wait for the elevator and possibly running into Abby. That's all I would need. I jumped in my Chevy and, two minutes later, pulled into the parking lot. Driving around, I spotted Mo's bike and parked a few spots down from it. I turned off the engine and sat staring, alternating between the bike and the store. My heart was pounding, and the sweat was already trickling down my back. I couldn't recall ever feeling this nervous over someone before.

What is happening to me?

I pulled the keys out of the ignition and got out, the back of my shirt damp with sweat. I hesitantly walked toward the store, pushing myself forward, and when I got to the doors, I paused briefly, my hand on the door handle. Taking a deep breath, I pulled it open and went inside. The store was busy for midday, and I didn't see Mo at first glance, so I strolled around the outer edges, trying to catch a glimpse of her, all the while trying not to look like someone casing the joint. I moved up and down the outer aisles, casually looking at the price tags on wooden skis, a stereo system and cassettes from the eighties, and tweed sports jackets that would have looked great back in 1968. I was disappointed though, no eight-tracks.

As I made my way up towards the front of the store, I saw Mo behind the jewelry counter. She was speaking with an older man, probably in his seventies, and he was trying on watches. Instinctively, I felt for my wrist and realized mine was gone. It had come off in the fight the other night, and I had completely forgotten about it.

Perfect.

There wasn't a better time than this to get a new one. I stood for a moment watching Mo. Her hair was up on the sides and tied back, and she was wearing glasses, dressed in jeans and a white top. There were several watches laid out on the counter and she was showing the man one, but he appeared befuddled. He took it off, then tried on another one, holding his arm out, twisting and turning his wrist. That was my cue. I sauntered over, Mo not noticing me until I was standing beside the man at the counter.

"That's a nice one," I offered.

The man dropped his arm and turned toward me. He looked confused, his eyes darting about. Mo looked up, surprised to see me, but she gave me a warm, friendly smile, my heart instantly melting into mush. The man was dressed in his Sunday best, and he was short, maybe five five. His hands were gnarled, the fingers bent at different angles, probably from a lifetime in the mines, his thick wrists stuck out from under the sleeves of a white dress shirt covered by a brown tweed sports jacket.

"Oh my," he exclaimed in a squeaky voice. "Do you think so?"

Looking over at Mo, I winked and looked down at the man. "It sure does."

"Oh, I don't know. Martha did all this, you know. She looked after all this. Every three years, she would come here and buy me a new watch," he said, his voice cracking.

"Where is Martha?" Mo asked.

"She's gone. She's not here anymore. And now I have to do this. Oh … oh, I just don't know."

"Well, what kind of watch did Martha get you?" Mo asked, looking at me and shrugging her shoulders.

"Oh, I don't remember. I don't … don't remember. She got me the same one every time."

"Where is your watch now?" I said. "We can get you the same one."

He looked down at his wrist. "I don't know … I don't know where it is. One morning I looked down and it was gone … I can't find it," he said, agitated.

I looked at Mo, and we were both frowning. This could be us someday.

"Well," I offered, "how about we find one that fits you now? What do you think?"

The man's face brightened, and his eyes opened wide. "Yes, yes that would be nice. But I don't see one that would fit." He looked at the watches spread out on the glass counter. Mo shrugged her shoulders again.

"Okay, let me see," as I scanned the display case. "Hmm …"

I crossed one arm across my chest and placed my hand under my chin, looking serious.

"Hmm," I tapped my chin as I gazed at the man, turning my head on an angle. "What do you do?"

"What do you mean?" the man asked.

"Well, where do you go every day? What do you do? Do you work? Martha's gone, but you must do something, go somewhere? You don't just stay in your house by yourself, do you?"

"Oh no … no, no, no, I get out … I help others." The man perked up, his chest puffing out. "I like to help others. I help at the church. I'm there every day. I just came from there."

"That's good," I said, patting him on the shoulder. Mo, watching me, smiled. "And I'm guessing the work you do at the church is important."

"Oh yes. It is important. I am important. I am very good at what I do. I help the others … oh yes …"

"So, for an important man, you need an important watch."

Turning to Mo, I said, "What is the most important watch you have?"

Mo, catching on, bent down and started going through the display case, pulled out a box, and strapped inside was a watch with a black leather band with a bright green aviator-style face. I smiled and looked at the man in approval.

"What do you think? Try it on. Let's see how it looks on you."

I took the watch from Mo, unhooking the strap, I asked the man for his arm, and I gently wrapped the strap around his thick wrist. It fit perfectly, the larger face and wide strap meshing perfectly with the white hair around his wrist. The man was beaming as he held his arm out, showing us.

"Oh my! It's perfect," he said, as he twisted and turned his wrist, admiring the watch.

"There! An important watch for an important man. Don't you think, Mo?"

"Ah yes, it's perfect," she said, all the while smiling at me.

"Can I wear it now?"

"You sure can," Mo said, and she leaned over and cut the price tag off the strap, placing it in the box. "Give the box to the cashier at the checkout and tell her Mo said it was okay." She gave him a smile.

"Oh, thank you, thank you. Martha would like this. Oh, I miss her … but she would be so happy. Thank you again." The man turned and reached out, pumping my hand. "You too, Miss," as he looked over at Mo behind the counter, "Thank you."

"You are very welcome, take care now," Mo gently patted his arm.

We watched as the man headed over to the checkout. I looked at Mo, who was still smiling.

"Maybe I should let you behind the counter," she said, as she started to gather up the watches and put them away.

"Hold on, not so fast. My turn. I need a watch too."

Mo looked up frowning. "Seriously?"

"Seriously. Mine got broken the other night."

Quickly her guard went up. "So, why are you really here, Pete?"

"I need a watch. Mine got busted as I said."

Mo studied my intentions, her eyes moving back and forth, not sure what to make of this.

"There are other stores that sell watches in Timmins."

"I know, but I landed here. What can I say?" I said, smiling innocently and shrugging. "And I'm not near as fussy as that gentleman just now. I just need a cheap watch that tells time. That's all."

Mo looked down through the glass counter, drumming her nails on the top, just loud enough for me to hear. "Hmm, let's see ... Where are those less important watches? Hmm, I know the five dollar ones are here somewhere."

I laughed nervously, not sure if she was serious, she looked up smirking. "Too easy."

Mo bent down, and I could see her hands through the display case, lifting the watches, finding one, she pulled it out and placed it on the counter. It was perfect. Black leather strap, black face, the ideal size. The dial lit up, the various smaller dials illuminated. I couldn't pick a better watch for myself. Then I saw the price tag and gulped. Two hundred dollars! Mo, noticing, reached for the scissors, quickly snipped off the tag, and handed me the watch.

"Here. Try it on, see how it looks."

I undid the strap, wrapped it around my wrist, and rehooked the strap. It fit perfectly. I held my arm out, just like the old man, twisted and turned my wrist, showing Mo.

"Perfect! And guess what? It's your lucky day, as it's on sale."

"Huh?" as I stared at my wrist. "I'm not sure ..." I said, hesitant.

Mo smiled, glancing around the store to see if anyone was watching, pulled out her pen, reached down under the counter, pulling up a blank price tag. She quickly scribbled $100 on the tag, then looped the string from the old tag through the hole and leaning over, reattached it to the strap. "There."

I looked at her, "Really?"

"Really," as our eyes locked. "And besides," she added, "I heard you tried to pay for the damages from the other night, so this should help."

Bree.

Mo put away the rest of the watches and motioned for me to hand her mine. I unhooked it, handed it over, and she placed it in the box and handed it back to me.

"You can pay over there, just like the man," she motioned with her head.

I knew she had to get back to work, and my heart started to sink.

"Do you like bowling?" She asked.

"Huh?"

"Do you like bowling?"

"Uh bowling, I mean sure. I haven't—"

"There's a bowling alley across the parking lot. I get off at eight. Meet me there."

50

I SKIPPED ACROSS the parking lot, holding out my wrist, marveling at my new watch. I had lots of time to kill until Mo and I played strikes, spares, and misses. So, it was the perfect opportunity to revisit the box contents, along with giving Teddy a ding. Parking in the garage, I took the freight elevator straight up to my floor. Once in my room, after carefully folding my shorts and T-shirt, I threw caution to the wind, leaving the curtains open, stretching out naked on the bed, all except for my watch.

I sorted through the folders, put the pages in order, and started once more from the beginning. Reading through the names identified in the report: Sara and Edward Polson. It was Sara and Teddy's parents who died in the fire that night. Then I saw the date at the bottom of the page—July 25, 1988. A shiver ran down my spine and I quickly got up and closed the curtains. I sat on the edge of the bed staring at the date. *July 25, 1988.* One year to the day my dad was killed.

How could that be? That was only a coincidence, right? I mean, people die every day. But one year apart? To the day? We didn't know each other, did we? How would we?

I thought back to Sharkees when I ran into Teddy. I had never met or even seen him before that day. Or had I? We were approximately the same age, but he didn't strike me as police material—but then again, that was said about me. It was doubtful our paths crossed at the academy, and I would have remembered if I had arrested him somewhere. Same for his sister Sara. I had never seen her before, except for the picture Teddy gave me. So, how did all this relate to me then?

The police files, containing Sara and Teddy's, or rather *Edward*'s, names confirmed what had been nagging at me all along—that day in Sharkees was no coincidence. That was no chance meeting. Teddy had picked me on purpose. But why? He certainly knew me from somewhere. And I must admit this was all a bit chilling.

I dropped the papers in my lap and stared out the window, the curtains apart enough to see out. I could hear voices and clomping, and every few minutes, a figure moved past the window, their hands carrying tools and ropes. I wondered what they did all day out there. I looked down, my penis poking out between the papers and giggled at the absurdity. *Talk about fucked.* I picked up the papers and something else jumped out. The penmanship.

It was neat and perfectly legible. There was no scribble or scrawl, no trying to guess what had been written. And which, by the way, 99% of us are guilty of. This handwriting was impeccable with its distinctive flair. Where had I seen this handwriting before? That's why it stood out, because it was so perfect, just like the actual notes themselves: meticulous, thorough, complete.

I flipped through the pages, scouring the bottom. They all contained the same signature, illegible, a childlike scribble at the bottom of each page. I scanned through the pages some more, scratching my head, where had I seen that handwriting before? I dropped the papers in my lap, burying my penis in them, feeling a little self-conscious.

What was with all the activity outside my window?

The burner phone buzzed in the corner, and I hurriedly gathered up the papers, dropping them loosely, along with the folders, in the box. I pressed the top of the lid down firmly and placed the box on the chair. Pulling the curtains shut, I retrieved the buzzing phone, placing it in my lap. I let it buzz once more, tapped disconnect, and waited. Thirty seconds later it started buzzing again. I waited through two more buzzes then I tapped connect.

"Why hello there, stranger. It's been a while. Guess you can follow instructions. Have you missed me? I certainly didn't miss you."

"Fuck you."

"Teddy, or is it, Edward? Come on, don't be like that."

"Edward? How did you know … fuck you, Humphries!"

"Sorry Edward, I mean Teddy. You look like an Edward to me that's all. Teddy, it is. Now, where were we?"

"I've been calling, as you instructed, for the past two days. Why didn't you answer? Where the fuck are you?"

"Oh, here, there, everywhere."

There was heavy breathing on the other end, and I knew I was flirting dangerously with fire and needed to be careful. I had been lucky once, being on the right side of the recent bonfire, but I didn't want to push it.

"How's your sister? Did she ever show? I mean, she was pretty cranky when I had her in my backseat. Ahh, I guess that happens when you don't put out, huh? And probably why she left."

"You are beyond fucking dead, Humphries. I am personally going to enjoy watching you die."

"Promises promises …"

"One thing with me, Pistol. I never fail to keep a promise. Never."

Suddenly unnerved, I had pushed things too far, once again. Would I ever learn?

"Okay, okay … sorry, Texas, I kinda got carried away. Let's start over, okay? We both have our issues with how this played out. How about we find some common ground, move forward, and reach a compromise? What do you say?" I asked hopefully.

There was silence and I could hear Teddy breathing along with rattling and voices in the background. He was probably at Sharkees, then I heard, "Hiya sis, I'm on a call and will catch up in a bit. Another drink would be great."

I didn't know what to make of that. Sara always seemed to be everywhere but where she was supposed to be.

"Ahh, sounds like your sister did make it back. Hope none the worse for wear."

"Yes, she's fine, but no thanks to you."

"True, very true. Okay, Teddy, let's get down to business. We both got off on the wrong foot, am I right?"

"If you say so."

"I say so. So, where do we go from here?"

"Well, you're the one calling the shots … for now."

Teddy was right, I was calling the shots, but for how long? It all depended on how I played my cards and looking over at the box, my hand had suddenly improved, and I needed to be wearing my best poker face. So, reverting to what I did best, though this time keeping my cards close to my chest, I winged it.

"What's in it for me?"

There was a long pause on the other end, and I started to worry, this time I might be flying on only one wing.

"Well, I paid you fifty grand to find my sister but funny, she's right here beside me, without any of your help. Then, I asked you to make a simple stop and pick up something and deliver it back. I even gave you extra for that, remember? And now, my sister is back with me, but not by your doing, and you have my box but won't bring it to me. So, what exactly more do you want?"

"*Au contraire mon ami, au contraire.* Your sister has returned, and I did do what you asked. I went looking for her, and it's not my fault she escaped from my backseat. I mean, did you want me to tie her up? She probably likes that stuff, but because I didn't, she escaped, and bonus, she's now safely back with you."

Dr. Jayne was right when she said my imagination knew no bounds. I continued quickly before Teddy spontaneously combusted.

"And yes, I do have the box, and you are right also, I should have returned it to you. But once I had a gander at all those papers inside … and by the way, I do think you look more like an Edward than a Teddy, just my opinion. Anyway … they must be pretty important because those bikers were interested in them as well. Did you know I took a beating for that? I went to a lot of effort to get the box for you, making a bonfire out of their bikes, though I honestly didn't think they would explode like that. And now you're sounding like an ingrate. You're hurting my feelings, Teddy."

"Sorry if I hurt your feelings, Pistol. I did hear something about that. So, a couple of bikes got torched, and a bar got busted up. What's the big deal?"

I almost leapt through the phone at the thought of Leia. Sweet, innocent, Leia and her .45. My stomach instantly went into a knot, and I hoped she was okay.

"So business is business, and the price just went up. It's nothing personal, just business. Never mind; you would do the same thing if you were in my shoes."

I heard a heavy sigh and waited to see if there was a nibble on the line.

"How much?"

"How much is it worth to you?"

Quickly, much too quickly, Teddy swallowed the bait—hook, line, and banker's box.

"How about another fifty grand?"

"Aww geez Teddy, don't come so fast! Good gawd man, women would hate you for that. Do you not have any stamina?"

The thought of another fifty grand was like a bomb going off in my head, but if Teddy was that quick with another fifty, that meant there was more, much more, to be had.

"Tell you what? Let me mull this over for a couple of days, and I will get back to you. Sound good? And don't worry, your box is in safe hands."

"When?"

"Just a couple of days, I promise."

I heard a voice on the other end asking, "Everything okay, brother?"

"Okay that's a wrap, Teddy. Nice chatting with you. We'll talk soon."

"Fine. And one more thing."

"Yes, Teddy?"

"I keep my promises. All of them, no matter how long it takes. Got that? So, you better keep yours."

"Yes, Teddy."

I tapped disconnect and lay back on the bed, resting against the headboard. That was easier than I thought. I had scored myself another fifty grand plus prospects for even more. But it came with a threat, that if I were smart, I wouldn't ignore. I looked at the clock, it was almost four, and I still had four hours to kill. I reached for the remote. Since this was Timmins, I was expecting to have a plethora of TV shows from the seventies and eighties to choose from. And maybe if I was lucky, there would even be reruns of *Joanie Loves Chachi*.

51

I JERKED AWAKE, and for a second, I didn't know where I was, the room dark, looking over at the window through the half-pulled drapes, I could see the lights outside. I sat straight up. The TV was on, but instead of *Joanie Loves Chachi*, it was a game show.

"Shit!"

Sighing loudly, I swung my legs off the bed, keeping my head down, refusing to look at the clock. I took a deep breath, shielded my eyes, and turned toward the nightstand. My heart in my stomach, I slowly spread my fingers, peeked through the cracks, and opened one eye.

8:10 PM – Gee, that's not so bad.

8:12 PM – I was out the door, licking my fingers, running my hands through my hair, as I raced down the stairs.

8:15 PM – Squealing out of the parking garage, the traffic gods were smiling, as it was clear sailing through the lights down Algonquin. I bounced into the parking lot and parked across from the front entrance of the bowling alley, frantically searching for Mo's bike, my heart sinking. It wasn't there.

8:16 PM – I ran toward the entrance, pulled hard on the door handle, barging through the double doors into the deserted lobby. I could hear the thump-thump of rock music, and up ahead, I could see a kaleidoscope of blacks and blues and purples all intermixing together. Good lord! Was I at The Club again?

8:17 PM – I slowed to a brisk walk as I approached the front counter. There was a teenager on the desk. I looked for Mo, but it was too dark, I could barely make out the lanes. The music stopped then started, the colourful lights matching the beat, along with—wait for it—a disco ball. The music pounding louder now, I recognized the song, clearly meant for me. Styx's *Renegade*.

8:18 PM – I leaned on the counter pounded the bell, trying to get the kid's attention, but he was buried in his phone.

"Excuse me, HEY!"

But he didn't move, oblivious. I banged harder on the bell, then started pounding the counter with both fists.

"HEY!" Finally, with all the racket, he looked up. He put his phone in his pocket and moved quickly over to me.

"Yes sir, sorry sir. How can I help you? Tonight is Rock 'n Bowl night. Five dollars."

He looked over at the empty lanes behind me. "It's not crowded, so you can stay as long as you like."

"I need shoes please, size nine."

"Coming right up." He went over to the cubby holes and retrieved a pair of size nines.

8:20 PM – I turned toward the lanes, looking for Mo but didn't see her. Frantic, all I could think of was that night in Peterborough and being late for my date with Syd—and *her* reaction.

"Here you go, sir." The kid placed the shoes on the counter in front of me. I handed him a five.

"Take any lane you want," he said.

"Aww fuck."

"Is there anything wrong sir?"

"Is there anyone here?" I asked, looking back over my shoulder.

"Just you so far, but it'll pick up later."

My heart crashed landed into my feet, and I considered handing him back the shoes.

"Oh wait, sorry. There is one other bowler here. A woman. She's down at the far end on the last lane. She came in about twenty minutes ago. Sorry, I forgot. She's a regular, and I'm so used to seeing her all the time I didn't count her."

8:21 PM – I grabbed the shoes off the counter and made a beeline towards the far lane. Scurrying along the back of the lanes, untying the laces of the bowling shoes, while at the same time trying to kick off my running shoes, I stumbled twice and forced myself to stop. Kicking off my runners, I carried both pairs of shoes, padding the rest of the way in my socks.

8:22 PM – Through the swirling lights, I could see Mo on the last lane, her arms out, holding the bowling ball and taking aim. I watched as she glided forward and threw the ball down the lane with authority. She followed her shot until the loud clacking of the pins could be heard. Easily a strike. Straightening up, she turned to see me looking like an idiot, carrying shoes in both hands. She broke into a smile as I walked towards her, shrugging and holding my arms out.

Time stopped – Mo was still in her white top and jeans, hair down, wearing glasses, she was beautiful. No makeup, no-frills, just pure natural beauty. I sat down on the bench and hastily started putting on the bowling shoes, all the while apologizing profusely.

"I'm really sorry, Mo. I'm late … man oh man … I'm so sorry. I lost track of time and fell asleep … up there. I don't know what it is about hotel—"

"Guess I sold you a defective watch," Mo laughed. "Stop, it's fine Pete, really. I knew you were coming, and it gave me time to decompress from work." She smiled at me, reassuringly.

"When I didn't see your bike out front, I thought … well I dunno."

"I left it over by the store and walked over," she said, touched at my concern.

Looking up at her, it was exactly like the moment on her couch, like we had been together forever. I felt this wave of peace and comfort wash over me, and I shivered and felt goosebumps. Mo was so comfortable to be around, acting natural, being herself, and I could just be *me*, and strangely, even though we were complete strangers, we fit, flaws and all.

"Okay, show me what you've got." Mo winked as I stood up and walked towards the ball rack and reached down, picked up a black, orange, and tan-coloured ball, held it up, prayer-like, inspecting it.

"No need to inspect it. Trust me, it's round," she smirked. "And since you are just going to throw it in the gutter anyway …"

"Fine!" I replied, in mock disgust and turned towards the pins, and peeked up at the ceiling.

If there were ever a time when I don't suck, this would be it, right, big guy? I promise never to ask for anything again, I mean it.

"The place closes at midnight."

Putting my feet together, I stood perfectly straight, holding the ball up to my nose. I took a deep breath, exhaling loudly, then slid forward, one step ... two steps ... uncoiling, I swung my arm back and unleashed the ball, my follow-through forcing me to my left, my back leg off to the side, high in the air behind me. I stayed in that position as I watched the ball roll down the shiny wooden floor toward the pins. The ball hit to the right of the center pin, exploding backward and taking down all the other pins with it.

"Steerrrike!" I drawled out. I turned back to Mo and stuck out my tongue, then I bent over, bowing, my arm sweeping out with an exaggerated flourish. "Okay, that's a wrap," I said. "I'm good, see ya."

I walked over to the bench and sat down, pretending to untie my shoes.

"Bye," Mo said, as she got up from the score table and moved towards the rack. "Oh, and before you go, can you get me a beer, please. Since you're buying, grab yourself one."

Walking over to the snack counter, I turned to see Mo fire another strike, and returning with our beers, we spent the rest of the night finding out how competitive we were. We went strike-for-strike, spare-for-spare, miss-for-miss, with the only exception being those damned gutter balls. The chemistry between us was undeniable; with each turn, we passed on the floor and lingered a little longer, a little closer—the sexual tension and energy between us palpable.

Hands reaching out, fingers touching lightly, the sensation sending shock waves through our bodies, we stopped on the floor just as Alice Cooper's *Only Women Bleed* started playing, in tune with the disco ball lazily spinning overhead; our bodies lightly touched then we were lost in a kiss of a lifetime. We stood in our warm embrace, gently rocking, arms around each other, her mouth warm, and her tongue felt hot, and I could feel stirring below and surrendered to the fact that she would notice soon.

"Strike," Mo whispered in my ear, as she pulled away, looking down at the bulge in my jeans.

"Certainly not a miss."

She giggled and we kissed again. Hips, slowly grinding in sync, our kissing became more intense, arms wrapped tightly around one other, we didn't care if anyone was watching or not. We made some futile attempts to bowl, but gave up, and remained stationary on the floor, kissing, hugging, and slow dancing to the music. Mo's head on my shoulder, our bodies locked in a warm embrace, it felt like the high school dance, except we were adults and not teenagers, and what awaited us, beat the grilling from our parents and that cold, lonely, single bed.

When the clock struck midnight, I remained a prince, the house lights flashed, and the music abruptly stopped. And not a moment too soon, as my jeans were ready to burst, the friction from Mo rubbing against me. We quickly changed, dropped our bowling shoes on the counter, hoping we hadn't scarred the poor kid. Outside, it was cool, and the streets were deserted. I decided to let Mo drive this bus.

"So, here we are again," Mo murmured, between kisses, looking over at my car.

"But this time, the cops aren't after us," I said, kissing her.

"Well, if you hadn't started that fight, and if I hadn't had to jump in and save your ass …" She patted it lightly. "And nice ass it is, worth saving." She ran her tongue across my lower lip.

"I had them, you know."

Mo pulled back. "Will you let that go! Next time you're on your own, how's that?" She playfully punched me in the chest.

We kissed and hugged, the smell of her hair intoxicating, and there was an awkward silence, and I wasn't sure what came next. Looking into Mo's eyes, we sensed this was real, but we knew that once we went forward, there would be no turning back. We could walk away now, go our separate ways, none for the worse for wear and knowing we had that magical moment, on the bowling lane of all places. Was that enough?

It was getting chilly, and Mo shivered in my arms. My heart started to sink at some imagined ill omen, but then she looked up and winked.

"Back to my place?" Her tongue flicking out and sliding slowly across my lips.

"Race you!"

Her eyes flew open. "You're on!"

She let go of me, turning toward the other side of the parking lot where her bike was.

I hopped in my Chevy and slowly followed Mo over to her bike, my headlights illuminating her behind. She straddled the bike, pulled on her helmet, and slipped on her gloves. Flipping her visor down, she gave me a thumbs-up, twisted the throttle, and tore out of the parking lot, running the red light. Following suit, it took me a block to catch up. She was waiting for me at the next light.

Looking over at my hotel, sorry Abby, that chocolate you left on my pillow is not going to get eaten tonight.

The light turned green. Mo twisted the throttle, the bike lurching forward, the front wheel high off the pavement. Quickly correcting, she was gone before I could react. I punched the accelerator, tires spinning and squealing, trying to catch her, and up ahead was the railway overpass, and just below, her taillights. She slowed and stopped at the next light, pulling alongside, I motioned for her to lift her visor.

"Hey, isn't your place back *that* way?" waving my hand over my shoulder.

"Yes, it is," she laughed, "but I thought we could go for a little run first. You keep saying how fast your car is, and I wanted to see for myself."

The light changed, and she roared off again. In tandem, we tore along Algonquin, the road twisting past the empty strip malls and dark fast-food joints. We passed the arena and raced along the long open stretch of 101, side-by-side when she found another gear, and with a wave, she was gone, her red taillight getting fainter in the distance. Looking down at my speedometer it read 125 mph. When I saw the sign for South Porcupine, I slowed, and up ahead, I could see Mo stopped on the side of the highway, waiting. I pulled alongside, her visor up, she was wearing that same maniacal smile.

"What took you? I've been here for twenty minutes."

I smiled and shrugged. "I'm missing a gear."

"Yes, I'm well aware. Let's head back," she said. "I promise to go slower so you can stay with me. Wouldn't want you to get lost and miss out—"

"Miss out on what?"

Mo had spun her bike around and was back on the highway. I quickly caught up, only because she let me, and we motored back at a much more leisurely pace this time, my speedometer hitting 100 mph briefly. I followed as she turned onto Pine, passing the cemetery, then she slowed and turned down the pot-holed road-to-hell. I decided to take it at my own pace, when I pulled in, the gate was open, and the bike parked, but I didn't see her. I got out, swung the gate shut, the front door open, lights on inside. As I walked up the step, Mo was standing in the doorway, holding two cans of beer, naked except for a red and black lumberjack shirt.

52

THE NEXT DAY, I checked out of the Ambassador, much to Abby's disappointment, and checked in with Mo. Bandit was now in his glory, Mo no longer jealous of his connection to me. It was effortless, we all fit, plain and simple, there was no other way to describe it. The three of us would snuggle on the couch, the blanket spread across, Bandit curled around our legs, and we lived life. It was heavenly. We talked for hours at a time, sharing our past relationships, triumphs and failures, and everything in between.

Well, sort of.

Mo told me about growing up in Sudbury, her dad teaching her how to ride a bike at age nine. How she met Rick, finally marrying, then their decision to move to Timmins. She told me about Gina, and I didn't let on that I already knew. She missed her parents and she would visit them every few months on her bike, but she had no interest in returning to Sudbury to live. Mo still wanted to open a dance studio in town, but it seemed more of a pipe dream now.

I shared my journey and that I became a cop, in Barrie, when I turned twenty, and how Dale purchased my white picket fence and my all-too brief marriage to Joanna. I told her the history with my Chevy and how it related to my dad. I wanted to tell her about what happened to my dad, but I casually fluffed it off with my parents living up in Barrie. I wasn't ready yet and I wasn't sure if I would ever be. And for now, I left out my starring role in *The*

Wizard of Oz; Teddy, Sara, the bag of money, and the rest of the colourful cast of characters.

We shared our love of music, though the whole eight-track thing was lost on her. One night channel surfing, we came across the movie *Roadhouse*. We discovered that it was our favourite movie, and one day I found the DVD in the drugstore and brought it home. That set things off on an entirely different level.

One rainy Saturday afternoon, I popped in the DVD, and we hunkered down on the couch to watch. Well, one thing led to another, and we started having sex. So much so that the movie seemed to be perpetually on pause. Then we got bored and started practicing the fight scenes with each other. We moved the coffee table off to the side and both learned we could take a punch. Of course, there was blood, mine and hers. Mo connected on an uppercut, cutting my lips and tongue when my teeth jammed together, and I lashed out in reaction nailing her square on the nose. We laughed and giggled as we wiped each other's blood away.

We became regulars at The Club and Bree was happy for our company. However, I could see the look of concern in Bree's eyes that things were moving too fast, which I completely understood.

The nights Mo covered behind the bar became more frequent, so tiring of fighting with the white ball, I started helping Adrian, the cook, in the kitchen. Tall, average build with black hair and a goatee, quick-witted and down to earth, we connected instantly. I started to wonder if there was something in the water up in Timmins, as overnight, I had acquired this instant family—Mo, Bandit, Bree, and Adrian.

Adrian started teaching me how to cook short order stuff, and washing dishes was fun, as we made up these crazy rhymes and poems, seeing how silly we could be while trying to maintain reality. I dunno, guess you had to be there. Late at night, we would sit out on the back stairwell and share a joint, it was just so peaceful. One unexpectedly mild night, after Adrian had gone back in, I sat on the stairwell, gazing up at the stars, when it hit me.

I was happy.

It made no sense, but I guess it made perfect sense—Timmins of all places, washing dishes in a bar, life with Mo and Bandit.

Overnight, I had stumbled on to what I had been searching for all my life, and without realizing it, I had found it. And it wasn't anything like I had expected or had drawn out in my head. Mo, Bree, and Adrian teased me about the silly grin plastered across my face, saying, I needed to stop smoking that stuff. But I knew different.

A few days later I pulled into The Club just past noon and parked beside Mo's bike. When I got out, I stood for a moment. Ever have that feeling something isn't right? Something bad was about to happen?

As I walked through the front doors of The Club, taking the stairs two at a time, suddenly, alarm bells started going off in my head. Looking up, Maurice, the burly bouncer wasn't there. Oh, and by the way, we still weren't friends and doubt we would ever be. He still hissed and glared whenever our paths crossed, and I guess I couldn't win everyone over. A strong sense of foreboding came over me, and I stopped as my hand clasped the door handle.

Don't be an idiot!

I pulled on the door handle and walked inside. In a way, I wished I hadn't.

I stood at the top of the railing and the sound of silence was deafening. Usually, inventory days were filled with laughter and loud music, Bree finding it easier to cope with the mundane task. Along with the silence, there was no laughter or sounds of any kind. Looking over at the bar, Mo and Bree were behind it, clipboards in hand, silently counting bottles. Their heads were down, even from this distance, their body language indicated something wasn't right. I walked down the steps and over to the bar. I could hear faint sounds coming from the kitchen and figured it was Adrian. I slid on a stool at the end of the bar, the atmosphere was so oppressive I was unnerved.

Is it me? Have I done something wrong?

"Hey, guys. What's up?" I asked tentatively.

"Nothing," Bree spat, her head down. "We're working, that's all."

I looked over at Mo, her back to me. "Hi, babe."

Mo stopped what she was doing, standing up, turned toward me. She was wearing a look I hadn't seen before, and I couldn't for the life of me figure out why.

"You okay?" I asked. "What is it?"

Bree stood up and slammed her clipboard down on the bar.

"Him. It's him. He's here." She opened the cooler door and pulled out a beer. Twisting off the cap, she slammed it down in front of me. "Here! You're going to need this."

Just then there was a loud crash, the sound of pots banging coming from the kitchen followed by another loud crash.

"Adrian, okay?" I asked.

"He's not here," Bree said. "Good thing."

"Then who?" I asked.

Bree, swearing under her breath, picked up the clipboard and turned back the bottles on the wall.

"Just wait…you'll see…"

I heard more banging and rattling, I saw movement through the porthole windows of the kitchen doors, and a big shape passing by. I looked again at the two of them and could feel their tension.

"What the fuck is going on?"

Angry, I started to move off the stool to see for myself, when the kitchen doors swung open, and a huge black shape backed through them. The figure turned toward me and was carrying a plate filled with food. Our eyes met, my blood froze, and I had to sit back down on the stool, grasping the edge of the bar. The figure broke into a broad smile, exposing the wide gap between his two front gold-plated teeth.

"Why howdy, pardner! I never expected to see you here, of all places. What the heck are you doing here? The last time I saw you, you were pointing a gun at my head."

Wishing I had it with me now, I remained frozen to the stool, unable to move.

"Well, what do you know. Usually, you're so chatty, so glib. Pardner, you disappoint me."

Tony looked at Mo and Bree, their eyes bugged out, mouths open wide.

"Girls … girls … pull yourself together now. It's okay, we're old friends, aren't we, Pistol? Tell them how we're friends and where you know me from. And Teddy too. By the way, Teddy's looking for you, and he's none too pleased. There is unfinished business between the two of you, which is why I'm here. Well, that and—" he stuck his tongue out at the girls, flicking it grotesquely back and forth "to see my favourite pair of sweet cheeks, right girls? Remember you promised I could watch you two kiss this time."

"Fuck you, Tony!" Bree said, visibly shaking.

Mo walked over and stood beside her, probably to keep her from doing anything she'd regret. She shot me a look demanding to know what the fuck was going on.

But I was glued to the stool, unable to speak or move. Bug-eyed, mouth open, I watched as Tony walked past me, carrying the heaping plate of food, and sat down at one of the tables behind me.

"Care to join me, Pistol?" Tony asked between mouthfuls, as the stomach-turning smacking and slurping sounds echoed off the walls. A wet rag smacked me between my eyes, snapping me out of my stupor. I shook my head, wiped my face with my arm, and tossed the rag in the garbage. Bree and Mo watched as I went over and sat down across from Tony.

"What do you want?" I asked, keeping my voice low.

Tony wiped his mouth with his sleeve and looked up.

"Always a Pistol. Teddy was right, always the games." He spat partially chewed pieces of food across the table as he spoke. Eyes narrowing, Tony stopped chewing and looked me straight in the eyes. "You know why I'm here, Pistol. I'm here for the box. Just give me the box, and we'll be done with it. And you can …" He looked at Bree and Mo, still motionless behind the bar. "Well, you can go back to your nice little life here with your two little playmates."

I remained silent, Tony was still leering at Mo and Bree. "Do you bang both of them? Or do they just let you watch as they go down on each other."

My fist flew across the table, catching Tony below the eye, and despite his heft, he fell backward off the chair, landing heavily to the floor. I was already across the table, food flying, on top of him, my fists flailing away. Grunting, I landed punch after punch until Tony recovered and, with one swing, hit me square on the temple, sending me sprawling.

I rolled on the floor, stunned, head spinning, my eyes watering. My side was numb, and I could feel tingles down along the back of my legs. I lay on the floor, unable to move. Mo screamed out and came running over.

Mo helped me to my feet, groggy, my legs wobbly, she lifted the chair upright and helped me sit down. Tony had gotten to his feet and righted his chair. He sat down, leaned over and picked up the knife and fork off the floor, wiped them on his pants, and started eating again. Coming around, Mo went behind the bar and stood beside Bree, looking at me, distressed, wide-eyed, confused.

"You pack some mean punches there, eh Pistol?" Tony slurped between forkfuls of greasy bacon. "Funny though, I only needed one punch. Remember that for next time."

"There won't be a next time," I growled.

"That's up to you, pawdner," he drawled like Teddy. "Hand over the box and I'll be on my way."

"Fuck you, Tony. I don't deal with you."

"Suit yourself, pardner," lowering his head, he resumed eating from the trough.

I needed to buy some time. I walked over to the bar, refusing to look at Bree and Mo, and reached for my beer. I downed it and turned toward Tony, wiping my mouth.

"Teddy can have the box when I'm done with it."

"When's that gonna be?" Tony stopped eating and put his fork down.

"When I'm ready."

"You already told Teddy that and look what happened."

"I need a week."

"A week? No can do, pardner. Teddy needed that box yesterday."

"Come on, Tony, that's bullshit, and you know it. He's waited this long; he can wait another week. I'm asking, please one week, please. Then I promise you can have it. The box is yours."

Tony paused and lifted his napkin to his mouth, burping into it, wiping his mouth. He motioned with his hand, "You know, Pistol, looking at you, I believe you. A week it is, though I'm going to have a hard time selling that to Teddy."

"That shouldn't be a problem for you, Tony," I said. "What with all that unmistakable charm and wit of yours."

"Ha! That's my Pistol. Always with the jokes. Okay, a week it is. I'm sure Teddy will be pleased, despite the delay."

"Oh, there's one more thing."

"What is it, pardner?"

"When I give you the box, you leave and never come back. You leave them alone. You leave them be. They have nothing to do with this. You never set foot in here again."

Tony looked at Bree and Mo, flicking out his tongue. "And if I don't?"

"I'll kill you."

Tony cackled loudly. "You had your chance. That is until Syd rescued you, again." He turned to Mo. "Did he ever tell you about Syd?"

Mo stared at Tony blankly.

"Syd's gone, you know. She left right after you did. Went back east. I heard it was a broken heart. You didn't have anything to do with that, did you, pardner?"

Ignoring the huge chunk that had fallen in my stomach, I fought off the urge to lunge at Tony again.

"The box. Do you want it?" I hissed.

"Tsk, tsk, so touching, breaking hearts wherever you go. Isn't that sweet. And now, look at you protecting your new playmates. You really crack me up at times, Pistol. This whole honour thing you have going, right out of the movies I tell you."

"Do we have a deal?"

Tony picked at the food on his plate, pulling apart two thick strips of bacon, the grease dripping down over the pancakes.

"Sure, we have a deal. It gives me a week to hang out here with my favourite pair of sweet cheeks, right girls?"

"Fuck you, Tony," said Bree.

"Hoping so, could be a long week. I may not be able to keep up." He turned his gaze back to Mo. "Hmm, Bree are you okay to watch?"

Bree picked up a vodka bottle and threw it, the bottle whizzing past Tony's head, landing harmlessly behind him, rolling on the floor. Tony flicked his tongue at her, and Bree was so enraged that if Mo hadn't grabbed her, she might have climbed over the bar.

"Tony," I said, "you touch them, and I will blow your fucking head off. You got that?"

Tony sat back and placed his hands up in defence. "Whoa, whoa, whoa there, pardner. Just having fun. A week it is. I will sleep in the office. This is my bar after all."

What?

Bug-eyed, I stared at Bree who nodded slowly. Disgusted, I turned toward the kitchen and left. My body on autopilot, I stumbled down the back stairwell and got in my Chevy. Tearing out of the parking lot, squealing and fishtailing wildly, I drove through the countryside, roaring up one gravel road and down the other for hours. Long past dark, I returned and pulled in the lane at Mo's. I knew there wouldn't be a naked body in a lumberjack shirt waiting for me this time, and when I went in, the house was dark, the gentle tick-tock of the clock on the wall, the only sounds. Heading straight for the fridge, pulling out a beer, I slumped on the couch, opened the beer and drained it. I got up, retrieved another, passing the blanket fort, thinking the answer lay in there.

After two more trips to the fridge, the blanket fort starting to look promising. I heard stirring coming from the hallway. Bandit came trotting out, Mo close behind, wrapped in her housecoat and thick socks. Her hair fell over her face, she pushed it back, and sat down on the other end of the couch, purposely maintaining the distance between us. Bandit jumped up on the couch and curled up against my hip, but I ignored the urge to pet him. Mo glared at me, and I sensed right then and there, what I said next would determine both our fates. It was no time for glib horseshit and my usual stickhandling. I knew I was going to have to be honest and forthright in ways I had never been. Mo continued to glare at me, and I couldn't blame her. Should I have told her? Probably, as I had the opportunity, more than once. But I didn't, and I guess I fell back into old habits. I didn't know what to say, or how to say it.

I mean, gee Mo, there's this guy named Teddy, who I randomly met a few months ago in a bar in Ottawa, and he offered me fifty thousand dollars to find his missing sister. Since I was feeling down on my luck that day, and I was greedy, I took it, but she wasn't missing. Then he offered me more money to pick up this box full of useless papers and deliver it to him, in effect, becoming his mule. Then these bikers appeared, and they beat me up and took the box, but I chased them down and got it back by blowing up their bikes. And along the way, there was Syd, the girl bouncer at a pool hall in Peterborough, and not the hockey player. Then there was Leia the server in Havelock, who just for fun carried a .45 in her purse. Then there was this guy Dave, who I beat to a bloody pulp. Finally, there was Tony and the time I pointed a gun at his head, threatening to blow his brains out. But you know what, honey? All this led me here to you, and now we can get married and have kids and live happily ever after. That's it in a nutshell. What do you think?

Strangely, Mo believed me. I think. When I finished talking, dawn poking through the curtains, Mo laid her head in my lap and fell asleep. Proving you just never know, and honesty is always the best policy. Sometimes.

53

"HE HAS IT."

"Well, I already knew that, asshole. Fuck! Did you not do as I instructed?"

"Yes, I did, boss," Tony answered nervously.

"Well, if you did, then you would have been calling me to tell me *you* have it, and not that *he* still has it."

"You're right boss, he still has it. But I am going to get it, soon."

"When, Tony when!?" Teddy demanded, having lost all patience with Tony.

"Soon boss, soon."

"When is soon?"

"A week."

"A fucking what?"

"A week. Pete said he needed a week, boss."

"Why the fuck a week? Why would that fucker need a week? It's a fucking box, for Christ's sake! Make him hand it over or fucking take it from him! I don't care which. Jesus fucking Christ, Tony!"

"Um, yeah, I know, um, it was just um, he um, asked for a week. So, I figured I was going to be up there for a bit anyway, and I didn't think it would hurt."

"You didn't think it would hurt? You didn't think that he's playing you, buying time, delaying things. Are you even sure he has the box? Did you see it?"

"No, boss. But he said he had it. Why would he lie?"

"Oh, I don't know, Tony, I can think of a hundred reasons right off the top of my head, but hey, you're there, and I'm here, what do I know?"

"He promised, boss."

"Well, that makes it all right then. He promised, and you believed him?"

"Yes, boss. Yes, I did."

"Did you not think that he's stalling so he can get rid of what's inside? Destroy the box? Burn it? And that's why he's asking for a week?"

"Um … no … um, actually no. I didn't think of that. He wouldn't do that, would he?"

"Gee, Tony, I don't know, would he? I mean, you know. You gave him a week, so he has plenty of time now."

"I'm sorry boss. I didn't think. Do you want me to go get it? Take it from him? I can, I know where he stays."

"No, no, that would just cause another scene. I can't afford another one. Leave it. A week it is."

"Okay, boss. I promise, one week, and I will have the box for you."

"You better. And Tony?"

"Yes, boss?"

"If you don't get me that box, you're a dead man, plain and simple. And if you were smart, you would do it yourself and save me the mess. But any way you look at it, you're a dead man without the box. Got it?"

"Yes, boss. I got it."

Teddy placed the phone face down on the bar, staring straight ahead. Dale was not going to be happy when he told him the news. He was furious when he found out he had been after it, and now that it was missing, he would be even more furious. That was something he didn't want; dealing with him when he was like that. It was bad enough dealing with Dale period, and this could send him over the edge. There was no telling what he would do. It all seemed so simple initially. How the fuck did things get so screwed up?

"You okay?" Sara asked.

"Yeah, I'm good, why?"

"You don't look good. Are you sure, is everything okay?"

"Yes, I'm just tired."

Sara reached over the counter and placed her hand on his arm. "I love you."

"Me too, sis." Teddy smiled.

Sara's mouth tightened, lips quivering, her voice cracked. "Teddy, if I ever lost you. I couldn't bear it … I can't … I can't lose you. Not after Mom and Dad. Please Teddy, whatever it is you're doing, be careful. Promise me, okay?"

How she wished she could find the courage to tell him what happened that night.

"I promise, sis," he squeezed her hand. "I promise everything will be okay."

Patty walked into the bar. "Teddy, can you give me a hand out back, please?"

"Sure, Miss Patty," he said, giving his sister's hand another squeeze before sliding off the stool.

"Amy, honey, there's a takeout order ready to go. Can you get it? The person should be here any minute for it."

Turning toward Patty, she curtsied. "Why sure, Miss Patty, right away," she drawled in her best southern belle accent.

"Oh, you …" Patty laughed. "What would I do without you?"

54

THE FOLLOWING WEEK could be best be described as the week from hell. The days and nights filled with tension, we all had our moments with it, but surprisingly, we all found a way to coexist in the bar. It wasn't easy though with Bree's outright disgust and hatred toward Tony.

The time she came out from the kitchen, arm raised, brandishing a carving knife, it took both Mo and me to restrain her, and we had to forcefully send her home to cool off. Mo hid her disgust with Tony and his lewd comments, remaining silent for the most part, but I could see it was eating her up inside. And though things seemed to be back on the mend, after I finally spilled my guts, there was still a distance between us. Wisely, I just let her be, following that age-old sage advice and giving her lots and lots of space.

Tony and I warily eyed each other, as I was painfully aware of his strength and maintained a safe distance at all times. Still, he unnerved me and held power over me, unlike any adversary from my past. He remained a condescending, male chauvinist prick, continually firing sexual innuendo and insults the girls' way, never mind eating non-stop. I still wasn't sure if I could kill someone in cold blood, and Tony sensing this, made sure to provoke me just enough to keep me on edge. The only one that managed to escape this was Adrian, who coincidentally had left the morning that Tony showed to visit family in Sudbury. Lucky him.

I felt like shit and stopped sleeping. I was no closer to tying the loose ends together of how Teddy supposedly knew me, and how maybe it was just a coincidence that our fathers died a year apart to the day? I had hoped that buying some time, I would be able to get us out of this mess. I was shocked when I proposed a week and Tony readily agreed. But as time marched on, it didn't seem to be on my side, and I felt lost. More than once, I thought of handing over the box to Tony and wiping my hands of it. But each time, the little voice inside poked me, saying, "not yet."

The peaceful, easy feeling from nights on the stairwell had been replaced by doubt, fear, and rumination. A couple of mornings later, after spending another sleepless night in the blanket fort, I crawled out and still prone on all fours on the floor, looked up to see Mo coming down the hallway, carrying the box in her hands. She sat on the couch, the box on her lap, looked over at me and smiled.

"Time we figured out what all this fuss was about, huh? I hope you don't mind." She flipped off the lid. "I got curious and found it in your trunk."

I was relieved that she didn't stumble on my .45, or had she? I let it be.

"Babe, make us some coffee," she said, while starting to lift the papers out, "and let's see what's in here."

Returning with the coffee and slipping on the couch beside her, the distance between us noticeable, we poured through the papers, as I explained what all the police jargon meant. Her eyes widened when she saw the names Sara and Edward Polson. Tears formed in her eyes, reading about their parents and how they died tragically, and she couldn't comprehend something so awful happening to her parents.

I told her what I knew about Sara and that they had something in common: street bikes. Mo asked if she was pretty and if I liked her. I said no, as I had never actually met her, only seeing a picture of her. I got up and retrieved the picture from my wallet, Mo remarked enviously how pretty she was, but I replied that no one could hold a candle to her. Corny as it was, it broke the ice between us, and for the next few minutes we hugged and kissed. Returning to the papers, now wrapped in the blanket, snuggled in close, legs and arms intertwined, we soldiered on. Then Mo noticed what had been disturbing me. The neatness of the handwriting and thoroughness of the notes, the signature at the bottom of each page, with its illegible scribble, and how it didn't seem to match the writing.

We were forced to stop there, as lust took over. The papers spilled over the couch and onto the floor as we embraced, the cloth belt on Mo's bathrobe slipping away, her skin soft and warm, as I rolled on top of her. It was over quick, after picking up the papers, we put them safely back in the box, and adjourned to the blanket fort.

55

"YOU LIKE HOCKEY?"

"Sure," I said. "It's all right, I guess."

"Let's get out of here, game starts in an hour. Let's go."

Mo was right, a night out would be nice. I hadn't thought about hockey or played in years. We jumped off the couch, and twenty minutes later, we were ready to leave but almost didn't make it. When Mo came down the hallway wearing a leather jacket, tight jeans tucked into long brown leather boots, my jaw dropped.

"I'm okay if we miss the puck drop," I said wearing a mischievous grin, "and you can leave your boots on."

"Later," she said. "Promise."

We parked and walking with the crowd, McIntyre Arena, home of the Timmins Rock, was like every small town in Canada on a Friday night—Junior Hockey. It had been so long since I had been in an arena. We had no problem scoring tickets and plopped in our seats just as the warm-up ended. Nothing had changed, and it felt like yesterday, the crowd and its Friday night vibe; the rush of it, the sights, sounds, and smells of small-town hockey.

The odour of popcorn as you enter stimulated your taste buds even if you had already eaten. The tasty aromas of coffee and pizza blend, and they're strangely appetizing. And just as appetizing, every other person carrying hot dogs as they casually moved about the concourse. Kids playing tag, zigzagging through the lobby and out the doors on each side, running along the rows of seats, chasing each other up and down the concrete steps that made up the arena bowl.

The fans arrived in groups of twos and threes, greeting each other like long-lost relatives, forming circles, all chatting excitedly and catching up on everything that had transpired since they last saw one another (just a short week ago at the previous game). The barking of volunteers—retirees and high school students putting in their hours, hawking 50/50 tickets and wandering around the concourse and the arena bowl. "Get your 50/50 tickets … $2,500 jackpot tonight but could go higher …" enticing the fans to dig deeper in their pockets.

I easily picked out the married hockey guys—in their minor hockey jackets, with 'COACH' embroidered on the sleeve, all who probably drove an F-150 or Dodge Ram, huddled in the corners of the lobby with the other coaches. Juggling their beer, they were animatedly discussing tomorrow's 6:00 a.m. practice plans, and no doubt sharing the latest drama involving their problem kid and overbearing parents.

I had forgotten those memories, nice memories too. But the other memories—of my friend, Billy and our last game together … and my dad—well, they weren't so pleasant, and I was taken aback at how easily stirred they were. I thought I had done a good job of burying them. I guess I didn't after all.

"You okay, babe?" Mo asked, noticing me slumped in my seat, eyes glazed, staring straight ahead.

"Sure, sure, I was thinking about the box."

Mo patted my thigh, leaning over, she kissed me lightly on the cheek. "Let it go, for tonight at least; it will be there tomorrow."

"Promise?"

"Promise what?"

"Promise that it will still be there tomorrow?"

She looked at me.

"I mean, I'm having so much fun with all of this I wouldn't want it to stop."

Mo laughed and punched my shoulder. "Tell you what. Think about this instead." Then she leaned in and whispered in my ear. "Think about fucking me later in nothing but these boots." Then she lifted her leg and started rubbing mine with her boot.

"Promise?" I said, breaking into a grin.

"Promise."

"Shake."

Mo laughed, as we shook hands, shaking her head.

"Remember, you promised."

The Rock and Rayside Balfour took to the ice, and the game started. Right away, something caught my attention, and ignoring the play, I focused on the visiting team's bench. Squinting, I saw a familiar figure. I watched intently as the figure paced back and forth behind the bench, animated, patting players on the back offering encouragement, barking at the referee.

Coach Billy.

"Well, I'll be."

"What? Who?" Mo asked.

"Coach Billy."

"Coach who?"

"Coach Billy."

I shifted forward in the seat pointing to the visitor's bench. "There! Behind the bench. That's him behind the bench. That's Coach Billy! Fucking Coach Billy." I sat back in amazement.

Mo, alarmed at my outburst, asked, "Do you know each other?"

"We sure do! We played together when we were teenagers. He was my d-man. He and I were inseparable, on and off the ice."

"That's great, babe." Mo patted my leg. Nodding, ignoring the game, my eyes remained glued to the bench.

The last time I had seen Billy was when I ran into him one winter's day in Barrie, a couple of years after our last game together, and I was in training to become a cop. He was in town, playing, and we had a brief catch-up in the sports bar across from the rink, then I never saw him again. I would hear about him from time to time whenever he was called up to the Show.

Like a lot of hockey careers, Billy's faded before it ever got started. He had talent, just not enough to play in the Show on a regular basis, so he started preparing for what lay ahead next: coaching. That was what he was good at. So, he started coaching minor hockey, then slowly worked his way up through the ranks, but got stuck as an assistant coach at the minor pro level. Finally, he got his break and landed a head coaching job in junior, but his timing couldn't have been worse. The team's ownership was in a mess, and as he suspected later, that was the only reason he landed the job in the first place. He was fired at Christmas and returned to being an assistant coach. But that experience had stirred something, as he wanted to be a head coach, somewhere, anywhere, it didn't matter. He was head coach material through and through. So, he started looking for head coaching opportunities, no matter the level, and once more worked his way back up. And here he was now.

"You never told me about him," Mo said, curious.

"Oh, there's not much to tell really. We played together."

"It's more than that. I can tell by your reaction."

"No … no, I just haven't seen him in a long time, that's all." I deliberately turned my attention back to the game.

"Spill!" Mo poked me in the side.

I turned to Mo and provided the Coles Notes version and, once again, deflecting an unpleasant memory from my past. In this case, what happened in our last game together, and my dad not being there, missing my game for the one and only time.

"We played together when we were teenagers. He was good, and I wasn't. He treated me like a brother. I miss him. We had fun. You know all those good memories when you are a teenager."

Mo looked at me. "That's nice," she said, as she turned back to the game, detecting that I wasn't exactly forthcoming about Billy.

I didn't realize how much I had missed Billy. He'd had such an impact on me. He grounded me just like my dad, keeping me on the straight and narrow. Seeing him here was completely unexpected, and I certainly wasn't ready for it. That was such a long time ago. We didn't have a falling out or anything. Our lives had simply gone in different directions—make that completely *opposite* directions.

As the game progressed, I went back and forth on whether I wanted to seek him out after. My stomach was in knots, and I was torn. On one hand, it would be great to see him. It had been years. But what did I have to hide in order to see him again, and would it be worth it afterward? I don't know about you, but did you ever catch up with someone you had a history with and hadn't seen in years, and it didn't go the way you hoped? Like those high school reunions. You think it will be great, all those wonderful memories and good times associated with the past. Then, when you do finally meet up, you don't look the same, you don't act the same, you both have changed. Attitudes, outlooks, and perspectives are replaced by maturity and life experiences. There's an awkwardness, as you sadly realize that all this time, you were living in a fantasy world about the past.

So, I wasn't sure this was a good idea, especially with everything that was going on around me now. I honestly didn't know if I could handle it, if Coach Billy was no longer Coach Billy, or worse, if Pete Humphries was no longer Pete Humphries. I also knew the first thing he was going to ask was, *Pete, what in the geezus fuck are you doing up here?* Or worse, he'd ask about my dad.

I wasn't prepared to answer either question. I had already been through one attempt with that recently, and I wasn't feeling very good about a second time. The second period ended, and Mo nudged me, asking if I wanted another beer.

"Sure," I responded, still staring out at the ice, the Zamboni slowly circling.

I nursed my beer through the third period, silent, Mo letting me be, sensing something was up. My eyes remained on the clock as the minutes ticked down. The score was 3–1 Timmins with eight minutes left, and I knew I had a decision to make. If I sought Billy out, I could wind up regretting it. I knew if I didn't, I would regret that also. Lovely, a rock, and a hard place. I still wasn't sure what to do as the clock fell under five minutes left to play.

"Why don't you just go?" Mo said, squeezing my arm. "You know you want to. I'm sure it will be fine, and he will be happy to see you."

"Will you come with me?" I asked, turning my head to Mo.

"Sure, babe. I love the smell of sweaty hockey players and dressing rooms. Maybe we could have sex in one, and I can wear your smelly old jock."

Smiling, relieved, I reached for Mo's hand holding it tightly in my lap. I was still anxious at going down to see Billy, but at least I had a wingman—or wing*girl*—with me. The game ended, and I told Mo we had to wait a bit until things cleared out before we could go down.

"Are you sure they will let us through?" Mo asked.

"Yes, it's not the Show," I laughed.

Finally, the crowd had dispersed, the seats empty, and the hallway down below appeared clear.

"Okay, let's go!" I said, reaching for Mo, fighting off the huge knot in my stomach.

Stepping over the rows, working our way on an angle down to the glass and the entrance to the player's area, I held Mo's hand as she stepped over the last seat, and then we were standing near the glass and the entrance to the hallway.

"It's much cooler down here. How come I don't smell anything? Maybe my sense of smell is numb already."

Rolling my eyes, we started down the long hallway looking for Billy, Mo holding my hand and tagging along behind. We passed some open doorways, stopping and allowing half-dressed players and other staff to move in and out.

"Can I help you?" the team trainer asked, poking his head out of an open doorway.

"Coach Billy. I'm looking for Coach Billy."

Looking me over then seeing Mo behind me. "You know women really shouldn't be down here. Lots of naked guys."

"It's okay," she said. "I like naked guys, especially *this* one," she grinned, pinching my butt.

"I'm looking for the coach. Is he around?"

Giving us another once over, the trainer hesitated, and just as I was thinking this was a mistake, I heard a booming voice coming from down the hall.

"Bomber? BOMBER! Holy fuck, Bomber! How are you?"

Walking towards me was Billy, his big booming voice matching his big booming frame, his face lit up in a huge grin, hand already out. As I stepped forward, he grabbed me in a bear hug and lifted me off the ground. He squeezed me hard, then letting go, stepped back and started pumping my hand.

"Pete, what in the geezus fuck are you doing up here? I haven't seen you in years."

"You look good in a shirt and tie. Your mom still dressing you?"

Billy laughed hard and hugged me again, pounding me on the back. He stepped back and looked me over.

"How've you been? You look good."

Then Billy saw Mo standing behind me.

"Please don't tell me you're with *him*," he said to Mo, then punched me in the shoulder. "Good job, Bomber. I didn't think you had it in you. Nice to see you finally moved on from all those puck bunnies."

Billy moved around me and extended his hand out to Mo. "Hi, I'm Bill. Nice to meet you. How did you end up with this guy?"

"Blind date on a bridge," Mo said, winking at me.

"I'm hoping not on the ledge. Pete always liked to live on the edge." He chuckled and poked me on the arm.

I was beaming and grabbed Billy again, hugging him tight, knowing this was the right call. We were forced to shift to one side to allow players to pass, and Mo squeezed my hand.

"Babe, I'm going to let you guys catch up, okay? I can get a lift back. You take your time and catch up. See you at home."

Mo extended her hand again towards Billy. "Very nice to meet you, Coach Billy."

"You too," he smiled warmly.

We watched Mo walk down the hallway, and Billy punched me again in the shoulder. "Good job, man. Good job. Any place we can grab a beer?"

"There's not much around here, but there are a couple of places up the road. I can drive and drop you back after."

"Sounds good. Give me a few minutes to finish up here. The bus will take the team back to the motel, and I can get one of my coaches to cover for me."

"Are you sure?"

"Absolutely Bomber," he said with a broad smile on his face. "Meet you upstairs."

Twenty minutes later, Billy came bounding up the stairs, still wearing a huge grin. He slapped me on the back as we walked out the doors into the chilly night. My car was parked around the corner, and Billy was impressed when he saw it.

"That's so you, Bomber," he said, as he got in the passenger side. He noticed the eight-track player in the dash and turned serious.

"Your dad, right? How are you doing? How have you been holding up, Pete?"

56

IT WAS AFTER two thirty when I came in the door. The house was quiet, the stove light on in the kitchen. Kicking off my runners, flipping my jean jacket on the hook, I walked over to the fridge, reached for a beer, then moved to the couch and flopped down. Sitting forward, I looked over at the blanket fort and thought of shifting to it, but it was too far away. Flicking the tab on my beer, taking a sip, I sat back. Then I leaned forward again, restless, unable to stop the noise swirling around in my head. I bit my lip, fighting off the wave of emotion that threatened to swamp me at any moment.

"Babe? You okay? Everything okay with Billy?"

Mo was standing in the hallway, and I fought back the tears, biting my lip harder.

"Yes, I'm fine, Billy's great. I was so happy to see him. He likes you. Thinks you're great. Great for me."

"I like him too. Then what is it, Pete? What's wrong?"

Mo walked over, a worried look on her face. I sighed, took another sip, and leaned back against the couch, running my hand through my hair. It was time. Finally, this was the time, and this was the place.

"We need to talk."

Mo's face dropped.

"It's okay. Um uh … ah shit, there's something I need to tell you. I haven't been completely honest with you," I said, reaching out for her hand.

Mo stood perfectly still, her hand limp as I held it.

"Sit down. Please. It's okay, it really is. I need … I mean, I want to tell you about my dad."

"I thought you said your parents lived in Barrie? Do they?"

"I know, sorry. I should have told you. I just didn't know how …"

Mo sat down cross-legged on the couch, and I turned and faced her. Her hands were in her lap, her eyes darting about uncertain.

"I'm not good at this. I never was. I wanted to be. I wish I could be. But I can't. I don't know how."

"Try."

"Easy for you."

"No … no, it's not. Remember that first night when you came here? And you saw the blanket fort and thought it was cool. You understand me. You listen to me. You let me be just me. You make me feel comfortable and safe."

"I know."

"So, here's your chance, spill. I'm not going to bite."

Mo was right. I felt comfortable around her and had never felt like that with anyone else. It had always been about the sex and good times, and once it moved beyond that, I cut the lines on the dock and drifted away.

"And just so you know. I've been waiting. I know you have been keeping a lot from me, and I can only imagine why. I just figured when you were ready, you would. But did you have to pick three in the morning?" Then she leaned over and punched me on the arm. "You're interfering with my beauty sleep and STOP! I don't want to hear any of your corny comments."

"I wasn't going to," I said. We both knew that was a lie.

The best place to start was from the beginning, so that's where I started, back at the beginning. I told Mo my mom, Debbie, left when I was three. "It was the only thing he would never talk about. My dad raised me by himself, sacrificing so much, but that's what dads do, right?

"He was always there. He never missed a school event or game. He took me anywhere I wanted or needed to go. We did everything together. We went everywhere together. On Saturday mornings, we would sit at the kitchen table, and he would pull out the road atlas and say, 'Where do you want to go today, Pete? Pick a place.' And off we would go just like that. That's where my love of fast cars, music, and eight-tracks, came from."

Mo had sat back on the couch, legs crossed, listening.

"At times, though, my dad could be distant and quiet. He never got angry, but he could be distant. I'm guessing it was due to my mom and that she had left. But he wouldn't talk about it, and I was too afraid to approach him. I could see that he was lonely, and as I got older, I started to worry, knowing that at some point I would eventually move out, leaving him all alone. He had devoted his life to me, so what was he going to do then?

"When I was fifteen, my dad met Lisa. It was a chance meeting one day in the grocery store. Their carts collided in an aisle, and that was that. That chance meeting, completely out of nowhere, that instant connection."

"Sort of like us that day on the bridge," Mo said with a sleepy smile.

"You knew then?" I asked, surprised.

"Totally."

"You're my favourite brat, you know."

"Uh-uh, keep talking," she said.

"Dad and Lisa started seeing each other, but he never told me. I just knew he was starting to go out more often at night. About six months later, he brought Lisa home and introduced her. She was younger than my dad and I took a shine to her immediately, and her to me. But it wasn't the mom thing, and she was like the sister I never had. I felt so comfortable around her and could talk to her about almost anything. And I saw that she made my dad happy. Despite the age difference, they just fit, like they had known each other forever."

"Like us," I said.

"Like us." Mo smiled, reached over and rubbed my leg.

"A couple of months later, Dad asked if it was okay if Lisa moved in with us, worried that it would affect our dynamic. But seeing how happy she made him and knowing that I had only a few more years living with him, I was all for it. He was so happy and changed overnight, more open and loving. We still did everything together, but I saw the change in him. How could anyone feel threatened by that? Lisa fit into our lives perfectly. She kept her own life, did her own things, spent time with her friends, but she always made time for Dad. She just had this knack."

I must have paused just a moment too long because Mo spoke up.

"Nice," she said, stifling a yawn. "But where does Billy come into things?"

"Right, sorry, I'm getting to that. My dad signed me up for hockey when I was seven, but he had never played and didn't know how to skate, but he wanted me to learn. He took me to every practice and game, no matter the time, or the weather. He never missed a single one. He would sit in the cold stands, alone, drinking that godawful arena coffee from a Styrofoam cup. He was my biggest supporter. I was pretty good, played defence. My dad used to make me watch old films of Bobby Orr."

"Who's Bobby Orr?"

"Seriously?" my eyes bugging out at Mo.

"Too easy," Mo grinned.

"When I was twelve, I got noticed and jumped from house league to the travelling team. It was harder on my dad because it cost more, plus we were away almost every weekend, travelling to all these small towns all over Ontario. His work was good about it, and when Lisa came along, she was a saint about it. That took so much pressure off us. She looked after our clothes, food and drinks, packing our bags and the cooler on Fridays then cleaning it out Sunday nights when we returned home, usually very late. She spent the next week doing laundry, never complaining.

"She always asked me how we did, and though she didn't care for hockey, she cared about me, and my dad. She would write out these notes and place them in his bag, telling him how proud she was of the both of us, and how much she loved him. That kept my dad going. Every once in a while, I got one too, reminding me not to take it too seriously, that it was just a game.

"When I was fifteen, not long after Lisa came into our lives, I met Billy. We landed on the same team that fall, and we got paired together on defence. He would sit beside me in the dressing room, plopping his big butt beside me, teasing, making fun of me. I'm moody at times, and he was always making me laugh."

"No. You? Moody?" Mo smirked, unable to control herself. I made a face, sticking out my tongue at her.

"I was always there early, and he was always late. So, I would spread my stuff out on the bench, saving his spot. Over time we became inseparable, and he was like the brother I never had. We made quite a pair on defence. He liked to rush the puck, and I liked to stay back, and I guess that's why I never became the next Bobby Orr.

"We drove the coaches crazy, which became a game in itself. Billy and I would take these long shifts, and I was always covering his ass, which I never let him forget, and we rarely got scored on. Oh sure, we lost our share of games and had the odd bad one, but we were clutch, and the coaches knew it. We always played the last five minutes of a period or game, if the score was close either way. And tough. We were tough, all right, but we were never mean. We played hard but never dirty. I don't know why, we just didn't. Early on, I sensed it wasn't Billy's way, and I picked up on that.

"During the games, when we were on the bench, Billy would search the stands, pointing out the local puck bunnies, and we would rate them. We would laugh and giggle, pointing to them in the stands, right in the middle of some intense games too. Then the coach would bark at us, and we would jump back on the ice, still laughing and giggling.

"When we turned seventeen, our birthdays two months apart, we started hearing rumours about scouts and stuff. We both thought we were too old already, but it seemed we weren't. That spring, we made it all the way to the Ontario finals of our division. My dad had changed jobs at Christmas, moving into a management role with IBM, better pay, fewer hours, but it meant more travelling for him. He had to travel to other cities more frequently, and he started worrying he would miss one of my games. As the playoffs wound down, it was becoming harder to determine the upcoming dates. Sure enough, we made the finals and got the schedule. But then my dad was asked to travel to Pittsburgh at the last minute. He always drove.

"He hated flying and preferred driving, though it took longer, it was less expensive, so work was okay with it. Plus, most of the travelling was in Ontario and to Binghamton, New York, so it was manageable. But if he drove this time, he would miss not only a game but most of the finals especially if we only went four games. So, he went to his boss and asked to fly. Flying, he wouldn't miss any of the games, as he was certain he could schedule the flights around the breaks in the schedule. Amazingly it worked. The series went seven games, and as luck would have it, there was a three-day break between games six and seven, so my dad flew to Pittsburgh the morning after game six.

"When my dad travelled, he always called when he arrived to let us know he had arrived safely, no matter how late it was. That came from the very first time my dad travelled after Lisa moved in. He arrived at his destination but didn't let us know until the next day. I was used to it, but Lisa was having none of it. The only time I ever saw her mad at him. She told him that if he ever did that again, she wouldn't be there when he arrived back home.

"When he left that morning, we never heard from him again. We checked the flights and saw he had landed. We called the hotel, but they said he hadn't checked in yet. So naturally, we were worried. This was so unlike him. My dad loved his newspapers and subscribed to the local paper, which was delivered every morning on our doorstep. The next morning, after getting up, I got the morning paper from the doorstep. I never read the paper, I wasn't a paper guy, I guess. Anyhow, I picked up the paper and looked up to see a police car pulling into our driveway.

"My world changed in that instant. I started shaking, and I began to cry. I dropped the paper on the step and went inside slamming the door shut behind me. I started yelling for Lisa, and she came running in. I kept saying over and over, 'Dad, Dad, Dad, Dad.' Then I fell to the floor. I couldn't comprehend it. Lisa started screaming also. It was a nightmare.

"We were both lying on the floor screaming and crying. The police did their best to console us. They said my dad was in his rental car driving into the city when he was hit by a drunk driver going the wrong way on the turnpike.

"Life was never the same after. How could it be? Lisa looked after my dad's stuff as best she could, but she had no legal ties because they never married. What was worse was playing game seven without my dad, two days later. It was a blur. People tried to tell me not to play, but I knew my dad would have wanted me to. Billy stuck by my side like glue, supporting whatever decision I made.

"I played, skating out on the ice with such a heavy heart. I couldn't look up in the stands, and see my dad sitting in the same spot, well it was awful. On the bench, all I did was cry. Near the end of the game, it got worse, as if things could get any worse. We were down 4–2 and play was in our end. They had this goon, who had been after Billy all game, trying to goad him into a fight, but Billy wouldn't bite. The two of them were going into the corner for the puck, and the guy waited a split second longer then cross-checked Billy in the back, sending him headfirst into the boards. It sounded and looked way worse than it was, the rink going abruptly silent.

"Billy finally got up and skated off, but something inside of me snapped at that moment. I guess the pressure of losing my dad had become too much. I stayed on the bench the rest of the game, and we lost 5–2 on an empty-net goal. The other team celebrated then we lined up to shake hands. I purposely slipped into the back of the line and waited for the goon to come along. Typically, once the game is over, no matter how intense, you shake hands and it's over. But not that night. As the goon approached, I slipped my left glove off, usually you'd slip off the right so you can shake hands. When I reached him, I held out my gloved hand and as he went to tap it, I suckered him, shattering his plastic shield and sending him sprawling. I jumped him and started flailing away, all hell breaking loose.

"Everyone was into it. The fans poured over the glass and joined in. It was insane. The fight spilled into the Zamboni entrance and then into the hallway. At one point, I was fighting two guys at once. We were all grappling with each other when we fell through an open dressing room door. It was me, two of my teammates, and the goon. I jumped up and shut the door, and it went silent at the sound of the lock clicking shut. Three on one. My teammates held the guy, bent backward over the bench, and I beat him senseless.

"It wasn't my finest moment, and I regret it and would take it back if I could. It was the loss of my dad …

"I got suspended, of course, but what I didn't expect was a lifetime ban. That effectively blackballed me from playing competitive hockey ever again. And with that, Billy and I went our separate ways, life now taking us in opposite directions. In time, I realized I didn't care, and with my dad gone, hockey lost all meaning, and I had never set foot in a rink until tonight.

"The next few years were a struggle. I buried my dad, never shedding a tear, and I worried that maybe there was something wrong with me because I felt that I didn't or couldn't grieve. After the first anniversary, I stopped visiting my dad at the gravesite, it was too difficult, and I hoped he would understand. So, imagine at seventeen and growing up without your dad? No mom either. Lisa tried and did the best she could, but she was awash in her own grief. Adding to the fact that they had never married, she couldn't receive financial support of any kind. They had talked about getting married, many times, but they never did. Too afraid to wreck a good thing, I guess.

"When I turned nineteen, I moved out and bounced around from place to place for the next year, then I decided to become a cop, thinking the structure and authority would ground me. My dad had loved all those cops shows from the seventies, and maybe it was my way to remain connected to him. Lisa initially stayed in the house, not wanting to start over again. Losing my dad crushed her, a fresh start wasn't what she wanted or needed. But now that I was of legal age, I sold the house, and due to the housing market downswing at the time, I didn't get near as much as I had hoped. So, I gave it to Lisa and told her that she had to find a new life for herself, with what time she had left."

I stopped, too exhausted to continue further, and looked over at Mo, unsure how she would react. Tired, worn out, strangely I felt better. I felt lighter, a sense of relief as I had finally got this burden off my chest.

Mo reached out and, taking my hand in her lap, stroked it. Her eyes were wet, and she leaned over and hugged me. We sat quietly, feeling each other's rhythmic breathing. She squeezed me then sat back, still holding my hand.

"Sounds like your dad was a good man, Pete."

"He was, but I don't think I am," I said. "Not anywhere close to him."

"Why? Why would you say that?"

"Because I don't think I am." Tears started rolling down my cheeks.

"I don't understand."

"I failed. I can't forgive myself for it. It's all my fault. I didn't have the courage to tell Dale and Karen that Joanna and the white picket fence life wasn't what I wanted. I started to resent them both for it and eventually pulled away. I loved them. And, I just up and walked away from my career as a police officer. To me, they were all linked together somehow. But now, I'm seeing they weren't."

The realization of all of this finally hit home, and I collapsed into Mo's lap, the grief pouring out, unable to stop it. I cried and cried.

I realized I still hadn't accepted my dad was gone. I was still lost without him because I had never grieved for him, instead allowing denial to work its magic and locking it away, so it wouldn't allow me to move forward and become strong on my own. Becoming a police officer was my way of remaining connected to my dad, thinking if I did this would he magically reappear? The footsteps had finally caught me, and I was now forced to deal with it, and it fucking hurt.

Mo stroked my head and rubbed my back. "It's okay ... just let it out ... get it out ... it's going to be okay."

57

I MOPED AROUND for the next couple of days, Mo letting me be, while I processed my chance meeting with Billy and finally coming to terms with my dad. Unable to sleep one night, I moved out to the blanket fort, where Mo found me the next morning.

"Babe?"

"I'm in here," I said. I could hear shuffling, then rustling and the flap opened, Mo poked her head inside.

"Comfy?" she asked, looking at Bandit lying beside me.

"Very."

"Sleep okay?"

"Yes, you?"

"Yes," Mo said, smiling. "Seriously, are you okay?"

"Yes, I am, now. Thank you."

"For what?"

"Listening," I said.

"It's what we do, why we fit," she said, her eyes shining.

"Bree told me why you started the fight that night."

I frowned.

"It's okay. I understand. I wish you had told me and not her, but I get it."

"I'm sorry," I said." I promise from now on—"

"Shake on it," Mo reached down and we tapped fists.

"Care to join me?" I asked, feeling frisky.

"No, I better shower. We should go soon. I don't want to leave Bree and Tony alone for too long. Yesterday had its moments and remember what happened earlier this week," recalling Bree coming out of the kitchen, brandishing the carving knife and waving it at Tony, pretending she was Jack Torrance.

"Can I join you then?" licking my lips.

"Normally, yes, but we better not, okay? I worry about Bree."

Mo backed out, the tent flap closing over, but she quickly pulled it back, poking her head through.

"You changed your mind?" I asked.

"Is that all you think about?"

"Yes, but so do you."

"I know, busted, what can I say?" Mo shrugged. "Pete, why did you tell me your parents lived in Barrie?"

"Um ... easier, I guess ... I didn't know how to tell you, as you found out the other night."

She nodded. "Just curious."

She backed out again, the flap closing over. I could see the bottom of her housecoat through the flap, and she started to stand up but bent down and poked her head through.

"What now?" I said. "And no, too late! I've changed my mind. I won't have sex with you."

She rolled her eyes. "The other night, Billy called you Bomber."

"Yup. It's a guy thing, a hockey-guy thing."

"Good lord, I'm glad I'm not one of you."

"Me too," I said, the image of Mo with stubble, hairy arms and legs, wearing goalie equipment, floating in my head.

"Babe, hockey guys go by last names but mostly nicknames. And we get the nicknames from the stuff that happens at the rink, mostly in the dressing room," I explained.

Mo shook her head, trying to wrap her mind around what I was saying. "He called you Bomber?"

"Yup."

"I'm afraid to ask."

"I was always dropping farts see? On the bench, in the dressing room. Bombs we called them. Hence Bomber."

Disgusted, Mo backed out, the flap flopping over, her fuzzy slippers moved past the opening. I listened as she went down the hallway. " … bomber … fart bombs … fucking fart bombs … I'm with a guy who drops fart bombs …"

"Mo, wait!" I called out, snickering, "come back and let me show you how I got my nickname."

"UGH!" as the bathroom door slammed.

An hour later, we left in my Chevy, but not before I made a quick stop at the trunk, my intuition raising the red flag, and retrieved my gun and tucked it in the back of my jeans. We were finishing up a game of punch buggy as we walked up the stairs into The Club.

"Did not."

"Did too."

"Did not!"

"OW!"

"Did too."

"Did not!"

"OW! Geez, that hurt!"

"Say it."

"Say what?"

"OW!"

"Saaayy it."

"No."

"Say it, or I will hit you harder."

"Fine."

"Then say it."

"Fine … you win," I sighed heavily.

"Why is that so hard?" Mo asked, grinning.

"Because you win every time."

"I know, but—"

"Brat!"

"What?"

"Nuthin ... I hate you."

"No, you don't."

"Yes, I do."

"Okay! STOP! Seriously, I mean it."

Suddenly, coming from the kitchen, we heard screaming, banging, crashing, the sound of something breaking, and we looked at each other. "Bree! Shit!" We started running, plowing through the kitchen doors, to find Tony's back was up against the grill, and Bree, her top ripped open at the front, was holding a giant rolling pin over her head, ready to strike.

"You fucking pig! You, you ... FUCKER! You fucking no good cocksucker! You fucking ugly pig ... I am going to fucking kill you, you, you, fucker!"

The rolling pin dangling in the air, Bree started toward Tony, he tried to back away but had no place to go. Wide-eyed, Tony looked to us for help.

"We were just playing is all, just having a little fun. I meant no harm. Aw, come on sweet cheeks, you know I was only funning."

"You call humping me from behind fun? You fucking mother fucking fucker, I am going to give you some fun, all right."

Bree, incensed, spit at Tony, and started toward him. Mo lunged at Bree and pushed her back against the sink, reached up and pulled Bree's arm down, grasping the rolling pin and holding it against Bree's side. I moved into the gap between them, glaring at Tony.

"Bree, Bree ... it's okay Bree honey, it's okay, calm down," as Mo placed her hands firmly on Bree's shoulders, centering herself in front of her, trying to make eye contact, and blocking her view of Tony.

"What the fuck is wrong with you?" I said, turning to Tony.

"Nothing pardner, just having a little fun," Tony defended, innocently.

"I told you if you touched them, I would kill you, didn't I?"

"Aw Pistol, you had your chance that day on the roof. You don't have it in you, pawdner," laughing, mocking me.

I started to reach behind my back when Mo calmly walked over, stepped around me, and punched Tony flush in his mouth, his body rocking back against the grill, a frying pan crashing to the floor. Stunned, he recovered quickly, feeling his mouth, inspecting the blood on his hand. Smiling, he leaned forward and smeared his hand across the shoulder of Mo's top, leaving a long red stain, her body twisting at the force of his hand.

Mo, eyes ablaze, chest pounding and breathing heavily, struck again, her fist catching him square on the side of the head, sending him sideways to the floor, pots and pans clanging, spinning on the floor. Then it was quiet, deathly quiet, only the sound of dripping coming from somewhere.

Bree was by the sink, leaning against it, panting, her face pale, the front of her shirt ripped open, one of the buttons missing. The side of her top was stretched, hanging off her shoulder, exposing bare skin, and a pink bra strap. Mo, fists clenched at her sides, chest still heaving, glared down at Tony. Tony, smiling, slowly worked his way to one knee, using the grill for leverage, wiped his mouth, checking for more blood. My hand wrapped around the handle of my .45, thumb on the hammer; I slowly lifted my gun out.

In a guttural tone so unrecognizable, it made me shiver, Mo said, "You fucking gutless prick. This ends here. Now. You and me, asshole. I've been wanting this for a long time."

Tony, unfazed, smirked at Mo, "Works for me, sweet cheeks. I am going to enjoy this. I heard you like it rough."

Mo, fists clenched at her sides, stared hard at Tony. I slipped my gun in the waistband of my jeans, letting go of the handle, turned to face Mo. My hands out reaching for her, swallowing hard, "Mo, baby, Mo. You can't do this," I choked, almost gagging, "You can't," I pleaded, "you can't."

"Why not?" she snapped at me, her eyes burning.

"Because he could kill you, that's why!" I squeaked.

"Aww, ain't that sweet. The big protector fighting her battles, such a man."

"Fuck you, Tony," Mo hissed.

"Please do," winking at her.

I reached for Mo's arm, but she turned, snapping, "You're not the only one who fights in bars you know."

I reached for her arm again.

"Leave me alone!" twisting and pulling away, turning back to Tony, "You and me asshole. Right here, right now, let's go!"

Quickly pulling myself together, I knew I couldn't stop her, and had to think fast.

"Not in here then," I said, looking at the war zone the kitchen had been turned into. "We need a level playing field. Let's take this out on the dance floor."

I started to step over the pots and pans littered on the floor. "Come on, let's go!" I ordered, looking at Mo and Tony, pointing at the doorway, "Out there on the floor. Let's go! Bree, can you give me a hand?" moving toward her, "I need help to clear the dance floor."

Bree nodded, reached up, took her sweater off the hook, wrapped it around her, and followed me out the doors. We cleared a space on the dance floor, moving the tables and chairs off to the side, trying to give them as much room as possible, and hopefully more of an advantage to Mo.

Mo came out, took off her glasses and placed them on the bar. Tony followed behind, still smirking, reaching out to pat Mo's behind, but sensing, she reached behind and slapped at his hand growling. They took up positions on opposite sides of the floor, as Bree moved behind the bar, and I hopped on the counter, facing the floor.

"Bree, can you get me a beer, please?" I asked, over my shoulder.

Bree reached down, flicked open the cooler, pulled out a beer, and placed it on the counter beside me, whispering, "Aren't you going to do something? You can stop this."

"I have a plan. I just need to let things play out a bit," I said out of the corner of my mouth.

"It better work because she could get hurt … or worse."

"I know," the fear rising in the back of my throat. "Plan B," reaching behind, I felt for Bree's hand and guided it to the back of my jeans, letting her feel my .45.

"Wish it was plan A," Bree said ruefully.

The scene was surreal—rock music playing, the only thing missing was the disco ball spinning overhead. I was perched up on the bar, beer in hand, lazily kicking my feet, with Bree beside me, leaning on the counter, picking at her fingers and biting her nails. Tony and Mo were on the dance floor, warily eyeing each other, and had taken up street fighting positions. They started circling clockwise, looking for an opening, waiting for an opportunity; who would strike first? It was insane and very, very real.

And just like that, the main event got underway. Mo, overcome by emotion and too eager, struck first; but Tony easily sidestepped her fist, and his hand flashed out, slapping her hard on the cheek, making a loud smacking sound. She grunted but remained on her feet. Her hair fell into her face, and she pushed it back and moved in again. Connecting, her fist slid across Tony's chin and off his shoulder, surprising him. They both reset and shifted around the floor, looking for an opening.

Tony's hand flashed out, smacking her other cheek, this time even harder. Mo's hands dropped on the impact, and his fist caught her flush in the mouth, staggering her. Falling roughly to the floor, her hands out behind she was unable to break her fall. Rubbing her mouth, checking her hand, she wiped the blood on her jeans and slowly got up.

"Had enough sweet cheeks? Too bad because I'm just getting started," Tony taunted.

Mo readied herself again. Her face taut, grimacing, grunting loudly, "UGH!" she lunged straight at Tony, but he easily sidestepped her, hitting her in the back of the head with his open hand, pushing her roughly into one of the tables ringing the floor, crashing hard against the edge of the table, her chin taking the full brunt of the impact.

"Do something! STOP THIS! Please, Pete, please," Bree pleaded, as Mo slowly pulled herself to her feet.

"Babe?"

Mo, using her sleeve to wipe the blood from her mouth, was leaning on the table to support herself. "Yeah?"

"You okay?"

"Yeah," she said, wiping at her mouth.

"Babe, do you remember that rainy Saturday afternoon when we watched *Roadhouse*?"

"Huh?" her head turning, eyebrows raised.

"That Saturday, that rainy Saturday afternoon, when we had the marathon."

"Huh? What marathon?" Mo asked, confused, wondering where this was coming from.

"You know. The sex marathon that went on all afternoon and night, then spilled over into Sunday. That marathon ..." I teased, my eyes glued on Tony.

"What are you fucking talking about?" she said, irritated, wearing the biggest what the fuck expression I had ever seen.

"Remember we started watching *Roadhouse*, and we kept pausing the movie to have sex. That Saturday ... remember?"

At the word sex, I watched for Tony's reaction. Since he only thought with his dick, I hoped it would get his attention. Sure enough, he was all ears, or was that, all dick?

Looking at Mo, "Don't you remember? We had sex off and on for almost twenty-four hours. Well, maybe it wasn't that long, but it sure seemed like it. If I recall, I came four times, and I think you came seven times or was it eight? That last time was a double for you, wasn't it? Anyways, you won the contest. That was quite the marathon, huh?" I smiled devilishly, wearing a big, fat, shit-eating grin

Thoroughly pissed now, I thought Mo might start fighting me instead.

"Gee Pete, that's such a lovely memory, but now is not the time, you know?" As Mo swept her arm out at Tony.

I looked at Tony, who was keenly enjoying our exchange. Ignoring Mo, focused on Tony, "Man, it was great! Fucking mind-blowing and the one where you got me with your mouth. I think that was my third ... no ... no wait! That was my fourth. I had five in total. I forgot. Wow! But you still won though, right?"

"So, I won the orgasm contest. Big fucking deal! I hope you enjoyed it mister, because it was your last one," Mo said angrily, her eyes burning through me, thankful she wasn't holding my gun. "Are you done here? I'm kind of busy. What's your point to all this?" pushing her hair back and wiping her hands on the front of her jeans.

Tony was now sitting on the edge of one of the tables ringing the floor.

"Remember what we did after?"

"After what? After sex?" shaking her head in disgust, sighing, "Infuckingcredible."

"What did we do after we moved the coffee table off to the side?" I asked calmly.

Tony was thoroughly enjoying the free entertainment, though I may have gone too far. And it's not like that's ever happened before.

"What did we practice after we moved the coffee table?"

"How to be nice? Jesus fucking Christ, Pete! I don't fucking know!"

"Babe, after that," I continued, undeterred.

"You're killing me ... you are fucking killing me here. There better be a point to all this ... SOON!" glowering at me.

A quick glance at Tony, and I was almost there. Just one more little hint; this better work.

"Remember how Dalton was teaching the bouncers how to take on someone bigger than them, and we were practicing that?"

Bingo! A thin smile crossed Mo's lips, as the light went on, and not a moment too soon, and ever so slightly, Mo winked. *Good lord! That was painful.*

Mo pushed her hair back, gathered herself, and moved back onto the floor. Tony jumped off the table and faced Mo, and I was hoping his mind would now be on sex; sex with Mo.

"Thanks for the intermission, I needed that. I was getting tired from hitting those sweet cheeks. The two of you make quite a pair. All that sex must make you tired. Watching movies together. BAH! That *Roadhouse* movie is really stupid. Pistol, sounds like you can really shoot with that thing; bet they're all blanks. What a pistol. All this movie stuff. Come on, sweet cheeks, let me hit you some more. That pussy of a man … I can give you what a woman wants … a real man."

I nodded and casually waved at Tony with a sly grin. Mo moved in quickly, Tony slow to react. Mo's leg lashed out, catching the outside of Tony's knee, caving in his leg. He screamed out, falling to the floor. Grunting, Mo connected with a vicious uppercut, catching Tony flush on the chin, snapping his head back. Stunned, Tony tried to get up, groaning and rubbing his chin, when Mo stepped forward, kicking him squarely in the balls. He groaned, slumping to his knees, falling forward, prayer-like to the floor. The three of us watched, as moaning softly, hands between his legs, he curled in a fetal position.

Mo, silent, breathing heavily, suddenly stepped forward, boot raised, poised to stomp on Tony's head. Bree screamed out, and I jumped off the bar, racing over, grabbing Mo from behind and roughly pulled her back, legs kicking wildly, screaming, "Let me go! … I will fucking kill him … let me go … LET ME GO!"

Mo thrashed and squirmed, twisting wildly, trying to escape my grasp, and I had to hold on with all my strength. Holding tightly, refusing to let go, Mo tired and collapsed in my arms. I let us slide to the floor, my arms still wrapped around her, both of us panting.

"It's okay Mo, it's okay, sshh … it's okay. It's going to be okay. Just breathe. It's over … you got him … you did good."

I held Mo in my lap, my arms across hers, as her head fell back against my chest. I gently wiped the hair from her face, leaning in, I kissed the top of her head softly. Mo looked up at me, eyes glassy, both sides of her face red with hand imprints. Blood was trickling from the corner of her mouth, along with a wet squiggly red line running from her nose; her knuckles were scraped raw. Barely audible, "Take me home … now … please."

58

MO WALKED THROUGH the front door, leaving a trail of clothing in her wake, as I followed behind, stooping to pick up her blood-soaked top.

"Burn them!" she hissed. "Burn all of them ... I don't want any of it."

She kicked off her tan boots, the fronts splattered with blood. Bending over, she rolled her jeans down her legs, kicking them in the air, then her socks, bra, and panties came flying next, as I stumbled, trying to grab them before they hit the ground. Gathering the discarded clothing against my chest, tucking my chin against her jeans, I leaned down and picked her boots up with my fingers, went into the kitchen and pushing the back door open with my hip, dropped everything in the garbage can.

Mo went straight to the bathroom, stayed in the bath for over an hour, and I let her be, checking occasionally by tiptoeing down the hallway and putting my ear to the door. When I heard the bathroom door open and the bedroom door close, I made a coffee and waited a few minutes, then went down the hall. Bandit was at the bedroom door wanting in. I gently turned the knob, scooting through the opening, he jumped up on the bed, curling into her legs.

Mo was on her side facing me, legs bent, the covers tucked under her armpits, her wet hair spread out evenly on the pillow. Padding softly across the room to the other side of the bed and gently lifting the covers, I slipped in and snuggled up behind her. She was still awake and, reaching for my hand, pulled it across her chest. I rubbed my face against the back of her head, kissing it lightly, squeezing her.

"Are you okay?"

Mo nodded. "Yes. Just hold me."

Her body pushed back against mine. I held her close, feeling sick inside, knowing this was my doing and was thoroughly disgusted with myself. We lay quiet until I could feel her rhythmic breathing, then I carefully slipped out from the covers and tiptoed out of the bedroom.

Returning to the couch, checking my phone, there were multiple texts from Bree. She said after we left, she went into the kitchen to clean up, leaving Tony where he lay on the floor, and when she came out an hour later, he was gone. She didn't know where he went and didn't care. But I knew he wasn't far, losing to a woman in a bar fight, even if it was a fair fight—sort of—was not something he would let go of easily. He was going to be a problem again, and since I couldn't kill him, or anyone, for that matter, what was the alternative?

Leaning forward on the couch, looking over at the blanket fort, I thought, *screw this.*

I reached for my phone and coffee, then I moved over and crawled inside. I quickly set up shop, moved Mo's magazines to the side, folded the blanket into a small table, crossing my legs and locking them, I balanced the blanket-table on my lap, then placed my coffee and phone on top. Searching through my phone, I found the number, tapped the screen, and waited.

"Yup."

"Call him off."

"Not even a hello? I'm disappointed in you, Pistol."

"Call him off," I demanded.

"I've been waiting for you to call."

"Call him off, Teddy. I mean it, call him off!"

"How is she?"

Strange, Teddy almost sounded genuine in his concern. "Uh, she's fine, thanks for asking. Tony though, I'm not so sure."

"He had it coming. I had warned him before about this."

"Finally, something we agree upon," I said.

"Look, Pistol, the choice is yours. Give me what I want, and all this goes away. You and Tony can stay up there with your cute little girlfriend and play house until you die, for all I care. I just want what's mine."

Teddy was right, I wanted this gone also, I was sick of this, a bad idea right from the get-go. But every time I thought of handing over the box, something inside held me back. There was something bigger going on here, and I needed to know. Plus, I had failed to deliver on my original promise. And yes, a lot of shit happened along the way, leading to the stalemate we were now in. But still, at the end of the day, I had failed to deliver on my promise. My pride was taking a direct hit.

I couldn't help but think that *if* I had found Teddy's sister, and *if* when I picked up the box that day I had been paying attention like I should have, then *maybe* those bikers wouldn't have got the jump on me. And *if* I hadn't run into Tina on the dock, *maybe* I wouldn't have melted down, losing valuable time. And *maybe if*... suddenly, I could hear children singing:

"If's and Maybe's and Maybe's and If's

Let's bake a cake and fill it with

If's and Maybe's and Maybe's and If's."

Hovering dangerously close to the edge of the rabbit hole, I managed to pull myself back. I remembered Jackie telling me to stay in the now.

"Pistol? You there? Pistol?'

"Yes, I'm here," sighing, drained, my head spinning.

"Good. What's it going to be then?"

"You're right, the box is yours, and I have it. But—"

"But what? What's the problem then?"

"Teddy, you went to a lot of trouble to get the box. There's nothing in there but an old police file on your parents' death and—"

"Wait, you read the file?"

"Yep, and for the life of me I don't know what you hope to find in it."

A pause. "Does it matter? I just want the damned file. And besides, I paid you to get it for me."

"Certainly not a princely sum and more like a pauper's penny, don't you agree?"

"Yes, you're right."

"And if I had more of a heads-up maybe I'd have been more careful, but I was caught flat footed in Havelock. I still don't know why those bikers wanted it. I suppose you're not going to tell me that either."

I could hear shuffling in the background, a glass banging followed by heavy sighing.

"Those bikers, this much I can tell you, I have no idea who they are or what they wanted. So, tell you what, Pistol."

"I'm all ears, Texas," sensing the tables were about to turn in my favour.

"We seem to be at a stalemate here. We both want something, am I right? I want the box, and you want me to call off the dogs so you can live happily ever after though, for the life of me, why anyone would want to do that way up in that armpit Timmins, is beyond me."

"Gee Teddy, what took you so long? And what's wrong with Timmins? I like it here. It means I am far away from the likes of you."

"Look, Pistol, I have a proposition for you."

"Shoot, Texas," I drawled.

"I will trade you the box for what I have on the table."

"What is this, Teddy, *Let's Make a Deal* with you as Monty Hall?"

He ignored that. "There's a meet coming soon, a week Friday in Halifax. I need someone, yes a mule, to pick up a package, and bring it back to me. Are you interested?"

"Maybe," I said, as a giant red flag instantly shot up the pole.

"It's simple. You fly out the night before, meet up the next morning, then straight to the airport from there. And before you know it, you are back here by noon, and we are doing shots one last time at Sharkees. And if you hustle, you could be home, fucking your girlfriend, by midnight."

The red flag was now flapping in a gale-force wind, I wasn't sure what to make of this; trading what I knew for what I didn't know. Lovely. This, I wasn't expecting.

"Well?" he said. "Sound like a plan? We wipe our hands of each other, and you are free and clear. I promise. And no more Tony."

"What is it? What am I picking up?"

"You don't need to know that."

"Uh, sorry there, big guy, yes I do. I don't mule drugs for anyone."

Teddy laughed hard, that same unmistakable high-pitched laugh from that day in Sharkees.

"No, no … no drugs. You have my word on that."

Strangely, I believed him on that part.

"Teddy, come on, you gotta throw me a bone here at least; otherwise, no deal and the three of us can continue to play Russian roulette."

"Bearer bonds."

"How much?"

"Ten mill."

I stared at the phone, trying to telepathically see Teddy on the other end and determine if he was serious or not.

"Five hundred thousand," he said.

"What's that?"

"Five hundred thousand to you. Two fifty upfront, another two fifty when you deliver. I will cover your flights, hotel, and car. All you have to do is meet the guy and come back, with the bonds of course."

"Of course."

"So, what do you think? Are you in?"

"That's it? I get five hundred grand for ten million in bearer bonds?"

"Take it or leave it."

"Can I sleep on it at least?"

"Sure, but I need your answer first thing tomorrow."

"That I can do."

"Okay good. And, Pistol?"

"Yes, Teddy?"

"This is a one-time offer only. If I don't hear back from you tomorrow morning that you're willing to do it, the person I send to collect the box won't be some useless muscle-head pussyhound like Tony. There won't be any discussion involved, no negotiations, and no happily ever after in the cards for you. And needless to say, if you do agree to do it, and you try to fuck me on the deal like you've done thus far with the box, then you, your girlfriend, and that other one, Brill? Breezy? Are all dead, and there will be nowhere to hide where I won't find you. Is that clear?"

This sounded different from the bluster and bullshit I was used to from Teddy.

"Got it, big guy. Until tomorrow."

The line went dead. It was a trap. I knew it was a trap, and Teddy had to know I knew it was a trap. It had to be, right? But this was the corner I'd painted myself into. Either I hopped in the car right now, drove the box to Ottawa and called Teddy tomorrow morning with a place to pick it up ... or I was going to Halifax.

The upside was I had just bought myself a little bit of time. I scrolled through the list of contacts on my phone, found the number, and tapped it.

I hope he's awake.

59

I FELT A hard kick, jerking me awake.

"Jesus! What the …?" Rubbing my eyes, I sat up, hitting my head on the side of the chair. "OW! Fuck!"

I could hear giggling. "That'll teach you to sleep with your feet hanging out."

Groggily, I poked my head out the flap.

"Morning slugger."

Scowling, Mo flashed me the finger and went into the kitchen. I could hear her filling the kettle and the familiar tinkling as she filled Bandit's bowl. Crawling out of the fort, the couch was too far away to make it safely, so I stayed where I was, prone on the floor. *So, this is what death feels like.*

"Mo baby, do you think you could move the couch closer? I don't think I can make it." I heard the kitchen drawer open then ducking, I covered my head, bombarded with flying cutlery. "I'll take that as a no then."

With herculean effort, I managed to make it to one knee, then crawled on all fours across the carpet, groaning loudly, pulled myself up on the couch. So, maybe this is what a beach landing felt like. Falling back against the soft cushions, I called out to Mo once more—this time positive she was going to offer a helping hand or at least, sympathy.

"Babe, I made it to the couch, all by myself without your help. I didn't want you to worry, since you hadn't heard from me. I'm doing okay though I am a bit tired. Do you think you could prop up the pillows for me?"

"I wasn't worried," she said. "Prop them yourself!"

She scowled as she came out of the kitchen carrying two mugs and handed me one. Leaning over, she kissed me on the mouth, her tongue running across my lips, then bit down hard on my bottom lip.

"OW! What did you do that for?" My head jerking back, rubbing my mouth.

"*Don't* call me slugger."

Mo sat down, crossing her legs, pulling the blanket over her lap. We sat quietly, sipping our coffee, enjoying the peaceful morning, and the realization that yesterday was more than just a normal day, even for us. Putting her mug down, she started massaging her hand.

"Ice?"

"Please."

I got up and returned with a cloth wrapped with ice cubes, Mo held it in place, grimacing, her hand tender.

"I'm done with these bar fights. I'm done. That's it, that was my last one," Mo said, wincing, adjusting the cloth.

"Me too," I nodded solemnly.

Mo looked at me skeptically, eyebrows raised. "Really?"

"Really. That's it for me too."

"We'll see," she said, not believing me in the least.

We continued to sit quietly, lost in our respective worlds, still trying to wrap our heads around the day that was yesterday.

"This has got to stop," I said, wearily, watching Bandit paw at the clothes peg on the flap.

'I know." Mo adjusted the cloth on her hand. "I can't keep doing this." Mo sat up, alarmed, "Bree! SHIT, is she okay? SHIT! We left ... where's Bree? Is she okay?" reaching for her phone.

"Wait, Mo. She's okay, she's fine. She texted us both last night. All is well. Sorry, I forgot to tell you." Mo breathed a huge sigh of relief and fell back against the couch.

"If anything happened to her ... I don't know what I would do. Do you think Tony will come back?"

"Yes, I do. He'll be back, sooner or later I'm afraid, but *when* is the question. You put him out of commission, for now at least. Nicely done."

"No thanks to you. But if you ever tell anyone again about our sex life, it will be your balls next time."

Feeling unnerved, I tried to read Mo's face, and I couldn't tell if she was kidding or not. I made a mental note to put our sex life in a box and park it way out back. I rewound last night's call with Teddy, and my gut instinct told me I didn't have much choice, it was Halifax or bust. But I wasn't ready to have that conversation with Mo just yet. I still had a couple of hours before I had to let him know.

"Everything okay?" Mo asked.

"Why?"

"You keep checking your watch."

"Was thinking we should check on Bree."

Mo pushed back into the cushions, wriggling her hips, lifted the blanket, turned and stretched her legs out between my back and the cushion. Shifting, I did the same, snuggling, Bandit jumped up and wiggled himself between our legs.

"Can't we just stay here for like forever?" Mo playfully whined.

"So, this is heaven ..."

"Better than death, huh?" Mo winked.

Giggling, we lay stretched out on the couch, and a few minutes later, I flicked off Mo's fuzzy slipper and started playing with her toes.

"For Pete's sake, what are you doing?" she said, her foot suddenly cold.

"Practicing my counting."

"How old are you again?" she asked, her eyes closed, while keeping her foot in place.

Twenty minutes later, Mo suggested we better go. "But the last piggy ... he hasn't got to the market yet."

"Fine," rolling her eyes, "Hurry up."

I quickly got the last little piggy to market and blankets were shed and dropped to the floor as we headed the bathroom and jumped in the shower.

―

Thirty minutes later, after our mini-submarine race went an extra lap, we were out the door. Hopping into my Chevy, I pushed in a tape.

"You like Chicago?"

"Never been."

I looked sideways at Mo, who was grinning, and started to reply then thought, *what's the point?* We drove in silence while Chicago ended its beginning, tight-lipped, both worried about what we might walk into this time. We parked and went up the stairs and were greeted by Boston blasting on the sound system.

Coming through the double doors, hearts pounding, we stood at the railing. The music was deafening, the floor vibrating to the beat. We looked over at the bar, and Bree was behind it, singing at the top of her lungs.

" … close my eyes and slip AWWWAYYY …"

Breathing huge sighs of relief, we walked over to the bar, and Mo had to reach over the counter, turning down the volume to get Bree's attention.

Bree looked much better and was back to her old self, full of life, playfully joking about yesterday's events. Adrian was still down in Sudbury, so she was wearing two hats, and went into the kitchen, while Mo started rearranging the bottles on the wall, and going through the coolers below. It was no wonder I was happy here.

My gaze shifted down, and I could see something black and metallic on the shelf below the register, a shiver ran down my back, and I jerked involuntarily.

"Babe, what is it?" Mo asked, alarmed.

Turning my head toward the kitchen doors then turning back to Mo, I tilted my head, and motioned with my eyes down to the shelf below. Mo following my gaze. Then she spotted it too.

"What the fuck?"

Just then, the kitchen doors burst open, and Bree came out carrying a tray of glasses, still happily singing to the song that had ended three songs ago.

"Someone's happy," Mo teased.

Bree laughed, and I slid off the stool and made my way over to the pool tables.

"Remember, the object of pool is not to sink the white ball, right slick?" Bree giggled.

"I think he's colour blind," Mo added.

Flashing the two lovelies the finger, I racked the balls. Unsettled, at what I had just seen under the bar, I needed to keep moving. I kept checking the time, and I had about an hour until I had to call Teddy. Part of me lived for this stuff, I couldn't deny that, it was who I was, after all. But I was also tired, tired of it, tired of constantly living on the edge. Death's door was getting too close for comfort, and I preferred *life*—the quiet life, up here, with Mo, Bandit, and Bree. I aimlessly banged the balls around the table, not caring what colours I sank, and go figure, I didn't drain the cue ball once.

"See ya guys, back in an hour, going to run some errands," Bree shouted, as she bounded up the stairs, keys jingling.

Mo, carrying two beers between her fingers, walked over, picking out a cue along the way.

"So, is this the moody Pete, Coach Billy was always teasing you about?" Mo winked, handing me a beer.

"Huh? I'm not moody."

"Then what is it?"

"What do you think?" I said, irritated, as I leaned over to shoot. "No wonder she's happy. She's got a fucking loaded gun behind the bar."

"How can you tell it's loaded?"

"I just can." I took my shot, draining the white ball in the corner pocket. "This is not good."

"I know …"

I could see the fear in Mo eyes.

"What do we do then?"

"Fuck." I let out a long sigh, reached for my beer, and moved over onto a stool. "Last night, after you fell asleep, I called Teddy."

"Bet he was thrilled to hear from you."

"Hardly, but he seemed genuinely concerned about you, asking if you were okay."

"News travels fast, huh?" Mo said, grimly.

"No doubt he heard from Tony, though I bet he told Teddy his version of events."

Mo smiled at the thought.

"Mutts like Tony don't go away unless you permanently put them down," I muttered, wishing I was capable of murder.

"What happened that day on the roof?"

"Couldn't do it. I couldn't do it … had my finger on the trigger, started to squeeze, but I couldn't do it."

"Just as well." Mo said, wearing her familiar mischievous grin. "I don't date cold-blooded killers."

"So, what did Teddy say?" Mo asked.

"He said all this goes away if I just give him the box."

"Naturally."

"So, are you going to give it to him?"

"Yes, I'm seriously considering it."

I took a long drink from the bottle, feeling the cold beer wash down inside, the familiar buzz starting to work its magic.

"There's no point in keeping it any longer. Those police reports are tied to something bigger than just a simple fire and the two deaths that came with it. Teddy and his sister's names were on the reports, but that could be strictly a coincidence for all I know. And if they were tied into it somehow, I just can't figure out what or where. So, maybe if I do return the box, it would lead to something else," I said, grasping at straws.

"But you're not going to just give it back to him, are you?"

"No, there's too much at stake to just give it back and walk away empty-handed."

"What then?" Mo slid onto a stool beside me.

"We talked a bit more, and he offered me a proposition. He wants me to fly out to Halifax and pick up a package for him."

"Um, babe," Mo reached out and placed her hand on my arm. "You tried that one already. Havelock right? And look at what that got you."

"I know … I know," I said, feeling a sharp pang at what Leia went through.

"Honestly, there are moments when I wished I had just walked away that day in Sharkees. I just said no and walked away. Then there's none of this, you know? You, Bree, you in that fight with Tony yesterday," winding myself up. "And now, Bree's carrying a loaded gun … shit! I hope she didn't take it with her."

Dropping my bottle on the table, the pool cue clattering to the floor, I raced over behind the bar. My heart pounding, I looked down on the shelf. I looked over at Mo—who was white as a sheet—and shook my head.

"It's still here."

Reaching down, I pulled the gun up and ejected the clip, sticking it in my pocket. I checked the chamber, then ensured the safety was on, and placed it back on the shelf. Nerves stretched, I grabbed two more beers from the cooler and walked back to the table, my hand trembling as I handed Mo hers.

"Fuck ... I'm so sorry for all this," my head down as I twisted off the top.

Mo reached for my hand. "Don't ... don't go there. What's done is done, and if you had walked away that day, you wouldn't be here now, with me. We'll figure this out. Together. It's what we do, right?"

Leaning over she kissed me.

"You're right. I'm not liking how things have played out is all."

"So, fix it then." Mo smiled, stood up and moved over to the table.

I got off the stool, picked the cue up off the floor, and went over to the table. Looking for an opening, I took aim and drained the eight-ball in the side pocket. Standing beside the table, I started chalking the cue, as Mo leaned in to take a shot.

"Like I said there's this meet soon, a drop they call it, in Halifax. These drops happen all the time, way more than people think. But they're not like what Hollywood makes them out to be. They're boring, and nothing ever happens. No giant dudes in black leather jackets carrying assault rifles, no bulletproof SUVs facing each other in the dark, the exchange taking place under hazy headlights."

"Then what *does* happen?" Mo asked, looking up.

"Nothing. Two cars meet in some out-of-the-way place, the package passed from one window to the other, and that's it."

"So, nothing could go wrong then? You couldn't get hurt or anything?" Mo asked, concerned, standing up, leaving her shot on the table.

"No, not usually."

"Not usually?"

"When I was doing this stuff back when I was a cop, we always had back-up just in case, so that if something did go wrong, you had protection."

"But you're not a cop anymore."

"Exactly," I said, leaning in to take another shot. "I hadn't forgotten, which is why, after calling Teddy last night, I called my friend Dale. Remember, I told you about him? We were partners years ago in Barrie. He was my best friend, besides Billy that is. He's in Peterborough now, and I called asking for his help. He has contacts in Halifax, so he's putting together a team, and they are going to shadow me every step of the way."

"So, how is this drop going to work then?"

"It's pretty simple. I fly from Ottawa to Halifax the night before, rent a car, grab a hotel, then early next morning, I do the meet, get dropped the package, then it's straight to the airport, and I catch the next flight out. I drop the package off to Teddy, and voilà! I'm back up here no later than the next day."

I looked hopefully at Mo, who was understandably skeptical. "Easy peasy," I added, trying to sound convincing.

"It sounds to me you've already made up your mind, calling Dale. Did you tell Teddy yes?"

"I hadn't made my mind up yet. I was sitting on it and wanted to talk it over with you first. And this morning on the couch was just so nice. I didn't want to interrupt that. I never want that to end."

"Me either." Mo smiled.

"Then when we got here, Bree, with the loaded gun, well, I have no choice now."

"I'm curious, what's in the package? What are you bringing back?"

"Ten million in bearer bonds."

Mo's eyes flew open. "Geezus, Pete!"

"Yeah, I know. But I get five hundred for doing it. Two fifty upfront and another two fifty when I deliver."

Mo looked at me in shock. "You're risking your life for five hundred bucks?"

Smiling, "five hundred *thousand*," I said. "Two fifty upfront and another two fifty after."

"If there is an after ..." Mo muttered grimly. "And excuse me here, I'm no math expert, but there's still a huge difference between ten million and five hundred thousand. I'm hoping your math is as good as mine, and you see this?"

"It is, and I do," I said, trying to sound reassuring. "I would be more surprised if the bonds existed."

"Then why are you even considering this?"

"I don't have much choice, do I? I don't see any other way out of this. Yesterday, Tony attacked Bree, and then you and Tony fought. Today, Bree has a loaded gun under the bar. What's tomorrow going to bring? Shit, look what happened the day Tony first showed up here. That shit will never stop. And don't forget you are dating someone unable to kill in cold blood."

"We could go to the cops."

"No. No, trust me. It will only make things worse, plus it will drag on for months. Those wheels of justice turn slow." I decided it was better not to mention Teddy's not so thinly veiled threat.

"So, this plan, that in all likelihood is a trap, is going to fix everything?"

"Yes, I believe it will. I believe Teddy, that if I do this, things will be square, and he will leave us alone—no more Tony, no more BS, I truly believe that. I don't know why but I just do. The problem is, it's all that stuff in front of it. That's where I don't trust Teddy."

"You really believe this?" Mo asked, incredulously, "You really believe this will work?"

"Yes, I do. It can work if—"

"If what?" she was frustrated now and anxious.

"If my instincts are correct, that it could be a setup, that means, I already know what's going to happen. So, I'm already one step ahead of things, and Dale with his team would be in position to intercept them. Mo, this is the stuff I'm good at, what I have always been good at. Dale said I was the best he ever saw at this."

Mo was still understandably skeptical.

"So, between Dale and me, and that Teddy doesn't know about our plan, I think I can pull this off. I really do. And worst case, we're $250,000 richer. Your dance studio."

"I don't care about that."

"I do, and I don't believe you."

Then, with no idea where it came from, or maybe I did, things suddenly became very real, maybe too real, and I was unable to stop myself.

"I want a life with you, and this is the way for us to get it, never mind putting an end to all this bullshit with Teddy and Tony. I want a home, and a house full of kids, a yard full of toys, and you can have your dance studio. You could buy that storefront on Third Street that you showed me, or we could build an extension off the house, I don't care. Whatever makes you happy. And I can, I could, I mean, maybe I could join the force up here and become a cop again."

Lightheaded, I had to reach out to the side of the pool table to steady myself. Holding on to the table, staring straight into Mo's eyes, unable to stop myself, I delivered the coup de grâce. "And I think, you want the same … with me."

There was a long pause, and everything was quiet. My head was spinning, and I was pretty sure Mo's was too. She was staring at me with a vacant look, and goosebumps appeared on her arms as she shivered and hugged herself. What I couldn't have known, of course, was that all her life, Mo had waited for this very moment when she would hear those words—*whatever makes you happy*. And here it was, not Rick's cabin in the woods (nor Dale's white picket fence) but an open promise, free of expectation or design. Neither of us saw this coming though maybe we should have. Because we did fit—we fit perfectly—and we both knew it. That is why we both denied it at first, denial being such a safe place after all.

"What makes you so sure?" Mo replied sternly, her head down, the temperature dropping sharply in the room. I watched as she started to back away. It felt like a movie, and looking up at the screen, we were playing parts from a script.

"Tell me you don't," I said, my voice shaky, my stomach in knots.

Mo retreated a few more steps, now up against the other pool table, nowhere to go, figuratively and literally. Holding the pool cue upright, she remained silent, her eyes dark, staring straight at me. I hoped I was right, and she felt the same, and that my instincts weren't wrong, but it was too late, and I couldn't take it back. Taking a deep breath, I cannonballed off the diving board, eyes shut tight, afraid to check if it was the shallow or the deep end.

"Tell me you don't," I said. "Go ahead and tell me …" my voice cracked.

Mo remained silent, staring at me, back up against the pool table.

"Tell me you don't want the same things as me, with me, and I will leave right now," I said. "I will go, and I will do this to get Tony off your back, and then I will leave you alone. Just tell me."

Time seemed to stop. *Again? The other time was way more fun.* The bar was silent, the wailing guitars of Supertramp's *Goodbye Stranger* fading out, and it seemed to take forever for the next song to play. Mo continued to stare at me. After what felt like an eternity, barely audible, Mo spoke.

"I don't … I … don't."

Stunned, my mouth dropped, staring hard her.

"Huh? What?" as my stomach plunged forty-stories.

Lifting her eyes, looking at me, "I'm scared Pete ... I'm—"

"I know," I said. "Me too."

Mo spoke softly now, looking straight at me, fixing me to my spot.

"You are right, Pete. We do fit." She took a deep breath and gathered her courage. "This is exactly what I want, what I've always wanted, a life with someone like you. It's what I've dreamed of, for someone like you to come along. I knew it that first night when we sat on the couch. Remember? Bandit jumped up on your lap, and you watched me sleep. I knew it then. Even that morning on the bridge, I didn't want you to go. I want a life with you, here with me, us, kids, toys, dance studio, everything."

As if almost knowing, the bar remained silent. We made quite a pair: Mo backed up against the pool table with me holding on for dear life to the edge of the other one. Both outwardly so strong and impenetrable. Our walls intact, we only let our guards down enough to look out occasionally but never enough to letting anyone else in entirely. Pride and fear trapping us in our own defences. But now the walls had finally come down.

"I guess we're not very good at this, huh?" I replied.

"No, we're not."

Playfully rolling my eyes, "Why didn't you say this then? Tell me ... tell me that night even. How come I have to do all the dirty work?"

Mo shrugged. "Oh sure, that would have been so easy, right? I rescue you from a barroom brawl, and we run from the cops, then next thing you know, we are sitting on the couch, and oh, by the way, I think you're really cute, and I want to have your baby."

I smiled, put my cue down, and walked over and stood in front of Mo. Her eyes were moist, and so were mine. Reaching, I took her cue away, then I took her trembling hands and pulled her close. Her chest touching mine, we could feel our hearts beating. Looking into her eyes, her eyes searching mine, though we both knew it, and had known for quite some time, we had never said it until now.

"I love you."

"I love you."

We hugged, breathing huge sighs of relief, knowing the worst-kept secret was finally out. We fit. Perfectly. On cue, the music started playing again, the Doobie Brothers South City Midnight Lady, holding each other, we danced slowly to the song, two finally becoming one. We kissed, long and tender, having crossed over, and since there was no turning back, it was better to enjoy it and reap all its wonderful rewards.

"I had them you know."

Mo laughed. "I know you did."

Coming up for air, we searched for our beers, and tapping bottles, downed them. Mo went back and got us two more.

"So, when again is this meet-thing supposed to take place?"

"Ten days from now, a week Friday, the 19th."

"You better let Teddy know," Mo said smiling.

"Right away, ma'am." I snapped to attention and saluted.

"Okay, as soon as you're done there, Mr. Mule, rack 'em! I haven't beaten anyone, in what?" she said, looking down at her hands. "The last twenty four hours?"

I went over to the bar, sat on the stool, and texted Teddy with the news. Then I texted Dale the same, with details to follow. When Bree returned from shopping—not before Mo had kicked my ass twice in pool—we told her the plan. I forced Bree to hand over the gun, and she was dismayed to find the clip had been removed. However, she grimly reminded me that she could easily locate another one.

We left Bree, gunless and pouting, to get the club ready for opening, and said we would be back in a few hours. When we got outside, it was raining, a late summer sun-shower, so naturally, we chased each other around the parking lot, running through the puddles trying to jump-splash each other. Just because we could.

60

TEDDY WAS PERCHED on the stool impatiently waiting for his phone to buzz. Sharkees was busy, and it only added to his anxiety. Usually, when the joint was busy, he took pleasure in mingling, interacting with the other patrons, watching people and learning what made them tick. But today all he wanted was quiet. He thought of going out on the patio, but the deck was filled with a baseball team. He stared at the phone lying on the bar, willing it to ring.

Finally, as if hearing him, the phone buzzed, and he quickly tapped the button.

"Yup."

"Hello. I hear you have been keeping busy."

"Is she there?"

"I'm fine, thank you for asking, you?"

"Is she there?" Teddy demanded.

"Yes, she is, but she is riding back soon for her shift. She's in the shower."

"Right," said Teddy through gritted teeth.

"Why does it always bother you? I thought you would be used to it by now."

"I don't know what she sees in you."

"I give her what she needs," Dale said matter-of-factly.

"One of these days, I'm going to find out the hold you have on her, and then—"

"Then what, you'll kill me? Come on, Teddy, don't go getting all weak-kneed on me, have a backbone. She is an adult, and you are too, so try acting like one. Why should you care who she is sleeping with?"

Dale was right, Teddy had no say over who his sister slept with. He just never understood the hold he had over her. That was the part that bothered him, not that she was having sex with someone, but because it was Dale. Sara was better than that, she could do much better than that. Teddy had pushed many good guys her way, handsome, clean-cut, respectful, solid incomes ... and she had pushed every one of them right back.

Teddy thought back to the night his parents perished in the fire. The guilt he felt after hitting his father in the heat of anger then never getting the opportunity to make amends after and obtaining closure. And poor Sara, trying to play peacekeeper, then being unable to do anything but watch as their home burned to the ground in the middle of the night. That was why he played those stupid games with all those poor lemmings. It was his way of coping and feeling in control. Having a sense of control over someone else's life the way his father had over him. But then there was Dale. He was just like Teddy's father and controlled him the same way. Teddy hated himself for it. He hated who he was and who he wasn't. Was he even capable of managing his own life? The question haunted him.

He tried to manage Sara's life but was failing miserably, same for Tony's. And now his latest charade, based solely on revenge, had gone completely off the rails. It felt like everything and everyone was crumbling around him.

Oh, for that night the summer after his parents' death. Staggering out of a bar at closing, Teddy got behind the wheel of his car and, twenty minutes later, on a dark country road, plowed into a couple out for a late-night stroll, killing both instantly—the impact forcing his car off the road and into a tree. The airbag deployed and he escaped without a scratch, the permanent mental scars the only reminder.

The first cop on the scene was Dale Simpson, coincidently, the same cop who showed up the night his parents died. He had no choice but to let Dale take charge. He remembered Dale's calming voice instructing him to do and say exactly what he said and nothing more. Just like with Sara, he was a free man—charges dropped, along with three months in Bermuda. He took a buddy with him, lying to Sara about cracking up the car. Again, just like with Sara, the pied piper came calling once more, this time bearing his name. And ever since, and just like with his father, he was under someone else's control.

He wanted to tell Sara what Dale was really like, but he could never bring himself to do it. So many times, he would start to tell her, then back off. And now his games had lost their luster, and he'd decided Pete Humphries was his last victim. No more, he was going straight. He wasn't going to fess up to anything from the past, but from now on he was done. He would wash his hands of his old life. He was secretly in love with Patty, and though he knew he wasn't her type, he longed for someone like that. He knew he had to tell Sara about Dale, and more importantly, he wanted to get himself out from under Dale's thumb—and he thought he had found a way.

Originally, Teddy felt the answers lay in the box, the box that was filled with the police report of that fateful night. It was the key to Dale's involvement, along with what really happened to his parents. For the longest time, he had wondered if it was Dale who had murdered his parents, for his father had shady dealings and maybe they had finally caught up to him. But now, he was caring less and less, losing interest, tired of the game and its players.

He thought he might be able to buy his way out now. The $250,000 he promised to Pete, instead, he would flip to Dale—at Pete's expense of course. This would mean Pete could get killed in the process, but he didn't care anymore about Pete. He could never forgive him for that day on the docks, but now it was a case of revenge best served cold, letting someone else, or fate, take care of it.

"Teddy? Teddy? I'm losing patience. Sara's almost done, then we won't be able to talk."

"Uh, what? Yeah … sorry … yes, he's in. Pete said he would do it. He texted me a few minutes ago."

"Yes, I knew he would. He couldn't pass this up."

"How do you know each other again?" Teddy asked, curious.

"We just do. Leave it at that."

"Okay, he's coming down for next Friday."

"Coming down from where?"

"You don't know where he is?"

That surprised Teddy. Especially if Dale and Pete knew each other.

"No, the last time we spoke was in Peterborough, and I hadn't heard from him until …"

Dale, caught himself, not wanting Teddy to know that Pete had called him the previous night.

"Until?"

"Nothing … I just hadn't seen or spoken to him in a while."

"Thought you were a better detective than that," Teddy said. "He's driving down from Timmins and said he would meet me at Sharkees next Friday."

Timmins? Dale thought, *Why would he be way up there?* Then it hit him, his dad. Just to be sure, he would put out some feelers and see what he was up to.

"Are you still there?" Teddy said on the other end of the line.

"Yes, I am here, but I better go. She just turned off the water." He glanced over at the shut bathroom door.

"Okay."

"Keep me posted."

"Will do."

"Oh, and Teddy?"

"Yes?"

"Just remember, I know where your sister is at all times. So don't go getting a backbone and becoming all noble like."

Teddy felt a shiver run down his spine.

"Never." Teddy ended the call then slammed the phone on the bar.

Patty, now behind the bar, glanced up. "Everything okay, Teddy?"

"Yes, Ms. Patty. Things are fine. My phone slipped out of my hand that's all."

"When you have a moment, can you chop some wood for this afternoon, please? Probably a good idea to make sure your hands are dry. Wouldn't want you to slip and have an accident."

"Sure, Ms. Patty. I have to make a quick call, then I will, okay?"

"That's fine, Teddy. You haven't seen or spoken with your sister, have you? Her shift starts in a few hours."

"No, I haven't," Teddy lied.

"I don't know what's got into her of late," Patty sighed, shaking her head.

Teddy picked up his phone and turned it over. The face was cracked down the middle. He tapped it to life and searched for the number. He downed his drink as he waited.

"Yes, boss?"

"He's in."

"Okay, boss."

"And Tony, that means you back off as of now, got it?"

"Yes, boss."

"And Tony?"

"Yes, boss?"

"I mean it. You go anywhere near any of them, you're a dead man. Got it?"

"Got it, boss."

"Same for once this is done. They are to be left alone. Pete and I will be square. You never bother any of them again. I gave him my word."

"Yes, boss."

Teddy disconnected and dropped his phone on the bar. He hopped off the stool, rubbed his hands together, smiling at the prospect of splitting wood for Patty. Each block would be Dale's, Tony and Pete's heads. He figured he might as well chop enough wood for the coming week, making him and Patty happy.

61

DALE SAT AT the small table by the window, facing the street. Sipping scotch from a tumbler, he scrolled through his phone. Oh, how he despised Teddy and his childish games and having to constantly bail him out when things went too far. He wanted away from him, away from this, he was tired of it all. But all of this had been his design, his creation, and it wasn't that easy to just step away. Not after all this time.

He held power over Teddy, far too easily, but he had been unable to do the same with his sister, Sara. She held power over him and worse, she knew it. She knew what buttons to push, how to poke, prod, and hit a nerve—and she owned him in bed. He had no control over that, control of himself, his cock. The others he had manipulated over the years, and the control that flowed from it, was intoxicating. Then, after meeting Sara, the sex was a high unlike anything he had ever experienced. A high that he was completely powerless to control.

He remembered the first night he ever set eyes on her—the night of the fire.

When he arrived on the scene it was chaos. A five-alarm blaze, the house engulfed in flames and burning out of control. The people trapped inside. Firemen racing about. People crying and screaming. Then he saw her, standing in the driveway, watching her family home burn, no emotion, nothing, just watching it burn. That had surprised him. He walked over and stood beside her, but she remained motionless, watching. He introduced himself, but she didn't respond, and he thought maybe she was in shock. He could hear voices in the background talking desperately about the couple trapped inside and deduced they were her parents. So, why no emotion then?

Then out of the dark, a figure ran straight for the house, and if Sara hadn't stopped him, he would have gone into the raging inferno. That was the only time she had shown any emotion— forcing her brother to the ground, she held him tightly, shaking, crying. Dale fell in love with her at that moment, with her innocence, her beauty, how fragile and strong she was at the same time.

The following summer, he arrived on the scene of a late-night accident. Two people dead on the side of the road, their bodies mangled beyond recognition, the driver, laying in the bushes, whimpering like a baby, drunk and not a scratch on him. He was disgusted at the sight of him. Ready to slap on the cuffs and haul him away, it was only when he started to read him his rights, that he recognized the name on his licence. Polson. He used Teddy as an excuse to remain close to Sara.

What was his long time friend, Pete, involvement in all of this?

How did they, Teddy and Pete, know each other? Dale always had a soft spot for Pete. Childish at times, thumbing his nose at authority, swimming against the current—all the things he couldn't, or wouldn't, let himself do. He had taken Pete under his wing at the academy, and they became inseparable, despite their differences. The only thing they had in common was they were natural born cops, making a perfect team. Pete was fragile, losing his dad, he had no mother, no love life to speak of, and he was a dreamer, lacking the grounding and security he needed. So, Dale did his best to provide that, bringing him around to meet Karen, and then ultimately introducing him to Karen's co-worker, Joanna.

Dale had thought Pete then had everything he needed to survive. But Pete let it all fall apart, and Dale could never understand why. Then, things slipped even further, when Pete abruptly quit the force, the same time he was transferred to Peterborough, breaking off all contact and, finally, disappearing altogether—save for a text a few years later when he had bought the Chevy. Did he quit because of my transfer he asked himself many times? That had been Karen's idea. Getting back to their roots. Make that her roots. Almost immediately he was bored and started looking for an outlet. And then he found his drug. Power.

⁓

Sara came out of the bathroom, her hair wet, hanging down her bare shoulders, the short towel tied at the side across her chest, barely covering her buttocks, the opening parting just enough for Dale to see everything clearly, as she walked toward him.

"Hmm ... looks good." Dale licked his lips, turning in his chair toward her. "I bet you taste good too."

Sara stopped in front of him, towel open at mouth level, and she could feel his hot breath on her, as his hands moved around to her cheeks. He pulled her in closer, and just as he started to open his mouth, she pulled away, bringing the towel across.

"Who was that on the phone?" she asked. "Who were you talking to?"

"No one."

"It was someone," she said. "Who was she?"

Dale laughed as he tried to pull her toward him. "There is no one. There is only you."

"Says the married man. What about Karen, is she no one?"

He flinched as that well-aimed dagger pierced his heart.

The room went quiet. There was only the sound of the cars from the street below. Then, like a snake strike, his hand lashed out, catching her on the side of her face, the loud slap echoing across the room. Sara didn't move, tears forming in her eyes, as she bit her lip, refusing to display any reaction.

Dale reached for the tumbler, downing rest of the scotch, and rapped it back down on the tabletop. Wordlessly, he got up, his shoulder brushing roughly against hers, pushing her back as he moved past.

She followed him. "She has a right to know. I'm going to tell her. And I'm going to tell my brother too. *All* of it."

Dale stood by the bed, silent, and started to dress. Sara, visibly shaken, walked over and grabbing his arm, roughly spun him around. Her eyes dark flashing.

"Are you listening? I am going to tell ... I can't do this anymore."

But Dale remained silent, turning away, and continued dressing.

Sara reached for his arm again, when Dale spun around, gun in his hand and pointed it straight between her eyes. He slowly cocked the hammer, the metallic click echoing like a sonic boom, the barrel lightly touching her forehead. Sara, in shock, didn't move a muscle.

"You will do nothing," Dale hissed. "You will do absolutely nothing because, if you do, I will blow your fucking pretty little head off. But not before I put a bullet in that spineless piece of shit brother of yours. You got that?"

Sara nodded, unable to stop the tears streaming down her cheeks, her body shaking uncontrollably.

"Good! And now that we are clear, there is one more thing …"

Dale moved the gun down her front and pushed open the towel with the barrel, inserting the cold barrel into her slit. Sara, eyes wide open, gasped out loud, as Dale slowly twisted the barrel inside her.

"The next time I want to eat your cunt, I will do so, and you will let me. You got that?"

Sara nodded, shaking, and as Dale started to withdraw the barrel, he pulled the trigger, the loud click sending shockwaves through her body, she collapsed to the floor, breaking into heavy sobs and turning on her side.

Dale finished dressing, ignoring Sara on the floor beside him. Once outside in his car, he pulled out his phone and placed a call.

"Yes, boss."

"I have a job for you," he said.

"Of course, what is it?"

"I need you to get up to Timmins and check out someone for me. Can you do that?"

"Sure, boss."

"How fast can you get up there?"

"Tomorrow fast enough?"

"Okay, good. His name is Pete Humphries. Dark hair, six feet, wiry. He drives a red '73 Chevy Nova SS. He should be easy to find."

"Okay, got it."

"I don't want you getting too close, okay? I only want you to see what he's up to and report back."

"Will do."

"And watch yourself. He's smarter than he looks."

"Got it. Leave it with me, boss."

Dale started his car, pulled out, and looked up at the window. Sara stared down at him from behind the curtain.

62

TIME SEEMED TO crawl, Mo and I were both restless, buried in our own thoughts of what lay ahead. One afternoon, Mo took me over to Gillies Lake, a local conservation area, saying it was the town's hidden gem, and she couldn't have been more right. The setting matched the weather, the fall colours spectacular, and I was seeing another side of Timmins—a side I could easily embrace. We strolled hand in hand around the lake three times, sharing the trail with other couples, dog walkers, and joggers. What struck me—and all the more for the life we had been leading—was how calm and peaceful everybody else's lives seemed. Oh, trust me, I knew everyone's outside story didn't always match their inside one. No one's lives were perfect by any means, but what struck me was this was just a normal day to them. Their normal day. And I longed for the simplicity of just their normal day, and not the normal day that our lives perpetually were.

"Babe? You okay? Where are you?"

"Right here," I lied, squeezing her hand.

"No, you're not. Where are you? Halifax? The drop?"

"No, I'm here … it's just how peaceful all this is. It's just so nice."

"I know." She squeezed my hand then hugged my arm, her head dropping against my shoulder.

∽

When we got back, I landed on the couch and sat quietly, unable to shake the images of our afternoon at the lake. Mo busied herself in the kitchen, her turn to cook, and I could see her glancing at me from time to time. I was lost in thought when she plopped down on the couch beside me, purposely hitting my hip, and leaned forward in a deep male voice.

"Whassup, Bomber?" She snorted, wiping her nose and sniffing loudly. "Big game tonight, huh?"

She punched me on the shoulder, then puffing her chest out, she let go a long, loud belch that would have made any guy proud.

I laughed.

"Sorry," she said. "I can't fart like a guy."

She smiled. "We're almost there. You said so yourself. Our normal day … it's just around the corner."

"I know," I said, returning her smile but unwilling to share how scared I was at what the cost of obtaining it could turn out to be.

The rest of the time flew by, neither of us mentioned what lay ahead, and Mo kept busy, picking up extra shifts at the diner and Village Mart, and I understood why. I was helping Bree and Adrian at The Club but instead of spending the nights hanging out and shooting pool, we raced home and hung out in the blanket fort, trying to squeeze out as much time together as we could.

I had been texting Mary, and my landlord, and made arrangements to get my stuff out when I got down, so I decided to leave two days earlier to make it that much easier.

Our last full day together was typical of what Mo and I did best, taking an hour and squeezing it out like it was an entire day. We assumed our respective places on the couch and played rock, paper, scissors, to see whether it was beach blanket bingo in the blanket fort, or the submarine races in the shower, one last time.

I dropped Mo at the diner, then I went over to the club. It had been a busy week, and I guess I hadn't been paying attention, for I found Bree and Adrian behind the bar, locked in a lengthy embrace.

"Allo, what's all this then?" I said in my worst cockney accent, startling them. They separated and tried to act like nothing was going on. "Good gawd, man! 'Ave you no couth?" I bellowed at Adrian. Looking at Bree shamefully,

"And blimey look at what happens when you don't have parental supervision. You should be ashamed of yourself."

Bree fired a wet rag in my direction and scored a direct hit.

"Whatever ..." she muttered, then kissed Adrian, and they went into the kitchen.

It turned into a hectic day, and I never got a chance to catch up with either one, forcing them to spill. I left the club around five and headed home. It had turned cool, the sky filled with heavy grey ominous clouds, and I could smell the impending storm in the air.

Pulling out of the parking lot, I immediately picked up a black F-150, pulling out behind me. Sure enough, when I turned, he turned. I crisscrossed up and down the main drag, going up one street and down another. At a light, I was able to catch a glimpse in my mirror at two lumberjack dudes in their twenties. Honestly, it was child's play, and two lights later, I was doing the following. But it became alarming, when I followed them out toward our place, passing by the lane. I turned around a few klicks later, doubled back, and parked on a side street nearby. The truck never came back, but I was shaken by it.

Mo wasn't home yet, so I went out to my trunk, brought in my .45, and carefully laid it out on the coffee table. I unwrapped it, rubbed it down with the cloth, double-checked the clip, flipped the safety back on, and left it out on the table. I figured now was as good as time as any to teach her how to protect herself. And since I couldn't fly with it, it might be safer in her hands.

When Mo came in, she spied the gun on the table, walking over, she picked it up and in one motion twirled it, checked the safety, ejected the clip, inspected it, snapped it back in, cocked it, pointed it, uncocked it, then double-checked the safety, and placed it back on the table.

"Cool!" she said, walking down the hall to the bedroom. "What's for dinner? I'm starving! Your turn to cook."

Returning, I was busily preparing dinner in the kitchen.

I glanced up from my chopping. "Babe, your last boyfriend, what did you kill him with?"

Mo grabbed a piece of carrot from the cutting board.

"Kindness," she smiled sweetly and popped it in her mouth.

63

WE WERE AWAKE well before dawn, lying in the blanket fort, playing shadow puppets with our fingers and toes. Neither of us had slept, sex not on the agenda, it wasn't that we weren't interested or were too worn out though God knows we should have been. We knew what lay ahead, me much more than Mo, and the weight of it held us down to the point where we just wanted to lay quietly. That was enough, and sometimes that was the best way. Mo snuggled in, her head on my shoulder, and I wrapped my arms around her, kissing the top of her head.

"Be home before you know it," I said.

Bandit pushed his nose through the opening, meowing. We tried to grab him, but he ran away. Sitting up, we looked through the flap to see Bandit chasing a toy along the wall under the side window.

"If life were only so simple huh?" Mo sighed.

I nodded, and we took a deep breath, tapped fists, and crawled out of the blanket fort, ready to face the day … and the subsequent days filled with life-or-death uncertainties—just our normal day.

Mo watched as I packed my bag, fussing when I tried to jam everything in, and made me stand back as she took over. I watched as she packed my bag, just like Lisa used to, and I thought how lucky I was *despite* the present-day insanity we were living. And my heart melted when I watched her slyly slip her hand in her pocket, pull out a note, and place it in the front pocket of my bag.

My packed bags sat alongside the banker's box at the front door. We took our respective places on the couch one last time. We talked about our first encounter on the bridge, giggling about our run-in at the diner, then later that night at the club. I shared how I felt that moment when Bandit hopped up on the couch. Mo got a kick when I told her how, the next morning, I was full of doom and gloom.

"Coach Billy was so right," she teased.

And she shared how she stood at the foot of the couch watching me sleep that morning. I never knew. And how she quietly pushed her bike to the top of the road before starting it, not wanting to disturb me, and how, on the way to work, she thought it was just the best day ever despite the rain and dark clouds and gloom above.

I looked at my watch, the one that Mo had picked out for me, and it was time. Bandit was nowhere in sight as Mo and I stood at the doorway. We were smart enough to keep the goodbyes short. A quick hug and kiss followed by one *I love you* apiece, and that was a wrap. I was on my way—with the box—to whatever lay ahead.

I made a stop at the club, and Bree and Adrian were behind the bar, once again locked in a lengthy embrace.

"Get a room!" I barked.

At the sound, they looked up, and there was a *thunk*, and I could see them fumbling with something in their hands. I couldn't see over the bar, but I could see them push whatever they were holding down, then placed their hands on the bar, looking very guilty.

"Okay, what's up?" I looked behind the bar. "Geezus!" I threw my hands in the air. "Fine! I give up. Kill each other for all I care. It means I won't have to now."

I moved back around to the front and slid on a stool facing Bree and Adrian.

"What can I say?" Adrian said, raising his hands in defence.

"Do you have sex with them?" I asked, looking at Bree.

"Wouldn't you like to know?"

"Matching Glocks. Good lord!"

Bree shrugged. "I told you I could get one easy."

"That's how the two of you met?" I said, giving them the stink-eye. "Over guns?"

Bree and Adrian looked at each other sheepishly and smiled.

"Fine, see if I care."

Then I turned serious.

"Guys, last night I was followed after I left here. A black F-150, two guys in lumberjack shirts. I gave them the slip, but still, I'm guessing they've been hanging around."

Bree's face dropped, alarmed.

"And I wouldn't count Tony out of the picture by any means," I said. "Trust me, he's lurking around here somewhere."

Bree and Adrian nodded solemnly.

"Mo has my .45 just in case. You two be careful okay?"

I looked at Adrian, then at Bree, and back at Adrian. "No matter how much I hate her, she doesn't leave your sight."

"Not to worry, Pete. You take care. Be safe and see you in a few days," Adrian said, wrapping his arm around Bree's shoulder.

"I better get back in the kitchen," Adrian said, stretching his hand over the bar, shaking mine. "If you need anything, just text me. I wish I were coming. I miss that stuff."

I wished he was too—Adrian was exactly the type of person you wanted having your back.

Looking at Bree, she wiped away a tear, and a huge lump formed in my throat.

"You know, I was perfectly happy hating on you when you first got here. Why did you have to go and wreck that?"

"Just my overall natural charm and good looks, I guess," I said, ducking as the wet rag flew past.

I slid off the stool and moved around behind the bar to where Bree was standing.

"I hate you. I really do," she said, hugging me.

I hugged her back, so lucky to have found such a good friend.

"Please keep an eye on Mo."

"Absolutely."

Another quick hug, and as I made my way up the stairs, Bree called after me, "If you don't come back, I will hunt you down, and if you are dead, I will *unkill* you, then *rekill* you myself. You got that, slick?"

I got it, loud and clear, a huge lump sticking in my throat, as I made my way up the stairs.

The trip along 101, then down Highway 11, was quiet, no music. I was feeling pensive, everything on hold until I got back. I was determined that there would be no IFs and MAYBEs this time, only WHENs. Looking in the rearview mirror, I guess what bothered me most was that there was more than just my past in that mirror. There was all three—past, present, and future—and the irony of it; all in the rear-view mirror. And there was something else, too. My losing battle with what I had kept hidden from Mo and the overwhelming sense of foreboding that washed over me the moment I texted Teddy to let him know I was *in*.

Fortunately, the farther down Highway 11 I drove, the better I started to feel. The roads were clear, devoid of the big rumbling trucks that rattled my Chevy's windows when they roared past, giving me a false sense of security. I kept looking at the box on the front seat beside me, recalling the dust-up with the bikers—I didn't want to go through that again, so it wasn't leaving my sight until I got to Sharkees.

Carefully keeping one eye on the road, I flipped off the lid, and felt for the papers inside. They were no longer neatly in order, as Mo and I had hurriedly stuffed them inside, when lust won out that morning on the couch. I ran my hand over them, selecting one at random. Then, checking the road, I took a peek.

It was the same as all the others, both sides filled with impeccable handwriting, almost like it wasn't real, but the blue ink indicated it was. I scanned the bottom looking for the signature, and there it was, the unintelligible scrawl. I flipped the page over, and it was the same. Where did I know this handwriting from?

Suddenly, the blaring of a horn made me look up, and to my horror, I had drifted over into the oncoming lane.

SHIT!

I jerked the wheel to my right, narrowly missing an oncoming semi as it roared past, its horn blasting angrily at me. Once my nerves had settled, I reached for the sheet and dropped it in the box, pushing the lid back down then putting both hands on the steering wheel. A few minutes later, reaching behind the seat, feeling for the eight-track case, I pulled out a tape, not caring who it was, pushed it in the slot and cranked the volume.

The opening guitar licks to Blue Öyster Cult's 'Don't Fear the Reaper' came pouring through the speakers, and I laughed at the irony.

The rest of the trip was uneventful, but as I got closer to North Bay, it started to rain lightly at first, then more heavily, as the wind picked up. Coming down the long steep hill into North Bay, the sky was pitch black with bright intermittent flashes, the scraggly lightning bolts covering the horizon like a cracked foundation. I watched in awe as long bands of rain swept across Lake Nipissing.

Lovely. I didn't think it wise to be going any farther than here tonight.

I turned right at the lights and headed towards the downtown core. Years ago, I had stayed at this dinky motel just past the main drag and right on Lake Nipissing. I had a room at the edge of the water—a perfect view—and I had slept with the windows open, the sound of the waves lapping up against the shore, better than any sleeping pill. I wondered if it was still there.

The flashing green vacancy sign peeked through the wipers, the motel under a different name now, guiding me into the parking lot, and ten minutes later, luck clearly on my side, my old room vacant, I flopped on the bed, the box safely on the chair beside me. The rain teemed against the windows and thundered on the tin roof overhead, as I texted Mo, who had sent me three texts, the first one starting with "Hey stranger", which made me smile. So her.

I told her I was stuck in North Bay for the night due to the weather, which she already knew— her other texts had been weather warnings. We both said how much we missed each other already, and she said Bandit appeared a bit out of sorts. I texted back with what I thought was front-page news about Bree and Adrian, only to have her respond right away.

"I've known for ages. Where have you been?"

We signed off for a bit, and I got up and flung open the curtains and, to my surprise, the rain had stopped, and the dark clouds were already dispersing. The storm had passed as quickly as it started. I thought of getting back on the road, but I liked better the thought of sleeping with the windows open and the water lapping at the shore.

I went for a walk and found the liquor store, and inside, strangely Dan Fogelberg's 'Same Old Lang Syne' was playing overhead. Though, it was only late September, I decided to play along, and moved stealthily through the aisles looking for my high school sweetheart. I bought a six-pack, and unlike the song, the snow wasn't falling, and it wasn't Christmas Eve. I didn't touch anyone's sleeve in the frozen daiquiri aisle, and I didn't bump into anyone, spilling their purse. I didn't laugh, though I wanted to cry, as the love of my life was up in Timmins, right about now lounging in the blanket fort in her tattered housecoat and fuzzy slippers.

Back at the hotel, I grabbed a blanket off the bed and adjourned outside to the breakwall, and after spreading out the blanket over the top, plopped myself up. Staring out on the water, popping open my beer, I raised my can to the sky.

"Please keep an eye on me will you there Mr., or is it, Mrs. Universe?"

I worked through the six-pack, trying to drink away the feelings of dread. I jumped off the breakwall, went inside and speed-dialled a pizza, returned and waited. When the pizza arrived, I polished it and the rest of the six-pack off, then went inside, spread apart the curtains, opened all the windows, and crashed.

I awoke at dawn, raring to go, the good night's sleep in the picture-postcard Hallmark location the perfect tonic. I texted Mo, who had slept in the blanket fort with Bandit, and she said during the night he kept going to over to my spot on the couch.

Twenty minutes later, I was out on Highway 17, headed for Ottawa.

The drive went quickly, and I mentally ran through what needed to be done. When I gave my landlord my notice, I had lucked out, as he had someone already lined up, and—bonus—they wanted my furniture. So, all I had to do was pack up my personal belongings and stereo, and that was it. Mary had always liked my stereo, so I sold it to her at the home discount rate, throwing in my red and white plaid aluminum lawn chair.

As I drove across the city, it didn't feel like home. Even though it had only been two months, it felt like a lifetime. Pulling into my driveway, nothing had changed. Mary was sitting on her front step, beer in one hand and a cigarette in the other. I looked for the cast on her foot, thinking she had been sitting there all this time, but fortunately, the cast was gone. I got out and went over and sat beside her, exchanging warm hellos. She went in and brought me out a beer, then caught me up on all the news that was.

Fortunately, there was no news to speak of. Nothing ever happened now, and I guess that was a good thing. She had kept up my place, and I was grateful beyond words—she casually waved that off with her cigarette. But still, I decided to give her my stereo and the matching aluminum chair; they came as a set, and it was the least I could do. Cat was doing great, and she loved him dearly. She got up and brought him outside for me to see, but he didn't recognize me, and I felt a sharp pang. We went through a couple more beers, so naturally, when the beer flowed, tongues did the same.

"Remember that night on my front lawn and how you came over and took care of that guy?"

"Yes."

"And after, you just let me be. I was expecting you to hit on me, you know? That's what most guys would have done, but you never did. Why?"

"Didn't say it didn't cross my mind."

"But you didn't. You respected me and gave me my space."

Mary took a long pull on her beer, turning and looking at me. "You need to do that for yourself. You need to look after yourself."

I nodded, wondering where this was coming from and if it was more than just the beer talking.

"Do you know, after that night, I never worried again. I felt safe because I knew you were there. Even after you left, I knew you were still there. I want to think I am making better choices now, better choices with my life, and men. And it's all because of you. You let me be and didn't treat me like some damsel in distress—though that night I was. But you didn't, and from that, it gave me time to find my self-respect. And if it had been any other guy that night, I would have kept repeating the same patterns over and over."

Stunned by Mary's words, I didn't know what to say.

"You need to do that for you," she said, pointing her beer toward me, tapping me in the chest. "You are back for a reason, and not just to clean out your place. Something big is going on, I picked up on that as soon as I saw you. It's written all over your face. I hope she's worth it."

Startled at the word *she*, my head dropped. Noticing my reaction, Mary reached for my arm.

"It's okay. I didn't mean for it to come out like that. What I meant was, are you doing whatever it is you are doing, for the right reasons? Besides her, and knowing you, I bet she's drop-dead gorgeous with a personality to boot … but besides her, who are you doing this for? Because no matter what happens, and no matter how wonderful she is, the most important person in all of this is you."

I tried to reply, I wanted to, but I couldn't because I didn't know. Sensing this, Mary shrugged.

"Don't answer me. I'm not the one looking for an answer. The only person you have to answer to is yourself, and there's no timeline with that. You will know when you know," she smiled at me reassuringly.

Between Mary and the beer, I was feeling fuzzy, and knew I better get in my place and gather up my belongings while I still could. I thanked Mary for the beer and told her I would drop by in the morning with the stereo as I wanted one last night with Pink Floyd in my lawn chair. Mary laughed.

"Sure. Hang on."

Then she went inside and came back out with a joint and matches.

"'Us and Them' sounds much better after a few hits," she said.

I went around, room to room, gathered up my belongings, throwing them in two large suitcases and taking them out to my Chevy and squeezing them in the trunk. I slammed the lid and rubbed my hands together in glee. It was time for one last trip around the dark side of the moon, Pete Humphries style.

64

SARA TRIED TO stay busy and out of sight of everyone, especially Patty, but one could only do that for so long when working in a bar. After Dale had left, she had tried her best to cover up the red handprint that covered her cheek, and now that the side of her face was noticeably swollen; unless she remained out of the public eye for the next few days, someone was bound to notice.

"Amy, honey, the condiment caddies on all the tables need to be filled. They weren't done again last night," grumbled Patty, walking in behind the bar.

"Sure, right away. I'm just going to finish up here," she said, keeping her back to Patty.

Patty sensed something wasn't right. "Amy?"

"Yes?" Still refusing to turn around.

"Amy, look at me," Patty asked, softly.

"I'm fine," she said, keeping her head down. "I'm just busy,"

Patty stepped forward and reached out for Amy's arm, and gently pulled on it.

"Amy."

"What?"

"Amy, look at me. Please," Patty's hand lay firmly on her arm.

Sara knew she had no choice, and reluctantly turned and faced Patty, head down, hiding her face. Patty reached out, tilting her chin up, her eyes instantly filling with tears, her voice cracking.

"Oh my God, who did this to you?"

"It's nothing. I slipped in the bathroom and fell against the cabinet," she said, turning away again.

"I didn't know the cabinet could leave handprints," Patty said, eyes narrowing.

"Leave me alone, okay? Please."

"Amy, you're my best friend, and I love you." Patty was now overcome with emotion. "What happened? What's wrong? You haven't been yourself in ages. I love you, and I want to help, but you won't let me. Did Teddy do this?"

"No! No!" Sara waved her hand. "No, Teddy didn't do this."

"Then who?" Patty asked angrily. "Who did this to you?"

"Please don't. Please, if you are my best friend and you love me, you will just let me be," she pleaded, tears rolling down her cheeks.

Patty gave up, reached out and hugged her hard. Sara's hands remaining at her side.

"Honey, I'm here, okay? I will always be here. You know that, right?"

Sara nodded, sniffling, wincing as she wiped away the tears with her hand then reached for Patty's hand and squeezed it. "Thank you."

Patty went into the kitchen, leaving Sara behind the bar. She fought off more tears and tried to push everything away, but like a dam that had broken, everything was coming out, all at once.

The night she killed her parents and covered it up ... no that wasn't right; it was Dale who covered everything up. Since that night, the price had become too much for her to keep paying. She couldn't live with it any longer and didn't care anymore if she went to prison for it. She couldn't continue to live in hiding. Amy. Sara. Sara. Amy. There were so many times when she or Teddy almost slipped up. It was at the point she could barely keep herself straight. She felt bad lying to Patty.

Was she Sara or was she Amy? She honestly didn't know anymore. If they were one and the same, why did she feel like she was two distinct and very different people trapped in the same body? At times, she thought she might be going insane. She wanted all of it to stop.

And she wanted away from Dale.

She despised him. Everything that he was and everything he pretended to be but wasn't. She hated him to his—and her—very core. Early on, she came to understand that he fed off power, he was drawn to it like a moth to a flame. He had a loving, doting wife and two beautiful children plus a big home in the country overlooking a lake. A picture-perfect family—things that anyone would kill for, yet to him, they were nothing more than possessions. What floated his boat was power. Pure raw power.

She sensed Teddy had fallen under his spell also. Was her brother under Dale's spell because Dale had told him what she had done that night? She didn't think so, but she couldn't be sure. He had something on her brother, but she didn't know what.

And she hated Dale for the power he had over her sexually. No one could fuck her like he could. She hated herself for that too. Around and around the merry-go-round went, unable to make it stop, wanting off.

She felt trapped and needed to find a way out. She tried to tell Teddy many times but had been unable to. Just *another* reason to hate herself. And it wasn't the first time she had threatened Dale that she would tell—and it wasn't the first time he had hit her either. But it was the first time he had pulled a gun on her, then ... what he had done. That was a whole new level of terror and his calculated intention. Make her so scared, there was no way she would talk. She was now seeing the pattern, each hit, each threat, was a little stronger than the previous one.

The fear building in her stomach worked its way up into her throat; reaching for her water jar, she took a long drink, water splashing down her front, but she didn't care. Tilting the jar up, she finished it off, sighing heavily. Smoothing her top, wiping away the water droplets, there was a rush of air followed by the loud bang, and she looked up to see Teddy coming through the door.

"Hey, sis!" Teddy bellowed, plopping himself on the stool in front of her, head down, he pulled out his phone.

She didn't say a word and waited.

Teddy scrolled through his phone, not looking up. "Beer please."

Nothing.

"Hellooo," he said playfully, still buried in his phone. "I haven't got all day, beer please."

Still nothing.

"Okay fine, I will just get it myself."

Chuckling, he leaned forward, reached over the counter, head down, when he caught a glimpse of his sister. His mouth dropped, and he went white, falling back on the stool. He stared at her, speechless. She stood across from him—silent, trembling, hands folded across her stomach, the mark on her face standing out like a bright red flashing beacon.

Patty came out of the kitchen, but when she saw the two of them, quickly turned and made a hasty retreat.

"I'm sorry, Teddy. I'm so sorry. I am so sorry."

Teddy, staring at the mark on her face. "Why are *you* sorry?"

"For all of this, for all of it. I wish, I—"

"For what? All of what? Wish for—"

"Oh my God . . ." as tears started rolling down her cheeks. "I'm so sorry."

Breaking down, shaking, holding herself, she leaned against the bar for support. Teddy moved behind the bar and took his sister in his arms, wrapping his big hands and long arms around her frail shoulders. Holding her gently, she fell into his chest, sobbing uncontrollably. He let her cry, then he guided her to the oversized chair beside the fireplace. Kneeling beside her, he placed his arm around her shoulder and waited. When the shudders ceased, Teddy pushed her head up so she could see him.

"Who did this to you?"

"Dale," she whispered.

She leaned against his side. A little brother consoling big sister because that's what loving families do. Teddy softly stroked her hair, lightly kissing the top of her head, then peeked at his watch. Giving her a reassuring hug, he said he had some business to attend to, and would she be okay if he left? She nodded and hugged him again and said she would be fine. As he started to get up, she reached out for his hand.

"I love you."

Teddy smiled. "Me too sis." He kissed her head, then he went outside, already placing the call.

⁓

"Yes, boss."

"I've got a job for you."

"What is it?"

"I need some muscle."

"Absolutely."

"I need a cop roughed up."

"Sure thing, boss …"

Patty cautiously poked her head out of the kitchen and saw Sara sitting by herself by the fire.

"You okay?" she asked, sitting down cross-legged on the floor in front of her.

Sara nodded then reached over and patted her hand. "I am so sorry," she said looking into Patty's eye. "I am so very sorry."

"What for? I don't understand."

"There is something I have been wanting to tell you."

"What is it, honey? You can tell me anything, you know that, right?"

"I know, and that's why I'm sorry. I should have told you sooner, a long time ago. I'm so sorry." She was again fighting back tears.

"Hey *hey*, that's okay," said Patty. "It's okay. I'm here now. That's all that matters."

Sara took a deep breath, shuddering involuntarily. "I'm not who I say I am."

Patty smiled. "Oh honey, none of us are who we really say we are."

Sara shook her head.

"No, no, I know that, but this is different," she said trying to compose her thoughts. She sighed. "I'm, well, I mean my name—"

Just then, there was a loud bang, and they turned their heads toward the front entrance. There was another loud bang and in walked a customer who looked familiar. The figure in the jean jacket looked to the right and then to the left, searching for an open seat, spotted one, casually moved around to the empty stool.

Patty looked at Sara again.

"What were you going to tell me?"

"Nothing. Just leave it," she said, and then by way of diversion. "Wow, is that who I think it is?"

"Yes it is. Haven't seen him in ages. Are you okay?" Patty asked.

"Yeah, of course. I'm just … it's okay."

Sara looked to the guy at the bar. It had been months since she had seen him. The last time outside of the Lucky7evens, looking very much the worse for wear. She had been surprised to see him and figured it had something to do with Teddy's latest scheme.

And he was the one who had followed her that night when she left the bar, the chase unnerving her. She asked Dale to check him out, but Dale never spoke of it again. And so, she had forgotten about it.

Now, here he was.

Patty helped her to her feet, and after another hug, Sara went behind the bar to serve him.

65

I WAS EARLY for my meeting with Teddy, sitting in the parking lot for the past hour observing. Teddy came out, phone up to his ear, and even from a distance, I could tell it was something serious. The phone was glued to his ear as he walked to his truck, got in and sped off. I sat for a while longer, watching as I wasn't sure what, if anything, was going to happen next. Eventually, I decided I could learn more inside.

I didn't realize how much I had missed Sharkees until I walked through those doors, the loud bangs of the outer and inner doors, and the rush of air, comforting. The crackling and smell of burning wood wafting in the air had a nostalgic feel now. Sharkees had been my escape. It had grounded me. And now I was back. I realized it had given me what I needed at the time, and what I had now up in Timmins, was a more permanent grounding. In life, there is a reason for everything, and Sharkees had given me what I needed, when I needed it.

So, I was home, temporarily, and it was nice to see the regulars perched in their usual spots on each side of the bar. Nothing had changed.

I took a seat at the bar across from the piano. There was no one behind the bar, and the other servers were bustling about. But then, as though on cue, Amy came walking in and headed straight toward me. She looked awful, and it was all I could do to not react. I felt sick as I knew someone had laid a beating on her. She dropped a coaster on the counter in front of me.

"Barking Squirrel, right?" Amy asked weakly.

"Please."

Amy reached down to one of the coolers, pulled out a bottle, twisted off the top, and placed the beer in front of me.

"Long time no see," she said. "How've you been?"

"I think I should be the one asking you that."

Amy didn't respond, so I tried to make light of things.

"Pardon me, but you look like shit," I teased.

"Ha. Nice, thanks. Just what I needed."

"Hey, I'm sorry. You know I was kidding. Are you okay?"

Nodding, Amy reached for her water jar.

"How are you?" she asked. "The last time I saw you, you were being carried out of a bar by a girl. That seems the norm for you," she said, smiling again, her old self quickly returning.

"That *was* you! That night at Lucky7evens in Peterborough. I thought that was you."

"Yes, that was me, all right. I haven't seen you there or here since."

"No. I've been up north. I just got back in town last night. I'm meeting Teddy here. You haven't seen him, have you?"

"Hmm, you're early. He's just stepped out, but he said he won't be long. Are you hungry? How about our grill cheese special? It's delicious. And if you're meeting Teddy, it should be on a full stomach."

It took three beers before I felt better, and the Sharkee's Special hit the spot. It was only eleven thirty when I finished it and I had an idea. I waved to Amy for another beer, then scrolled through my phone looking for the number, created a text, tapped send, and waited. I sipped on my beer, inwardly teleporting the short distance to the airport and Meghan's phone. I hoped she was there.

Meghan was like the daughter I would have had if I were older and hadn't screwed up that picket fence years ago. In her early twenties, cute, outgoing, full of life, she had the perfect job, working for Porter Airlines at the airport. Despite all those unruly flyers, she had the perfect temperament and it suited her.

We met when I briefly dated her mom, Janet, someone Mary set me up with—her one and only attempt at matchmaking. We weren't a match, but I connected immediately with her daughter Meghan. Meg was a kindred spirit, so we naturally fit. There was nothing romantic, but we became fast friends, secretly going out for beers, not wanting to upset her mom, who still had an interest in me. She told me that anytime I needed to fly, she could get me on standby dirt cheap. I hadn't seen her in months, but I figured I'd take a chance.

A few minutes later, my phone dinged, and there was a reply from Meg. She was pleased to hear from me and hoped I was doing well. She said she was working and asked what I needed. I texted back that I was flying to Halifax later that night, but I wasn't sure of the exact time or airline, and if it was hers, could she do me a favour? She said to tell her what I needed and that she would be there until the last flight of the night arrived.

Perfect. That was a start. Now, if the flying gods would only cooperate. With time still to kill, I realized I had forgotten another important detail. Where was I going to leave my beloved Chevy while I was away? I was only going to be gone twenty four hours, but I wasn't comfortable leaving it in the parking lot or at my now *old* place.

Just then, Patty walked by, and the light bulb went off. Back in the summer, I watched her leave one time, driving a souped-up Pontiac Grand Prix. This tiny thing, wheeled it out of the parking lot, smoothly punching through the gears better than any race car driver. She would be perfect, my only concern being that she might drive it better than I did. I didn't have much choice, hoping my ego could stand it. Getting Amy's attention, I told her I wanted to speak with Patty when she had a moment. A few minutes later, Patty came out and stood across from me.

"Hey stranger, long time no see."

"Been busy," I said, trying to keep it short, thinking Teddy would be here at any moment.

"We miss you, not near as many orders for grilled cheese sandwiches with a pickle on the side."

Looking at the clock behind her, I got right to the point. "Patty, I need a favour."

"Sure, Pete. What is it? And it better not be wanting the recipe for those grilled cheese sandwiches."

"No, no, nothing like that. You know I drive that red Chevy."

"Yes, the metallic candy apple red 1973 Chevy Nova SS 350 cubic inch

V8 4-barrel with the Mickey Thompson slicks and four on the floor Hurst shifter. Why?"

Yup, she would be perfect.

"I need someone to look after it for me. Just overnight. I have to leave from here in a bit, and I'll be back tomorrow sometime in the early afternoon. Would you be interested?"

Patty's eyes opened wide and her mouth dropped—it was probably the first time I had seen her at a loss for words. You would think she had just won the lottery.

"I'll take that as a *yes*," I said smiling, not sure if she heard me, as she was wearing a thousand-yard stare, already shifting through the gears and doing bleach burnouts.

"Okay, great! I'll give you the keys before I leave. Sound good? Patty? ... Patty ... sound good?"

"Oh God, yes! Absolutely! You can trust me. I will treat it like it's my own. Thank you!"

"That's what I was hoping you would say."

Patty returned to the kitchen, and behind me, there was a loud bang, a whoosh followed by another bang, more whoosh, and there was Teddy in all his glory.

Lovely, I hadn't missed you in the least.

He still looked the same, and I was disappointed he wasn't wearing that ratty orange tank top. Teddy caught my gaze and ambled over, plopping his big butt on the stool beside me.

"Well, howdy, Pistol!" pounding me on the back, no doubt sending a message.

"Nice to see you, Texas!" I drawled, as message received, I punched him back, hard.

"Still the same funny guy."

"How was the trip?"

"Uneventful."

"Just what is it about up there in the north? Timmins, isn't it? That's where you are now, right?" Teddy knowing full well he knew exactly where I was.

"Yes, it's a lovely place. I don't think it's for you, though."

"Why?"

"Normal people live up there."

Teddy looked at me, unsure if I was serious or not, then started to laugh again.

"Ahh, Pistol! Such a Pistol. And you have a girl. Look at you go all domesticated."

"Living the dream, what can I say?"

Amy came in behind the bar and not a moment too soon.

"What'll it be, Teddy?" she asked formally.

"Beer and a whisky chaser, and another for whatever my friend here is drinking."

Amy turned away to get our drinks, and when she placed them in front of us, Teddy suggested moving to a table, but looking around, there were no tables to be had. We tapped glasses, Teddy downed both his drinks, while I sipped on my beer. He waved to Amy for another.

"Where's the box?" Teddy asked, getting straight to the point.

"I have it."

"Did you bring it?"

"Yep."

"Where is it?"

"I have it."

"Do you have the two-fifty?"

"Yes."

"Where is it?"

"I have it."

"Look Texas, we could do this all day, but I've got a plane to catch, courtesy of you, so maybe we should get to it and move out of the sandbox."

Amy placed the drinks in front of Teddy, and he took a sip, squinting as the whiskey chaser hit the back of his throat.

"You're right, Pistol."

Teddy unzipped his jacket, lifted his shirt, fiddled underneath, the sound of vinyl ripping, pulled out a money belt, and placed it on the bar.

"I see your appetite has changed," Teddy said, expecting that I would have gone all glassy-eyed at the sight. "I'm disappointed."

"I'm not. Not near as hungry as before."

"Look at you. That place up north has changed you."

"More than you know," I said, thinking about the normal day that awaited Mo and I once this was finally over.

"The box, please."

"Once I count it."

Teddy handed me the belt, placing it in my lap, I quickly checked each pocket, and it appeared to be all there.

"Give me a minute," as I slid off the stool, and finished my beer. "Can you order me another one, please? The box is in my Chevy, and it will take just a minute."

I started toward the door.

"No tricks," Teddy warned. I stopped, annoyed.

"Geez Teddy! This is just like the movies and the tricks don't come until the exchange takes place."

"Ahh, such a Pistol."

I walked quickly out to my car, fumbling with the keys in the lock, I reached inside for the box, making sure the lid was on tight, then grabbed my shoulder bag, shut the door, and locked it. I made my way over to the entrance and lucked out, as someone held both doors open for me. I walked around to Teddy and dropped the box on the counter.

"It's all yours, big guy," as I leaned and let my bag slide off my shoulder onto the floor.

Teddy stared at the box, wide-eyed, unable to hide his excitement. Now it was my turn.

"Hmm, look at you, such a big appetite. Hopefully, it's not a case of your eyes being bigger than your stomach. You know what happens if you eat too much."

I could see Teddy fighting the urge to open the box, and I couldn't blame him. Undoubtedly, he had gone to great lengths to get it, and now there it was, in front of him. Sort of like meeting your hero. Sometimes it was better not to, as you could wind up disappointed, and worse, no longer seeing that person in the same light, or in Teddy's case, careful what you wish for.

So, I let Teddy be, and sipped my beer. I gazed around at the patrons and wondered what was going on in their lives at this moment? Were they living normal lives? Was today just their normal day? Were all their days normal?

I thought of Meg and tapped Teddy on the arm.

"Hey, big guy, I've got a flight to catch, remember?"

Still staring at the box, he turned to me. "Yes ... sorry there, Pistol."

He reached in his pocket and pulled out an envelope.

"Everything you need is in there. The address is written down. At 6:00 a.m. tomorrow, drive to the address, park, and wait. A white Honda Civic will pull up and pass you the case with the bonds inside. That's it. A car is under your name at the airport, and I've booked you a room downtown at the Marriott. The address is written down inside. The flight is tonight at 9:15 p.m., direct to Halifax. The return ticket is tomorrow at 9:15 a.m. Sorry, it's not first-class, all I could get was a cheap flight."

I fought off the feelings of dread. This was now real. Acting nonchalant, "Aww, it's okay. It's a short flight anyway, what with the one-hour time difference. Be there before you know it. If they serve beer on the plane, I don't care where I sit."

I took the envelope from Teddy, flipped open the flap, and pulled the ticket out far enough to see the airline. Porter. Bingo!

"Listen, Teddy, I gotta make a quick call to the missus. Do you mind watching the money for me? I trust you."

"Sure, Pistol. I'm not going anywhere.'

I hopped off the stool and searched around the bar for a quiet spot to talk, but it was too noisy. I headed towards the can, and walking inside, I looked along the row of stalls and saw an empty one at the far end. I locked the door, searched my phone for Meg, and tapped connect. *Please answer, please answer.* Meg answered on the third ring, and I got right to the point.

"I've got a ticket with you for 9:15 tonight to Halifax. Can you switch it for me?'

"Give me a second and I'll look."

I could hear typing.

"I've got a 5:15. That work?"

"Perfect!"

"Okay, you're all set."

"Great! I owe you."

"Beer. It would be nice to catch up."

"I promise, soon."

"I will hold you to it. Anything else?"

Then it hit me. "Yes, there is."

"What is it?"

"Can I fly as a John Doe?"

There was a pause, and I wondered if I had asked too much. "It's okay Meg, I don't want you to get in trouble."

"No, it's not that. It's what I've always liked about you. You've always got stuff going on, and I'm betting this one's a doozy?"

"Yes, it is," ignoring the gnawing pit in my stomach.

"Okay, let's do this."

There was more clicking.

"When you check-in at the counter, show the person your ID, but I want you to say this code word: Guinness. Then just follow their lead. Got it?"

"Yes, Guinness. I got it."

"I'm working near your gate, so I will keep an eye out for you just in case."

"Thanks a million, Meg."

"Anytime, Pete."

"My mom says hi," Meg giggled.

"Very funny."

"I will look for you. Bye!"

It was twenty past one, and I had just the right amount of time. I was certain Teddy would have someone waiting for me when the plane landed in Halifax, but now—four hours early—I highly doubted it. I texted Dale, giving him the new flight and waited for his reply.

I didn't have to wait long

He said to meet him at the Mooseheads game, downtown, when I landed. Though that intense feeling of impending doom was still present, I wondered if it was just nerves having been out of the game for so long. Plus, I had slain that hockey dragon, and the thought of seeing another game was appealing, despite the circumstances it was under.

I stood up, pushed the handle, and looking at the tank, the light bulb went off again. I made my way back and sat down beside Teddy. The box was still unopened in front of him, and the money belt lay beside it. *Strange*, I thought. *All right out in the open, and no one noticed.*

"Shots for old times?" Teddy asked.

"Sure, why not? One won't hurt," I said, quickly falling into old habits because they are hard to break after all.

Teddy bellowed for Amy, and three shots later, I had to use the can again. I slid off the stool and stumbled towards the bathroom, discreetly grabbing the money belt off the bar and tucking it under my shirt. Walking by the entrance to the inside of the bar, I looked down on one of the shelves and saw man's second-best friend—duct tape.

When I came out of the can, I looked over to where I was sitting, and Amy and Teddy were in an animated discussion, her hands gesturing and pointing. I dropped the duct tape back on the shelf and lazily wandered along the other side of the bar. Looking over, Amy looked in my direction, and our eyes locked.

Sara.

Amy was Sara, or Sara was Amy, it didn't matter which because they were one and the same.

How could I have missed something so obvious?

I plopped down beside Teddy. "No more shots!" I said, waving my hand at the glasses on the bar. "You can, but I'm back to beer."

"Sure, Pistol. You're a real trouper, though. Three shots!" Teddy mocked.

"I know, guilty as charged. Lightweight city, what can I say?"

Teddy hollered for Amy and when she came over our eyes met again. I didn't say anything, and I could see the fear in her eyes. She brought us our drinks then moved away to serve the others, but not before turning back and looking at me. She needed to know. Glancing at Teddy to see if he was looking, I brought my hand up to my mouth and made a locking gesture. She smiled and turned away.

When Teddy went to the can, I slipped outside and checked on my Chevy to make sure I hadn't forgotten anything, then I went back inside looking for Patty. I handed her the keys and made her pinky swear she wouldn't squeal the tires or play my eight-tracks full blast.

"What's an eight-track?" she asked.

I liked Patty, as she reminded me of Bree. I thought they could be sisters as they were so much alike.

It was time to make my exit, but Teddy wouldn't let me go so easily, the alcohol clearly winning. It was also having its own effect on me, as I was making frequent trips to the can. Teddy had started to look like a slinky-toy, and it was my chance to duck out, as I started to leave, he said something that made me stop.

"You know we've met before."

"No, I don't believe we have. I mean, I thought the first time was back in the summer here."

"No," he slurred. "We've met before. A long time ago. You don't remember, do you?"

Puzzled, I had no idea what he was talking about, even after quickly powering on the old mental VCR and inserting the tape from my childhood.

"A long time ago ... such a long time ago," he reminisced, slurring.

"Teddy, I don't recall meeting you. Like I said, not before the summer, at least."

"The boat," he mumbled. "It was on a boat."

Quickly, I ejected the tape, searching for the tape when I had my dad's boat. Pressing the FF button, it only contained Tina, and I had made peace with that weeks ago.

"Honestly, Teddy, I don't know ..."

Teddy waved his hand. "It's okay, Pistol. It doesn't matter anymore."

I was confused and didn't know where this was coming from, but the way he spoke gave me pause, and it was more than just the alcohol talking. I made a mental note that when this was over, and my head was clear, I would figure out what he was talking about.

"Listen, Texas, I gotta run. Big day in the morning, and I will see you this time tomorrow," I said, trying to sound confident, and fighting off the fear and uncertainty that came with it.

"Sure thing, Pistol," he waved. "Keep me posted and have a safe trip. See you tomorrow."

I called for a cab and waited outside by the entrance, looking across the parking lot at my baby and praying this wasn't goodbye.

66

TEDDY, FEELING THE effects of the drinks, watched Pete get into the cab. When it pulled away, he reached for his drink then made his way over to the piano and slipped outside through the patio door.

So, it was done. He had the box—though he had no desire to look inside now. He'd left it on the bar and watched through the window as Sara reached for it and tucked it away out of sight.

My poor, sweet, innocent Sara.

What would he do without her? So caring, so fragile, always concerned about his well-being. She probably had no clue what really happened that night.

Teddy was certain Dale had something to do with their parents' death, and it wasn't just an accident, and he was sure the answer lay in that box, but he didn't care anymore. And just now, when he tried to tell Pete where he knew him from, Pete's expression told him that he didn't know. That didn't change anything about getting revenge for that day on the dock, not in the least. By this time tomorrow, there would be no more Pete Humphries, no more of his smart-ass wisecracks, and no more of that fucking honour thing, and he thought that was what bothered him the most about him—he wasn't capable of being that honourable.

He downed his drink, then looked through the window to get his sister's attention. Sara was watching him, smiling, he raised his glass, jiggling it, and she nodded. He pulled out his phone, texted his contact at the airport security gate, informing him Pete was to be screened through when he arrived for his 9:15 flight. Receiving confirmation, he debated texting Dale. The hit he put out on Dale was only hours old, and knowing Tony, things usually got done later rather than sooner. Still, he wondered if he should contact him, strictly for appearances' sake?

Was the hit the right call? He had ordered it based solely on emotion. If Dale had smacked Sara that hard, it probably wasn't the first time and certainly wouldn't be the last. Except now maybe it *would* be the last time.

Fuck him.

Pete's flight wasn't for a few hours yet, and nothing was going to happen between now and the morning anyways, so he decided to leave it for now.

Teddy heard the patio poor open. Sara, carrying two drinks, handed Teddy his. They clinked glasses and stood quietly looking at the blinking lights, listening to the thump-thump of the music from inside, along with the occasional whoops and hollers.

They turned to watch the pink sunset in the distance, and if you could ignore the bright neon sign of the grocery store just below it, it felt like the paradise that one dreamt about. Your normal everyday paradise.

Teddy moved over and put his arm around Sara, her head dropping against his shoulder.

"Teddy, there's something I need to tell you."

"Sure, sis, and I have something to tell you. Who wants to go first?"

The timing was right, the setting perfect. Brother and sister were finally going to unload their respective burdens.

Sara's phone dinged, looking down at it, she froze in horror and started shaking. Alarmed, Teddy stepped back, and his jaw dropped when she showed him her phone. Quickly, they looked around to see who was watching them, then hurriedly went inside.

67

MEG WAS WAITING for me at the gate, and just for fun, I used a low dramatic voice when I gave her the password, which broke her up. We exchanged quick pleasantries, and I thanked her again, and walking down the ramp, I heard her call out and turned back to see her running towards me.

"Everything okay?" I asked.

"Sure, sure," she said, catching her breath.

Turning serious and checking to see if anyone was watching.

"Look, it's not my place, but are you okay? For as long as I've known you, I've never seen you scared. But today, you look scared, and I could even sense it in your voice when you called earlier," she said, her eyes full of concern.

I didn't know what to say other than she was right; I was scared, more like terrified.

Thanking Meg, I told her I was doing something important, but not to worry. I could tell she didn't believe me, but to her credit, she let me be. But she did make me promise to check in with her, and touched by that, I promised I would. I headed back down the ramp, stuffing my hands in my pockets, not wanting anyone to see how badly they were trembling.

Fortunately, the flight wasn't full, and I had a row all to myself near the back. I couldn't sleep and tried counting eight-tracks, alphabetically. I dozed off when I got to Chicago and was jerked awake, when a flight attendant gently tapped me on my shoulder, informing me that we were on final approach, and to raise my seat up.

Groggily shifting forward, I looked out the window. It was amazing how pretty a city looked from above, especially when night fell. The twinkling lights of roads and buildings spread out below as far as one could see, everything looked so calm and peaceful—the vehicles like toy cars as they travelled along the shiny thoroughfares.

Disembarking was a breeze, and I followed the signs through the concourse leading to the car rentals. I stopped and texted Mo, letting her know I landed safely, and her instant reply was exactly what I needed.

Who's this?

Do I know you?

I started to text Meg, but noticed someone suspicious and quickly moved through the concourse. Stopping at a newspaper stand, I watched as the suspicious person passed, nothing more than a traveller like myself. Switching flights had worked. I found the car rental terminal on the bottom floor and approached the counter, where a pretty, young girl stood behind.

"Hi, Emy," I said reading her name tag. "How are you tonight?"

"Well, hello sir," she responded cheerily. "So, how can I help you?"

"You have a car with my name on it, Pete Humphries. But I'm a few hours early. I hope that's okay."

"Oh, let me check. It's probably ..."

She started typing on her computer. She reached over and pulled out an envelope, reached down and pulled out a printed sheet. Folding it and placing it in the envelope, she handed it over to me.

"Here you go, all set. Your car has already been picked out for you, sir. A bit strange, usually, we let the customer pick any car from the aisle."

Teddy. And I knew why.

"Take the door over there and when you get outside, turn right, and your car will be on the right, third down the row. Can't miss it."

I thanked her and following her directions went outside. Just as she indicated, there on my right, the third car down the row, sat a tiny bright-yellow piece of shit.

"Absolutely no fucking way!" I blurted, shaking my head, I headed straight back inside.

Emy looked up. "Is there anything wrong, Mr. Humphries? Was the car not where I said it was?"

"What, the dinky-toy that barely covered the oil stain underneath it?" I frowned. "Any chance I could pick my own?"

"Why sure you can! Just pick any car from that row or the row right across from it. No extra charge either. And I am sorry about that car. For some reason it is our least popular." She gave me a wink. "Happy hunting, sir."

"Thank you, Emy."

Two minutes later I was back.

"Hi, Emy."

"What's wrong?" she asked. "Can't find a car to your liking?'

"No, I did, but um, it's down along the back wall of the garage. The black Chevy Camaro. Any chance?" I put my hands together and hit her with puppy dog eyes.

Emy thought for a moment, and when I whimpered, she smiled and relented.

"Why not? Give me a sec. I have to get the keys for it. We don't leave the keys in those cars."

While I waited, I texted Dale to let him know I had arrived and was on my way. He replied that he had a seat behind the Halifax net and included the section and row number.

After thanking Emy for the third time, I was finally on my way. The Camaro was fun and very fast, and I must admit a bit more modern than my Chevy. I drove in silence, as I had no iPod-thingamajig, and the radio had never been my thing. Too many commercials.

Reluctantly, I turned on the GPS and let it guide me into Halifax, and all I had to do was follow the signs along the highway, as they led me across the Mackay Bridge and downtown. There was a left turn along the waterfront, then a right, and up ahead, the unmistakable glow of lights above the buildings—the Halifax Metro Centre. I purchased a ticket, in the section Dale had texted, and, once inside the arena, could hear the last strains of the anthem. The crowd was thinner than I expected and I made my way easily along the concourse. Passing a merchandise stand, two young girls behind the counter were waving. Curious, I wandered over.

"Hey mister, you look like you could use a hat." She was a tall, thin blonde wearing a green Mooseheads hat and flirty smile.

The other girl, just as thin, had shoulder-length brown hair concurred. "You look like a hat guy."

Though I wasn't, I thought what a better way to fit in than with a hat. "Well, what have you got that says *Me*?" I asked, returning their flirt.

They giggled and turned back to the wall of merchandise behind them, and the trays of hats hanging off each side. Fighting with each other they tried to find the exact right hat. After a moment they returned, each holding out a different hat.

"Here!" they squealed in unison, handing their selections to me at the same time. Not wanting to disappoint, I took both of them and placed them on the counter in front of me.

"Hmm …" my hand under my chin.

"Try mine!" the blonde girl said excitedly, holding out the same hat she was wearing.

I tried on the hat, but it didn't have a strap at the back, and it fit snug, sitting uncomfortably on the top of my head.

Shaking their heads, the girls frowned, and the other one said, "Here! Try mine now."

I adjusted the Velcro strap in the back and put it on. It fit perfectly.

"TA-DA!" swinging my arms out wide and spinning around, the girls giggling and nodding approvingly.

"How much?"

"Forty!" they said in unison.

Gulp!

I reached in my pocket and pulled out two twenties. The girls fought briefly as to who would take the money, the brown-haired girl the victor. I thanked them, adjusted my hat, and continued along the concourse.

The sights and sounds of the rink, though similar to Timmins, had more of a corporate feel. Which made sense, as this was the top level for junior hockey and the last stop before the Show. Well, if you got drafted that is. Right Billy? Fewer kids were running around, and even the 50/50 hawkers were more professional. I peeked through the entranceways to see which end was the Mooseheads end, watching white jerseys flash by, chased by black jerseys, and I deduced I was heading in the right direction. Reaching the end of the concourse, I purchased a beer, then started around the circular end of the rink. Checking my ticket, I located the section and row number, the lower bowl behind the net not as full, and quickly spotted Dale.

I plunked down in my seat, leaving an empty seat between us. Dale was wearing a black leather jacket, holding a coffee in one hand and a bag of popcorn in the other.

"Popcorn?" he offered, staring straight ahead.

I shook my head, taking a sip of beer from the plastic cup.

"How was the flight?"

"Good. It's great to see you," I answered, enthused.

But strangely, he wasn't, eating his popcorn, still staring straight ahead at the game.

"It's nice to see you," I tried again.

"Nice hat," he grunted, his eyes still on the game.

Ooookaaay.

"Who's winning?" I asked innocently, making another attempt at small talk.

"The other team," he answered, still watching the game.

"Hey Dale? Is everything okay?" When he didn't respond I tapped him on the shoulder.

"What?" he growled, turning and glaring at me.

"Sorry. Geez, I was trying to get your attention. We've got work to do tomorrow morning. It's why we're here," I said.

Dale nodded.

"What happened to Syd?" he asked.

"What?" surprised, or more like shocked, at his question.

"What happened to Syd? I heard you are up in Timmins now. Did she go with you?"

What the fuck? I never told Dale I was up in Timmins.

"Oh, you know me. She stopped being all shiny and new."

"Why?"

"Why what?"

"Why didn't she go with you?"

"Because Dale, it's like you said. Once you get past shiny and new, they see the real me, and she saw the real me," I said trying to sound flippant. "But I've met someone else, and she's real and I, well I love her. She's great."

Shifting forward in my seat, I scanned through my phone for a picture, locating the selfie we took that day at Gillies Lake, and proudly showed it to Dale, who barely glanced at it, not taking his eyes off the game.

"She looks nice. Just like all the others. Has she seen up underneath yet, with all the dirt and rust and cracks?"

"Yes, she has, Dale," I said, annoyed now at my friend's interrogation. "She has, and she was okay with it, and the best part was I showed her, and she didn't have to wait to see it. I showed her first, and I'm proud of that."

We sat in silence, watching the game, and I would peek over at Dale every couple of minutes, trying to figure out just what in the fuck was wrong. A few more minutes went by and having lost patience, angry at Dale's attitude, I stood up.

"Fuck this!" I said. "And fuck you, Dale! I thought you were my friend."

Dale reached out with his arm and stopped me. "Sit down."

"Why?" I glared, looking down at him. "I don't need this shit, especially from you."

"I'm sorry, Pete. Please sit down. I am sorry. It's been a fucking awful day."

They say big things come in threes, right? Well, that was number two. A curse word from Dale Simpson's lips, and an f-bomb no less.

I sat back down. "What's going on?" I asked, concerned.

"Oh, just stuff at home. Karen went for her checkup recently, and they think they found a lump, and now we are waiting to hear back from the tests."

"Oh my God, Dale. I'm so sorry," I said.

Karen really was wonderful. She was perfect for Dale, and maybe that's why Dale had tried so hard to find the right match for me. She was the heart and soul of the family, the glue that held it—and Dale—together. I couldn't imagine Dale losing her and what it would do to him.

"I'm sorry. Is there anything I can do?"

"No. Thank you, I have it covered. The best doctors are looking after her, and depending on the tests, there is a clinic out in Arizona that supposedly has a high success rate with this, so we are just waiting on the results."

That was so like Dale. He had everything under control. But specialty clinics were big bucks, and with insurance, even with Dale's salary, it was not even close to covering the costs. But it wasn't my business to ask, and the thing with Dale was he could make anything happen, especially when it came to his family. I think that's what I admired about him the most.

"Look, Pete, I'm sorry. It's not my place to question where or with whom you live your life. I must admit, I was surprised to hear you had gone up to Timmins."

"How did you know I went up there? I haven't seen you since the day we ran into each other back in the summer on George Street, and when I called the other night, I didn't tell you."

Dale turned his attention back to the game.

"I think your area code came up when you called the other night. And I ran into Syd after you left, and she said you had gone up there."

And that ladies and gentlemen was number three. Dale had just lied to me.

I hadn't changed my phone, it was still on the 613-area code, and I know I never told Syd I was going to Timmins because the last time I saw her I was heading to Havelock with no idea what lay ahead. I was in uncharted waters now, wary of Dale.

Things took a turn for the worse, as when I showed Dale the information about the drop in the morning, he barely read through it.

"So, do you know where this is?"

"It's down by the waterfront. The Halifax Curling Club parking lot."

How was he so familiar with Halifax?

"Okay, so how are we going to set up the team, should we go—"

"No team. Just me. I'll have your back."

I was in shock.

I was about to ask about communications when, as though reading my mind, he reached into his pocket and handed me a burner phone. What was going on here? I was expecting some sort of two-way set up so I could keep in contact with him while things were in motion. A burner phone was useless for this sort of job.

"So, do you have a gun for me?" He'd know that I couldn't fly with one (though he could).

"Don't worry," he said. "You won't need one. I'll have your back."

I'd have raised hell, but obviously I couldn't do that in a public place—not about what we were discussing. It wasn't lost on me that Dale was the one who decided to meet here.

"Dale," I said, pitching my voice low, "I'm not getting a good—"

But he was already starting to stand.

"Where the fuck are you going?" I asked as casually as I could manage.

"Meet me across the street from the curling club tomorrow morning at five thirty," he said. "We'll talk then."

"Dale—"

"Don't follow me." And with that, he abruptly got up and left.

To say I was shaken was an understatement. This was wrong on every level. What had made Dale and I good with this stuff—and more importantly what had kept us alive all those years—was our planning and preparation. Before any operation, we would do a walk-through, run-through, and every other kind of through-through until we could recite our roles in our sleep. It was like a football playbook, and though you were one player, you had to know the play for everyone else.

I didn't have much choice and had to quickly accept this was going to be how it went down. At least, I had the Camaro, and shuddered at the thought of pulling up in that bright-yellow shitbox. I was numb, and it was all I could do to fight off the fear that threatened to overtake me. Forget about ever finding normal, tomorrow would be my last day, period. My phone dinged, and it was a text from Mo.

How are things going?

My heart sank, what was I going to say?

I hated lying to Mo. That was one huge change I had seen in myself. I had stopped hiding, deflecting, lying only so no one could get too close. Being with Mo had changed all that—changing me for the better. I was about to lie once more, and I truly hoped for the last time, swearing to myself that, once this was over, I would never put myself in any position like this ever again.

All good ... Dale & I are set for the morning.

She immediately asked about his team. I lied, texting back that they were ready to go and would be in place. I felt a sharp pang of guilt. To offset it, I texted saying only two more sleeps until our forever normal day. She told me to be careful, and said, 'I had them,' which warmed my heart.

I texted Teddy, informing him I had landed, and he replied that I hadn't gotten on the plane yet. He was not very pleased when I told him I caught an earlier flight, lying about wanting to do some sightseeing first. He asked if I had picked up the rental car yet, but I said piss-yellow wasn't my favourite colour, and I had taken the airport shuttle instead. Ending the conversation, I said I would see him at Sharkees around noon tomorrow, and I'm sure that didn't warm the cockles of his heart.

I tried to watch the rest of the game, but I wasn't paying attention, so I looked up the drop address on my phone and just about fell over when I saw the map of where it was. An industrial area near the Port of Halifax across from some sand and gravel company. Lovely. Sniper heaven.

With five minutes to play, I left my seat and made my way out ahead of the crowd. I entered the curling club address in the GPS and drove toward it. Parking out front on the dark side street was even worse than I thought, one-way in and one-way out. Worse, the sand and gravel company was directly across the street with giant silos stretching into the sky. I drove around the block, and it was perfect for blocking someone in from either direction.

I attempted to scope out the surrounding area but ended up hopelessly lost even with the GPS. Forty-five minutes later, back downtown, I found the Marriott and hoped they hadn't given away my reservation.

At least Teddy got the room part right, I had a nice view of the Halifax waterfront. I stretched out on the bed and stared up at the ceiling. Around 4:00 a.m., still staring up at the ceiling, I got up; rummaging through my bag, I found Mo's note. Sitting on the bed, I unfolded it and started reading. I reread it multiple times, each time wiping my eyes a little more, until trying to read the note was like trying to see through your windshield during a torrential downpour.

I texted her, telling her how much I loved her, and that no one had ever made me feel the way she had, then powered off my phone. I found some needle and thread in the bathroom and sewed my phone, the note, and my wallet into the inside pocket of my jean jacket.

An hour later I checked out of the hotel and pulled up in front of the curling club at exactly 5:20 a.m., texted Dale, and waited for his reply.

68

"WHAT DID YOU say?" Dale asked.

"Said I would, boss."

"Are you going to go through with it?"

"I'm not sure. That's a lot of money. It all depends."

"All depends on what?"

"What's in it for me."

"Your life."

There was a long pause on the other end.

"Let me think about it."

"Don't think too long, Tony."

"I won't, boss."

Dale quickly dialed again.

"Is he with you?" Teddy asked.

"I can see him. He's parked across the street from the curling club."

"He took an earlier flight," Teddy said. "He wasn't supposed to."

"Yes, I am aware. People do that all the time."

"So?"

"So what?"

"Is everything still on?" Teddy asked.

"Well, the fact I'm calling you from the location, means I guess you could say it's on. Nothing has changed, at least not from my end. Yours?"

"No. Nothing has changed here. Do you think he suspects?"

"Probably, he's not stupid."

"So ... then what?"

"Then what, *nothing*. The plan is still the same. That is, if the guys you hired don't screw it up. They are already late."

"They'll be there."

"Promises, promises ... we've both been down that road before, haven't we, Teddy?"

There was silence on the other end. "Teddy? You still there?"

"Yes."

"Don't worry, things will be fine," Dale said confidently. "I have it covered. Even if your guys screw it up, and I would be more surprised if they didn't, I will finish it. The two fifty is in the money belt, and he is wearing it, correct?"

More silence.

"Teddy? Teddy. You better tell me he's wearing it or at least has the money on him. That was the plan. He would breeze through airport security wearing it."

"Um ... he didn't get on his flight. He didn't board the 9:15 and took an earlier flight instead."

"Yes, you told me. But he still went through security. They would have seen it and let him through?"

"Um no ..."

Dale exploded. "What the fuck do you mean *no*?"

"I told airport security his flight was at 9:15, so they were only checking for that time."

"You fucking moron!" Dale yelled into the phone. "Did you ever stop to think that anyone who flies arrives early for their flight?"

Teddy's stomach dropped, realizing he screwed up, and big-time too. He had been so rattled yesterday at seeing the picture on Sara's phone, after coming inside, he forgot to inform his contact at airport security that Pete had just left in a cab, most likely taking him straight to the airport.

"I'm sorry," Teddy replied meekly.

"Well, sorry is not going to make my two fifty appear, is it?" Dale took a swig from the flask, the straight whiskey burning the back of his throat.

"Teddy, if Pete doesn't have the two fifty on him, I will come back, and I will cut off your balls and stuff them down your throat, but not before you watch me fuck your sister up the ass, and I stick my gun up her cunt and pull the trigger. And none of it, absolutely none of it, will cause me to lose even a wink of sleep at night. So, you better hope Pete has the money. And by the way, I liked the sweater Sara was wearing yesterday. Powder blue is a nice colour on her, but you need to do something about that jacket."

Dale abruptly disconnected, leaving Teddy alone with those thoughts. His head spinning, Teddy slid off the stool and made his way towards the can, using the bar for support. Walking inside, he staggered, reaching for his stomach, bending over. Looking along the row of stalls, he spied the empty one on the end and made his way over to it. Closing the door, he had enough time to lift the lid, falling forward, spewing vile liquid inside the bowl and around the edges. When he was finished, he reached up, pulled the handle, wiped his mouth, and started to stand. If he had been paying attention, he would have noticed the end of a lone strip of duct tape sticking out from behind the tank.

69

AT FIVE MINUTES to six, the burner phone buzzed.

"Where are you?!" I answered nervously.

"Don't worry, I can see you."

"Well, I can't see you!"

"Maybe you should move into place. It's almost time. And gosh dang it, stop being so jumpy. Everything's going to be fine. I have your back just like old times." Dale's calming voice soothed my nerves momentarily.

But this wasn't the good ol' days, this was today, and despite that familiar, comforting feeling washing over me, it was all too brief, a wave crashing into the shore and pulling back just as fast. I missed the crackle of the two-way radio chatter, and now with the burner phone, it just wasn't the same. I felt a slight tinge at being back in the game, but this wasn't like before. And yes, not every operation or stakeout ended in our favour, but each one did end with us intact and alive.

I pulled across the street into the curling club, drove around back, coming back down the laneway, stopping twenty yards from the road. I left the engine idling and waited. My phone buzzed again, with Dale telling me to pull forward so he could see me clearly. I thought it strange, wondering where he was, and felt vulnerable. Now my car was sitting out in plain view of the silos and buildings across the street.

6:10 am – Nothing.

6:20 am – Still nothing.

6:31 am – *No show?* I texted. Dale replied to wait a little longer.

6:52 am – I was getting ready to call it a day when my phone buzzed and Dale said to give it until 7:00.

At 6:59 a.m., approaching from opposite directions, two black SUVs slowly came toward me. I put my foot on the brake, shifted the Camaro into drive, switched feet, putting my left foot on the brake and my right foot on the gas.

Watching the SUV's approach, I thought, *no fucking way, I'm not going to be anyone's SUV sandwich* and hammering the gas, letting go of the brake, the Camaro jerked forward, and tore straight across the road and down the lane towards the silos. I heard loud pops and ducked when my rear window was riddled with bullets, shards of glass flying everywhere. I kept my foot to the floor and could hear the pinging and splattering of bullets, as they riddled the back of the Camaro. I crashed into the fence at the end of the lane and stopped dead, the hood crumpled and smoke billowing out. I had no idea who was what, or where—without the two-way radio, I was blind. I ducked back down again, when the popping and pinging got too close for comfort and threw it into reverse. I pushed harder on the accelerator, the tires smoking and squealing, but I was stuck. Taking my foot off the gas, the roar of the Camaro instantly stopped, the car jerked forward, everything going quiet.

I tried to open my door, but I was blocked in. I crawled across the gearshift, reached for the passenger door handle, pushed open the door, and wriggled forward like a snake, push-pulling myself onto the pavement. Now on my stomach, I looked underneath to see if there was any movement. I reached inside for the burner phone, then crawled on all fours towards the break in the fence at the foot of the giant silos.

The phone buzzed. Dale told me to get moving towards open field and the train tracks behind the silos.

"Get going!" Dale yelled through the phone.

"Get going where?" I yelled back.

"Straight behind you. Follow the lane between the silos towards the tracks and the open field. I'll cover you."

This didn't feel like the best choice. I was a sitting duck. But the choice was made for me—coming toward me was a black SUV. I tore down the lane, hunched over, body tight, bracing for the bullets.

At the end of the silos there was a gate to the right. I threw myself at it and fell through the opening, rolling on the ground. I was up instantly, and it was eerily quiet, all except for the trees swaying in the wind and the tweeting of the early morning birds. The sun was up, a bright yellow ball, and if it were anything other than this, one would think it was nothing more than a clear, crisp, fall day.

Checking my phone, there was a text from Dale telling me to follow the line of silos that ran parallel with the railway tracks. I ran towards the first silo, stopped, and looked behind me.

That's strange, I thought. *Why am I not being chased?*

Cautiously peeking around the corner of the first silo, I looked down the line.

The railway tracks ran parallel to me, but it was wide open, and no trains were in sight. In the distance was a viaduct where the tracks merged underneath it. There was a text from Dale to head towards the viaduct and look for his blue truck waiting on the bridge. My gut instincts were screaming to go in the opposite direction, but either I trusted my best friend—despite my suspicions—or I made my way on my own.

Looking behind me, I was on my own and usually, that would make you happy as someone wasn't chasing you, but it was the opposite. Bad guys carrying guns should have been on my tail long before now, maybe even howling bloodhounds on leashes. Taking a deep breath—and ignoring my gut instinct—I started running towards the viaduct. I tried to keep low and ran hunched over, breathing hard, waiting for the burning sensation. The sun was blinding, and I stumbled and fell a few times on the hard ground. I got to the end of the line of the silos, and all that remained was wide open ground on either side.

Panting hard, shielding my eyes against the sun, I looked up at the bridge, but I couldn't see Dale's blue truck. I turned and looked behind me, but there was nothing but wide-open space, and I felt like a sitting duck. I called Dale, but there was no answer.

What the fuck, Dale?

I tried texting him, but where there should have been an instant response, there was nothing. Turning in a circle, shielding my eyes, I frantically searched for Dale, when suddenly there was the sharp cough of bullets hitting the ground near my feet, specks of dirt kicking up, as the bullets tore into the ground. Instinctively, I ducked, but I had nowhere to hide. Dancing, covering my head with my arms, trying to get out of the way of the bullets, I was forced to start running toward the tree line that lay two hundred yards off in the distance.

Zigzagging across the open field, I hurdled the single set of train tracks, forced to slow at the double ones, bullets whizzing all around me, chunks of dirt kicking up, flying in my face as I ran. I was amazed I wasn't hit and if I had time, I would have stopped and thanked my lucky stars. The tree line was getting closer, and I was almost there when a bullet grazed my thigh, sending me spinning to the ground. I rolled, grabbing at my leg. Fortunately, it was just a graze. I pushed myself up and continued making my way towards the trees, and the safety of cover. I was half running, half limping, my hand holding the phone against my leg for support, when I reached the tree line, the ground underneath crackling as I trounced over the dirty brown leaves, stumbling, I rolled and sat straight up.

The shooting had stopped, and it was quiet again. My chest was heaving.

I sat in the leaves, panting like a dog. Where the fuck was Dale? Checking the phone, there were no calls or texts since our last communication. I tried calling, Dale picking up on the second ring.

"Where the fuck were you?" I hissed.

"Got stuck in traffic."

"I was fucking target practice!" I screamed into the phone.

"Calm down, there Pete-boy. As always, you are overreacting."

I looked down at my leg, the thin line of blood oozing from the tear in my jeans. *Really?*

"Focus, Pete. Stay focused. Where are you now?"

"I'm in the tree line on the other side of the viaduct."

"Can you walk?"

That's when I was hit by a bolt of lightning. How did Dale know I had been shot?

"Sure," I lied.

"Okay, good. Follow the tree line until you come to a two-lane road, then follow that for about two hundred yards, and it will take you to a public park. You will be safe as no one is going to mistake you for target practice there."

"You've been wrong before."

"Just make it there, and I will meet you at the base of the Anchor Memorial."

"The anchor what?"

"Follow the signs when you get to the park. The memorial will be straight ahead. It should only take you a few minutes."

I waited another five minutes to be certain, which also gave me time to catch my breath.

I pulled myself up, my thigh stinging, the blood oozing out thicker, and felt light-headed, but I knew I had to keep moving. Following Dale's directions, I moved along the edge of the tree line until I came to the two-lane paved road. I swiped at the blood on my thigh, wiping my hand on the back of my leg, trying to hide it as best I could. Each step was becoming more painful, and though not serious, I would require medical attention soon.

The memorial was just up ahead, and I started toward it, keeping my head low, as joggers and walkers passed by in the opposite direction. I ignored their strange looks. About fifty yards from the memorial, I heard rustling and turned to my right, the sound coming from the trees. A figure emerged from a clump of bushes. Dale.

I started toward him. "Dale … what the fuck happened back there?"

Dale remained silent, and I watched as he lifted his gun and pointed it at me. There was a flash, I felt a searing pain in my shoulder, then everything went black.

70

5:33 AM – Mo tossed and turned all night, first on the couch, then to the blanket fort, then to the bedroom, and back again to the couch. Curled up in the blanket, she stared at the other end, fraught with worry. She hadn't heard from Pete, and she knew something had gone wrong. He hadn't responded to her texts, and there was nothing she could do now but wait. Horrible, awful thoughts raced through her head.

Pete had been beaten up, or shot, and was lying somewhere, left for dead.

The thought of him dead stung like a hot poker, her throat so tight she felt like she couldn't breathe. A paper bag, sides slit open, lay crumpled in front of the blanket fort; she'd been forced to use it when she had a panic attack around midnight. Her mouth was dry, and she wiped it, small pieces of vomit catching on the back of her hand from when she had thrown up an hour later.

Uncomfortable, Mo shifted, and stretched her legs out, her foot slid down the back of the couch and she felt something with her toe. She sat up, poking between the cushions, pulled out a single sheet of paper. Tossing it on the table, she started to sit back when the paper caught her eye. It was one of the police reports from the box, and it must have fallen between the cushions.

Sitting up, she leaned over and picked it up. Her eyes moved down the page and settled at the bottom where the signature matched the impeccable handwriting.

What!?

Flipping the page over, she looked at the signature there. The familiar, unintelligible scrawl. Turning the page back, she looked at the signature again and gasped, her hand coming up to her mouth.

"Oh my God!"

The paper slipped from her hand and fell to the floor at her feet. Jumping up, Mo searched for her phone, her hands shaking so badly it took four tries to take a picture of the side with the matching signature. It was all she could do to send it to Pete. She tried texting Bree but gave up, calling instead, even that an arduous effort

"Hullo?" Bree answered groggily.

"Can you come over now, please," Mo's voice cracked.

"Have you heard from Pete?'

"No."

"Then what is it? Is everything okay?"

"No."

"What's wrong?" Bree asked, now wide awake.

"Can you just come over now, please? Hurry."

"Be right there, honey. Just be a few minutes."

Mo leaned forward on the couch, holding the paper in her shaking hands, staring at the signature at the bottom. Dale Simpson.

9:17 AM – Dale looked out at the city below, watching it disappear behind him as the plane slowly gained altitude. Everything was a complete mess, and he didn't know if he would be able to get himself out of this one. Teddy's boys had messed up the approach, which didn't surprise him, nor did Pete's reaction and abruptly driving away. He was mad at himself mostly. He had forgotten that his best friend had a knack for detecting the obvious. He was like a goddamned boy scout, never unprepared, period.

Because of that, he had been forced to shoot his best friend, something he didn't want to do. To cover his tracks, he had driven the eight hours around to Saint John, Pete's body in the trunk, dumping it on the side of the highway near the airport. Pete wasn't wearing the money belt, and now, he had no idea where the money was.

Considering it had been a day of nothing but mistakes, Dale started the morning off with a whopper. Waiting to take off, based solely on emotion, he ordered a hit on Teddy, effectively destroying any hope he had of finding the trail to his money.

1:15 PM – Teddy maintained a vigil at Sharkees—sleeping on the cot in the kitchen—ever since Pete had left in the cab for the airport. Patty just let him be, considering what was going on between him and his sister, it was a hill she didn't feel like dying on at the time.

Constantly checking his phone, he hadn't had contact with either Pete or Dale, and he was frantic. He hadn't heard from Tony either and had no idea whether the hit on Dale had taken place. Had Tony done it or was he planning a double-crossing at that very moment?

He wouldn't put it past him, suspecting Tony was someone who could play both sides, without so much the blink of an eye. And where was the money, the two fifty? Was Pete dead yet? Maybe they both were? There was nothing he could do but wait.

71

IT WAS LIZZY'S turn to drive and Dex, her partner, occupied the co-pilots seat. They were returning from a call out at Willow Grove, an elderly couple, the husband short of breath, the wife scared out her wits. Just another routine call.

"Do you think your mom will like me?" he asked.

"Of course, she will," she said, reaching over and patting his thigh. "What's not to like?"

He gave a fretful sigh.

"It will be fine, I promise," she reassured him.

He stared straight ahead, not believing, the trees flashing by the road making wet swishing sounds underneath.

"What time is dinner again?" he asked.

"The same time it was when you asked the last time. Thanksgiving dinner starts at noon when our shift ends. We are going straight there so make sure you pack a change of clothes. My mom won't like you if you sit down at the table wearing these blue T-shirts."

"Hmm, there's an idea. Then when she doesn't like me, I can get up and leave," he said, still staring straight ahead, wearing a sly grin.

"Don't you even consider it!"

She turned to look at him just as something caught her peripheral vision. Something in the bushes crawled out onto the road.

"Jesus Lizzy, look out!"

Slamming on the brakes, swerving in time, the loud screeching echoed through the tall cedar trees that lined both sides of the highway.

"Hit the lights!" Dex barked, already out the door.

"I'm on it."

Opening the rear door, reaching in, he pulled out his bag, and ran to the lump lying on the road in front of the bumper. "Call it in!" he yelled over his shoulder, approaching the body, fearing this wasn't going to be good.

Lizzy reached for the mic and called in their location. She jumped out, ran to the back, reached for her bag, then came up behind her partner, who was leaning over the body in the road.

"Who is it? Do you know? Is he alive?" she asked, opening her bag and putting on her gloves.

He didn't answer, bent over the figure, but she knew to wait, as no one was better than Dex at first response. Peeking over his shoulder, she could make out a jean jacket that was covered in blood.

"Male, Caucasian, mid-thirties … multiple gunshot wounds … one to the upper right shoulder just below the collar bone … exit wound appears clean … gunshot wound to the right thigh but just a graze … vital signs are good … some blood loss … cuts and abrasions across the face and neck … no bruising or swelling in the back of the neck and head area … lower extremities are responsive … hands and fingers respond to pricks."

Dex reached around underneath the body, this time feeling for any further signs of trauma. He moved the jacket and it fell away, the left front pocket exposed. He felt something lumpy, becoming alarmed when the eyes opened wide at the touch. The victim groaned, his hand lifted and pointed. Dex carefully felt around the lump, gingerly with his fingers, lightly touching it, unable to determine what it was. It wasn't an injury, it wasn't sticky or wet, then he felt the pocket lining. He lifted the jacket then the T-shirt just enough to feel the damp skin. Using his fingers, he gently felt around, satisfied it wasn't an injury, he went to caring for the gunshot wound. Five minutes later, they were enroute to St. Joseph's Hospital, lights flashing, siren blaring, interrupting the stillness of the quiet morning countryside.

The medical staff were waiting when Lizzy backed in, pulling open the rear doors before the vehicle had stopped, Dex hopped out and helped pull the stretcher down, the metallic clicks pinging as the wheels and legs fell out and hit the ground. Dex walked alongside the stretcher, and the hand started tugging on his arm. Looking down, he saw the eyes open wide and pleading. The hand kept pulling on his arm, and he was trying to speak. Dex leaned in as they moved along the corridor.

"Inside my jacket … my stuff … please … take my stuff … please …" The man was pleading, tugging on Dex's arm, trying to push it against his side.

"Your what?"

"My jacket … my stuff … please, please … take my stuff, please."

Dex couldn't make out what the person was asking, and he had to pull away as the stretcher stopped at the front desk, waiting for an exam room. Lizzy had parked and met up with Dex at the desk.

"Is he okay?" she asked, concerned.

"Yes, he's going to be okay. He's fortunate."

Lizzy heard murmuring and turned toward the stretcher. The hand reached out and pulled on her arm.

"My jacket … inside my jacket … my stuff … please … take it."

"Huh? Your what?" leaning in closer.

"My jacket!" the voice said urgently, the hand tugging at her arm.

"Inside my jacket …" trying to turn on his side. "Underneath … behind … in my jacket … please."

Lizzy looked down at him, confused, and gathering what strength he had left, he roughly grabbed her hand pushing it against his side, then tried to push it underneath him.

"My jacket."

He pulled at her hand, and she felt something lumpy against his side. Reaching inside further, she could feel the lump. Something was inside the pocket. She looked at his face, eyes pleading, and he nodded. She felt around and found a loose thread and pulled on it as it tore away from the fabric. She pulled away the rest of the material with her hands and reached through the slit. She fumbled around then pulled out a phone. Reaching in farther, she pulled out a wallet and a crinkled piece of paper, holding them in her hand.

"Are these yours?"

He nodded then reached out and pushed her hand towards her.

"Take them … take them, please," he whispered weakly.

"You want me to take them?"

He nodded.

"Take them where?"

"Just take them … please!" he hissed, his eyes blinking rapidly, he pushed against her hand again.

Lizzy knew she shouldn't. She could get in serious trouble taking someone's ID, never mind that he would now have to be admitted as a John Doe. But there was something about him, and quickly looking to see if anyone was watching, she stuffed the phone, wallet, and crinkled paper in her jacket pocket and zipped it shut. He looked up at her and nodded. Then, his head fell back as he passed out.

72

LIZZY STOOD AT the foot of the bed, holding a folded newspaper, looking down at the sleeping figure. He lay on his side, sleeping peacefully, the intravenous tube taped to his forearm, the line dripping slowly above his head. Thick black hair covered his forehead, his hands covered in bandages, and she could see the black stitch lines that crisscrossed just below his left eye. She wondered who he was.

She had gone through his wallet, of course, finding his licence, but she didn't know anything else. She had been reluctant to go through his phone, even though it wasn't locked—after tapping the button, she could see text messages but went no further. She had accidentally tapped the photos button, discovering two pictures.

A selfie with a woman and one of him posing in a garden.

She had read the crinkled note, smoothing it out on her kitchen table, and felt guilty for doing so, but she was hoping it would provide a clue as to who he was. The note made her cry, and she thought how lucky this guy was, whoever he was, that there was someone who loved him as much as the note said. Lizzy loved Dex; they were getting married soon. Like in the note, she hoped she would always feel that way toward him in the years to come when their white-picket-fence took the inevitable direct hits.

At the same time, she wasn't sure if she *wanted* to know who he was. Her partner Dex was waiting downstairs and thought it best to perhaps let things be—to return his stuff and move on. She moved around to the side of the bed, gently placed the folded newspaper on the tray and, with one last look, turned toward the door.

———

The woman at the door was one of the paramedics, at least I was pretty sure she was. The one who took my stuff.

"Thank you," I said, my voice sounding strange and a little hollow.

Stopping, she turned. "Huh?"

"Thank you," I smiled weakly, trying to sit up in the bed.

She looked at me not sure what to say.

"You were supposed to say *you're welcome*." I shifted, trying to get comfortable.

"Could you raise the bed for me?"

She walked over and adjusted the bed. "Better?"

"Yes, thank you."

Moving back to the foot of the bed, she stood silent, watching me.

"And now you owe me two."

"Two what?" she asked, her head tilted, curious.

"You're welcomes," I teased.

She laughed. "I'm sorry … your welcome, your welcome."

"Thank you."

"I'm not giving you a third," she smiled, shaking her head playfully.

"We'll see," I answered slyly.

She moved around to the side of the bed.

"You're lucky. My partner is the one that spotted you. I almost ran you over you know."

"I'm glad you didn't."

She twisted her head, looking down at me. "Who are you?"

A head poked in the doorway. "Hey, we have to go." Looking over at me. "Hey. Hope you're feeling better."

"I am. Thank you."

"Oh! not that again," Lizzy broke out laughing.

"Meet you out front," he said.

"Be right there."

The head backed out of the doorway, and she started to leave. "Bye, take care, whoever you are."

"Thank you, I will."

At the doorway, she stopped and turned. "I'm off tomorrow night. How about I come by and see how you are doing? And besides, I don't think you're going anywhere soon."

"Thank you. That would be nice. Um … I didn't get your name."

"Lizzy. It's Lizzy."

"Nice to meet you, Lizzy."

"Nice to meet you, Pete."

Lizzy turned to leave, quickly turned back, and in rapid-fire, "You're welcome, you're welcome, you're welcome, and just in case I missed one, YOU'RE WELCOME!" giggling as she went out the door.

I noticed the folded newspaper on the tray. Ever since my dad I would become nauseous at the sight of a folded newspaper. Tentatively, I reached for it, and as I lifted it, my phone, wallet, and the crumpled note slid out on the tray. I brought the newspaper down into my lap. With a heavy sigh, I flipped it open and stared at the headline.

Whew.

73

AS PROMISED, LIZZY dropped by the next night, her partner, Dex, in tow. They made quite a pair. Lizzy was short, outgoing, full of life, chockfull of energy and wore a permanent radiant smile; while Dex was moody, a straight shooter, assertive, tall, and athletic. But anyone could see they fit perfectly, finishing each other's sentences, doting, caring, and that was all that mattered. The visit did me a world of good, the company nice, and Lizzy talked my ear off. Dex found the TV remote, searched for the hockey game, and sat slumped in the chair by the window, looking over during the breaks and giving us the stink eye with our animated discussions. I asked Dex who his team was and laughed when he said Boston.

"Bobby Orr, right?"

"My dad," he said.

"Mine too!"

Lizzy brought something out in me, or maybe, she just restored what I had pushed away to protect myself. It wasn't on a romantic level, but it was her energy and playfulness and her outlook on life that was so similar. I guess I had forgotten, and in a lot of ways, she was similar to Mo. A nurse poked her head through the doorway, telling us to lower our voices. Snickering like little kids when she left, Lizzy promised to come back, and we both poked fun at Dex, still slumped in the chair watching the game. As they walked out the door, I called a thank you out after them.

"You're welcome, Pete," Lizzy said. "Anytime."

I forced myself to get up and go for a walk around the floor, my leg stiff from the stitches, still unable to move or bend it naturally. My shoulder screamed in pain, despite the painkillers that had been prescribed, the ones I refused to swallow—hiding them under my tongue and spitting them out when the nurse's back was turned. The doctor said I was lucky, the bullet went clean through, leaving a small hole just under the collarbone, the exit wound just as small. A millimetre either way, he informed me, and I would have lost too much blood, not surviving the trip.

Speaking of the trip. I still had no idea how I had gotten to Saint John. When the doctor told me, I was incredulous, I had no idea. The last thing I remembered was running across an open field and jumping over train tracks. That was it. The cops had been in twice, grilling me, but I stood firm playing my temporary, and hopefully not permanent, amnesia card. The hospital was also grilling me. It seemed they didn't like calling me JD anymore.

After completing three laps around the floor, I became tired and returned to my room. The sun had set, and through the window, I could see remnants of reds and pinks still lighting the sky. I walked over and stood looking out the window, and I don't know why, but it reminded me of Timmins. And with it, I felt a sharp pang at what I had been avoiding.

And at how I had screwed everything up. And at how stupid and short-sighted I was, blinded by greed. And at how gullible I was. And at how easily I had been influenced by the money and Teddy's promise. And at how I had been blinded by the thought of that bright white picket fence and all its promises. And at how I didn't listen to Mo or Bree but should have. And, and, and …

I had ignored my basic gut instinct. It could not have been screaming any louder. To drown it out, I had put on my headphones, and turned the volume up—chalk up another victory for denial.

I crawled back into bed, checking to see where my tail was. I picked up my phone, surprised that it had any juice—probably Lizzy had charged it for me. I tapped the button, checked my texts, a mountain of them from Mo. The most recent one was the picture she had sent of Dale's signature.

That's when things fell into place.

Dale and Teddy were in cahoots all right, and it had something to do with the tragic death of his parents in that fire. No doubt Sara had a part in it too.

So that's why Teddy was so determined to get the box, the lone piece of paper with Dale's signature the key. Dale had covered up what happened that night, for reasons known only to himself, but missed one teeny-tiny spot. Dale's handwriting had always been so neat and meticulous, and that's where I knew it from. And for him to make a mistake like that and miss a single solitary side? That was so unlike him.

I needed to get out of this hospital ASAP, as the longer I stayed, the better the chances of the cops finding a reason to transfer me to a hospital room with bars. I was safe so long as I went by JD, but the timeline on that ruse was just about up. Also, things could start going bump in the night, as the bad guys might want to make their own house call. That was a genuine possibility, what with the money unaccounted for. I could only imagine Teddy right about now angling to react to what had happened. Dale too, and that frightened me because I knew Dale was smarter than Teddy. I would have liked to have known myself, and my memory was returning, I was starting to have flashbacks, and it was only a matter of time. I just hoped I would like what I saw.

Sadly, I knew I couldn't trust my best friend anymore, and that was heartbreaking, but it was a grief I would have to put aside for now. Realistically, I was still too weak to travel, so I had to be careful. I wanted to contact Mo, the ache of missing her burning bright, but I couldn't trust anyone—fearing Mo could now be in danger herself. Never mind that Tony was due to resurface or maybe he had already. There was an upside, I wasn't worried about Bree and Adrian, the mercenary couple, figuring they already built a bunker under the club, hopefully with enough room for Mo.

I needed to fix this quick, but how? Especially, from here in Saint John. I had no car, I was shot up, I was weak, and hitting on the trifecta, I was on the lam from the cops, Teddy, Dale, and possibly others.

Then, it hit me. I had one crucial thing going for me. I was supposed to be dead. The bad guys won't come looking for a dead man, right? I searched through the contacts, Meg picked up on the third ring, but she didn't seem happy to hear from me. Didn't she know yet I was dead?

"Hey, sorry. I know what you're going to say."

"Oh, do you now?"

"Please," I sighed, "please ... I need your help."

There was a reluctant sigh and a long enough pause to make me feel even worse than shit, which was probably her point.

"What?" she asked coldly.

"I need a flight to Ottawa."

"From where?"

"Saint John."

"Saint John, New Brunswick? How did you get over there?"

"I don't know."

"You don't know? You don't know how you got to Saint John? You flew to Halifax, then you drove, maybe?" Meg snapped.

"I honestly don't know. Look, Meg. I haven't got time to explain. I need to get back to Ottawa. Can you help? Please. "

I could hear clicking in the background. "Okay, you're all set. But the best I can do is 9:15 a.m. on Monday. Sorry, all the flights are booked up."

"Same codeword as before," she said. "Guinness."

"I didn't ask about that."

"Really? You're in some deep shit out there," she said. "I can just tell."

"Yes."

"Be careful. I'm working Monday, so I'll look for you."

"Thank you."

The call ended abruptly, and I sensed Meg was mad at me. I had to make all this stop once and for all. I couldn't live like this anymore.

74

LIZZY AND DEX were back the next afternoon, and it was nice to have a diversion. Dex made a beeline for the TV remote, resuming his position in the chair by the window, while Lizzy and I caught up. She loved all those TV crime shows and told me all the intricate ways people went about killing each other. She was quite the chatterbox and revelled in the gory details of the latest TV show, and part of me itched to tell her what happened that morning with the black SUV breakfast sandwich.

Then, as though sensing my itch, Lizzy lowered her voice and leaned in.

"Pete, what happened? I don't want to pry, but we did find you left for dead in the middle of the road with multiple gunshot wounds. And I did as you asked, taking your stuff and holding it for you. But you know, I could have lost my job over it, taking a big risk, so I do have a right to an explanation."

Lizzy was right, and I had to decide how much they needed to know. With anything, there is an inside story for every outside story, and the tricky part is knowing what to reveal. I spilled. Sort of.

I told her that I was supposed to meet someone in Halifax, that I was a mule who would receive an envelope, and that was supposed to be it. But it went sour, a trap in the making. Lizzy's eyes lit up at the word mule, and she rubbed her hands together in glee at the thought, no doubt thinking back to season 7, episode 15, of one of her TV shows.

I told her I had been double-crossed, escaped, and in the process, shot (twice) and left for dead.

Lizzy, sitting on the edge of the bed, listened intently. I wanted to tell her more, but I knew I couldn't. The less the better for both their protection. And I was completely truthful in that I had no idea how I had ended up in Saint John. I told her how grateful I was that they had found me, and I wished I could have said more, or found a better way to show my appreciation.

Lizzy asked why I made her take my phone and wallet, and I explained that I didn't know who to trust—but that she and Dex looked trustworthy—and if she had it, that would protect me. She apologized and told me she had read the note from 'that girl Mo,' and I said it was okay, I understood. She said it was the most beautiful thing she had ever read and how lucky I was.

"Where is she?"

"Timmins?"

"That's where you are from?"

"Sort of, I guess. I have been there since the summer. One morning, we met on a bridge as my car had broken down, and she drove by on her motorcycle and stopped to see if I was okay. And the rest is history."

"I bet your car is fast too."

"Very."

"Ooh ... so romantic," Lizzy cooed.

Turning her head at Dex, immersed in the game "And that's *my* knight in shining armour."

"Does he love you?" I asked.

"Yes, he does."

"Does he make you happy?"

"Yes. We are getting married November 7th."

"Does he make you feel small?"

Lizzy looked at me, puzzled, unsure what I meant.

"What I mean is, does he respect you for who you are?"

"No, never! No! I mean yes! Yes, he does," her eyes lighting up.

"Then you have everything you need, kid." I smiled, reaching out and patting her arm.

Dex stirred, the game on a break, and it was perfect timing. I needed their help, and I knew Lizzy would jump at it, but this wasn't a TV show, and it could mean both their jobs.

I lowered my voice. "Guys, I have a favour to ask," I said, glancing at the doorway.

"What is it?" Lizzy asked.

I checked the doorway again and the coast was clear. "It's a big one, and it's serious, and it could mean your jobs, so you have to think about it."

Dex now leaning forward, listened intently, while Lizzy suddenly seemed uncertain.

"What is it?" he asked.

"I need to get out of here tonight, I can't hold off the cops much longer. I have a flight back to Ottawa first thing in the morning, but I can't stay here until then. The person who wrote me that note, her life is in danger, and if I don't get back, I can't save her. I can't go to the cops with this. Too much has happened, and the trail runs all the way from Timmins to here. If I can get back to Ottawa—"

"Why don't you go straight to Timmins? What's in Ottawa?" Lizzy asked.

If there was ever a loaded question, that was it.

"My car," I said, which was technically *true* just not why I needed to get to Ottawa. "My car's there, and I need it … it's complicated."

I looked at Dex. "Can you help me? Can you help get me out of here?"

"Where would you go? Where would you stay?" Lizzy asked, worried.

"My place," Dex said. "He can stay at my place."

"That's right!" Lizzy said, looking at me. "Dex has been living with me, and the lease on his loft is up at the end of the month. It would be perfect!"

"Great! Where is it?"

"Near the waterfront," Lizzy said before Dex could speak. "It would be perfect. This time of year, no one's there."

"Perfect," I said, "so, how do we get me out of here?"

For the next thirty minutes, the three of us went back and forth trying to come up with a way to get me out without being seen. You would think Lizzy, with all her TV crime experience, would come up with some elaborate foolproof plan but she had nothing. Finally, we settled on Dex and Lizzy wheeling me out at midnight in a stretcher.

They quickly left, Lizzy whispering excitedly to Dex as they walked down the corridor to the elevators. The next few hours crawled by while I prepared as best I could. I located my runners in the bottom of the closet. They were serviceable, but my jean jacket was toast, and my jeans were now shorts—the legs having been cut off when I first arrived.

The doctor came by, on his nightly round, to check on his handiwork, informing me that unless I could provide proof of my identity by morning, the hospital would have no choice but to turn me over to the police.

I kept checking the clock and started to worry when the hands got to the twelve but the big hand kept on moving. Pacing beside the bed, I looked up when I heard the elevator doors open, and the clacking of the metal wheels coming along the corridor. Dex and Lizzy, grim-faced, wheeled the stretcher in the room and busily got me ready for transport. Lizzy flipped back the sheet and, underneath, was a bag of clothes. I broke into a wide grin, as she threw the bag at me, and said to hurry up and get dressed.

Dex's light sweater fit perfectly, but his jeans were loose at the waist, so I grabbed the tie from the hospital gown and fashioned a belt from it. I tried on his shoes, but they were too big, so my blood-stained runners would have to do. Dex handed me a slip of paper with his address and security code, a key not required. I hopped up on the stretcher, and Lizzy covered me over. She placed a clipboard with official-looking forms on my chest. They wheeled me out, down the corridor, Lizzy whispering to stay silent and follow their lead.

Passing the nurses' station, eyes averted, heads down, we needn't have bothered, as it was empty, and luck was our side when Dex pressed the button for the service elevator, the doors opened immediately. The trip down was fast as no one else got on. Smiling at each other, I said it felt like we were in a movie, and Lizzy totally dug that.

The elevator doors opened, Dex pushing me out, while Lizzy ran ahead. Straight ahead were the loading docks, Lizzy going down the steps and out the side door while Dex wheeled me to the loading dock on the left. Pulling on the chain, the door squeaked loudly as he pulled it open. He pushed the stretcher to the edge and said I could sit up.

The rush of cool air took my breath away. The night was beautiful, the black sky crystal clear, a full moon overhead, stars shining brightly from one end to the other. There was a peaceful stillness about it. The parking lot was empty, and we watched as Lizzy got in the van and started backing up, the loud beeping piercing the night. I looked at Dex in alarm, but he nodded it was okay.

Lizzy swung the van into a straight line and started up the ramp. I couldn't believe it. This was going to work. I was going to be back before I knew it—back up to Timmins and Mo so we could finally start *our normal day*. It felt so close, I started to get shivers down my spine. The van inched closer to the edge of the dock, Dex leaned forward, reached for the handle.

"All right stop," he called out to Lizzy.

Twisting the handle, Lizzy jumped between the seats and pushed the stretcher toward the doors. Dex held my arm as I stepped down and crawled onto the stretcher. It was so easy. Lizzy never stopped smiling the entire time. Dez jumped in and sat beside me as Lizzy returned to the driver's seat.

Ten minutes later, the ambulance pulled up in front of Dex's loft. Lizzy got out and opened the rear doors, stepping aside to allow me to exit. I couldn't thank either one enough. Dex leaned out and shook my hand.

"Thank you for everything."

"Don't mention it, Pete. Good luck."

I turned to Lizzy. She wore an expression of sadness, the realization our little adventure was at an end.

"Thank you," I said.

Lizzy smiled, stepped forward and kissed me on the cheek. "My pleasure, Pete."

She moved around me and walked to the driver's door. Opening the door, she looked back.

"And no! Thank *you!*" Giggling, she jumped up on the seat inside.

I waved as they pulled away and stood watching until the van got to the end of the street and turned.

75

MO SAT ON the couch looking over at the empty spot, the pillow and blanket piled neatly on *his* cushion. Her brain was on fire, a never-ending tennis match, back and forth, back and forth. She hadn't slept a wink, up all night, staring out the window. Bree texted to see how she was doing and said that she and Adrian were at the club cooking breakfast and to join them. She knew Bree meant well, not wanting her to be alone on a Sunday, and she texted back that she would be there soon.

It had only been two days since Pete last texted, but she knew that things had not gone according to plan. He was supposed to have been home yesterday, worst case late last night. But it had been nothing but crickets since his last text early Saturday morning. What had happened?

Was he okay and his flight had been delayed? That happens all the time. Maybe his phone battery had died. He would drive her crazy, always forgetting to charge his phone. Maybe that was it? But she couldn't stop herself from thinking the worst.

Did the drop go bad and he got into a fight and now was lying hurt somewhere? *So him*, she thought. The floating images swirled around in her head: Pete lying injured, beaten, broken, dead.

She sat for a while longer, staring straight ahead then shifting her legs, she stretched, rubbing her feet on his cushion, then got up and walked over to the window and looked outside. The grey clouds and overall gloom reminded her of that first morning, after Pete had slept on her couch, and how to her it was beautiful, glorious day. She refused to let herself believe anything different this morning.

The day has just started. Keep working your magic. I can wait.

She knew it sounded hokey, but she had always believed in the power of the universe, and she knew Pete did too—one of the many reasons that had drawn them together in the first place. Something told her he was okay, maybe a little battered and bruised, but okay still the same. It was a feeling she was willing to trust for the time being. She showered and headed over to The Club, the short spin on her bike helping clear her head and refusing to let her mood match the gloomy weather overhead.

Bree and Adrian were sitting at the bar eating when she came down the stairs. They both turned and waved a garbled "Hello!" their mouths full, and it made her laugh. Bree hopped off her stool and went into the kitchen as Mo took off her leather jacket and threw it on one of the tables. She reached for a stool, took it around behind the bar, and slid onto it facing Adrian.

"Happy Sunday," he said, earnestly.

"Happy Sunday to you," Mo replied, weakly.

"Want a drink?"

"Sure. I can get it."

"No, here, let me get it for you," he said putting his fork down, jumping off the stool, moving around beside Mo.

"How about a Peach Blow Fizz?" he said, picking up a silver shaker.

"A peach what?"

"A Peach Blow Fizz," he said, pretending to be serious.

"A glass of white wine will be fine, thanks."

"Are you sure? The Peach Blow Fizz only takes twenty minutes to make."

Mo turned her head sideways at him, grinning. "Wine please … next time."

The kitchen doors swung open. Bree carrying a plate in her hands, placed it down in front of Mo. It was a feast that would have made Tony envious. Scrambled eggs, bacon, pancakes, fruit, toast, cranberry, stuffing, and two thick slices of turkey smothered in gravy. Mo looked it over and then at Bree.

"Turkey? Stuffing? Gravy?"

"Sure! It was Adrian's idea. Dig in!"

The three of them sat eating, and though the ache of missing Pete was unbearable, to be surrounded by her friends was, in a way, its own unique version of the white picket fence. Bree's phone buzzed, and looking down at it, she stared at it for the longest time, frowning.

"It's from Pete."

"Pete? Why would he…what's wrong, Bree?" Mo asked, confused, a huge knot immediately forming in her stomach.

"It's a picture of … oh shit, Mo … I'm really sorry."

Bree immediately thought the worst. Pete was dead and someone had his phone. She went to delete the text, but Mo reached over and snatched the phone from her hand.

She stared at the phone, her eyes moving up and down. A wave of relief washed over her as she studied the picture. Nodding her head slowly, she handed it back to Bree.

"Mo? Are you okay? I'm sorry. I think something bad has happened …"

"It's okay, Bree."

Mo pushed her hair back from her face, smiling and taking a couple of deep breaths.

He's fine. I knew it.

"Mo?"

"Pete's fine, Bree. That's his way of letting me know he's okay. My sense he is afraid to contact me directly. Don't worry, he'll be back."

"How do you know that?"

"I just do." Looking at Bree's phone, "It's an old picture of Pete that he used to go on about to me. That was the only picture he had on his phone until the selfie we took that day at Gillies Lake. That picture meant so much to him. Said he had it taken when he was in San Francisco years ago, and it was the recreation of his dad's favourite band's album cover. He grew up listening to his dad's music, and this was his way to remain close to him. So that is his way of telling me he's okay."

76

DEX'S LOFT WAS beautiful. At the top of stairs sat one large room. There was a massive, and very shiny hardwood floor, and an art deco spaghetti pipe ceiling layered overhead. Red brick lined the inner walls, and there was nothing but windows on the outer wall, the light streaming through. There was a kitchen along the wall to the left, an island perched in front of it with two high-back chairs tucked against it, moving boxes on top. Farther along the wall, past the kitchen, was a hockey net with hockey sticks lining the wall, a basketball hoop, and at the very end, a king-size bed. Behind the kitchen was a doorway that led to a bathroom. Straight ahead, hanging on the red brick wall, was a massive TV. In the middle of the room, an L-shaped black leather couch sat over a Persian rug, along with a coffee table, with various remotes and video game controls scattered on it. There were no window coverings, and the wall below the windows was bare except for half-filled boxes of sports jerseys and hats, along with more moving boxes scattered on the floor.

There was a photo of a smiling Dex and Lizzy in a silver frame on the nightstand beside the bed, and I walked over and picked it up. Studying it, I was envious, wishing I had their normal days.

For some reason, I was feeling uneasy about this. Maybe because it all had been too easy. I was restless and couldn't sleep. Unable to unplug the mental VCR, taking one of Dex's jackets off the hook, I ventured outside. I needed air badly, my stomach not happy with me either.

I poked my head out the door, looking up and down the cobblestone alley and finding it deserted. I headed left along the alley, which ended about fifty yards up. Cautiously peeking out, I checked in both directions, and the two-lane boulevard was quiet. To my left, I saw some lights, then cars passing in opposite directions. My heart stopped, and I froze. I looked in the other direction, but it was dark, and I couldn't make anything out. I returned to the loft and dozing off and on, my head jerked up at the slightest noise.

I checked the time—1:00 a.m. and once more ventured out, coming across a bar nestled on a dead-end street near the waterfront. The beer and whiskey chasers went down like melted butter, and bonus, I had made another new best friend.

"Do you know what the sound of one hand clapping is?" asked the old man.

"Um, I think so," I slurred.

"Then what is it?"

I scratched my chin, thinking. "Hold on … it was right here a second ago." I dropped the whisky chaser into my beer. Chugging the beer, holding the shot glass against my teeth, I finished, pounding the mug on the counter.

"I got it!" I said. "It's when someone is missing a hand and they try and clap, right? That's … no … no wait, that's not it … it's when you bang your hand on the table like you're clapping."

I demonstrated, the glasses bouncing at the force.

"That's it! I'm sure of it," grinning proudly, looking at the old man sitting beside me.

"Barkeep! Another round for me and my friend! What was it you were drinking? It doesn't matter. Whatever he's having, I'm having. What's your name again?"

But he didn't say anything, just looked at me amused.

"No don't tell me. Bob? Jim? Pete … no that's me! Floyd, right? And I bet your last name's Pink. Another drink for my pal Floyd Pink! He's teaching me how to clap you know, with one hand and it's much harder than it looks," I said knowingly to the bartender, leaning back.

Waiting for our next round, I looked around the bar. To my right, a small band was playing; a guy on acoustic and electric guitars, while a young woman was seated behind an electric piano, singing mournfully about paved paradise, parking lots, and losing stuff. Her voice was haunting, the song's mood matching mine perfectly.

There were maybe half a dozen people in the bar. A middle-aged couple sitting at a table beside the small stage watching the band, two older fisherman types perched down at one end of the V-shaped bar, swapping stories about the big one that got away, and there was me … well me and my new best friend Floyd, sitting opposite of each other by the entrance. The bartender placed the drinks in front of us. I picked up mine and turned and toasted Floyd.

"Thanks for teaching me this new trick, Floyd!" I said and pounded back the beer.

Floyd was wearing a torn and faded brown satin jacket with buttons down the front and sat quietly on his stool, looking at me. His face was made of leather, weather-beaten after years at sea. His hands were gnarled, and I wondered if he ever harpooned a whale? His longish hair hung over his ears, flowing down over the collar of his jacket. It was thick on the top, messy and unkempt, needing a visit to the barber. His pug nose stuck out, a round bulb at the end, thick and red with tiny black pimple pricks. His eyes sparkled, and there was something about them, the way they glowed. Despite his years and the hard nautical miles he had travelled, there was life in those eyes. He sipped on his beer, wiped his mouth with the back of his hand and spoke.

"You have been telling me your story about what happened, and I listened to it."

I nodded solemnly.

"And you promised you would listen to mine once you were finished."

"Yes. That was the deal."

"So, for the past hour, I have been talking, but I don't think you have been listening. You still have not heard a word I said."

"No, that's not true. I heard you. You're trying to teach me how to clap with one hand, right?"

Floyd sighed and took another drink.

"You need to listen, not only with your ears, but with your heart," he said, tapping his chest. "And your eyes." He tapped the sides of his face with his fingers. "And your skin," he said, pinching the back of his hand. "And your bones," tapping his forearm. "And your mind," tapping his temples.

"Especially your mind. You need to listen with your entire body. Your body is always talking to you." His eyes narrowed, staring straight into mine.

"Every single part of it. Your body never stops talking to you, and even when you are sleeping, it is talking to you. And it's talking to you right now, pretty loudly from what I can hear. So, it is up to *you*"—he pointed and then tapped me on the chest—"to listen. It's a choice. Listen or don't. It is entirely up to you."

He tapped me on the top of my head.

"You had all these things go wrong, and bad things happened as a result. Your best friend betrayed you, you have left a trail of broken hearts in your wake, you blame yourself, and that is true for the most part. You were greedy, and you paid the price. But there are good things still, and there is someone who loves you and is waiting for you, yet here you are, crying and drowning your sorrows in beer. You can't change it. You can't go back, but you can go forward. And that is what your body is trying to tell you, but you won't let it. It is trying to help you, and it's telling you there is a way forward if you will listen. But you're not, you won't," he sighed, frustrated with me.

Au contraire, I am but I can't.

I had heard every single word, loud and clear. I really had.

Tapping him on the sleeve, I told Floyd I had to take a piss and would be right back. He nodded, telling me to take my time; he wasn't going anywhere. Walking slowly past the stage I made eye contact with the singer. I smiled, and she smiled back. I mouthed, "great song," and she smiled and inserted "thank you" into the lyrics as she sang. It made me laugh, warming my heart, and in that instant, I felt a spark, and a shiver running down my spine. I staggered punch-drunk the rest of the way to the men's room.

Finished, I stood in front of the sink, staring at my reflection in the mirror. It shocked me to see I looked like I was on death's door. Turning the tap, I let the water run over my hands, rubbing them vigorously, then leaned over, cupping the water in my hands, washed my face. Wiping my hands down the front of my jeans, I stood back and stared at myself in the mirror.

Ol' Floyd was right. I wasn't listening, and I had stopped moving forward. I'd been stopped dead in my tracks. Without realizing it, once more I had entered the room of denial. Old habits are hard to break. But that's the strength of denial—protecting one from listening, from hearing or seeing the truth, from reality, because the truth fucking hurts, doesn't it? Living in denial shields and protects you from life, preventing you from moving forward.

Dale had betrayed me, and that stung. Never mind he shot me, and that hurt figuratively and literally. But if I really thought about it, best friends don't betray best friends, period. The best friend I *thought* I had was actually from somewhere back in my long ago, when my white picket fence was still intact. Maybe that was the only reason he was my best friend in the first place. I guess I couldn't see it. Once again, denial working its unique brand of magic.

And that's what the old man was saying. There were good things still. One very good thing: Mo. And once more, I had to remind myself that without this journey, there would be no Mo. Along the way, I had made a mistake, or two, or three. The biggest one being greed.

I had so many chances to walk away from Teddy or go to the cops about Tony. Hell, all I had to do was deliver the goddamned box once I had my hands on it, and that would have been that. I could have mailed it to him from Timmins. But I didn't. I was right in that I couldn't kill Tony in cold blood, or anyone else, for that matter. Maybe the only good thing. Mo and the others had been right in telling me to walk away, go to the cops. But the lure of the money, along with a misguided chance at redemption, was too much for me to pass up. Pride sucks. So, here I was, in a dive bar in Saint John, broken, bruised, and battered, but I wasn't dead yet. The old man was right. Looking at myself in the mirror, I didn't like what I saw, but recently I had.

So, what had changed?

Simple, I had stopped listening. I had stopped listening to myself, to my gut instinct. And as much as my pride hurt—along with the rest of my body—there was a way forward. It was the only way. I took a deep breath, swallowed my pride, hopefully for the last time.

"You can do this! YOU CAN DO THIS." I said to the mirror.

Returning, I passed the singer, stopped, and took out a fifty-dollar bill. I folded it and pushed it through the slit of the tip jar. I smiled and mouthed a "thank you." Her infectious smile warmed my heart, reminding me everything was still possible. Approaching the bar, Floyd wasn't there, and I hadn't passed him along the way. He didn't smoke, so where was he? Sitting down, I motioned for the bartender, who came over.

"So, where is he?"

"Who?"

"Floyd. The old guy that's been sitting here drinking with me."

"Who? What old guy?"

"Christ," I said pointing to the empty stool beside me. "He was sitting right here!"

"Buddy, you've been sitting here by yerself. It's almost closing and time to settle up and head out for some fresh air there, boy."

She turned and moved to the other end of the bar where one of the fishermen was trying to get her attention. I slid off the stool, tucking a fifty under the coaster, and went out the door.

77

TEDDY PUTTERED AROUND Sharkees nervously, constantly checking the front door. He split some wood, tidied up the patio, and much to Patty's surprise, helped Danny in the kitchen. He was still shaken by Dale's recent text and had been on guard ever since. He didn't know who was coming for him. Dale? Tony? He hadn't heard from Tony, meaning the hit on Dale never took place, and he was worried the tables had been now turned on him.

Dale's text announced that Pete was dead, the money was missing, and Teddy was next. Pete's death, surprisingly, left him with feelings of remorse, and he wasn't sure why. Maybe, it was because the money was missing. He had no idea where the money was now and was angry at himself for screwing up the airport security check, and more concerned if the bloody trail found its way back to him. Most of all, he feared for his sister's life, and at his urging, she had been staying at his place.

Teddy slipped onto a bar stool and fiddled with his phone. His head jerked up when the house lights flashed, signaling closing time. His stomach was in knots and he was sweating profusely. He got off the stool and walked behind the bar and poured himself a tall glass of bourbon. Returning to his seat, he studied the glass in front of him on the bar.

"You okay, brother?" Sara slipped onto the stool beside him. She rubbed his back then pulled her hand away in disgust.

"Yeewww! Geezus, Teddy, your shirt is soaking wet!"

Teddy's stomach clenched, and he mumbled, "Yeah, I know. I got hot when I split the wood."

Patty came in behind the bar and noticing Teddy's soaked shirt, "Everything okay? Not used to hard work?" she teased.

Teddy smiled weakly, still staring at the glass of bourbon. Patty mouthed, *What's wrong with him?* to Amy but she shook her head.

Patty reached for the keys on the shelf and started to head around closing the doors when there was the familiar loud bang and whoosh. In walked Tony, much to everyone's surprise, no more than Teddy's.

78

I STUMBLED BACK to Dex's loft, shaken by my encounter with the Old Man from the Sea. Morning had broken, and I was restless, my flight still hours away but I couldn't stay here, so I called for a cab and waited, staring out the window. Though I had found my resolve again, I wasn't in the clear by any stretch, and just wanted to be done with everything. I no longer cared about the story in Teddy's box, even if it did connect all those pretty dots. Though, so long as I remained dead, I had more options. Go figure.

I had thought about talking it out with Teddy, cutting both our losses, taking the two-fifty as a Pass-Go. I felt I had earned that at least. I had no interest in going to the authorities about him or Dale and whatever scheme they were running. I genuinely felt bad for his sister, Sara, and the double life she led as Amy. That must have been extremely difficult to maintain, and I think she got in too deep and couldn't get out—loyal to her brother, afraid of Dale.

All I wanted was to return to Timmins and spend the next fifty years painting our white picket fence. I hoped that possibility still remained.

On the cab ride to the airport, I'd kept turning and checking the rear window, positive I was being followed. There was absolutely no reason for me to feel this way, *was there?*

I entered the airport, keeping my head low, wearing a black ball cap courtesy of Dex, and slumped down in the far corner on one of the benches across from my departure gate.

When my flight was called, the flight check-in was a breeze. The person at the check-in counter, head down, didn't ask for the code word, punched out my ticket, and pointed over her shoulder.

"Boarding now, follow the lines," she grumbled, Monday morning not agreeing with her.

The flight went quick, disembarking, Meg was waiting for me at the gate, wearing a big smile, and I was relieved. The smile looked good on her, and she wore it well. But her face dropped as I got closer, and I looked behind me, thinking I was being followed. Turning back, I realized it was me. I was limping noticeably, a red streak oozing from my jeans again, bloodstains were on the front of Dex's sweater, and my face pockmarked with red scratches, and tiny black stitches. Meg ran straight towards me, arms out, hugging me gently, careful not to touch anything.

"OMG! Pete. I didn't know. I'm so sorry. I didn't know. What happened to you? Are you all right?"

She wrapped her arm around me, helping me walk along the concourse. It was busy, so we moved off to one side, and I made her stop. Paranoia had taken over and breathlessly, I started peppering her with questions.

"Has anyone contacted you recently? Phone call? Text? Anyone following you? Where is your mom?"

Meg looked at me, frightened. "What do you mean? What's all this about?"

"Have you noticed anything strange going on?" I asked, becoming more intense.

"Pete, stop! You're scaring me."

I felt bad for scaring her. "Look, it's probably nothing. Sorry, I'm not myself right now. Forget it, okay?"

"Okay. Are you all right, Pete? What happened out there?"

"Not right now, Meg. I have to get to Sharkees. In time. I promise."

She smiled like she didn't believe me, walked me out to the cab stand, and hugged me tightly. Once again, it reminded me of how lucky I was, and I waved as the cab pulled away from the curb.

The cab pulled up to the entrance of Sharkees. I paid up then hobbled out into the bright sunshine. There was no one else around. Teddy's pickup and another car beside it parked in front—no Chevy—and I hoped Patty had it under lock and key somewhere. I quickly reviewed in my head what was next, which wasn't a lot. Part of me wished Teddy wasn't there and that I could get my keys from Patty, collect the money, and head up to Timmins lickety-split, and that would be that. I hadn't contacted Mo because I couldn't trust, instead sending the picture to Bree and hoping that was enough to let her know I was okay.

Taking a deep breath, I reached for the door handle and pulled open the door. The loud bang and rush of air didn't feel so comforting, and as I moved through the doorway my gut instinct immediately went on high alert.

The place felt like a morgue. The lights were on, but nobody was home. The fireplace was dark, and where wood was constantly burning, I could see faint orange amongst the grey ashes and charred pieces of wood. The bar and seating area were empty, and what struck me was the silence. No music playing in the background.

"Hello? Is there anyone here?"

I walked past the bar, the wood floor creaking eerily underneath, when the kitchen doors swung open, and I jumped back in fright. Coming straight out toward me was Patty swearing a blue streak.

"GODDAM FUCKING PEOPLE! WHERE THE FUCK IS EVERYONE? I told that fucking brother of hers a hundred fucking times to lock the fucking front door at the end of the fucking night!"

"Patty?"

"Oh, shit! Sorry, Pete. I didn't see you. Where have you … Oh my God! What the fuck happened to you? You look like shit."

"Nice to see you too."

"Sorry there, Pete, but you look like roadkill. What happened?"

"It's a long story. Where is everyone?" I asked.

Patty started speaking rapidly. "Good question! When I got here a few minutes ago, the front door was unlocked, the fire was out, no music playing, and we open at ten. I've told Teddy countless times never to leave the front door unlocked after closing. I'm so pissed because he's let the fire go out, and now trying to relight it, it will get smoky, meaning we have to open the front and patio doors, meaning the hydro bill is going to go up in flames. I am so fucking pissed and there he is sleeping it off, didn't even move when I came in."

Turning to follow her gaze I saw Teddy, fast asleep, hunched over the piano. There was a loud bang and rush of air, as someone came through the front entrance. Keys jingling, head down, hearing the silence, Sara stopped and looked up. Our eyes met, her expression changing from surprise to confusion.

"Hello," Patty said coldly.

"What's going on?" she asked.

"You tell me."

"Tell you what?"

"You tell me. I walked in here a few minutes ago, the place dead, not a soul in sight. No fire, no music, your brother's passed out on the piano. I slept later because you told me you would be here for eight."

I watched the fear envelope Sara, and I knew she was thinking the worst.

"Why were you late?" Patty demanded.

"I'm sorry, Teddy didn't come home and—"

Patty, fuming, her hands crossed tight against her chest, "Well …?"

"I don't know!"

"Okay, okay. Take it easy, slow down," I interrupted, stepping forward. "Here … sit," I said, motioning to a stool.

Sara nodded, staring at Patty, whose laser-like stare was burrowing a hole straight through her chest. She sat on the edge of the stool, placing her purse on the bar. Her hands were shaking, and as she looked up, she let out a loud shriek.

"TEDDY! OH MY GOD OH MY GOD OH MY …" as she leapt from the stool knocking it over. Running around the bar toward the piano she was crying, "Oh my God, oh God, ohmygod …"

I grabbed for her but missed and I ran, grabbing Sara by the arm, just as she got to him, roughly pulling her back. Holding her tightly from behind, my arms wrapped over hers, she was screaming and thrashing, kicking in the air wildly, crying hysterically. I held her, forcing her to the floor, her legs thrashing about.

Teddy wasn't breathing. He was slumped over the piano, dead. His left temple rested against the upper cabinet, and there was a thin red line running down his nose from the small bullet hole squarely between his eyes. His right hand was resting on the keys like he was playing, his eyes were open, grotesquely staring straight ahead.

Patty cried out, "OH no, no, nooooo ..."

I tried to calm Sara, as Patty reached for her phone. That was the last thing we needed.

"Patty, no. Hold on. Wait."

"What. No, what ... we have to call 911. Dead. Oh my God. No, no, no ..." Patty, in shock, couldn't take her eyes off the piano.

"Yes, just wait. Just wait a bit, okay?"

Patty stood glassy-eyed as I held on to Sara tightly.

"Patty, you need to lock all the doors, so no one gets in. And quickly."

Zombie-like, unable to take her eyes off Teddy, Patty went around to all the doors, locking them, only looking away when she had to. Once Sara had calmed enough, I was able to get her to her feet, and led her back to the bar, forcing her to sit down, facing away from the piano. I walked behind the bar and stood opposite her.

"Sara, just look at me. Okay? Only at me."

Slowly, she lifted her head.

"Your brother's dead, and I'm sorry, but nothing is going to bring him back. The next few minutes will dictate how you go forward. I am sorry, and I wish there was an easier way. Are you listening, Sara?"

"Yes."

Patty had returned and looked ashen and confused. "Amy?"

Sara looked at her. "No, I'm so sorry ... that is what I've been trying to tell you. My name is not Amy. It's Sara. I hope you can forgive me."

Patty, in shock, her mouth open, stared at her.

I gently pulled on Sara's hands. "Sara, who do you think did this? Was it Dale?"

Sara looked at me, shocked. "How do you know about Dale?"

"He's ... It's not important. And there's no time. Was it Dale?"

"I don't know! It could have been him. He threatened to kill Teddy and me a few days ago. That's why I had been staying with him."

I felt like a detective on a TV show. Things were finally coming together, appearing to be some sort of perverse love triangle; linked together with the death of Sara's and Teddy's parents, the box, and that piece of paper.

"Who was here last night? Was Dale here?"

"Yes, we all were. But, no, not Dale."

"Who then?"

"Me, Teddy, Patty, and Tony."

"Tony was here?"

"Tony. Yeah. He showed up at closing out of nowhere. We were all surprised. No one had seen or heard from him in weeks."

"What happened when he got here?"

"Nothing. I don't know. They were drinking pretty hard, I guess. Teddy seemed surprised to see him now that I think of it."

"When did you leave?"

Patty spoke up, "We left together maybe two thirty. Me and Amy … I mean Sara. Teddy and Tony were still drinking pretty hard, and I told Teddy to make sure all the doors were locked when they were done."

"Sara, I need to ask you a question, and you don't have to answer it, but it would help."

Sara looked at me and nodded.

"Did Dale kill your parents that night, and then try to cover it up?"

"No," she said, looking down, shaking her head slowly. "No, he didn't."

"Do you know who did? Does Dale know who did it?"

Her head dropped farther and barely audible, "I did. I killed them."

And then she sighed heavily, and I could literally see the relief wash off her shoulders. Patty gasped and turned away.

"Did Dale cover it up?"

"Yes," she said, numbly.

"Why? How did you know Dale?"

"I didn't. Not until that night is. He showed up and took over. Told me to do as he said."

"Why?"

"I don't know. I have always wondered why. I think he got off on it. Over time, I watched him do it to others. It was like a power trip of some kind."

"Did your brother know? Was he a part of it?"

"No … no, he didn't. He never knew, but he was getting closer, and I think that's what did it. He got too close..." she gasped and started to sob again. "I had tried to tell him so many times, but I couldn't."

"If only I had. I'm so sorry for everything." She looked up at me, then over at Patty, whose back was still turned.

"So, Dale hid it. Dale covered everything up," I said, thinking out loud. "Can I ask why? Why did you kill your parents, were they abusing you?"

"No," Sara answered coldly, reminded of her mother's awful words that night.

"Our father was hard on Teddy. And that night, I guess Teddy had taken enough, and he slugged him in the face, knocking him over. I was watching, and I tried to stop it, and I was able to push Teddy out of the house. And when I came back, I saw my mother and father on the floor, and something inside snapped. I went out to the tool shed and came back with a pitchfork, and I killed them. And, I didn't care. I still don't. I cared about Teddy, and I didn't want him to know what I had done. I set fire to the house, trying to cover up what I had done, and when Teddy saw it, he came running back. Part of me hoped I could get away with it, but the cops would eventually figure it out. I didn't care, and I was okay with whatever happened because Teddy wouldn't suffer anymore.

"When Dale arrived, he took over, and everything was a blur, and before you know it, Teddy and I were on a beach, all expenses paid. He told us to lay low. I lied to Teddy, and said Dale wanted us to go away and get out of the limelight. When we got back, I thought that was that, but that was pretty naïve, huh? One day, there was a knock on the door, and opening it, there stood Dale. The rest is history," sighing and looking over at Patty, who had turned back but remained silent, staring at her.

"But if Teddy didn't know—"

"I'm assuming he had something else on Teddy. I don't know what."

I leaned forward and rubbed Sara's hands. "Sara, where does your brother know me from?"

Looking at me, she could tell I didn't know.

"Did we meet somewhere?" I asked.

"Sort of ... a long time ago ... something happened on a dock ... um, he said it was you that day. Did you do something to him? Teddy said *it was you*, but I didn't know what he was talking about."

That day on the dock. That was Teddy.

I felt like I had been struck by lightning only a hundred times worse. But I had to stay focused, stay in the present, or I would collapse just like Sara. The ball was in my court, and both our lives depended on what happened next.

"Sara is there anywhere you can go?"

"Teddy's place is—"

"No, I mean away from here. Is there anywhere you can go far away from here?"

She thought for a moment. "I have an old college roommate out in BC somewhere. I could maybe find her, I suppose."

"You have a choice to make, but you have to make it quick. Either wait for the cops to arrive and fess up or make a run for it and buy yourself some time. Your parents and brother are dead, and you will rot in jail if they find out you were involved. Big if. Or you can make a run for it, get a head start. Worst case, they catch you. That won't change a thing. It will take them quite a while to sort things out, and maybe they will, or maybe they won't. Unless you tell, of course, and your secret is safe with me."

I looked over at Patty, "You too, right?" Patty nodded dutifully.

"The way I see it, you're a prisoner either way. I don't know about you, but if I'm going to be a prisoner, I would prefer it not be behind bars. But you have to decide right now. Patty has to make that call soon, and once she does, that's it. There's no turning back."

"What about you?" Sara asked, concerned.

"Look, I'm sorry about your brother, I truly am. I may have to go in hiding myself for a bit, so I'm a prisoner just like you. Get out of here now and just go. Don't go back to Teddy's, just get going. Do you have enough money?"

"Yes."

"Good! Get on that bike of yours and don't stop until you see the ocean, okay?"

Sara nodded. "Pete, I'm sorry."

"Me too," I smiled weakly.

Sara stared straight ahead, lost in a thousand yard stare. I reached for her purse on the bar and handed it to her. "Come on, get going."

Sara slowly stood up, her hands shaking, and steadied herself against the bar. I felt awful for her. She was completely on her own. There would be no burials, no celebrations of life, surrounded by loving and crying family members, and friends. Instead, she would be running, once again from her past, in an entirely different direction. And she had betrayed her best friend, lying to her all this time. *All just part of her normal day.*

Sara slipped her jacket over her shoulders, and tentatively, moved towards Patty, her arms out, but Patty backed away.

"I'm so sorry," she began crying. "You're my best friend … I love you so much … I'm sorry I lied to you … I wanted to tell you so many times. I hope you can forgive me." She lowered her head and turned toward the door.

Sara stopped, looked over at her brother, and started crying harder, her body shuddering. I moved in front of her to block her view, hugged her, and could feel her trembling. I wanted to reassure her that everything was going to okay, but there was no point, and kissing her on the cheek, pushed her out the door.

"Wait!" Patty suddenly called out in a wail of anguish.

They fell into each other's arms, in between the doors, both sobbing uncontrollably. I watched the gut-wrenching scene play out, and I think at that moment, I hated Hollywood more than ever. Patty, holding Sara tightly, walked her outside, and they hugged some more. I watched from the entrance, as she got on her bike and sped away. Patty came back inside, and we stood in the empty, silent bar, Teddy's body mere feet from us. Looking at each other, neither of us uttering a sound, abruptly, Patty turned toward the kitchen, and following behind, I took a left at the men's room.

I walked over to the last stall, closed the door, and slid the latch. Facing the toilet, I said a silent prayer, bent down and reached around the bowl with my hands. I fiddled for a minute, then with a couple of hard yanks and a loud rip, pulled out the money belt. I held it up to the light, peeling off the rest of the duct tape, patting it lovingly. I lifted my sweater, wrapped the belt around me, securing it with the Velcro strap. Pulling down my sweater, I headed back out to the bar. Coming out the door, I was feeling heavier and laughed at that irony. I stopped briefly, listened for Patty, and could hear rummaging in the kitchen. I went behind the bar, poured myself a beer and whiskey chaser, pounding them down. The kitchen doors opened, Patty walking towards me, her phone out, when mine rang.

"Okay, to call now?" Patty asked, calmer now as she threw me the car keys.

"Hold on a sec," catching the keys, I answered my phone.
"I have her."
"Have who? Who is this?"
"Hello? Pete, I'm sorry, he surprised me."

79

I MOTIONED FOR Patty to sit down and put my finger to my mouth for her to remain silent. I placed my phone down on the bar and tapped the speaker button.

"Hey, stranger."

"Hey, it's nice to hear your voice. Sorry, he surprised me."

"It's okay. Nice to hear yours too. How are you? You okay?"

"Yes."

"Are you on speaker?"

"No."

"Okay, good. What's happening?"

"The money. Tony wants the two fifty. He thinks you have it. Do you?"

I tapped the mute button and sighed heavily, shaking my head, the fear washing over me. Tony. Patty was looking at me, eyebrows raised, with a confused look. I tapped the mute button again.

"Yes, I have the money."

"He wants you to bring the money to him."

"Where are you?"

"My place."

"That was the down payment on our white picket fence," I sighed, watching all that green flutter away in the sky.

"I know but, I don't care about the money, Pete. I just want you and our life here."

"Me too, babe, me too. How much time do I have?"

"As soon as you can get here, I guess."

I could hear rustling and clunking, then Tony's voice.

"Howdy Pistol! Sweet cheeks is looking mighty fine. I want the money. You know, you're like a fucking cat. How many lives do you have?"

"Quite a few. And I saved the best for last … you."

"Always the pistol. You've got until midnight, and then sweet cheeks here becomes dead cheeks."

"I can't make it there by midnight," I said. "It needs to be tomorrow morning at least."

"Nope. Midnight. After that anything I get up to is on you."

"Be reasonable, Tony," I pleaded, unable to hide the panic in my voice.

"Aw, pawdner, now don't be going all soft on me. It's only sweet cheeks. They're a dime a dozen for guys like you."

"I will fucking kill you, if you touch her!"

"Same ol' Pistol. Empty words, hollow threats. How many times have we been down that road? You ain't got it in you."

"We'll see," I said.

"You better haul ass, pawdner. Clock's a ticking."

"Put Mo back on."

"No tricks."

"Just put her back on."

There was more rustling and clunking, then Mo's voice. Mo sweet Mo.

"Hey, it's going to be okay. I'm bringing the money and should be there around midnight."

"He said *by* midnight," Mo replied nervously.

"I know, but a few minutes, either way, he won't care."

"Are you sure?"

"Yes, and—"

The call abruptly disconnected, and I sat there looking at Patty.

Patty, angry, started going off again.

"That fucking slimeball. He killed Teddy. I thought he and Teddy were friends! And now he's up in Timmins? There was something slimy about him, I never took to him right from the start. Teddy was a handful at times but Tony? There's something sinister there, Pete. I have no clue what any of this means, and I don't even want to try and figure it out. I'm still trying to process how my best friend lied to me all this time, and now she's like a what? A femme fatale? Is that what you call it? She's on the run, her brother is dead in my bar, and you're right in the middle of it. This life you lead it's something all right. Have you ever thought of maybe trying something less normal?"

While she was talking, I had reached under my sweater and tore open the Velcro strap removing the money belt. I dropped it on the bar.

"Is that what I think it is?" she asked, her hand reaching out to touch it.

"Uh-huh."

She patted the pockets, "Infuckingcredible! How much?"

"Two hundred and fifty thousand," I said.

"Dollars?" she asked, incredulously.

"Canadian. Sorry," I smirked, making her laugh.

"You're right. My life is certainly not for the faint of heart, huh?"

"Not if you want to see the sun come up when you're old," she smiled. "What are you going to do? And I don't want to rush you or anything, but I've got a dead body that needs removing because, I think that might be a bit much to handle, even for my regulars."

I asked Patty where my Chevy was, and she said it was out back under a tarp.

"Too bad you just couldn't fly," she mused.

"That's it!" I exclaimed. "That's it! I can fly!"

I leaned over and kissed Patty on the cheek, then searched on my phone for Meg and tapped connect.

"That was quick," she said

"How fast can you get me a flight to Timmins?"

"Huh?"

"I need a flight to Timmins."

"Timmins."

"Yeah, can you get me there?"

"For when?"

"Now?"

Meg checked and said she had a connecting flight through TO, but it left in twenty minutes, and could I get there? I said sure, tossing my keys to Patty, and said I would be there in ten. I thanked Meg, disconnected, and reached for the money belt.

"Come on Patty, Teddy can wait. He's not going anywhere. I need you to drive me to the airport, and then you can return to your normal."

Patty pulled up in front of Departures a mere four minutes after pulling out of Sharkees. She said not to worry, my Chevy was in good hands and to do what I needed to do. I thanked her, and as she started to pull away, I yelled out, and she stopped, the loud screech making heads turn. I ran over to the driver's side and handed her the money belt.

"I can't fly with this. It will take too long to pass through security. Just leave it in the Chevy; it will be fine."

"Are you sure?" she asked.

"If it can survive taped to the toilet tank at Sharkees, it can survive in my Chevy until I get back."

"It what?"

"I taped it to the toilet tank in the men's can before I left, the day I gave you the keys."

"You what? Oh my god, Pete, you are something all right," she laughed. "Do you know what you are going to do when you get there? Any plan?"

Who me? Plan? What plan?

Patty extended her hand out the window, shaking my hand, "Take care, Pete, and good luck. Mo sounds worth it."

"Thanks, she is. Listen, Patty, if something happens to me—"

"Nope!" she said, pulling her hand away, "see you when you get back."

Revving the engine, Patty popped the clutch, burning a strip of rubber ten feet long, smoke swirling, she roared off, as I watched my baby fall in love with someone else. I went inside and walked up to the counter. Meg was typing furiously on the computer, face scrunched, staring intently at the screen.

"I think I've almost got it. Okay, I think I can swing it, but you are going to have to do a bit of running and hope there are no delays."

The thought of missing the connecting flight filled me with dread, but I didn't have any choice. The fastest way there was this or nothing. Meg finished up, speaking fast now, holding out the tickets.

"Flight leaves from that gate over there," she pointed behind me. "I've got you in the first row so you can get off quickly when it lands. But you are going to have to haul ass to get the connecting flight, it departs fifteen minutes after you land. My friend, Katie, in T.O., knows you're coming, and she will be waiting for you, but she can't hold the plane. Her gate is at the far end where you get off, so don't stop for anyone, or anything. Just get there, got it?"

Looking down, she folded the tickets and put them in the envelope. I took them from her and nodded.

"I can't thank you enough for this."

"You're welcome. Now get going! You've got planes to catch and damsels to rescue. I assume she's in distress, right?"

"Very."

Meg moved from behind the counter and stood in front of me. "You look like shit, you know."

"I know."

"Pete, you can't keep doing this. This life, this stuff, you can't keep living like this. No one can."

Meg didn't have to tell me she was right, but it wasn't easy to get off once you got on this merry-go-round. "This is the last one, I promise," I said, trying to sound convincing.

She looked at me, not believing, and I couldn't blame her. But I was determined that this was it; it was over after this. Whatever normal day lay ahead would be better than this normal day.

When I got seated, I texted Adrian and asked him to meet me at the airport, not to tell anyone, and I would explain. The flight to T.O. was quick, Katie waving to me as I hurried through the concourse. Walking through the passenger door, it closed behind me, and I was hurriedly ushered to my seat by an annoyed flight attendant.

"We've been waiting ten minutes for you. I hope you're headed somewhere important!"

Landing, Adrian was waiting out front as promised, the engine running, and there on the seat staring up at me, was a Glock.

"How did you know I needed that?" I asked.

"Really?..." raising an eyebrow. "You know when Bree finds out what we're up to, we're both dead men, you know that right?"

"Maybe don't tell her?"

"I'm screwed either way," he sighed. "And if she finds out, I've given you her Glock …"

It was just past seven, night was falling, the roads were empty, and the trip into town was quick. Adrian asked if I wanted backup, but the thought of guns blazing, bullets flying, and bodies littering the front lawn … I reluctantly declined. He understood, and I didn't have to explain that I needed to do this on my own, no matter what happened. I told him to drop me off on the street behind Mo's, and I would take it from there. Adrian killed the lights when we got to the cemetery and turned down the lane before Mo's, driving slowly along the gravel road, trying to remain as quiet as possible. When he got near the end of the lane, I told him to stop. I got out, walked around to the driver's side.

"Do you know what you're going to do?" he asked.

"No clue, just wing it."

"Are you *sure* you don't want backup?"

"No … no. I have to do this."

"Be careful and remember the Glock kicks differently than your .45, so aim high and shoot low, as the song says."

"I will, and thanks. See you in a bit."

"Take your time. I'll be at The Club."

"Mum's the word on Bree."

"Got it. I'll wait to hear from you first."

I watched as Adrian turned around and drove off. I checked the gun, flipping the safety off. It was a full moon, similar to the night with the bikes, which took away any surprise element. It was still early, and I ran the risk of encountering dog walkers, but it was a chance I would have to take. So far, everything was quiet and the night still. I walked up the road about twenty yards, then cut left at a driveway, ducking low, I duckwalked alongside a car until I got to the front of the house. I stopped, waited, and listened. My hands were wet with sweat, and I wiped them on my jeans, carefully balancing the Glock. The moon overhead shimmered above the treetops. *What a beautiful night.*

Another quick check, keeping low, I moved past the house, there was no gate to the yard, so I hugged the tree line that separated Mo's property from her neighbour's. It was thick enough that I could walk upright, and when I got to the back of Mo's place, I jumped the wire fence, the metal pipe clanging and jiggling. Hunched down, I listened, but it was quiet, filled with just the normal nighttime noises.

I made my way through Mo's backyard and walked along the side of her house. The windows were too high to see through, but they were dark and closed, and there was no point in trying to get in that way. Up ahead, I could see the light coming from the kitchen window, and the light on over the back door, illuminating the small porch attached to the side. I approached, one step at a time, pausing and listening, but the element of surprise seemed to be still in my favour.

Quickly looking around, I cautiously placed one foot on the porch step, trying to keep my weight on my back foot. When I didn't hear a squeak, I shifted, and brought my back leg up, then placed my foot on the next step, and did the same. I turned and put my back flat against the wall beside the door. Turning my head, I carefully moved sideways until I could see through the window.

Mo was sitting on the couch straight ahead in the living room. Bandit, oblivious, was playing with a toy under the kitchen table. I couldn't see Tony.

I jerked back as he walked into the kitchen, heading straight for the back door. I braced against the wall and brought my gun up. Waiting to hear the door open, my heart pounding so hard I swear he would hear it, but there was nothing. I waited a bit, then cautiously peeked in at the edge of the window. He was gone, and looking through to the living room, I could see him sitting on a chair, his back to me, facing Mo.

This wasn't going to work; no way I could sneak in. The bathroom window was open, but the opening was too small for me to crawl in without being heard. So, my only option, the prospect of it unappealing to say the least, was to come in through the front door and see where things led.

I worked my way back along the side of the house to the backyard, and then over to the other side and walked past Mo's bike. I reached up, undid the latch, then pulled the gate far enough open for me to slide through. I didn't bother closing it as you never know, it might be an escape route. I took stock of my surroundings: there was a black BMW parked in the driveway, but there were no other cars in sight, and my sense was Tony was alone. I was standing out of the light, off to the side of the front door, and my hands were sweating so much

I had to hold the gun with two hands. My chest felt like it was going to explode. I had to force myself to slow my breathing.

Come on, big guy, you've done this a hundred times before, and you've never felt like this. Just like riding a bike, right? Wrong.

I forced myself to count to ten slowly; getting to ten, I took a deep breath, stepped out of the light, and walked up the front step. Pausing, I reached for the door handle, the aluminum door squeaking as I pulled it back; pushing down on the inner door handle, clicking as it opened, I walked in.

"Hi honey, I'm home," I said, my arm out, gun pointed at Tony.

Tony was sitting on a chair in front of the blanket fort across from Mo, a knife in his hand as he carved off chunks of apple, eating them with the knife. Looking up, between mouthfuls, his cheeks expanded like a chipmunk, he smiled.

"What took you? I expected you here, oh, about thirty minutes ago. How was your flight?"

Mo was staring at me in shock, the side of her face red, her nose bloody, courtesy of Tony. I looked at her then back at Tony.

"Aww, what's wrong, pawdner? Cat got your tongue?" stuffing a chunk of apple in his mouth. "I knew you couldn't make it here in that red shitbox of yours. Just 73 sss's of shit ... Mickey Mouse slicks ... that six-pack plastic music box from the 60s or is it the 50s?" he mocked. "I saw it parked out back of Sharkees. Fucking piece of shit it is."

"I guess you don't appreciate good cars. I mean, look at you. Driving a beamer. I had you more for a Tonka Truck."

Tony cackled, his gold teeth flashing in the light. "That's my pistol. Always the joke, and since you're early, hand over the money, and I'll be on my way. Well, after I rub those sweet cheeks a bit more," looking over at Mo. "That was fun, wasn't it? Do you squirm like that when he fucks you?" grinning at me.

I cocked my gun, the metallic click of the hammer making Tony briefly pause, then he broke out in laughter.

"For Pete's sake, pawdner. How many times do we have to play that game of yours? Will he or won't he, will he or won't he?" Tony, disgusted, shook his head slowly. "We both know the answer to that. Put the fucking gun down now, or I will come over and take it from you and stick it so far up sweet cheeks' snatch you'll need pliers to get it out."

"Fuck you, Tony," I hissed.

"That all you got?"

"That's it."

Tony waved his hand and motioned with his fingers. "Just give me the money, and you and sweet cheeks can play house." Pointing over his shoulder with the knife. "Did you know she has a pup tent here in the living room, or was that your idea?"

"It's a blanket fort!" Mo and I snapped in unison.

"Whatever ... I don't care anymore. I'm tired of this, tired of you ... tired of her."

Mo stared at Tony defiantly.

"I didn't bring the money."

Tony's face dropped. "You what?" his eyes suddenly growing wide.

"I didn't bring it."

Tony staring hard at me now, realized I wasn't playing games. "Pawdner, that might have been the dumbest thing you've ever done, and the last thing you will ever do," shaking his head sadly.

"We'll see about that."

"Yes, we will, because before I kill the both of you, I'm going to make you watch as I fuck sweet cheeks here, then I'm going to make you suck my cock while she watches and learns. Guys like you secretly suck dick, don't you? It's all show. And all just because I can. So, if you were joking like you always do, and you do have the money, now would be a good time."

"As I said, I didn't bring it, and if I'm going to suck cock, I want a meal. You're not even a snack. Those walls at Sharkees, they talk, you know ... tell stories ..."

Suddenly, Bandit jumped up on Tony, surprising him. Picking him up, he threw him against the wall, Bandit landing with a sickening thud, whimpering, emitting a stomach-turning undistinguishable low howl.

"BANDIT!" Mo screamed, racing toward him.

I spun my gun, throwing it at Tony, hitting him in the temple, knocking him sideways. I flew at him, fist out, punching him repeatedly in the head and face. Mo, kneeling on the carpet, tried to comfort Bandit, but he slipped away, limping heavily, his body slunk low, he crawled through the open front door.

Mo screamed out "YOU FUCKING BASTARD!" and turning, she

attacked Tony with her fists. The two of us pummeled Tony, as he covered his head, shielding himself from the barrage. We flailed away, both of us grunting loudly, when Tony reached out and pushed Mo roughly away. He gripped my sweater, stood up, as I continued to pound away with my fists, and threw me against the wall. Landing hard, gasping for air and groaning, my back screamed in pain where I hit the edge of the wall.

Dazed, I watched Mo kick out at Tony, but he remembered what happened in the bar, remaining just out of reach. He connected solidly with a right to her nose, then punched her hard in the stomach, a loud "oof" as the breath came out of her, doubling her over in pain. She fell to the floor on her side, moaning, blood coming from her nose. Tony turned and came over to me, picked me up like a rag doll, holding me by the scruff of my neck, threw me like a bowling ball through the doorway into the kitchen. I landed hard on the bare floor, my head stopping inches from the base of the dishwasher. I couldn't move, every inch of my body ached, my head was spinning, the sounds garbled and muffled, everything seemed to be happening in slow motion.

I tried to move my arm to push myself up, when I felt hands on the back of my neck, I was lifted straight up and roughly thrown face-first against the sink. Tony put his arm around my chest, and with his other hand I could feel him fumbling behind me. I heard the sound of a belt buckle and zipper, I froze, his hot breath on the back of my neck. I shuddered, my spine tingling, as he leaned in and licked my ear, his tongue wet and hot, as he ran it up and down, tickling the lobe.

"Gawd, I miss this," he whispered in my ear. "Fucking like this. Did you know I fucked Leia from behind like this? Made Jimmy watch too. Do you know he cried like a baby the whole time? But that Leia, she's tough, never said a word, didn't cry out, didn't make a sound, not even a whimper ... took it like the man she is."

At the sound of Leia, something inside snapped. "NO!" I screamed out.

I started pushing and thrashing, trying to get away, but Tony had me pinned tight up against the sink. I reached out with my left hand grabbing, reaching, stretching, trying to find anything to fight back with. My hand fumbled along the countertop, I grasped a knife lying in the sink, but Tony pulled my hand away and grabbed the knife and threw it behind him, it clattering harmlessly on the floor. Tony started grabbing at my jeans, and I fought back, and I could feel his erection against me. He was struggling to get my jeans down, and every time he touched the button to my jeans, I wriggled away. I tried reaching out again, but he grabbed my arm, but I twisted it away. I think I was yelling at him, but I'm not sure.

Tony tried to grab my cock through my jeans, but I twisted away, and reaching out again, I felt something sharp and was able to grasp it. I swung backward in a stabbing motion and kept swinging until I connected. Then I hit flesh and heard a slight "ugh," so I kept stabbing hard in the same spot. My hand felt wet and sticky, and I knew he was bleeding, so I kept stabbing. I was hitting home because his grip was loosening, and his breath becoming shallower. I twisted and thrashed, pushing back against him, and suddenly I had room. I kept stabbing and pushing back with my legs and hips. There was a louder "ugh," then I felt his hands drop, and I turned and pushed him hard in the chest, he fell back, holding his side. The colour was draining from his face, and he clutched his side, his shirt a dark red, blood seeping out between his fingers.

I looked into the living room where Mo was still on her side on the floor. I saw the gun lying near her, and I called out,

"Mo! Mo! Wake up! Mo! Get up. The gun … MO!" I screamed at her.

I was frantic, as Tony was just a few feet from me, dazed and holding his side, and I knew I had only seconds until he recovered.

"Mo!" I screamed again. "Get up! MMMOOO!!!"

Mo stirred, and lifting her head, looked over at me. Her eyes were glassy, and blood was covering the lower half of her face.

"Mo! The gun! Throw me the gun … MO!"

Tony was coming around, and I knew if he got in close, I was a dead man, the paring knife too small to stab anymore. I threw the bloody knife in the sink and looked around to see if there was anything else, when I heard "Pete … here," and looked up to see the gun in mid-air. I turned, catching it awkwardly, the barrel slipping between my legs and pointing into my crotch.

I grabbed at it, fumbling, then my hand found the grip, and I lifted my hand and pointed it at Tony, just as he was starting to come toward me. I squeezed the trigger, the loud bang echoing off the kitchen walls, and watched as the bullet hit Tony in the left shoulder, staggering him. I squeezed again, another loud bang, this time hitting him in the left thigh, and he dropped to the floor holding his leg.

I cocked the hammer, walked over and stood over him, holding the gun out, inches from the top of his head, the barrel lightly touching his forehead. Tonys' eyes were glassy as he looked up at me.

"You were wrong, pawdner," I drawled out as I pulled the trigger, the loud bang and muzzle flash, as the top of his head blew clean off, fragments of bone, tissue, brain, and hair splattering my face and the wall behind him. The top of his head was blood red, and I could see bits and pieces of his brain exposed as his head drooped and his body slumped forward against my knees. I pushed him roughly to the side, stepped back, put the safety on and threw the gun in the sink. I called out for Mo and headed towards the living room.

Mo, dazed and battered, was sitting on the floor, head down, watching the blood drip in small puddles on the carpet. I went into the kitchen, found some cloths and knelt beside her.

"Here," I said as I reached out and started to wipe. She grasped my hand and said, "I got it." I let her finish wiping then helped her up. She was unsteady on her feet, her face red, and she was wearing a vacant stare. I pushed her hair back from her face and pulled her into me. We stood there, holding each other up, and that was all we could do, both our bodies and brains numb.

"Let's get some air," I said. I held her against my side, as we shuffled over to the front door.

"Bandit," she whimpered, looking through the opening. "Bandit."

"We'll find him. He's tough, he'll be okay," I tried to reassure her. I walked us outside, the damp cool air hitting us immediately. Mo was still unsteady, and I held her as we stood on the porch, watching our breath make tiny white puffs in the night.

"Let's move into the light," I said.

I led her over near the tree, the one ironically surrounded on three sides by the two-foot high, badly faded, white picket fence. We stood shivering under the glow of the moonlight. We were both numb and in pain. My right wrist and forearm, if they weren't broken, were severely cracked. I had trouble breathing and feeling my ribs, I knew some were cracked. My shoulder was numb, and my thigh was sticky, and the back of my head ached. Mo was badly beaten up also. Her nose looked broken, and I worried about internal bleeding from the force of Tony's blow to her stomach. Mo looked over at the broken window and whimpered softly, "Bandit ..."

I squeezed her, rubbing her shoulder. We could hear dogs barking off in the distance, and I knew the cops would here soon; gunshots eventually draw attention. I was surprised we didn't hear sirens or see flashing lights yet.

"Baby … it's over … I'm sorry … but it's over … time for our normal day finally."

Mo squeezed me. "I know … I'm sorry too … I'm just glad you're here. I never believed for one moment you were dead."

I squeezed back, marveling at how I was so lucky. Despite everything, we had found each other, and now we could finally start living. I had never met anyone as beautiful, inside and out, never felt the depth of love as I did with her. We fit perfectly. It had all been worth it, every second of it, and I thought at that moment, I wouldn't trade any of it, because, each and every single bit of it, had led me to her, and her to me.

A chance meeting one morning on a bridge, all because of a stupid box.

"So, look at you. You finally got your white picket fence all by yourself, and you didn't need my help with this one. Look at you, all grown up like."

I froze, as I watched the body emerge from of the shadows and move into the light, turning and facing me. Mo, holding on to me, shifted behind me.

"Who's that?" she whispered.

I didn't respond, my eyes glued to the dark figure.

"Well … aren't you going to tell her who I am? Come on, Pete-boy, don't be so surprised."

"Pete? Who is he?" Mo asked.

"I'm his best friend. I'm the one that made him. Or didn't he tell you that?"

"You're Dale …"

"Give that girl a stuffed animal. That's what you lovebirds do, right? Give each other stuffed toys. All those token affections of your love."

"What do you want?" I asked blankly.

Dale laughed, a maniacal haunting belly laugh.

"What I've always wanted, and what I always get, power, buddy boy, nothing but power."

"If it's the money, I don't have it. If you're after Teddy's money, it's down at Sharkees in the trunk of my Chevy. Help yourself. Tell Patty to give you the keys, and you can keep the car too."

Dale exploded. "That stupid fucking car! You and that stupid car, and all those sob stories about you and your dad."

I looked on in bewilderment, having no idea where this was coming from.

"When are you going to fucking grow up?"

It was still a surprise to hear Dale swear.

"Yes, buddy boy. I swear. All the time. Just not around you."

Looking at Mo behind me. "It was me that taught him how to be honourable you know. Me!" Dale pounded his chest. "It was me …"

"I know it was you. You gave me a gift. But why? Why are you upset at that?"

Dale waved his hand. "Because you never listened, that's why."

"Huh? What do you mean I never listened? I always listened to you. You taught me the honour code. I did what you told me, and married Joanna. We bought a house and tried to have kids, just like you and Karen. I did everything you wanted."

And then it hit me. I had done everything *he* wanted, and it wasn't what I wanted, and why it had failed, why everything had failed. And why I had left the force. I couldn't breathe living under Dale's shadow on his terms. One couldn't continue to try and fit a round peg into a square hole.

"That's it, isn't it? Whenever I pulled away and lived on my terms, you couldn't accept it. That's what all this is about."

I thought back to when he met Syd and poked fun at me. And in Halifax at the game, when I showed him the picture of Mo, he barely looked at it. And why he had failed to back me up. None of it was Dale-approved. Dale provided, did something for you, but it came with a hefty price tag; you had to pay it back. You always had to pay, there was always a debt attached to it. Me, Teddy, Sara, we all owed Dale on some level, forever remaining in his debt.

I wondered how many others were out there, owing Dale? That's what made Dale tick: power. Dale was the Pied Piper, and we were his followers, the rats trailing behind blindly. He hated my car, because it wasn't his type of car. He hated the women I dated, because they weren't the women he thought I should date. He hated it when I thumbed my nose at authority, because it was something he could never do. And he hated my dad, because I had been close to him, and I guess after my dad, I never got as close to Dale as he wanted. It all added up and made sense.

"So, what now, Dale? Do you want to extract another pound of flesh? Just take the money and go."

There was a brief flash, as Dale holding a gun, the barrel came up. I reached around and pushed Mo further behind me, shielding her from Dale.

"Stay behind me, okay?" I whispered. I could feel Mo nod, her warm breath on my neck.

"I'm not going to tell, Dale. I don't care what you and Teddy and Sara did. I don't care. I'm finally happy, and for the life of me, I can't understand why you're not for me. I trusted you. I had your back, and you had mine. That's what best friends do. So, I don't understand and honestly, I don't care anymore. I'm sorry. I wish there were something I could do to fix it, fix this. I'm happy. I like who I am, and no one's going to take that away from me anymore. Not you, not Tony, not Teddy. I just want to stay here. I just want to live a normal day, do normal things. I'm going to apply here to get on the force; Mo is going to open a dance studio. All normal everyday things. You should be happy for me. So, if you're worried I'm going to spill, you're wrong. I can sleep at night, and that's all that matters to me."

"See? That's the problem, Pete-boy. I can't have you sleeping at night."

"Huh? What do you mean?"

Dale's arm came up, and the shot rang out before I could react. A soft pop and muzzle flash, then I felt something fall against my legs, and I knew she was gone. I froze in horror, unable to speak, as I stood staring at Dale, his hand holding the gun at his side.

"WHY!" I screamed into the night, falling to the ground, reaching for Mo. "WHY?"

Her body, lifeless, limp, I sat on the ground and lifted her head into my lap, cradling it, as it fell off to the side, and I lifted it back up. Her eyes were closed like she was sleeping, and I brushed the hair away from her face, rocking her gently.

"Why?" I said softly to my best friend. "Why? … WHY?" I started crying hysterically.

"Oh baby, it's going to be okay. He was just playing around, that's all … come on wake up please … come on Mo, wake up baby, please," I moaned, patting her cheek. "Mo baby, wake up! Oh, Mo, Mo, Mo … wake up, please?" as I shook her shoulders frantically.

"Help me, Dale. Help me wake her up, please? Come on Dale, please? Mo baby wake up … Mo baby …" holding Mo, crying and rocking, pleading to Dale.

"Oh God Mo … oh God no," I wailed.

Dale stood across from me, silent, watching. I rubbed Mo's head, caressed her face, ran my fingers over her mouth, lightly pushing them inside feeling her teeth. I ran my fingers over her eyes, gently touching her eyelids, pushing them open, but her eyes were lifeless, staring straight ahead. I ran my hands up and down her arms, trying to keep her warm. Her legs were bent, and I reached down, and pushed them out, rubbing her thighs; hoping somehow all the rubbing would revive her and bring her back to me. And then, we could start our normal day just like we had promised each other we would. It was going to start right now, I promise. I sat, rocking Mo, her head rolling off on an angle, and each time I would pull it up and position it. I tired from trying to keep it in place in my lap, so I gently placed her body on the ground, carefully placing her hands over her stomach and stretched out her legs so they weren't bent, adjusted her head, so it lay flat. Then I stood up and faced Dale.

"Why?" I pleaded. "Why?" tears streaming down my cheeks, my voice quivering and shaking. "Why?" slumping to the ground beside Mo, sobbing. "Why?" I mumbled, lying on my side, staring at Mo's body. I forced myself to get up and unsteadily moved closer to Dale. He remained silent, staring at me with a blank expression. Finally, he spoke.

"I can give you a thousand reasons why … but … I don't care, and I'm not sorry."

Before I could react, his hand came up, holding his gun under his chin, he pulled the trigger. Another soft pop and muzzle flash, I watched as the bullet went straight through his chin, up through his brain, out the top of his head. He fell face forward on the ground, the blood oozing out of the hole, spreading out over his head. It was like a bad dream, and I couldn't comprehend any of it. There at my feet, dead, was my best friend, who had just killed himself. Behind me, was the love of my life, also dead, courtesy of my best friend. And yet, here I was, the lucky one after all, alive. *I would rather have been dead.*

I looked up into the crystal clear night sky, filled with a bright white full moon and twinkling stars, but none of those stars bore my name; the sky overhead was filled with nothing but unlucky stars. I thought how beautiful the universe looked, from up there, not down here. I slumped to the ground, and crawled on all fours over to Dale, forcibly removed his fingers and hand from the gun, and took it in my own hands. I shifted to my knees and put the barrel under my chin, cocking the hammer. Putting pressure on the trigger, I slowly squeezed. *Almost home*, I thought. *Be right there, Mo honey. See you in a minute, baby, and I promise I will always be with you. I love you.*

I applied a bit more pressure, and I could hear the last faint click as the trigger locked.

"Don't."

"Huh?"

"Don't."

"Why not?" I asked. "Give me one good reason."

"You can do this," the voice said reassuringly. "You, me. We can do this."

"Who's me? We?"

My hand still on the trigger, one tiny slight pull away from freedom, and Mo. The voice spoke again.

"Me ... I'm you. We are We—Me and You," the voice said softly.

"I can't do this," I said, my hand trembling.

"Yes, you can," the voice responded. "I promise to be right here with you."

"But you will leave just like everyone else."

"No, I won't."

"How do you know that?"

"Because I'm You. I've been here all along ... I've been waiting. I knew one day it would be time to let me in. And I'm here now."

I didn't know what to think. *Was it my subconscious talking or maybe the universe?* I started to lower my hands but stopped and cried out.

"NO! I can't do this, I can't ... I don't want to be here anymore. Mo baby, I'm so sorry ... I love you so much ... Mo!" I wailed into the night. I put the gun up under my chin and started to squeeze.

"Please don't. Put the gun down, please," the voice said softly. "Please."

I don't know why but I did, and as I lowered my hands, the gun went off.

80

NURSE CASSIE WAS evil, pure evil, through and through. Anyone could see that, anyone but me, that is. But I could sense it. They say when you lose your sight, even temporarily, the other senses kick in automatically to compensate for it. So, I couldn't see her, but I could sense her, hear her, but that's where it stopped. I didn't want anything to do with touch or taste. At least not with her. She would stand in the doorway, at all hours, and just watch me. I could feel her, her eyes burrowing through me, and I don't know why she hated me. What had I ever done to her? Oh sure, when they first brought me in, I wasn't the best patient. And yes, maybe I was just a teeny bit defiant. Okay, fine, I was a little more than that.

But was that any reason to hate someone just because they threw their tray of food across the room, and where it left long dripping lines down the wall where the food stuck like plaster? I could see her being a little angry, as I did it four, no make that, five days straight. And I'm sure it was hard on her, and the others, when I wouldn't pee in the bottle for the tests the doctor had ordered, and instead, I tried to write my name across the bathroom wall, yelling at the top of my lungs, and making everyone come running, when I couldn't quite squeeze out the last *E*. Is any of that reason to hate someone? I don't think so.

And I could see her being a little miffed when I half-heartedly performed the mandatory exercises that would help me get back on my feet; sitting on the edge of my bed, swinging my legs and flapping my arms, instead of getting up and walking the floor like all the others. I mean, why give up your cozy warm bed, and live in total darkness, where you were completely safe and sheltered, protected from the big bad outside world? I had found a normal day to my liking, so I certainly wasn't going to wreck a good thing; no fucking way I was giving that up, for anyone, or anything.

Nurse Cassie. I heard her name mentioned so often, I did the math. Drill Sergeant + Nurse Cassie-this + Nurse Cassis-that = Evil. And I learned her last name quickly. Sigh. Sigh was her last name. Nurse Cassie-Sigh, because that was the only sound I ever heard coming from her. Well, besides her constant barking. She and the doctors would consult, just outside my room, talking in hushed tones about me. Just loud enough that I could make out the words.

"Temporary loss ... trauma ... broken something ... head ... denial ... permanent maybe ... long road ahead."

I don't know about you, but no one likes to be talked about. In my case, it wasn't behind my back, it was in front of me, sort of. I couldn't see them, but they could see me. And I could hear them, but they didn't want to hear me. That was getting mighty frustrating because, where I wanted a two-way conversation, all I got was one-way: orders, orders, and more orders.

Do this, do that, drink this, drink that, eat this, eat that; it's good for you. Get up, lift this, touch that, walk here, walk there. And it didn't seem fair, as I was supposed to listen to them, but they weren't listening to me. When I spoke, they, mostly Nurse Cassie, ignored me. They weren't listening, or maybe, they weren't hearing me. Funny, but I sure heard them. So naturally, I did what anyone would do, I tried to make myself heard, raising my voice until I was heard. And it was weird, because, that didn't seem to do it, finally giving up because all the yelling made me hoarse.

Hospital life was different, never mind the constant beeping, and I started to tell time by the movements in the corridor, and by the feeling in the air. I could tell when the morning came just by lying in bed and listening. How the stirring would begin slowly, coughing, rustling, doors opening and closing, carts banging, traffic in the corridor would get heavier, the rubber-soled shoes squeaking, and I could tell when someone came on the floor who didn't work there. Just by the sound their shoes made on the floor. I could tell if it was a visitor, male or female, even a child, all by the sound their feet made.

Traffic would tail off after breakfast, things would quiet down; then, as lunch approached, the pace picked up again. The food carts rattling and squeaking, as they made their rounds on the floor, people moving about from room to room. Then things would slacken, mid-afternoon pleasant, as it was nap time. Two hours later, dinner time, the hustle and bustle slowly building, peaking to a loud banging crescendo, then just like that, things settled in for the night, just the soft squeaks of the attendants making their rounds. Oh, did I mention the incessant beeping?

Which brings me to my constant visitors. Just like everything else, they ran like clockwork, always visiting at the same time. The elevator doors would open, out would come four legs, always four, striding with a purpose; heavy strides in soft-soled shoes, but not hospital shoes, the soles squeaked with a different type of authority. Soft-soled shoes of a different kind, the kind that wore a badge, visiting so often we were almost on a first-name basis, almost. Just as the visits were regular, so were the questions. Always the same questions, by the same person, the other one never spoke, and I thought maybe they were mute.

The questions always started with: We are sorry for your loss. What happened? Who were they? Where did you know them from? Where was the money? And it was always the same answers: I don't remember, I don't know, I don't know, and what money? You would think they would have gotten tired of the same answers and just left me alone. But they were persistent, and so was I, and around it went.

I also had another visitor. This went on for a few days actually. I couldn't see who it was, but I could sense their presence and quickly discovered the pattern, same time every day, and the same result. Someone, female, guessing by the footsteps, would come down the hall, and stand in the doorway. I could feel them looking at me. Whoever it was, remained silent, only the slightest rustle of clothing indicating their presence. When I called out, they didn't respond. By the fifth day, I was starting to become uncomfortable with it, so I asked Nurse Cassie. But she said I must be hallucinating, as no one was there, but I didn't believe her. Adrian popped by regularly, but I hadn't seen or heard from Bree, and I thought that was strange. Then on the sixth day, when the person was standing at the doorway, I could hear the person breathing followed by a quick click.

I called out, "Who's there? I know someone is there. Is that you, Bree?" But there was no answer, then I heard the person turn and leave, but this time they stopped just outside the doorway, and I could hear talking. More like whispers, in low, hushed tones. I couldn't make anything out, just that more than one person was talking. Then, I heard some shuffling, and it was quiet, and no one was there anymore.

This went on for three more days, I was now way beyond uncomfortable, which I speculated was the intention. The next day I decided not to call out and instead just listened. Everything was still, with just the usual normal hospital noises in the background. I heard some more rustling then a voice.

"Why?"

My insides froze at the sound of the voice, and I knew exactly what the question was implying.

"I don't know," I replied.

My stomach churned, my throat constricted, and I had trouble breathing. My eyes welled up, and I started gasping, searching for air, my chest heaving. I slowed myself down, looking in the direction of the doorway.

"I'm sorry. I know ... I know I screwed up ... I wanted a life for us so bad ... I couldn't see ... I never wanted any of this to happen ... I should've ... I should've just left, taking all this with me ... I should have left that next day after I came to see you ... I shouldn't have to come to see you in the first place ... I'm sorry ... I'm so sorry."

Overcome with emotion, heavy sobs wracking my body, I fell back into the pillow, tears streaming down my cheeks. I lay like that for a long time, then drifted off to sleep. I woke a few hours later to the sound of dinner, opening my eyes, there was no one there. The next morning, just after the orderly had taken the breakfast tray away, there was someone in the doorway.

"Hello?" I called out. There was rustling, someone was coming closer, then I sensed them at the edge of the bed. Reaching out with my hand, "I can't ... I'm sorry ... I wish ... I can't change it ... please stop punishing me ... I know ... trust me I know. We both loved her. I know who she was to you ..."

Bree, reached out, taking my hand in hers, and just like our first encounter, her hand was soft and warm. She squeezed it, remaining silent, then let go and stepped back. I could hear the sound of a chair being pulled forward, she sat down and reached for my hand again. She stroked it softly, remaining silent, then twenty minutes later, she got up, leaned over, kissed me on the top of my head, and said, "See you tomorrow."

Bree returned the next afternoon, and slowly, over the next week, I learned about her friendship with Mo. It was extremely difficult hearing how much Mo meant to her, the impact they had on each other, and my heart ached, which was Bree's intent, for me to feel her hurt. Bree said she had been speaking with Nurse Cassie and the doctors daily and was getting concerned, as I wasn't making any progress, and I would never get out of there at this rate. I told Bree how much I hated Nurse Cassie-Sigh, that she was always on me, and I couldn't breathe. I asked Bree about getting another nurse assigned, and maybe then, I would start recovering faster. Bree patted my hands and said she would check.

One night, it was late, maybe midnight or so, and the floor was quiet. I was lying in bed staring at the ceiling, thinking about how Mo and I used to play shadow puppets on the cloth walls of the blanket fort. A nurse softly made her rounds, stopping at each doorway, poking her head in, and checking. She must have been new because I had never *seen* her before, and when she stopped at my door, she just stood there. It was strange, because I could feel her presence. I waited, thinking she would leave. But unlike Nurse Cassie, I could feel the warmth and comfort emanating across the room. I looked toward where I thought she was standing.

"Hello?"

She remained quiet, and I thought maybe I was dreaming, but I knew I wasn't imagining Mo. That much I knew. So, I called out again.

"Hello? Is anyone there?"

"Yes, I'm here. Hello," she said, her voice gentle and warm.

"Are you new?" I asked. "I've never seen you before."

"Yes, I am. Right out of college. I started tonight. This is my first shift. My first floor. I'm walking around trying to become familiar."

"Nice to meet you," I said, shifting, sitting up in the bed.

"You're Pete. I read your chart."

"Yes, that's me. Bad boy Pete. I'm sure you've heard all the stories."

"Yes, I was warned about you. Nurse Cassie said you were a handful, but I think she's wrong. You don't seem like such a handful."

"Ahh, that Nurse Cassie. She hates me. Nurse Cassie-Sigh, that's her name you know."

"I don't think she does," she said. "She's just doing her job. We all are. We care about our patients. I know it doesn't always show, but we do. Or, at least I do."

She moved from the doorway stopping at the foot of the bed. I could feel her. I could feel her aura, and it was glowing. That's their aura. Everyone has one. She moved closer, inches from me, and though I couldn't see, I looked up towards where I thought she was. She spoke softly, and I could feel the power of her energy.

"Pete."

"Yes."

"Pete, the way is forward. What happened was awful, but you can't stay here, hiding. The way is forward. I can't imagine how hard it is, but you can't give up. You can't. And no one, me, Nurse Cassie, or any of the others, can do this for you. The longer you fight, the longer you resist, the longer it takes. Don't fight the universe. I know you know this. Let it work for you, don't resist, fight back, but fight back right. Fight back with a purpose. One day at a time, one step at a time. The universe has a plan for you, and it has your back, but you have to let it. Don't try and push that rope. Pull it, and it will guide you. The universe brought you and Mo together for a reason. Just because Mo's gone doesn't mean the reason still isn't here. Trust your instincts, trust in yourself."

How did she know about Mo?

I began to cry, embarrassed, but she said it was okay and understood. She said she had to finish her rounds and that someone would check in on me later. I listened as she turned away and walked out, and I could feel a slight breeze come from the doorway, her shoes making faint squeaks as she went down the corridor.

She was right. She hadn't told me anything I didn't already know. Denial, once more, had been lying in wait, latching on the moment I let it. But this was one time when I couldn't be angry at myself for it, it was the only coping mechanism I had available at the time.

Once again, I had been lucky. The gun had gone off, the bullet going straight up, burning the tip of my nose, and being lucky and all, landing harmlessly in a yard nearby; the bright flash temporarily blinding me. And I knew the trauma of that night had a hand in it also. Lying in darkness, refusing to get out of bed, was safe. I was protected by Nurse Cassie because the more I resisted, the more she pushed, and the longer I remained where I was, I remained safe and protected from living. I had to start living again, painful and scary as it was. The way was forward: life, living, surviving.

Next morning, I was up and out of my bed, stretching and feeling my way around my room. I made my bed, tidied up as best I could, found my way to the bathroom, showered and attempted to shave, but gave up, thinking one step at a time and not two. When I peed, I lifted the seat, then wiped the bowl; I was on a mission. Returning to my bed, I waited for breakfast. Nurse Cassie, as usual, arrived right on time, and I could sense she was surprised to see me up and dressed, waiting. She didn't say a word, as she checked my vitals and added them to my chart. When she left, she stopped at the doorway and turned, and I knew she was staring at me. I had no idea what she was thinking or feeling and didn't care. *I'll show you!* I yelled telepathically at her.

The days flew by, each day I was getting stronger, doing laps around the floor daily, cheerily greeting the other patients, as I passed by their rooms. I was soon bored with that, so with help from another set of eyes, I started a bedpan relay race with the other patients. We walked quickly around the floor, carrying bedpans, empty, then handing them to the next patient, waiting at the end of the lap. We were all cheering and laughing, and I wish I could have seen Nurse Cassie's face. Or, maybe not, wearing her perpetual frown, but I didn't care.

Bree noticed the improvement, and was much happier, lifting both our spirits. One night she snuck in after visiting hours were over, bringing me a donut and a chocolate shake. She sat in the chair at the edge of my bed, and we had a nice little party. I was worried as Nurse Cassie was on that night, and every time I heard footsteps coming from the corridor, my heart would jump. But if she saw us, she let us be. I was talking to Bree, and she wasn't listening, having fallen asleep in the chair. I called out to her, she stirred, jumping up, worried something was wrong.

"Come lie with me," I said, patting the bed.

"Where?"

"Here, come lie with me," I patted the bed again.

"Are you sure it will be okay?"

"Yes," shifting to one side, pulling over the blanket.

Bree gingerly crawled up on the bed and lay down beside me, cradling her head in my shoulder, snuggling in.

"I miss her," Bree started to cry.

"Me too. I'm sorry, I never meant for any of this to happen. I wish I could turn it back. Go back, you know? Oh, Mo … Mo sweet Mo, I miss you so much."

I began to cry also, and we lay holding each other tightly, just letting our grief pour out. We must have fallen asleep, woken the next morning by the sounds of the new day. Stirring, I felt a blanket over top us, placed there during the night.

Two mornings later, my eyes closed, but I was awake, playing possum; Nurse Cassie standing at the foot of my bed reading my chart. Stretching, my arms raised behind my head, yawning, exhaling loudly, I resisted the temptation to fart. Recalling, the time I did, purposely to annoy her, and after, she wouldn't speak to me for the next few days. I hated her, but I found I hated her more when she wasn't barking or growling at me.

Scratching my stomach, rubbing my eyes, I opened them, and there standing in the flesh was Nurse Cassie-Sigh. She was pretty. Her dark brown hair, streaked with white highlights, was piled in a bun on the top of her head, curly bangs stretching down the sides of her face. She wore a white sweater over a pink nurse's uniform. Her glasses hung loosely at the end of her nose and she would push them back with her thumb every few seconds, only for them to fall forward again. But I still hated her. I thought I was dreaming, rubbing my eyes, I shut them tight, counted to three, and opened them to Nurse Cassie-Sigh, live and in technicolour.

"Good morning," I said.

"Good morning," she replied in that same dreary monotone, her head down, reading my chart, not bothering to look up.

"You look nice today."

"Thank you," she said, her head still down.

"New sweater?" I asked.

"Yes, last week."

"White looks good on you."

"What?" her head jerked up, mouth open wide.

Smiling like a Cheshire cat, I stared blankly straight ahead. Nurse Cassie looked at me, tilting her head, searching my eyes. Her body turned, as she leaned over, looking at me, waiting to see if my eyes followed. She continued to look at me, my eyes straight ahead.

"Hmph," returning to her clipboard.

She started writing, my eyes following her, but she stopped and looked up. I remained staring straight ahead. Sighing, she started writing but stopped again, looking at me. Turning her head, checking if anyone was watching, she brought her hands up to her ears and started flapping them, sticking her tongue out at me. I remained stock still, staring blankly straight ahead.

"Hmph," looking down at the chart, she continued writing.

I looked over at the window, the trees almost bare.

"I wonder when the snow will fly?" I said to her.

"Soon," was her muffled reply, her head still down.

Carefully lifting the covers, swinging my legs out on the floor, Nurse Cassie was still at the foot of the bed, head down, writing.

"It's a perfect day for the wheelchair races," I suggested.

"That's nice," Nurse Cassie responded in her pitch-perfect monotone drone.

I covered my mouth, snickering, slid my butt off the bed and took a long side step to the wheelchair parked just to the left of the bed. I took hold of the handlebar, slowly turning the chair so it was facing the door and gripped the handlebars with both hands.

"On your mark! Get set! GO!" I yelled.

I ran out the door and down the hall, whooping and hollering.

Nurse Cassie didn't visit as often anymore, then eventually stopped altogether, another nurse taking her place. And strangely, I started to miss Nurse Cassie. I missed her barking and constantly telling me what to do. I missed her monotone drone and that she was always annoyed with me. *Careful what you wish for, huh?* The other nurse was nicer and gentler, but I missed Nurse Cassie. Despite this, I was progressing rapidly now, pushing myself, as if Nurse Cassie was there, and two weeks later, I was ready for discharge.

The morning of discharge came, and Bree waited for me downstairs. I told her to wait there, as I didn't want her pushing me out in a wheelchair. When it came time to leave, an orderly arrived with a wheelchair, but I flatly refused to get in. The poor guy was only doing his job, but I wanted no part of it. We were at a stalemate in the doorway, and I refused to budge. Nurse Cassie hearing the commotion came out of the nurse's station, walking towards me.

"What's wrong?" she asked the orderly.

"He refuses to let me push him in the wheelchair."

Nurse Cassie looked at me with her usual frown. "Is that true?"

"Yes."

Bracing for a barrage of some sort, instead, she calmly asked the both of us, if I walked beside the chair, and the orderly pushed it, would that work? I looked at Nurse Cassie, then at the orderly, and said yes, that would work for me. The orderly reluctantly agreed, no doubt fearing some union repercussions.

"Okay then. There you go, Pete. Problem solved," she said coldly, returning to her station.

I dropped my bag in the seat of the chair, and the orderly moved behind, and in tandem, we headed towards the elevator. As we passed the nurse's station, I looked over and saw Nurse Cassie's head buried in the computer screen. I heard squeaking and the sound of chair wheels and stopped. Nurse Cassie came out from behind the nurse's station and stood in front of me. We looked at each other, but I didn't have any words. I was almost going to turn away when she spoke.

"I'm curious, Pete. You were on the road to nowhere, and then overnight, you were on the road to recovery. What changed?"

I stepped toward her. "Your new nurse. She stopped in to see me the first night she started on the floor, and we talked a bit. I have been looking for her, to thank her, but I haven't seen her since. Would you thank her for me please, when you see her?"

Nurse Cassie looked at me puzzled. "What new nurse?"

"The new nurse you have. Um, I couldn't see her, I was still blind, but she said she was new and it was her first shift. So I thought …"

Nurse Cassie shook her head. "Pete, the trauma unit is staffed entirely by experienced nurses and doctors. No one sets foot on this floor unless they have a minimum of ten years service."

Too much had happened to make any sense of it. I turned toward the elevator and waited. Getting on, I looked out, Nurse Cassie looking back, as the doors closed.

81

I WASN'T READY to return to Mo's, and I didn't know if I would ever be able to. Bree drove by a few times to check on her place, and it was the same: the yellow tape covering the driveway, wrapping along both sides of the yard, strands of it that had let go blowing lazily in the wind. She hadn't gone inside, and I understood why. That was going to be a difficult day, as everything remained as it was. Bree set me up in her spare room, and she and Adrian went to great lengths to make it as homey as possible. I had a comfy bed, it was quiet, my room in the back, and we quickly got into sync sharing the one bathroom.

Their relationship was similar, in that they had their own unique schtick, constantly poking fun at one another. I was happy for them, as they fit perfectly in their own way. But it was difficult to be around, as there I was, on the outside looking in, my hands pressed to the windowpane, nose against the glass. Bree encouraged me to come to The Club, which hesitantly, I did, unable to look in the direction of the pool table. So, I hung out in the kitchen with Adrian, and at both their urging, started tending bar on the quieter nights. Bree said I was a natural, and I must admit I enjoyed it. It was nice to be on the other side for a change, especially at closing time. I was hit on a few times by the cougar crowd, and typically, would flirt back, but I ignored them for the most part and stayed busy.

I missed my wheels, so I texted Patty to see if she could come up soon. She texted back that she would be up the next afternoon, which was so Patty, and no doubt wishing it was a sixteen-hour drive instead. Sure enough, around four the next afternoon, Patty came breezing down the stairs, and once I introduced her to Bree that was it. They hit it off immediately, and before you know it, they were off in the corner of the bar, chatting and giggling like school girls. I joked with poor Adrian that he was now dating twins.

Patty asked how I was holding up. Then said the cops had been in a few times to question her, but everything seemed low-key for now. After she returned from dropping me off at the airport, she had called 911, and it was like a TV show she said. All these squad cars and ambulances pulling up, yellow tape everywhere, forensics people swabbing and dusting anything that moved. But her sense was it was just another unsolved murder to go along with all the others.

Patty learned someone came forward, looking after Teddy's funeral, but she didn't know who or where he was buried. She told me that when the Sharkees regulars discovered they had missed out on a dead body, they were genuinely pissed at her, and as a form of protest, they boycotted Sharkees for all of twenty-four hours.

I asked about Sara, but she hadn't heard from her, though she had texted her a few times. Give her time, I told Patty. Switching gears, Patty said my Chevy ran great and hoped I wouldn't mind that she adjusted the Hurst shifter, the problem with coming out of third gear no more. I laughed and thanked her. Then she said there was just one more teeny-weeny little thing, and I braced myself.

"Um … uh … yeah, your eight-track things? Did you know that if you insert the tape with the label upside down, it doesn't play? I didn't know that. And did you know the tape can unspool inside the deck, and it's like spaghetti everywhere? I'm sorry, but Blue Oyster something or other, went all garbled, then barfed. You can buy another one, right? And I'll pay you for it."

I waved it off, hiding my disappointment, and thought at least it was only Blue Oyster Cult who met the grim reaper, and it wasn't the Doobie Brothers or worse, Foghat. Patty was heading back in the morning, and I told her to use my room at Bree's, and I would bunk at the club, which took about, oh, maybe two seconds of convincing. The look on Adrian's face was priceless, and I spent the rest of the night teasing him about it.

The following day, the weather changed as a storm blew in, which disappointed Patty not in the least. She happily went to the club with Bree, then promptly took over, much to Bree's delight, readily accepting her suggestions. When the storm cleared the next day, Patty stayed on, as she was having too much fun, and they made a good team, working hard on the improvements. I must admit it was a nice reprieve from everything, and I found it healing in its own way, watching Bree and Patty run the club, much to Adrian's chagrin.

Patty was a carbon copy of Bree, in that she barked orders at Adrian and was constantly teasing him. One day, Adrian pulled me aside and said it was like dating the two of them at once, minus the sleeping and fun parts. Don't even go there, I admonished him, but I suspected he was only joking. Maybe.

Then, sure enough, it happened. The Two-for-Tuesday dance-n-beer night, where Bree and Patty waded out onto the dance floor to break up a fight. They separated two hulking lumber-jacketed dudes, who had started it over, wait for it, a girl. Adrian and I watched from behind the bar, playing lifeguard just in case, but they had everything under control, thoroughly enjoying the free entertainment it brought. Bree and Patty, up on their tiptoes, shaking their fists in the combatants' faces, giving them a thorough tongue lashing, the crowd cheering as they walked back to the bar.

Eventually, all good things must end, and Patty needed to get back. I texted Meg, who found her a standby flight back to Ottawa the next day. I picked Patty up at the club in the morning, but not before tearful goodbyes, hugs, and exchanges of numbers, with promises to stay in touch, and God knows what else instant friends like that do. I let Patty drive, and we took the long way, past Gillies Lake, out along the two-lane blacktop, then across to the airport. I told Patty to let her rip and that we did, roaring down the road, the windows down, the tunes blasting, high school kids out with Daddy's car. We parked in front the departure gate, and Patty got out, letting me get in, and gave me a long puppy dog face.

"Pete, don't ever sell that car unless it's to me."

I laughed and said sure.

"Pinky?" holding her hand out, as we pinky swore. Turning serious, she asked what was next? I told her I honestly didn't know. She could tell I was restless and unsettled, and she understood. She also said that I was a natural to tend bar and offered that I could come work at Sharkees and she would teach me the ropes. And she would help me set up with my own bar if I wanted. I thanked her, and once again, here I was, the lucky one. She patted my arm through the window and said the door was always open. I nodded and started to pull away when I heard her call out. I stopped and leaned my head out the window.

"The money belt is in the trunk under the tire cover."

I smiled, waved and pulled away, and watched her enter the terminal in the rear-view mirror. Funny, I had completely forgotten all about the money.

82

DRIVING BACK INTO town, I pulled over and texted Bree. It was time, and I told her to meet me at the cemetery in an hour. The weather fit perfectly with what I had to do. The sky dark grey, filled with clouds as far as the eye could see, the wind blowing from the north, alternating between rain and light snow. It was a Hollywood funeral made for the moment if there ever was one. I parked on the street facing the cemetery and waited. I stared straight ahead, unable to look to the right. A few minutes later, Bree pulled up, and we got out. She looked stunning with her hair up, in a dark blue dress and heels, covered by a long blue trench coat. Her bare legs must have been freezing and I know Mo would have appreciated the gesture.

"Ready?" she asked, and I nodded solemnly.

Reaching for my hand we turned right, and she led me along the gravel road toward the marker. The wind was blowing hard, it had started to rain, and we shielded our faces. About fifty yards down, Bree stopped and looked, then pointed to her left.

"It's just over there."

She gingerly stepped through the grass in her heels, trying to avoid the soft patches as I trailed behind. She reached back for my hand, finding it, she clasped her hand around mine and squeezed.

"Almost there," she said. A few more steps, then Bree stopped, and we turned: Mo. The grave remained fresh, dirt still scattered about, a temporary cross over it. We stood holding hands, looking down. I brought my hand up to my mouth, as the tears started streaming down. I started shaking, I couldn't stop, and there was nothing I could do but just be. Bree held my arm tightly, looking at her, she was crying also, large tears rolling down her cheeks.

"Oh God … Mo … I miss you so much … I love you so much … I wish … I wish …"

Bree held tight.

"It's okay, Pete. She knows … I know she knows …"

Time seemed to stop, as I wished and hoped and prayed, making every deal imaginable with the universe, God, and everyone else, pleading my life for hers, I would go right now, I begged. Please bring her back. I promise I will be good. I will do anything. Just please take me. Please. Take me instead. Just bring her back. Please. I begged and begged, promised and promised, pleaded and pleaded, but none of it was answered. Because that's not how it works, and I knew it. I would have given everything and anything to have Mo back. *Mo, sweet Mo.*

"Pete … Pete? Do you want me to say something?"

"Huh? Yes, please. I know she would like that."

Letting go of Bree's hand I lowered my head, closed my eyes, folding my hands across my front, I bit my lip, trying to stop crying, but it was useless. Bree looked up into the sky.

"Please God take care of her. She was one of the good ones. She was the best friend one could ever have, and this guy standing beside me, well he done fucked up big time. I know it, he knows it, and I know you know it. It is going to take time for all of us to forgive him. The only good thing he did, and please forgive me God, but that slimeball Tony had it coming. He did good on that so please be gentle with him. I hope God, you can find a place in your heart to forgive him, and to help him forgive himself. He is a good man despite of what happened. This guy, Pete Humphries, loved Maureen Ferguson in a way others couldn't possibly imagine, and I know she loved him the same in return. Their love will remain forever. Please remember that, God and the universe, and whoever else, please remember in case you ever forget why you chose to take her like you did …"

Bree broke down into heavy sobs, unable to finish, and I had to hold on to her, as her legs gave out. Composing ourselves again, I made sure Bree was okay to stand on her own. I knelt in front of the marker, kissed my fingers, then, reaching out, I touched the head of the marker and ran my fingers across it.

"I love you, baby … I always will. Remember that day out on the bridge, and you pulled up on your bike, and I dropped the spark plug wrench under my car? I fell in love with you right at that moment. And remember when you rescued me from the fight, and we sat on the couch after? We both knew it didn't we? You are the most beautiful person I have ever seen. Oh, baby, I love you so much. Be safe. You're home now, and I promise one day I will be there right beside you."

I let my hand slide off the marker, stood up, and stepped back. Turning to Bree, swallowing hard, I said, "Let's go." She nodded and reached for my arm. I wrapped my arm around hers, and we walked slowly toward the gravel road, when I heard a faint meow and rustling in the bushes to the right of us. I stopped, Bree asking, what was wrong.

"Ssshh."

There was another faint meow and more rustling; coming out of the bushes was Bandit, limping badly, his back leg dragging on the ground. He crawled toward me; the meows, though faint, were more frequent.

"Bandit!" I called out. I started crying as I moved toward him, and he stopped and laid down, I reached out with my hand and he rubbed his nose against it. I reached down and gently lifted him into my arms. Bree and I were both crying as she rubbed his back.

He was in terrible condition, his fur all matted, chunks missing, pockmarks all over his back and stomach, his back leg badly cut, his ribs poking through his sides from lack of nourishment. I wrapped him inside my jacket, and I could feel him shivering and shaking. I felt his rough tongue on my finger, as he licked it. "Leave my car," I said.

Bree drove, once again, I was lucky, as the Vet was right across from The Club, and we were there in minutes. The Vet said with time, Bandit would recover, and she asked how we found him. I said it was a chance visit to the cemetery, and she said that had I waited a day longer, Bandit would not have survived the night, most likely dying in the bushes. Bree and I shuddered at the thought and pushed it from our minds. I asked the Vet how he knew to come out as he did, and she asked if I had been talking? I said yes, Bree and I were talking.

"He heard your voice and my guess is, he was waiting for someone he knew. You are a lucky man, Mr. Humphries."

Lucky?

Bree dropped me back at my car, and before getting in mine, I stood looking at the cemetery, then across the road at Mo's laneway. Bandit must have been searching for Mo and ended up there. Then he heard my voice. I shivered hard at thought of all of it. Looking again in the direction of Mo's, I told Bree it was time to go to her place. She asked if I wanted company, but I said this was something I had to do on my own. She went back to The Club and said she would remain in contact with the Vet.

I pulled into Mo's and parked in front of the gate and sat looking at the yellow tape blowing in the wind. I looked over at the tree, and the two-foot-high fence that ringed it on three sides, broken in places, only a few slats remained upright, and I laughed at the irony. I got out of the car, pulling at the loose strands of yellow tape blowing about, then I walked around the yard, removing the rest of it. I gathered it up in a ball and threw it in the back seat of my car. I walked over to the gate and peered over the top. There was Mo's bike, untouched, the cover over it. I started to cry and forced myself to stop.

Turning, I walked toward the front door and up the step. I pulled away some more strands of yellow tape and reaching for the handle, pulled open the door. There was the familiar loud squeak as I pushed down on the latch, and it opened. I stood in the doorway as the door swung back. Everything was untouched.

The blanket fort had collapsed into the middle. The chair that Tony had been sitting on lay overturned beside it. The couch was intact like nothing had happened, Mo's blanket still covering her spot, my pillow resting against the arm at my end. I gingerly walked across the carpet towards the kitchen, passing the bloodstains that littered the carpet, from where Tony had hit Mo.

The kitchen was a war zone, pots, pans, and cutlery, strewn everywhere; blood still covered the walls where I had shot Tony, long red drips lining the wall like curtain lights. There was broken glass on the tiled floor in front of the fridge and stove, and it cracked under my feet. I stood in the doorway, surveying the damage, numb. There was no other way to describe it. I knew it needed to be cleaned up, and I was the one who wanted to do that. And maybe it would be therapeutic, but just not today.

I walked out, closed the door behind me, and drove to The Club. I went straight behind the bar, poured myself two beers and two whisky chasers, dropped them in the mugs, picked the first mug up and drained it; then did the same for the second mug. I made two more and did the same; two more after that. After two more, Adrian tucked me in the cot in the office, and I slept like a baby.

I was up at dawn the next morning and headed straight to Mo's. Around eight that night, I returned to the club, and played rinse and repeat at the bar, once again Adrian tucking me in afterward. This went on for the next two days until Mo's place was completely clean, with no remnants of any kind remaining.

The timing was perfect, as once Mo's place was cleaned, Bandit had recovered sufficiently enough to come home. The problem was, what did home look like now? I knew I couldn't stay at Mo's. I did try one night.

I tried sitting down on the couch, but that was as far as I got. All I could feel was Mo and looking at her spot was like looking at a ghost. Same for the blanket fort. I put the fort back together, but when I went inside, I had to come right back out, as I started to hyperventilate.

The day Bandit was ready for pickup, I met Bree as she was coming into The Club, and I suggested to go for a walk. Walking along the sidewalk, towards the main drag, we talked.

"Bree, I tried, but I can't stay here. I can't. I'm sorry."

"Where will you go?" she asked, fighting off the tears, wiping at her eyes.

"I don't know yet. I just know that, at least for now, I can't stay here. I love you and Adrian; you both have done so much for me. But it's too fresh, you know? Everywhere I look, I see her. She's in everything."

"I know Pete, but honey, you can't run … you can't run from this," Bree pleaded.

"I know, but I'm not running. At least, I don't think I am. I just need space from here. Everything feels so heavy. Maybe with time, I could come back. I'm going to miss you. I love you; you know that, right?"

"And here all this time, I thought you hated me," she sniffled, trying to laugh.

"I hope you understand."

"I do, Pete. I just want you to be happy."

Happy? Define happy. Please.

All this time, I had wanted just a normal day. And now it seemed I had it; this was my new normal. Careful what you wish for.

We got to the end of the block and turned back, Bree holding my arm as we walked. We stopped and turned as we heard someone call out. Running along the sidewalk, pushing a stroller in front, someone was waving at us.

"Hey! Stop! Wait, hold on."

"Who's that? Do we know him?" I asked.

"Yes, that's Rick."

"Mo's ex-husband?"

"The one and only," sighed Bree, afraid of another drama-like encounter.

Rick, out of breath, stopped in front of us. The two babies were wrapped in matching blue snowsuits, and stared wide-eyed, as they sucked on bottles.

"Glad I saw you," Rick said between huffs, hunched over. "I have been looking for you all over town."

"Rick, you know I work at The Club, and I'm there all the time," Bree answered, annoyed, already on the defensive.

"No, not you," he laughed. "Him."

"Me?"

"Yes. I've been looking for you."

"Well, now you found me," I said, apprehensively.

"I've been looking for you, as I wanted to tell you something, the both of you, actually."

"Okay …" Bree drew out.

"Look, Pete. It's Pete, right?"

I nodded.

"I'm very sorry about what happened to Mo. I loved her too."

Stunned, I didn't know what to say and remained guarded.

"I can only imagine how hard it is, but I am hoping it's okay." Rick looked at Bree. "I contacted Mo's parents when I heard. I felt maybe it was best if it came from me. It wasn't easy, and I ended up going down to Sudbury to see them. They're working through it, and I have made arrangements for them to have her body transferred down to Sudbury, so they can give her a proper burial. I hope that's okay, I mean, I hope …"

Bree wiped her eyes. "Thank you, Rick. That was very nice of you. I don't know what to say."

"There's more. If it's okay with the both of you, I will look after selling Mo's place. My name is still attached to it, but it was hers, and yours, and I have no claim to it. So, if it's okay, I can sell it, and it will help cover the funeral expenses."

Bree started to cry.

What was Rick to her?

"Rick, thank you," Bree walked over and hugged him.

"You're welcome," he said.

"There's one more thing," looking at me again. "Pete, I would see you around town with Mo, and I will admit I was jealous. She was happy, she was happy with you. I could see it, and it was hard for me to admit that I couldn't make her happy the way you did. But her happiness was most important, and if you were part of it, then so be it. I told her parents about you. I hope that was okay. They said if I ever saw you, to tell you, you are welcome there anytime, and they would love to meet you. I think you are a good man, Pete."

Rick extended his hand, and we shook, his grip firm, looking me directly in the eyes.

I didn't know what to say, uncertain, I was the man he thought I was. I thanked him and wished him well. Rick said goodbye, and turning the stroller, he started back down the sidewalk.

"Rick! Wait!" Bree called out, running to him. She spoke with him for a few minutes, but I couldn't tell what she was saying, all I could see was her patting his chest and Rick nodding. She reached up, gave him a long hug, then watched him as he moved along the sidewalk, pushing the stroller in front of him.

"What was that all about?" I asked.

"Oh, nothing really, just a boy turning into a man," she said proudly, looking on in admiration.

We stopped at the Vet, picked up Bandit, and I carried him across the street, gently placing him on Mo's blanket in the passenger seat of my Chevy. Home, for now, buddy.

I followed Bree inside, retrieving my backpack from the office, Bree was behind the bar when I came out, and I sat down across from her.

"So, this is it."

Bree, her head down, refused to look up or acknowledge me.

"Bree?"

"What?" her head still down.

"I have to go."

"Says you!" her head remained down. "I've always hated you, you know. Right from the very first time I met you, I hated you. So please just go will you, and leave me be," she said, sniffling, refusing to look up.

Bree was right; just go. Leave and get it over with. I slid off the stool, took one last look around; slinging my bag on my shoulder, I started toward the stairs, stopped and turned when I got to the landing. Bree behind the bar, was watching me.

"If you don't stay in touch, I WILL find you, and you know what that means right, slick?"

I waved, fighting back the tears, and watched as Bree fired the wet rag in my direction, it falling harmlessly to the floor. Turning away, she went into the kitchen, pushing hard against the doors, "AADDRRIIAAANNNN!"

I looked down over The Club, and thought back to the night, when some beautiful, unpredictable, biker-chick, rescued me from a barroom brawl. *Just all in a normal day.* Outside, it had started to rain again, and I thought *perfect.* I walked over to my Chevy, and ironically, I had parked in the same spot as that first night. Opening the door, Bandit was awake on the seat. I stood against the door, my hands hanging limply on the roof, and reflected.

The Grateful Dead were right, life was one long strange trip. I got in, started my Chevy, and instinctively reached for a tape. I hope you like it, I said to Bandit, the Doobie Brothers were my dad's favourite. Pulling out onto Mountjoy, I hadn't noticed the construction up ahead, the road down to one lane. The light changed at Algonquin, just as I started to go through, and I was forced to stop. I looked over at Bandit, who was still groggy. I drummed my fingers on the steering wheel, waiting for the light to change.

Looking to my right, I saw east. East was Ottawa. Home? Sharkees. My friends Patty, Meg, and Mary. My own bar maybe? Stability and security if I wanted it.

Just a normal day.

Looking to my left, I saw west. West was west, nothing more. Hadn't Sara headed west?

I looked over at Bandit.

"What do you say, buddy, which way?"

Looking up, the light turned green.

Acknowledgements

Dear reader, if you have made it this far, reading the complete book, thank you for being a part of my three year journey. I hope you enjoyed the ride and got something from it.

Back in December 2018, the seed was planted by Christine Denis, when I attended her workshop on how to write and publish a book in ninety days.

Approximately two hundred and ten days later I had yet to write a single word. Then fate intervened and a week later, thanks to the perseverance of Zoe Nguyen, the neglected seed was nourished back to life. Four days later, on a hot, humid, Saturday afternoon, a chance encounter in Moose McGuires with a complete stranger, the seed turned into a blossoming tree.

Mark Twain said, *write what you know,* so I did exactly that. But in order to do that, I needed a bit of help. Actually, a lot of help. So without further adieu, the envelope please.

The award for Best New Mentor goes to Christine Denis. Accomplished author, Public Speaker, Life Coach, entrepreneur. Our paths crossed for a reason and you were the shining light that showed me the way. Thank you.

The award for Best Inspirational Performance goes to Zoe Nguyen. Our paths crossed in 2018, when I was considering the Remote Year program, and she was my contact. The program wasn't for me, but she took an interest in me, and a year later reached out again. The phone call from Zoe, on July 16, 2019, was the final push I needed. And, the inspirational email she sent the next day, is framed, and hanging in my writing studio. No amount of words can express my gratitude.

The award for Best Location and Scenery goes to Moose McGuires. My second home. Grill cheese sandwiches, pickle on the side. Barking Squirrel, Bud Light, Wing night, daddy-daughter nights, freezing on the patio, writing at the picnic table. Twas the Night Before Mooses. On and on. A unique bar with its strange and colourful cast of characters – its own version of The Wizard of Oz. A writer's creative dream. Where do I begin? Shandy, Kristen, Adrian, Tanya, and Maggie. I can't thank Mooses enough for the book launch party. It's like winning the lottery.

The award for Best Musical Score goes to the Amanda Keeley Band. Our paths crossed in August, 2020, a year into my book. I was still finding my way and I happened upon Amanda playing in Prescott. Little did I know then that I would ultimately move to Prescott and purchase a home there. As I listened, her voice and musical style fit my story perfectly and I approached her after her set. I explained my book, and she asked if I had a social media presence, and/or website, and, did I have any biographical information? I had none, but two weeks later, my website was up and running, and the biographical handout on order. When Mooses offered to host the book launch party our paths crossed again. I am honoured that Amanda will be playing at it. Thank you.

The Peoples Choice award goes to everyone who I encountered along the way. Too many friends and acquaintances to mention here, who provided inspiration, feedback, opinions, support, critiques, you name it. All of you know who you are. Thank you, thank you, thank you.

And finally, the award for Best Everything Period goes to KC. Yes, I could have written just any book, but, I could not have written *this book* without your inspiration, support, and feedback. Thank you.

So that's a wrap. Maybe one day I will write a book about the writing of this book. For now, there's this one, and Tara, coming in the Spring.

Craig Baumken
Prescott, Ontario, September 15, 2022

Just Another Novel
Coming Spring 2023
by Craig Baumken

TARA

Another novel by Craig Baumken

Prologue

"HELLO?…IS ANYONE THERE? I'm scared…," the voice squeaked from behind.

"Shut up!" Tara yelled into the rear-view mirror.

"…I'm scared…I'm…I'm scared…I want to go home," the voice whimpered.

"Shut up! Just shut up! I can't think…just be quiet…please!" she barked, glaring through the rear-view mirror at the sniveling figure, zippered from head to toe, in a heavy black rain poncho, strapped in the wheelchair.

The wheelchair van suddenly swayed to the left, hit by a gust of wind, the radio cord swinging wildly and hitting Tara in the side of the face, and she swatted at it like a fly. She had to use both hands to jerk the sluggish van back into its lane, over steering; she almost careened off the road and could feel the van slipping on the soft shoulder. Hitting the brakes, skidding, she floored it, the back wheels spinning in the gravel, then the van jerked hard as all four wheels found pavement. She looked down at the speedometer, the van shuddering and groaning, the engine emitting a high-pitched whine, and she knew it would not hold at this pace much longer. Looking out at the large side mirrors, they were jiggling so heavily she could not make anything out other than the blinding glare of lights in them. The circular convex mirrors, mounted on each side of the hood, were useless, pointed down at the road, illuminated by the headlights, the grey pavement nothing but a blur.

The van rattled loudly, its hollow insides amplifying the road noises, the sounds unbearably loud and muffled all at the same time. Her heart pounded and her hands dripped in sweat and she had a hard time holding the wheel. The lights in the side mirrors blinded her, and she raised her left hand to shield her eyes. A metal water bottle rolled down the aisle and stopped against the wheelchair frame, then rolled the rest of the way, where it banged incessantly against the rear door. She swerved to avoid a giant rubber tread that appeared out of nowhere in the road, the force knocking the radio microphone from its cradle and hitting her on top of the head, then landing on the floor at her feet, the long cord swinging like a pendulum across her face.

"SHIT!" she swatted at the cord trying to grab it, causing her to swerve, jamming her elbow painfully against the door. Reaching out she finally grabbed the cord and yanked the handheld mic up into her lap. With one hand on the wheel, she fumbled for the mic and closed her hand over it. Her eyes still on the road, by feel, she reached up and placed it back in the slot. Then the van hit a bump, bounced hard and there was a loud bang and she flinched, ducking, and watched as the small fire extinguisher came loose from its mount overhead. She watched it fall into the stairwell, where it rolled lazily between the step and the passenger door, the clicking of metal like finger pricks against her forehead. She thought she was going insane, trapped in this rolling pinball machine from hell, the clanging and banging echoing like sonic booms in her head.

Tara saw movement in the rear-view mirror and frantic, looked up to see the figure, strapped in the wheelchair, trying to get free. She saw a hand poke out at the neck, grasping at the material of the rain poncho, and it reminded her of the movie Alien when the monster poked through the stomach. She watched as the hand grotesquely twisted and turned, the fingers reaching until they found the zipper and tugged at it.

"Stay still! Stay where you are!" she commanded, and turned her attention back to the road and pressed down hard on the accelerator, gripping the wheel tighter. The movement continued and she looked up again to see the figure emerging from their cocoon but she had to ignore it and keep her eyes on the road. Up ahead she saw the sign for Ontario and let out a gasp of relief, they were almost there. They would be safe soon. Sam would know what to do. Sam always knew what to do. She wished she could be strong like her, but she was who she was, and despite her parent's words – 'Heroes are created from fear', she was not feeling so heroic at the moment.

She slowed and took the Summerstown exit off the highway, checking the mirrors but no longer were they being followed. The van's headlights cut narrow tunnels of light as she wound her way along the dark country road. A few minutes later, she came to the bridge with the rusting steel arches and turned onto it, the van shuddering as it hit the jagged edges of the ramp, the tires bouncing, emitting loud click-clacks as it crossed over. Following the twisting narrow dirt road, guided by the full moon above, she reached the end of the lane, where she slowed, and at an angle, drove across the narrow ditch, the van bouncing and shaking violently, and parked on the grass in front of Sam's place. The cottage was dark, a long sliver of light illuminating the river and the dock where the boat was tied to it. She wished everything were as peaceful as it was here.

She kicked on the emergency brake and then instinct took over, and she automatically performed the post-trip inspection; checking her mirrors, then securing the door handle, and looking up, visually inspecting the instrument panel overhead. From left to right, she methodically flicked off the switches on the panel, then turned off the radio, and finally twisting the key, turned off the engine. The sound of silence was deafening and it only added to her anxiety.

She sat slumped in the seat, her head throbbing, fingers stiff and sore from gripping the wheel. Her body ached and she tried to turn her head but her neck was stiff and all she could do was look straight ahead. She could hear rustling but it was pitch-black inside the van, and then whimpering, "Where are we? Am I home now?"

Breathing heavily, she ignored the voice, her chest started to pound and she tried to slow everything down. Inhaling deeply and exhaling loudly, counting aloud, "one steamboat, two steamboats," it had no effect. She shuddered hard and suddenly she was cold. She felt a wave of nausea wash over her, her stomach clenching, and could feel the bile rising in the back of her throat.

At that moment the realization of what she had done hit her like a sledgehammer, coughing and sputtering, her body jerked forward, spewing chunks of vomit all over the steering column and dash, splattering on the floor underneath. She held on to the wheel for support as her stomach and back heaved in sync. Finished, she leaned her forehead on the wheel and looked down at the pool of vile liquid on the floor. She swiped at it with her shoe and rubbed the back of her hand across her mouth, breaking into a cold sweat, and sat back, staring straight ahead.

She didn't notice the cottage porch light come on or see the figure dart across the lawn, the rush of cool air startling her as the van door squeaked open. Painfully, she turned her head and looked at Sam who was staring at her, her eyes wide, mouth agape.

"Tara, are you ok? What in the hell is going on?"

"I just killed my daughter…oh my god Sam, I killed Emily."

Manufactured by Amazon.ca
Bolton, ON